GOLD OF THE LOST EMPIRE

A LOST ORIGINS NOVEL

A. D. DAVIES

CRATER OF THE NORTH PUBLISHING LTD.

www.addavies.com

NOVELS BY A. D. DAVIES

Lost Origins Novels:

Tomb of the First Priest

Secret of the Reaper Seal

Curse of the Eagle Plague

Guardians of the Four Shields

Gold of the Lost Empire

Adam Park Thrillers:

The Dead and the Missing

A Desperate Paradise

The Shadows of Empty men

Night at the George Washington Diner

Master the Flame

Under the Long White Cloud

Alicia Friend Investigations:

His First His Second

In Black In White

With Courage With Fear

A Friend in Spirit

To Hide To Seek

A Flood of Bones

To Begin The End

Moses and Rock Novels:

Fractured Shadows

No New Purpose

Persecution of Lunacy

Co-Authored:

Project Return Fire – with Joe Dinicola

Standalone:

Three Years Dead

Rite to Justice

The Sublime Freedom

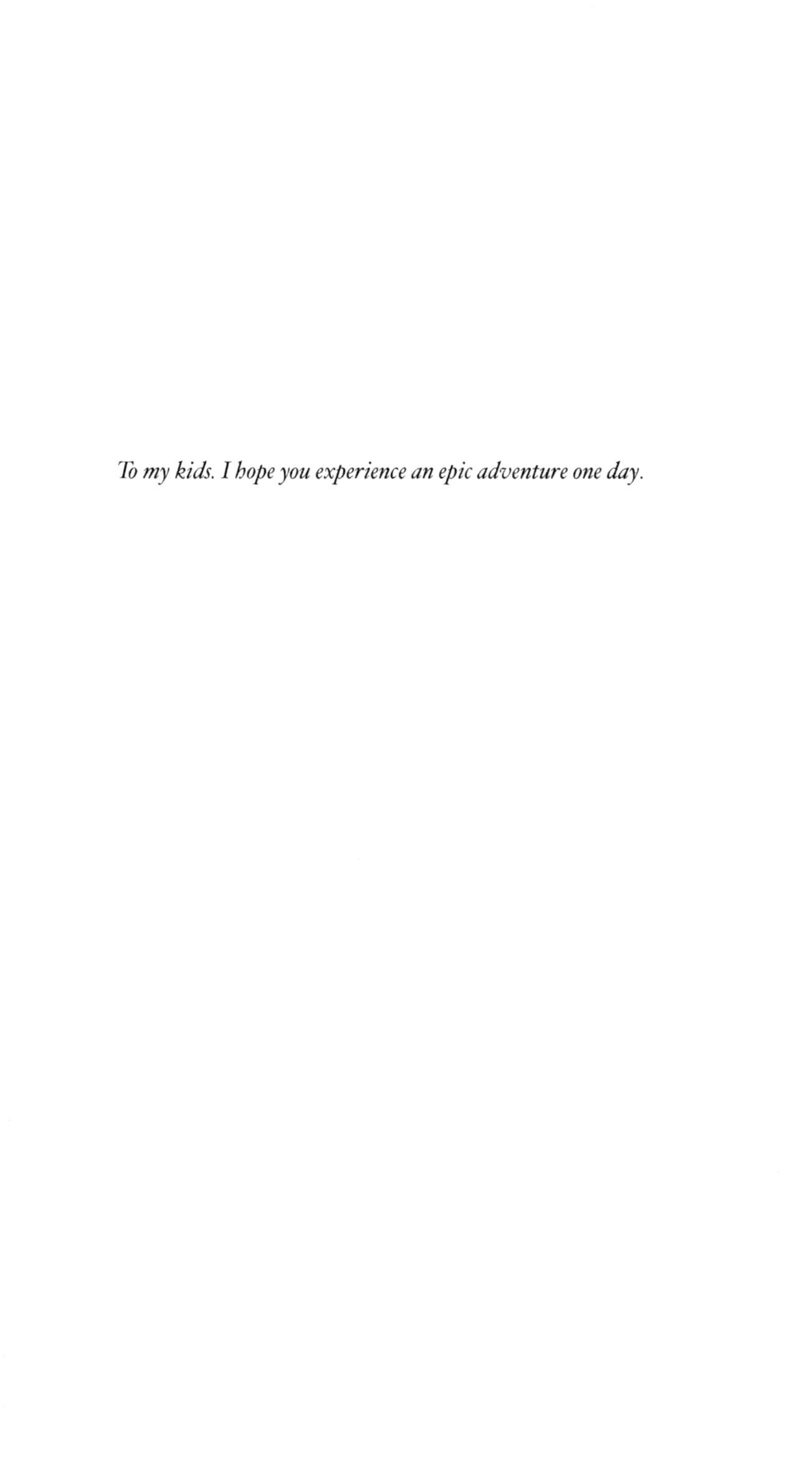

To my kids. I hope you experience an epic adventure one day.

"What can we gain by sailing to the moon if we are not able to cross the abyss that separates us from ourselves? This is the most important of all voyages of discovery, and without it, all the rest are not only useless, but disastrous"

- Thomas Merton

"Archaeology holds all the keys to understanding who we are and where we come from"

- Sarah Parcak

"Mistakes are the portals of discovery"

- James Joyce

PROLOGUE

1946

PETRIONION JARAMILLO HAD BEEN WALKING for hours, and his feet were raw in his thin-soled shoes. He had arrived in this precise spot in the Amazonian rainforest following an old map his uncle had given him, and sworn him to secrecy, shortly before his death.

"I must entrust this to someone who is true to himself and our people," Uncle Jomie had said as he pressed the parchment into the teenage boy's hand along with a long, old-looking key. "If you go here, people will know. They will come. You must trust they know what is best."

Even now, Petrionion wasn't sure what he was looking for, and he had almost given up hope when he saw it—a cave that practically called to him. One that had been forgotten by time. No different from the hundreds of others he'd passed on the way, but something deep inside the boy pulled at him like a magnet.

Petrionion walked closer and found the cave's impressive entrance infused with precious metal, well-hidden in the aged rock. Runes, which Petrionion couldn't read, were engraved in the surround, and when he placed his hand on the metal, a cold chill ran through him. When he squinted, it was as if the runes had lit up.

He knew then that he had to go inside.

A short way into the cave, where the air hung musty and stale, an old wooden table held a large book in its center.

Strange.

An actual table. In the middle of a cave. As if someone had been preparing dinner but got distracted, exited, and left their novel behind. Distracted, or too frightened to collect their things.

Petrionion walked closer and saw that the book was made of some kind of metal.

Should he touch it?

Why else would his Uncle Jomie have presented the map to him? It wasn't like he'd been warned off. Uncle Jomie had practically instructed him to come here.

Alone.

Without telling a soul.

Petrionion dragged the book toward himself. It was heavier than any he'd ever known. The first page was stiff as he opened it.

Page?

The pages were gold—actual gold, not golden in color—stiff yet pliable.

On the first image was an etched map of the jungle with a strange symbol at its center. The same as one of those runes at the door.

He looked closer.

Other symbols dotted the map. Symbols he didn't recognize. He followed them and soon realized they were leading him somewhere new.

Petrionion closed the book and slid it back to the middle of the table. He looked around. Now his eyes had adjusted to the gloom, he saw bookshelves filled with even more tomes. He wandered without touching and soon noticed doors on the walls. One in particular called to him. Not with a voice or a musical note, but with a pull similar to the cave entrance, a vibration in his fingertips, his toes.

He opened the door—unlocked—and found himself in a small room filled with statues and artifacts. He recognized some of the objects as local to his native Ecuador. Others were unfamiliar, some that must have hailed from farther afield, perhaps even beyond South America's many ages, which he had only heard about in stories. He was mesmerized by the beauty of the pieces, and simply had to explore.

At the back, he found another door, locked this time. It wouldn't budge when he tried to open it. He stepped back, wondering what was beyond, or whether he should even consider breaking in, when he remembered the key Uncle Jomie gave him.

Petrionion pulled the old metal key from his pocket, still cold despite the heat of the trek through the rainforest. He inserted it into the lock and twisted, the barrels turning with a smooth click as if freshly oiled, not an ancient door hidden in a cave in the jungle.

Peering into the room, something glinted on a plinth in the center. He stepped inside and approached the small golden box. His hands hovered over it, that sense of belonging, like he was meant to be here, soothing what should have been deep apprehension. It reminded him of a glamorous cigarette case, something a beautiful Hollywood star might snap shut as she fluttered her eyelids at the leading man.

I have come this far...

Without hesitation, Petrionion opened the box. Inside lay a small disc with a serrated edge, like the cog of a clock, only far smaller.

"You are Jomie Jaramillo's boy?"

Petrionion's heart almost burst with shock at the stranger's voice. He spun and felt for the knife on his belt, but he was facing an elderly man—at least seventy years old—with a pack on his back and holding a pistol at his hip.

"Do not fear this," the stranger said. "Give me your name, though. I was expecting someone older."

"I am not his son," Petrionion said. "I am his nephew. I do not know why he chose me."

"Petrionion?"

"Yes." How did this stranger know his name...? Only one answer: Jomie told him. "I am Petrionion."

"Then he must have judged you more worthy. You are true to yourself and your people, yes?"

"I swear." Petrionion's heart had slowed somewhat, but he was still dizzy with surprise. "What is this place?"

"It was built to protect a more glorious secret." The man pulled back the hammer on the gun, slowly uncocked it, then lowered it. "The secrets beyond this point are not for the eyes of modern man. Come."

The stranger walked past Petrionion to the back of the room. Unlike the previous wall, there was no door here.

The stranger unslung his backpack and lifted a C-shaped bangle from within. At first, it looked like dull rock, but when he removed a glove and held it in his bare fingers, a tiny pattern of green flecks glowed in the darkness.

He held the item to a rune shaped like the number eight, slotting it in to the top curve. Then he extended a hand to Petrionion. "The other."

"Other what?"

"Other key. Give it to me."

Petrionion held out the door key that his uncle had bequeathed him.

The stranger slapped it from his hand. "Not that one. The one that looks like this!"

He meant the bangle.

"I received no such item. I—"

The man raised the gun and cocked the hammer. "Give it to me, boy. I know he had it. I know—"

An impossibly loud *bang* rang out. Blood stained the older man's front, and he let go of the bangle, falling to the floor with a thud.

In the doorway, a trio of people had gathered. An African-looking woman was aiming a gun very similar to the stranger's.

Petrionion staggered, his legs jelly, his ears ringing.

The two men accompanying the woman were also African or Caribbean people.

The woman handed her weapon to one of the men and rushed toward Petrionion, speaking English at first, then switching to a Mexican-Spanish dialect which Petrionion could understand.

"You are safe, child. And we have retrieved the bangle at last."

Outside, as Petrionion found his balance, he recovered from his shock and managed to speak clearly again. His ears only rang instead of hurt.

"Who are you?"

"We are Guardians," one of the men said, his Spanish more formal than the woman's. "Child, did you have another bangle? Like this one, but with red stones?"

Petrionion shook his head as firmly as he could, maintaining eye contact.

"Good." The man blew out a breath and seemed less tense. "They have not found the Ruby Rock bangle. It remains safe. Whoever St Thomas trusted, it was a wise decision."

"We will hide this place better than before," the woman said. She had taken the golden box from Petrionion and opened it, removed what looked like a clock cog from inside, and held it before him. "This must never fall into the wrong hands. People far wiser than us concealed it here for protection. But when a worthy person comes along, they must be allowed to find this place."

"How does this help?" Petrionion asked.

The woman just smiled. She was wearing the bangle on her left wrist. Little green flecks had lit up when she handled it, but it was just a rock again.

She said, "If Jomie gave you the map and the door key, he trusted you. More than any other person."

Petrionion nodded, although he was both honored and annoyed at how Jomie saw him. He was a boy. He did not expect to be facing an old man with a gun or be confronted with Africans, who sounded American or British, and who seemed intent on preserving the discovery.

"You have it all," he said. "I do not want it."

"We cannot leave with this." The woman placed the cog in Petrionion's hand. "You must take it. To a site in Europe."

"Europe? I am only—"

"If Jomie entrusted this place's location to you, then you are a man. Man enough to do your duty to humankind and take this where only the worthy will find it. Will you do your duty? For your uncle?"

Petrionion struggled to believe he was the best person for this task. For this *duty*. "You are Americans? Surely you—"

The woman scoffed. "The Americans recently dropped a nuclear bomb on their fellow humans across the sea. Their allies approved of that action. The people who put this here would not want men like that to have this knowledge. The human race isn't ready for it yet. We must keep it safe."

"But it is just a cave. You say you will hide it, so it looks like any other, but... why? Why is a simple cave so precious?"

The two men laughed, and the woman scolded them with a harsh look.

"We must hide it. As I must hide this, until the right time." She lifted her arm with the bangle. "I will look after it and ensure my family knows its value as I pass it on. It is my duty. Let me show you yours."

She took Petrionion's hand and led him away from the cave mouth.

"We cannot go inside, not this way, not without the other half of this key. For now, thankfully, it is lost. But I can show you what we are protecting. The earth has given us a peek at what lies within."

In the same way he'd felt connected with the cave as he approached, as his instinct warned him away from the elderly man who'd clearly stolen the bangle, he trusted this woman. He trusted her and went outside with her, scaling a hillside that wound around a cliff and perched precariously over the Amazon river. Through a tiny fissure, unnoticeable if you didn't know it was there, the woman encouraged him to crawl in.

He did so.

Over centuries or even millennia, thanks to shifts in the land's geology, the rocks had opened briefly. Through a gash barely large enough for Petrionion's hand, he saw what they were guarding. And he could hardly get a breath as he scrambled back out.

His senses buzzed, fully alive, his heart thumping, his extremities tingling as if crawling with electricity.

The woman asked, "Will you help us?"

"Yes," he said without hesitation.

She smiled. "Then the Guardians thank you. And I will tell you where to go."

PART ONE

CHAPTER ONE

MALTA - MODERN DAY

THE EXIT BECKONED mere steps away, but Prihya Sibal feared she wouldn't make it that far. Her fingers were raw from scrabbling at the hard-packed earth, finessing what her trowel had found under one of the Hypogeum Hal Salfieni's walls, and her emotions were frazzled from what she hoped was paranoia, but tradecraft insisted was common sense.

They're watching you. Don't be naïve.

She'd hidden in the shadows of a six-thousand-year-old passage never frequented by tourists, and the groups she snuck away from had followed the guide beyond the main body of the temple. All she had to do was will her legs to move, to rush her across the stretch of sandy floor where sunlight beamed in from the domed ceiling—a ceiling that had survived a near-impossible length of time.

In recent years, she had learned many skills—some from a former boyfriend in the New Zealand intelligence service, others from a man she thought was once a British spy but who would never confirm it, and also from a man she hoped never to see again. Only... her cursory countersurveillance measures had hinted at eyes upon her as soon as her ferry docked. And they were not the leery, lingering gazes she was used to.

Despite no evidence, she was certain they were out there. She just hoped "they" weren't who she suspected.

Prihya took ten calm breaths, inhaling for ten seconds, exhaling for twenty. Nothing at all happened. No scuffle from a recessed doorway, no shadow passing above.

Afraid she would never move if she didn't go *right now*, Prihya set off at a brisk pace. Back straight, the purse with her prize bouncing on a strap across her chest, her legs propelled her like a large bird or, embarrassingly, like John Cleese in a classic Monty Python sketch, the name of which escaped her.

She made it across the domed chamber and paused by the exit ramp, the stairs worn smooth by years of tourists' feet. She heard nothing, saw no sign of people lurking, and found enough courage to speed walk out. With another brief pause as the fierce Maltese sun reminded her it was summer—another record breaker in Europe—she was thankful for the crowds as she stepped out, intending to lose herself among them.

Tourists came in two varieties: those who flaunted their foreign fish-out-of-water status with loud short-sleeve shirts, strappy summer dresses, and quite hideous floral shorts; and those who dressed for comfort, like Prihya, who'd chosen lightweight cargo pants, a hard-wearing cotton shirt, and sturdy but breathable boots that were distinctly inelegant but made tramping over uneven ground much easier than flipflops and sandals. The downside of this tactic was that it made spotting tails all but impossible.

As she returned to the old town, she had to choose between storing the cypher in her hotel safe and fleeing quickly, leaving her belongings behind, and claiming her reward. What was the option they'd least expect if she was being followed?

To remain relaxed. To play it as if she was still searching.

Yes, to pretend she'd found nothing.

If she'd recovered the cipher, surely, running or hiding were the only choices. Sticking around meant she'd failed.

Xander Madri was her best bet for appearing at ease. He'd smoothed the way for her arrival, arranging the visa and hotel with cash couriered to him by her employer, and they'd bonded over a shared view of the ancient world when meeting briefly behind closed doors to hand over the tools she needed. That, and being as good-looking and well-chiseled as a Calvin Klein model. But mostly, the shared worldview.

Probably.

Both had learned of a history that modern humans were either unaware of or stubbornly denied because it contradicted the narrative. Prihya because she'd lived it; Xander because he'd opened his mind years before and refused to let conventional wisdom shut it down. They were both in this business to discover the truths of the ancient world.

Who truly built Stonehenge?

How are the Pyramids of Giza so astronomically accurate?

What happened to Atlantis?

Why was the Colossus of Rhodes destroyed?

When did someone decide to obscure the real war at Troy?

How can the Hanging Gardens of Babylon exist in so much literature but leave no evidence behind?

Prihya had long been intrigued by these and other questions. And, despite academics dismissing her as a crank, she'd learned more incredible things than she'd hoped. Perhaps they did not simply hide those "conspiracy theory" questions for the sake of knowledge hoarding but were concealing humanity's history as legends because the truth was too dangerous. If that were the case, better people like Prihya uncovered it than the man she suspected had sent his best trackers after her.

Prihya was sweating by the time she arrived at Xander's quaint little cafe. She sat at a small table on the pavement overlooking the more modern plaza and adjusted the café's parasol, estimating the shadow's effect would last about ten seconds. Plenty for her to gather herself.

Within a mere five seconds, Xander sidled over, one hand in his immaculate apron, and fired her an expectant smile. "Ready to order, madam?"

She returned the smile, straining to keep the smug inside and to avoid staring too long into his deep, dark eyes. "Coffee. And water. And for you to stop playing it cool. You're not cool."

He relented. "Did you find it?"

Prihya tapped the purse in her lap, a touristy piece of crap with "MALTA" stitched across it—a gaudy accessory to her dusty cargo pants and sweat-stained T-shirt. The coins inside clinked alongside the cipher. "Right where the diary said it'd be."

"Does that mean—?"

As a pair of men drifted into her peripheral vision, a jolt spiked up Prihya's throat and her voice rose a notch. "It means I'd like water and a coffee, please. Not a conversation."

Xander stared.

Prihya hoped narrowing her eyes would ram the hint home. She couldn't risk even a sideways glance that would betray that she and Xander were more than server and customer. He knew of the hidden world, but not how dangerous that knowledge could be.

Xander gave a shallow bow and said, "Of course, madam," and retreated inside.

One of the two men Prihya had spotted taking seats at the next table rose to his feet, shifted aside, and sat opposite her.

How long was he listening?

Moses shifted the parasol, so the shade favored him, making Prihya squint.

"You've been working out," she said, forcing a calmness into the words.

Why him? If he's here, the others are, too.

"We all have." Moses rolled his shoulders as if self-conscious about her comment. He was an academic before training as a killer, and always preferred to act without violence but was more than capable of switching between the two as simply as opening a window.

"Who's the priest?" Prihya tilted her head toward the Caucasian man in the black robe and Roman collar.

Moses dead-eyed her. "Give it to me, Prihya."

Prihya frowned. "Give you what?"

Moses glanced at the priest, who gave no acknowledgement, then back to Prihya. "You know how we work."

"I do."

"Then give me the artifact."

Xander returned, somehow carrying the tray in a flamboyant manner.

How does someone make that *look flamboyant?*

With a chipper, "Your water, madam. Your coffee," he presented the espresso in a tiny mug on a saucer alongside a perspiring glass of iced water. Barely flinching, he asked Moses, "For you, sir?"

Moses remained lasered on Prihya. "The same."

"Very good." Xander headed into the café again.

Prihya sipped her espresso. Then she placed it down, willing her hand not to tremble. "You want the diary?"

"No, you left the diary behind, along with the bag of tools you were carrying. Therefore, I want what you found in the Hypogeum Hal Salfieni. The cipher."

"I didn't take anything. That'd be stealing."

Her bravado wasn't hitting the mark as Moses gave an impatient sigh. "You expect me to believe you were sightseeing?"

"Exactly."

"This is untrue. We know you are investigating a trail obtained from intellectual property owned by our employer."

"Valerio Conchin can't claim ownership of something he stole."

"Which you helped secure."

"Under false pretenses."

Moses gave the priest another look. Again, no reply. "Prihya, listen very carefully. Valerio sees you were scared. He understands. He will forgive your betrayal. If you cooperate. Willingly."

Prihya swallowed. Knowing the man before her, and who he was working for, the offer was probably genuine.

She asked, "Why do you think I have it?"

A fraction of a crinkle darkened at the corner of Moses's eyes, the closest he had to a tell. "What else would you be looking for in a six-thousand-year-old necropolis? We know that you know it is the oldest underground temple on Earth—thousands of years older than the Great Pyramids. We also know you have been studying the disappearance of the temple culture from fully two thousand years ago. So, Prihya, after what *we* have learned about the past, and what *you* know too..."

"Sir." Xander delivered Moses's drinks—less flamboyantly than he had Prihya's. She hoped it didn't tip Moses off.

When Xander moved out of earshot, Moses nodded toward her

filthy attire. "We believe you dug up the answer to something we have been searching for—the answer to what happened to them, and how they advanced so quickly."

Prihya needed something. An opening. Anything to find an advantage she might have overlooked. One she had to press home.

"I found it," she admitted, unsure how to test her theory.

Moses relaxed. Downed his espresso. Clinked the cup down. "Show me."

Prihya eyed the small cup and saucer. "I don't have it here."

"Why?"

Prihya formed a circle with her thumbs and forefingers, about the size of the espresso saucer. "It's this big and made of gold. I didn't think I could conceal it about my person."

"Where is it, then?"

Gotcha. You don't know what the cipher looks like.

Sipping her water, Prihya signaled Xander for the bill. "A locker at the port."

"We watched you leave the Hypogeum Hal Salfieni without the diary and tools. You came right here."

"I'm not stupid. It wasn't me who brought it out."

Moses frowned.

Prihya lifted her arms as if to say, *Search me if you don't believe me*. "I paid our fixer to pose as a tourist and handed it off to him before I left the temple."

"Madam." Xander handed her the bill on a small silver tray.

Moses didn't even glance at him. He hadn't identified Xander as an ally.

"I always assume I'm being followed." Prihya dipped into her purse, deftly wrapping the cipher—actually the size of a silver dollar—in a twenty euro note and took it out.

Moses reached for the bill. "I'll get it."

"No, I insist." Prihya snatched the tray.

"I think you'll find *we* insist," the priest on the next table said, a genial smile as he twisted to face her.

He had thick, gray hair and a craggy face that must have been handsome at one time. The smile had a steely firmness to it, and his ice-blue eyes sent Prihya into a shiver she couldn't explain. She quickly returned the tray, mustering all her willpower to keep from urging Xander to run, to get away from here.

Her fingers returned to the purse, where she swapped the twenty for a five. Moses passed the tray to Xander, which now held enough cash to cover only the bill.

Prihya withdrew her folded banknote and placed it on the shiny surface. "I know what a lousy tipper you are, Moses. Let me take care of that."

Moses and the priest exchanged shrugs as Xander bowed his head in thanks and accepted the small silver tray of money. Moses then extended his hand to Xander as he shifted to turn, aiming for the five euro note. Xander paused, showing puzzlement, as the sometime-assassin, sometime-scholar lifted the money.

Nothing underneath.

Moses motioned to the priest, and both men rose.

"Let's go," Moses said.

Xander headed for the cash register.

Prihya pushed back her chair. It scraped on the tiles. She didn't stand.

"Don't do it," Moses warned.

Prihya lowered her head, eyes still on his. "You know me so well."

She threw the table over, launched into a sprint, and bundled straight into Xander, grabbing him to stay upright, where she whispered, "Don't follow me. Find Toby Smith. Tell him everything."

Then, as Moses freed himself from the toppled furniture and leaped to his feet, Prihya ran.

In the four or five years since she met Valerio Conchin, she'd learned a lot, but she wasn't a super soldier. With the world on hold for nearly two years, cardio and physical fitness had become essential hobbies. But so was the tradecraft she expected to need once the planet's travel routes reopened.

Drawing attention and causing confusion was her best chance of survival, and she cleared a human corridor as she bustled into the crowded narrow streets lined with traders' stalls, shoving people, and yelling, "He's coming. Help me," then rushing on before some random hero offered support that could lead to his death. She'd gotten a jump on Moses, and the priest wasn't exactly a sprinter, but they might not be the only ones out there.

As she turned another corner, running as fast as she could in what was becoming a thin crowd, she looked back and ahead, and up, in case they'd used a drone or some rooftop spy to track her. She checked her trail again, saw no one, and slowed as she entered an indoor market full of flowery scents and earthy spice aromas.

She was sweating, breathing hard but not wheezing, her high-altitude ten-kilometer runs paying off. Her heart rate was now around 120 and would fall below 80 in three minutes. *If* she could keep the adrenaline at bay. And if she could hide until the assassins gave up or moved on.

Prihya slipped into a clothing stall, purchased a shawl and headscarf for thirty euros, and didn't wait for the change as she put on the new shawl and covered her head with the scarf. She altered her gait as well, hoping her boots would draw little attention as she took dainty steps rather than determined strides.

There was a staff-only door between a fishmonger and a butcher who specialized in lamb, and it looked promising enough for her to dart down the tiled path to try the knob.

Locked.

Damn.

She turned around and jogged back to the main drag of stalls, ready to adopt her feminine shuffle and blend back into the local crowd, when she was stopped by someone dressed similarly to her. The woman wore a headscarf, but her face was not obscured.

Prihya said, "Renata."

"Nice try," the woman replied, "but we tagged you before you even went inside the temple."

Prihya cursed herself for not thinking they'd have a way of tracking her beyond their eyeline. She'd been so careful. It must've been a tiny device that someone who appeared local attached to her as she hustled between her hotel and the Hypogeum Hal Salfieni. *Appeared* local, because it could have been any of the people she thought of as "scholar-assassins" if they'd concealed themselves as Renata clearly had.

Married to Moses, she was his intellectual superior, very close to his physical equal, and far more willing to kill if the situation warranted. Prihya had liked her when they first met, but soon came to fear her, more so than her husband or their boss.

Renata said, "Come along. Quietly."

"If you wanted me dead—"

"Yes, yes, you'd be dead already. I do not need to recite clichés to get what we need."

Renata jabbed something sharp into Prihya's belly. Not hard enough to break the skin but drew Prihya's eyes to the black tactical blade which could slice through a deer's hide with the slightest pressure.

"Walk by my side. Try nothing. And you may live."

Prihya obeyed, falling in beside Renata, who looped an arm through hers, so they looked like sisters or girl friends. As they approached the exit, two cops milled around, smoking, chatting.

Renata's arm stiffened. "Do not think about it."

"You don't want attention," Prihya replied. "No matter how well trained you are, some Maltese SWAT team—whatever they're called here—can pick you off."

"Valerio is not above collateral damage."

"Collateral damage," Prihya said. "Murdering civilians. And I know he doesn't mind. But only when it benefits him. It wouldn't here."

They were almost at the market's exit. The cops hadn't looked up from their conversation.

Renata said, "I do not have his qualms. Frankly, I'll take out this pair just to see you weep for them."

Prihya remained silent. She didn't look at the cops as they passed, and kept her cool as they walked a hundred yards down the street to a bar where the other scholar-assassins were waiting. Muzaffer pretended to smoke—a cigarette between his lips, but he didn't inhale. Hilla appeared strange to Prihya, and it took her a moment to realize why: the group's pilot was wearing a flouncy dress while nursing a soda. Not ideal for fighting, but with the wide-brimmed sunhat on the table, she made an effective lookout. Moses simply leaned forward, his elbows on his knees, scowling in annoyance.

Renata said, "I told you she'd come quietly."

"And no blood," Muzaffer said. "Kudos."

Renata gave a sarcastic curtsy and added, "Yet."

Moses stood, all false pleasantries extinguished. He didn't seem bothered that he looked every inch the intimidating brute, bullying a young woman outside a bar. "Give it to me. Now."

Prihya had no choice. She carefully lifted the purse with MALTA stitched on the front and opened it. Dipped her fingers inside.

"Slowly," Renata warned.

Prihya slowed her movements, her thumb and finger closing around the small, round object which she withdrew and placed gently in Moses's hand.

Prihya whispered, "Three."

Moses brought his hand up, squinting at the circular item.

Prihya said, "Two."

"What is this?" Moses demanded.

"One." Prihya dived aside.

The scholar-assassins moved too late. The mini flashbang—adapted from a former coworker—exploded. Prihya escaped the worst but knew it would burn their retinas and temporarily deafen them. Though only a fifth as powerful as US military and SWAT flashbangs, it distracted them enough for her to flee.

She could still hear them cursing and moaning as she sprinted away, seeing an opening, a way out of the winding streets, back into the modern part of town where there would be taxis, cops, and an escape to—

An enormous man stepped into her path. She hit him full speed and bounced off, her head whipping back as if she'd hit a wall. She curled up so her arms and side struck the ground first, rolled, got one foot under her to spring up, but a shovel of a hand landed on her shoulder to hold her down.

She looked into the face of a man she last saw comatose. Once a brilliant tactician and skilled soldier, she now saw a face scarred by injuries both internal and external, and eyes so dead she might as well have been staring at two lumps of coal.

She said, "Horse? Is that really you?"

"Stay," he said.

The word sounded forced, as if it were difficult for him to speak. Perhaps it was. After the injuries he'd suffered, it was a miracle he articulate words at all, let alone be here, solid as a mountain, cutting off any hope of escape.

The scholar-assassins caught up, blinking and not yet fully recovered, but more than capable of finishing her if they chose. If not for Moses elbowing in front of her, Prihya guessed Renata would have done just that.

"Last chance," Moses said.

Prihya lifted her purse.

Horse said, "Mine."

The man who made Muzaffer look positively weedy took the strap in both hands and yanked it apart, the fabric snapping with little resistance. He let Muzaffer pull Prihya to her feet and chuckled like a cartoon villain, looking down on her as a little drool escaped the side of his mouth. He wiped it on his sleeve and handed Moses the purse.

Moses opened it and took out another mini flashbang, a hundred euros in various notes, and a few coins. He squinted in irritation. "It's not here."

Prihya gave a tiny shrug, as much as she could manage under Muzaffer's grip. "Sorry. Must have dropped it."

Moses's face turned to thunder, fixing Renata with an expression that permitted her to stick that blade into Prihya, when it suddenly switched. His eyes widened, and he barked a single laugh.

"Oh, that was clever," he said. "The waiter. Go back. Get the waiter!"

Xander Madri had been waiting for someone like Prihya for years. Someone who shared his belief that the world was not as it appeared, that places like his home country held treasures and secrets that no one had even considered, let alone discovered.

He had often wondered how much of his free thinking was

because of the death of his wife. His mother had even told him he was insane, giving in to conspiracy theories and fantasy. Trauma had a way of changing your perspective on things, she explained. Anyone who believed in exaggerated conspiracy theories felt out of control, and this deep, dark secret that no one else could see made them feel special. He'd been on the verge of believing her when she pointed to his go-bag as proof of his paranoia.

But then he came across dark-web accounts of a group that even he thought was a fiction. People who had discovered evidence of civilizations tens of thousands of years older than those who built the pyramids, older than his native land's Temple Culture. He'd attempted to contact them, but they'd rebuffed him, citing the same reasons his mother had used to discourage him from pursuing his theories in the wider world.

But the name Prihya had used—Toby Smith—proved to Xander that he was on the right track. He had to flee with the little gold cog Prihya had palmed to him earlier. Not selfishly for himself or Prihya, but for the human race itself, and for one human in particular.

Kat held his hand as the ferry sailed for Italy, waving to the mainland from the deck. "Are we going on vacation, Daddy?" the eight-year-old girl asked.

"It's better than a vacation, baby," Xander said. "It's an adventure."

CHAPTER TWO

WESTERN CHINA, EXACT LOCATION: CLASSIFIED

JULES APPRECIATED the archaeological dig's quiet isolation the way a stressed mom might enjoy an afternoon at a spa—a relaxing change but one that couldn't last and, besides, he kind of missed the real world. In this forested region of China, the only outside chatter he had to deal with was from monkeys. He'd grown accustomed to the institute's habits and social mores, and could fake interest even when the subject was as interesting as a spent match. But they were good people, and he felt better around them. Despite the authorities blindfolding the group to transport them here and refusing to reveal its location, he'd found a home in the remote Chinese wilderness.

According to the flora and fauna, and the weather patterns, they'd set down in the west of the country, and Jules's lungs and senses told him they were at an elevation of around 10,000 meters, or 33,000 feet if you went imperial. Jules rarely did. Metric made more sense. He might lose his US passport if he said that.

So, a forested region closer to Tibet than Beijing, operating under a commercial license granted to the Carson Corporation. LORI's funders received bad news.

Toby Smith, the institute's de facto leader, showed Roger Carson through the camp's residential area, which had high-quality tents for living, eating, and cooking, rainwater showers, and surprisingly clean latrines. Dan Vincent, Harpal Singh, and Bridget Carson kept up with Jules in the late afternoon sun.

Bridget said, "He's not going to be happy."

Dan shrugged, carrying his H&K submachine gun. "We could lie."

Dan insisted on keeping an armed presence at the camp despite Charlie Locke's motion detectors, which could distinguish between animals and humans. The group carried sidearms "in case of tigers" when Dan wasn't around, but Jules saw them as a security blanket for a man who had spent his entire life on the lookout for danger. Toby called him their "man-at-arms," an archaic term that didn't mean he was in charge of shooting bad guys who wanted to steal their stuff and kill them, but Toby was an archaic kind of guy.

"Mr. Carson," Jules heard Toby say. "We are currently walking over what we believe was a stone-laid path to the, er, *monument,* as our benefactors call it, which we have partially excavated."

Roger Carson, in an expensive suit garnished with a comfortable-looking but not-very-hard-wearing brand-name walking boots, slowed, and looked down at the man in the beige shirt and cargo pants. "Partially?"

Toby met Roger's eye and gave a thin smile. "A lot of progress, given the nature of the location. And plenty to offer an update."

"Good."

Roger's strides lengthened and the shorter man hastened to keep up with him.

As the group also upped their pace, Bridget said, "His first concern will be potential loss of profit and reputation, then he'll try to fix it by pouring more money into the pot. After that, he'll start throwing blame around. Then, he'll think about poor ol' me and how I have to be back in Paris in three weeks."

"He'll want solutions," Jules said.

All looked at him.

Dan said, "You know Big Kahuna Carson better than his own daughter?"

"He's a fixer. Needs to find a way around every problem."

Jules made a conscious effort to keep his tone light and breezy, which diluted the arrogance he'd once displayed without due consideration for how he appeared to others. Like most Black parents in the US, his mother had taught him to soften his baritone around cops and anyone else who might be intimidated by his voice and what, even then, was his clipped, direct way of speaking. He was still adamant that he was correct, but the shift in tone meant that his friends didn't bristle, tut, or put up much of a fight.

"Mr. Carson'll make out like he's collaboratin' but he'll really be laying down the law."

Harpal said, "You can't know that."

"No, he's right." Bridget flashed Jules a wide smile. "Annoyingly so."

At one time, Jules had wondered if a relationship with Bridget was on the cards. But after several violent missions and numerous historical revelations that dwarfed trivial matters like love and romance, he'd abandoned that notion. But out here, on a normal, potentially exciting archaeological dig, he'd begun to wonder again: what if her Alabama accent and coy demeanor weren't surface characteristics that made her unique, but intrinsic features that meant Jules wasn't imagining his feelings for her? And what if her defending him to the others wasn't motivated by altruism or her natural peacemaker instincts?

He'd think about it after this was over. Maybe he'd show up in Paris once the new semester started. If she hadn't met someone else in the interim.

Someone else...

Huh. Was that... *jealousy* he was feeling?

Audrey Carson, who had the same long red hair as her daughter, was already at the dig site. She rose from her squat and smiled at her husband. They'd arrived by Land Rover and parked ten minutes away, leaving their personal protection agent in charge of the vehicle.

He wasn't cleared for the site.

"It's amazing," Audrey said.

The trench was twice the length and width of a school bus, with statues of men, women, and animals buried to their waists every two meters—or six feet. Several were strange hybrids, chimaeras that combined human and tiger, human and panda, or human and monkey, all in strange poses representing athleticism or fighting. Harpal and Dan had to compare them to Kung Fu Panda, but these were far scarier, with fangs and claws that Hollywood would never show children.

Roger puffed himself up and emitted a satisfied *harrumph* as he strode to the trench and tracked around one of several small diggers emblazoned with the Carson Corporation logo. "You seemed hesitant, Toby. From your manner, I was expecting bad news."

Toby shot a nervous glance at Jules and the others. "Well, this isn't quite what we were expecting."

"No, it's better." Roger spread his arms. "Look at this! They aren't all the way out of the earth, but..." He rounded on Toby with a huge grin. "Our clients are going to be very impressed."

Jules sensed the tension from Bridget.

As ever, Harpal compensated with lame humor. "Wait for it, ladies and gents."

Toby, as the spearhead charged with delivering the news, betrayed his worry with a lick of his lips. "This isn't what you think it is."

"What?" The ebullience from Roger remained, but he placed his hands on his hips then swept one of them toward the excavation. "This is like the Terracotta Army, only... better. Look at the detail. Look at this!" He pointed to what appeared to be a human-tiger hybrid holding a sword. "It's brilliant!"

"It's a child's playground," Toby said.

It took several moments of blinking and the Carsons exchanging frowns for Roger to reply. "I'm sorry. What do you mean?"

"It's, umm..." Toby was running out of the sort of words that usually flowed freely when discussing historical artifacts. "It's a delicate issue, Mr. Carson. While we will always keep an open mind, especially given your kind sponsorship of the dig..."

Having said nothing before because he was afraid of coming across as arrogant or superior, Jules approached the pair. "Your surveyors found heads poking outta the soil, right?"

Roger moved to his wife's side. "Yes, yes. You're supposed to dig them out. Date them. Send the full story to Beijing so they can..." He stuttered again, a piercing gaze finding Toby. "What are you telling me?"

Bridget stepped in. "Dad, I'm sorry. But this isn't a thousand-year-old monument to some great dynasty. It's an interesting find, but it's only a few hundred years old. Look, it's on a sloping section of land that's mostly flat, before increasing its elevation into the mountains."

The landscape rose far into the distance, largely obscured by trees.

"We think the land once had a grand old house," she went on. "And this was a training area, like a gym. Or, more likely, something for children to play in."

Jules crossed to a snake-headed warrior figure. "They're a bit scarier than we'd go with today, but we reckon two hundred, maybe three hundred years old at the most. A landslide must've covered the property."

Roger Carson still appeared confused, although his wife had deflated already. She sighed and faced Toby. "This was a home that got destroyed during a storm?"

"It seems that way." Toby sounded more confident now the news had broken. "We cannot tell if it was before or after whomever lived here fled, and we haven't located a house yet. It might even be—"

"A house?" This had perked Roger up. "Like... a buried family? People?"

Harpal butted in. "Or a village."

"Village?"

Bridget squinted at Harpal, annoyed for the same reason Jules was.

Dan said, "Yeah. Bit weird having a house all the way out here. Probably a business owner. Mining. Farming, maybe."

Roger was joining the dots, forming a narrative. "Let me get this straight. I risk hundreds of thousands of dollars to uncover what my partners here expect to be something as majestic as the Terracotta Army. I use my huge, expansive network to ship in digging and drilling equipment to this remote region..." He raised a finger to the air. "In record time, I might add. We promised them we would dig up something needed quite badly following the pandemic, lockdowns, war in Europe, and whatever else has hit this region's capacity to make a living. And all I have to show for these efforts is a children's playground."

"I'm sorry," Toby said. "We can only uncover what is here. We can't make it something it isn't."

Roger pulled away from Audrey and trod the ground across the longer side, turning back on himself as his wife took out a phone.

He asked, "Who are you calling?"

"The ambassador," she said. "We said we'd tell them as soon as we had news—"

"Not yet." Roger's raised finger became a wagging one, a gesture that appeared excited, as the solution to a problem dawned. "What would you need to excavate the rest of this hillside? See what buildings are here? If this is a child's playground, there must be an estate. And your security fellow said maybe a village?"

Toby stuttered again, palms up, reluctant to argue.

Jules said, "It's speculation. No evidence."

Roger pointed at the statues. "That's evidence enough for me. What do you need? How much will it cost?"

Dan strolled into Roger's eyeline, rubbing his chin like a used car salesman considering a lowball offer. "We got someone developing a more intense ground penetrating radar than anything on the market. Three times deeper than LiDar, and the software that comes with it is top of the line."

"Yes," Roger said flatly, a side-eye at Bridget. "I'm financing Charlie and Philip Locke's R&D project. She assured me it wasn't quite ready for field use."

"Then this would be perfect," Bridget said. "Wouldn't it?"

Jules modified his tone, covering frustration this time. "It's another delay."

"A delay to what?" Roger asked.

"The Witnesses."

Everyone quietened. As if on cue, a breeze picked up, although it may already have been there, and Jules hadn't noticed until the hush.

Roger said, "That's on hold."

"The world was on hold for too long," Jules replied as politely as he could. "Ask your masters if they really want to continue."

Toby approached him and made a calming gesture. "Jules, this isn't the time."

"His number must be in my other phone," Audrey said. When Roger gave her a questioning look, she showed him her screen. "It's not here."

Jules said, "Don't worry, if it's Mr. Xing, I know it." He recited the number.

"Okay, that's freaky," Roger Carson said.

"You think that's freaky," Dan put in, "try living with it."

Roger wasn't deterred. "How on earth do you do that?"

Jules gave a nonchalant shrug. "I hear a number or see someone dial it, put it on my mental screen and take a snapshot. Then I just pull it out when I need it."

"So, you read it back like a sticky note?"

"Yeah, ain't that how you do it?" Of course, he'd learned in his teens that wasn't how everyone did it, but eidetic memories—near perfect recall of facts and, in Jules's case, physical learning—came to people differently than normal folk.

"He's our freak," Harpal added, "but we like him freaky. He's useful."

Audrey had input the number on the sat-phone but hadn't pressed dial yet. "Oh, please. If you can define 'normal' in the next thirty seconds, you get away with labeling people freaks. Otherwise, concentrate on being kind." She hit the send button and retreated out of earshot.

Jules faced Bridget. "I always liked your mom. 'Normal' changes all the time, doesn't it? Maybe one day I'll be the normal one. I mean, haven't we *all* given up Netflix?"

"*We* never had to give it up," Bridget replied. "You're the one who got obsessed with TV for a while. Which wasn't exactly a good thing."

"No." Jules didn't like to rehash these matters, but for Roger's benefit and to pull the conversation back on track, he elaborated. "I got lazy locked up twenty-four-seven. One-more-episode stopped me concentrating on the origins of the Witnesses. Which we all agree is the more important business. This..." Jules waved at the chimera statues. "It's nothing."

"It's business," Roger said. "And, frankly, I'm not impressed by this extracurricular stuff when we are pretty much single-handedly funding your institute. So, instead of daydreaming about this theoretical race of super-men, how about you concentrate on working out what you'll need to ensure a site we thought would rival the Terracotta Army becomes a site to rival Pompeii."

Toby's brow crinkled in concern. "Mr. Carson, Jules is referring to our efforts to unpick several books and scrolls previously. And we are very grateful for you not cutting off funding, but I can assure you we are fully focused on the task you are paying for. It's just that—"

Audrey returned. "He's unavailable."

"Good," Roger said. "Toby, please continue. You were saying how this Witnesses business is nothing more than a hobby these days?"

"It's not a hobby." Jules had dropped his filter. Unambiguous certainty filling his voice.

"Hey, hey." Harpal circled Jules and Roger, hands patting the air. "We all had to do something during lockdown, and now it's a long time over, we have jobs to do. We can go back to it when we're finished with Mr. Carson, right?"

Dan said, "Yeah, I boned up on a lot of that history stuff."

"That history stuff?" Bridget echoed.

Dan nodded. "Even some boring bits."

"Okay, this is getting us nowhere," Roger said. "The bottom line here is, you need to tell me how much equipment you need, how many people to operate it, and what sort of timeframe I need to give Mr. Xing."

Jules had followed through on their agreement made in New Zealand, but logic demanded that they pursue the more important questions. Questions that had grown in importance because he had spent so much time investigating them from the comfort of his armchair. And now this dig appeared to be ending, his entire body felt compelled to investigate their theories further.

There wasn't much concrete evidence. However, there were many starting points.

"All our research," Jules said. "All Bridget's code breaking and translations, everything we worked out, and we're here sucking up to the Chinese in the hope the Carson Corporation can partner with them on some copper mine in Burundi."

"Three copper mines, actually," Roger said. "And now a new nickel seam has been discovered in Indonesia that we're bidding for."

"And if you don't curry favor with your Communist Party friend, you get nothing," Jules finished for him.

"I don't like your tone." Roger squared off with him, although he clearly had no intention of getting physical. "What I want is answers to how you'll approach the wider excavation. Or we'll cut off your funding once Bridget goes back to Paris. Then see if you can go cap-in-hand to your Italian friend for another handout. Remind me how many goose-eggs you brought him the past couple of years. How much did he spend for nothing?"

Jules bit back what he wanted to say. When no one picked up the diplomatic baton, he replaced his angry reply with a petty correction. "Alfonse is Sicilian, not Italian."

"Sir," came a Nigerian-accented voice. It belonged to a thickset Nigerian man emerging from the trail, his gun stowed much like Dan's.

Roger nodded for his close protection officer to go on.

"Sir, a man has arrived on a scooter. With a little girl. They must have travelled the same trail as your contractors."

"What man?" Toby asked.

"You weren't expecting anyone?" Roger said nervously.

Dan tensed. "He have a name?"

"Xander," the bodyguard said. "Xander Madri."

CHAPTER THREE

Dan quickly relaxed into mild irritation. "Xander Madri. Damn. How'd he find us?"

"Who exactly is he?" Roger enquired. "And what is he doing at our *hidden* location?"

Dan moved to leave. "Don't worry, he's harmless. Just someone who doesn't know what 'stay away from us or we'll shoot you' really means. I'll get rid of him."

Harpal said, "How the hell did he find us in *China*?"

"Oh," Toby said in a half-grunt, half-cough that fooled no one.

"Did you know about it?" Dan asked.

Roger's annoyance increased by a few degrees. "Yes, Toby. Did you tell a stranger where this place is?"

"Not quite, but..." Toby ran out of steam. "I'm sorry. We needed some precautions."

"I did it," Harpal admitted. "I had a friend satellite track us. Only Toby and I were aware. The others still have no idea where we are. Didn't think he'd mail our location to a stalker."

Bridget and Dan both opened their mouths to speak, but Jules got in first. "It doesn't matter right now. Is this Xander Madri the same as Xander M?"

Toby scuffed his feet. "He is."

"Then me and Dan'll get rid of him. Come on."

Dan and Jules ran down the worn path where they'd found tiles and brickwork. By the time they arrived at the camp's entrance—a cold war era image of a steel barrier, barbed wire, and two private security goons from one of the Carson Corporation's shell companies—Bridget and Harpal were coming up behind, and Toby was visible some way back.

A handsome man in his early thirties stood next to the armed goons who were dressed in army surplus fatigues, pointing their submachine guns at the sky. The contents of the man's backpack had been stuffed back in and protruded from the top. He shielded a seven- or eight-year-old girl with olive skin, black curly hair, and almond-shaped eyes, who peered around the man's legs as Dan and Jules approached.

"I don't want to hear it," Dan said, careful to keep his gun stowed away from the girl.

"Please." Xander Madri pressed his hands together before splaying them in the universal gesture of, *I'm not a threat, honest*. "Five minutes, then I deliver an item, and then I will leave. I swear."

"You expect us to believe some crazy cyber-stalker?" Jules said.

"You must. Please. Ask your Mr. Smith. He will attest to my character."

"Toby will vouch for you, huh?"

"My friend has gone missing. I believe she was taken by very bad people. Please. I require your assistance. In exchange, I have something extremely valuable to offer."

Bridget and Harpal arrived.

"Wow, this isn't what I expected Xander M to look like," Harpal said.

"No way," Bridget said. "Me neither."

Jules took her in, then switched to Xander and back. She stroked her hair and parted her lips slightly. Jules was determined to get rid of the man as soon as possible.

Again, jealousy?

Jules rolled his eyes and suppressed his petty feelings. "Do you mean the stereotype of kooky conspiracy theorists as forty-year-old whales in sweatpants clogging up their mothers' basements?"

Bridget shook her head and stopped touching her hair. "A bit. Yeah."

Harpal approached Dan and gave Xander a thorough evaluation. "He's like a Mediterranean Tom Cruise. But taller."

Dan threw Harpal a bemused look. "Need a room?"

Finally catching up with them, Toby led Roger and Audrey along, their beefy guard holding his sidearm in a two-handed grip, pointed at the floor but clearly ready to fire. Toby was still breathing hard as he extended a hand to Xander, easing Dan and Jules away until he could speak.

"Gentlemen, please listen to him."

Roger motioned for his bodyguard to step aside. "Toby, this had better be good. I'm almost out of patience."

Toby gave a single nod.

Xander took his daughter's hand in his, spoke softly to her, and reached into his bag for an iPad for her. While her father stepped into what had somehow become a semi-circle of people, she sat cross-legged beside a private contractor's feet to play a game. He reiterated and expanded on the fact that bad men had kidnapped his friend. "She was exploring the Hypogeum Hal Salfieni. In Malta. Seeking something more recent."

"More recent?" Jules said. They were accustomed to learning about millennia-old artifacts, out-of-place objects that defied conventional historical accounts, rather than more recent work. "How old?"

"She thought it had been buried in the 1940s. However, it was much older."

Jules noticed Toby fidgeting. His expression remained stiff. Jules was about to press him to speak, but Dan also sensed something was up and took a firm stance.

Dan said, "Just spill it, Toby."

"Spill what?" Toby said.

"You only act like this when you're trying to hide something. We know you had Harps track us despite promising not to, so... spill. What exactly is this Hypothermic Hal Needle-whatever?"

"Fine." Toby made a final apologetic glance at his institute and explained. "The Hypogeum Hal Salfieni is one of the best preserved prehistoric sites on the planet. Six thousand years old. To put that in context, the Giza Pyramids are only four thousand five hundred years old."

Harpal gave a quiet whistle of appreciation.

Toby went on. "It is thought to be a necropolis. The oldest underground temple ever discovered. Pre-Sumerian."

"Yes, yes, yes." Xander had a fanatical grin on his face, his lovely eyes wide. "It truly is a unique location. My late wife adored it, but so much of it defies description. It is what made me question the historical narrative we are fed as children—"

"Yeah, yeah," Jules said. "But your brand of nonsense ain't what we do."

"Do you want the facts?"

"Facts are what we live for."

"Okay." Xander pumped his fists and adjusted his collar, as if preparing to fight. He spoke instead. "The Hypogeum amplifies sound one-hundred-fold. It appears intentional, but nobody knows for sure. If it was, Malta's culture, when most humans lived in caves and clubbed their dinner to death, understood harmonics and building techniques thousands of years ahead of their time."

Jules had heard of the location but never investigated it. He'd listen if Bridget or Toby said this, so he'd let Xander finish.

"We're certain it was a ritualistic location. They discovered elongated skulls—"

"Like, aliens?" Dan said.

Everyone groaned as the man-at-arms circled back to his favorite theory.

Xander blinked it away. "No, not like aliens. Manipulation begins at a young age, when the skulls are soft. It has recently been observed in some tribes in Africa, Asia, and South America."

"Your friend," Bridget said. "What happened? You said she was following a diary entry?"

Xander sighed, his eyes dulled. "It was the final clue needed to send her... She refused to tell me where. A professor and a priest pursued her. But she passed this on to me."

Xander reached down his pants, fiddled with what Jules hoped was a secret pocket, and produced a leather drawstring pouch.

"Oh, my, it's true," Toby said. "She found the cypher. It was really there."

"Are you certain you're not going down another pointless rabbit hole?" Harpal asked.

Toby shook his head. "I admit, yes, I was a little too... gung-ho in chasing clues that led nowhere."

"Seven, by the way," Jules said, answering Roger's earlier question about how many times they'd wasted Alfonse's money. "If Toby starts gambling again, we got a problem, but let's hear the kook out first."

"Thank you," Xander said. "I think."

"I've been rash," Toby continued. "However, this..." He motioned to the iPad in the girl's hands. "Is that the same device that we delivered to the hotel?"

Xander took the iPad from his daughter, who pouted as he launched an app that appeared to be a CAD-style design program. It displayed a rotating 3D rendering of a machine, an ornate box containing a device with cogs inside, and a floating star map that appeared to be disconnected from the body.

"That's the Antikythera Mechanism," Bridget said.

Jules examined the graphics. "No. Similar. Very similar. That one was two thousand years old. Roman. Or Greek." Jules studied the mechanics. "Something's missing." Without understanding the device's function, his brain mapped it out and saw that it lacked one crucial component. "It needs another cog."

"Yes. Exactly." Xander untied the string, opened the tiny pouch, and inserted his finger and thumb. They emerged holding a gold disc with a serrated edge, similar to a clock's cog but with much smaller teeth. "Her last words to me before she vanished were, 'Find Toby Smith.'"

"What exactly is that?" Harpal asked.

"The cypher," Xander said.

"No, no." Bridget narrowed her eyes. "A cypher is used to decode things. This is... It's pretty, but it's unmarked."

The disc was about the size of a matchbook, with an uneven serrated edge that would fit perfectly into the 3D-rendered device.

"That's what's missing," Jules said.

"Yes," Xander said. "Prihya was very excited to slot it into the real machine."

The group fell silent in a stunned hush.

"Wait," Dan said. "Did you say Prihya? *Prihya* is your kidnapped friend?"

"Okay." Harpal clapped Xander's shoulder and took the cog from his fingers. "If Prihya is working with Xander, I say we get a cup of tea and hear him out. Okay?"

CHAPTER FOUR

SMALL TALK WAS THE WORST. Jules believed it should only be used to set the tone of a stranger-to-stranger conversation, and only then if it was absolutely necessary to break the ice. A person's, "It's raining," could be cheerful or depressing, foreshadowing the nature of the upcoming interaction. Even in those cases, inane chitchat should be avoided because most opening salvos can be conveyed through body language and words.

Pointless chatter also involved withholding important information. Xander wanted to reveal the mysterious part of his story rather than the most important part.

"Could've led with Prihya bein' in trouble," Jules said as they escorted Xander and his daughter—now introduced as Katrina, or "Kat"—to the dining tent.

Inside the tent, they elected Harpal chief tea-and-coffee maker since it had been his idea, and they made themselves as comfortable as possible at the two tables with folding chairs around them. Basic but functional.

"Do we have to?" Roger Carson said as he snapped the flap back.

Audrey stepped in behind him and touched his arm. "It's about their friend, Roger. Let them listen."

Roger bristled but complied. Bridget mouthed, "Thank you," and they all settled in as Harpal served.

Xander settled Kat down with the iPad once again, before

outlining the events in what Jules appreciated as sparse and to-the-point language.

He'd been contacted via his website, which offered tours and lectures on "the hidden truth of human history" based on his local knowledge (likely), expert research (doubtful), and independent verification (virtually impossible). Toby confirmed it had been Alfonse running the covert side via an intermediary, a double-blind arrangement, so the Carsons would not infer Toby was giving them less than one hundred percent.

"Except you *were* short-changing us with your time," Roger pointed out.

"Hush," Audrey said.

Xander proceeded with a series of events that included him paying cash for a hotel room where no photographic ID would be scanned onto a cloud server, meeting a woman at the dock who was arriving by the oldest ferry still in operation—which lacked halfway decent CCTV—and escorting her as if they were a couple.

"She was nice," Kat said without looking up from the screen.

"Yes, she was." Xander's smile shone with admiration. And more than a little fear.

"You involved your daughter?" Dan said.

"Dinner was needed. My childcare is the other wait-staff at the café where I work. But, no, I never involve Kat in anything that I believe is dangerous. It's the first time..." Xander made a tiny hiccupping sound, the sound of a man swallowing guilt or worry. "It was the first time anything I investigated became something the authorities needed to suppress with force."

Jules had met Xander online, and when he kept breaking through their blocking mechanisms, most of LORI had at some point answered his calls or emails. Although Charlie Locke's software and engineering genius meant that incidental images of the team were constantly scrubbed from the internet, their existence had made it onto several forums on both the dark and light web. Xander wanted to learn more about them, so he could decide whether they were on his side or the side of the World Order, which lied about Stonehenge, the Pyramids of Giza, Babylon, Damascus Steel, and even the moon landings being faked.

"Let's keep to the facts," Jules said. "What happened to Prihya? What'd she tell you about this cipher thing?"

"Not much. She suspected someone had hidden it in a place that had been fully investigated already. No one would go digging around there again. The diary said it was a cipher hidden inside an enigma."

"Very poetic. Facts?"

Xander accepted tea from Harpal and sipped it black. "She found it. She brought it out. She came to my café, and the professor and the priest scared her enough to make her slip the disk to me and run away."

"Which professor?" Toby asked. "Did she introduce you?"

"No, but he was clever. He spoke like the professors I have met with. Knew about the Hypogeum. But he was big. Fit. Like a... like him." Xander pointed at Dan.

"Sounds like one of Valerio's people," Harpal said.

"Who is Valerio?" Xander asked.

"A bad man," Bridget answered.

"With a lot of money," Toby said. "And resources."

Jules recalled the academics who trained as assassins and spies for the same reason Valerio Conchin had set out to discover the secrets LORI sought. He'd slaughtered dozens in order to reach the Tomb of the First Priest, which could cure his untreatable condition, but the structure had collapsed, nearly killing him. While he recovered, the man had what Prihya called his scholar-assassins do his dirty work.

Dan said, "If he's involved, Prihya might be dead already."

Toby fiddled with the disc. "We knew this held some provenance not associated with its resting place. We knew it slotted in to a machine described in a manuscript unearthed in Kenya—one of the few we managed to open. Valerio was on the same trail."

Bridget stared hard at Toby. "Why didn't you tell us you were working with Prihya?"

"Plausible deniability," Toby replied. "I didn't want you to have to lie to your parents." He glanced up at Roger and Audrey. "Especially since they have been so kind as to fund both your education in Paris and allow us to continue using Chateau Caché as our base."

Bridget huffed but kept on track. "Fine. What does it do?"

"We aren't sure. We *think* it represents a journey of sorts."

"Leading where?" Jules asked. "We been doing all that research, all that brainstormin' and storytellin', while you helped someone go out and find this, and didn't tell us?"

Toby adjusted his expression to enhance his apologetic manner. "You had grown rather... obsessive during those closed-in months. If I'd said this might have something to do with the Witnesses, would you have fulfilled our contract here?"

Jules said nothing.

"I didn't think so." A rueful look landed on Roger and Audrey. "And I believed simply employing people through subcontractors did not breach our agreement. You had my full attention and expertise."

"So, what's next?" Harpal asked.

Dan adjusted his grip on the SMG. "We find Valerio and shoot him in the face."

Toby took out a sat-phone. "But first, we have to find him. Let me do the talking."

He set the phone to speaker mode and hit a speed dial button. It rang twice before the recipient picked up, his plummy accent a thousand times more British than Toby's.

"Hello, Professor Smith. Nice to hear from you again."

Toby's head dropped. "Hello, Colin. How did you know this was my number?"

"We keep tabs on several people of interest," Colin Waterston replied. If smug had a color, it'd have radiated from the handset. "What can I do for you?"

"Thank you for taking my call." Toby's poshness amplified to the max when speaking with Colin. Always did. "Are you well?"

"I can't complain. You know how a change of management can often necessitate a refresh of the staff. But His Majesty has seen fit to keep me on following his mother's passing, for which I am exceedingly grateful. I would enquire after your health, Toby, but I can find that out if I need to. How about we get down to brass tacks, hmm? Why are you calling your favorite protégé from a dig in deepest, darkest China?"

To his credit, Toby kept his posh voice firm. "It's about our mutual friend, Valerio Conchin. Am I presuming too much to expect he is also someone you keep tabs on?"

"Oh, him, yes. Our miracle man is up and about again. Funnily enough, I received a security update recently. Something about his oddball enforcers causing a ruckus on Malta."

"Yes. He kidnapped someone we would like to reacquire unharmed." Toby frowned at the awkward phrasing, picking up the same as Jules: he was overcompensating, given the imbalance of power between the former student and his mentor.

"From what I can gather," Colin said with an exasperated sigh, "he is on a wild goose chase in Ecuador."

Jules leaned in. "Whereabouts in Ecuador?"

"Ah, is that Jules Sibeko? Am I on a party line with the rest of the gang, Toby?"

Toby narrowed his eyes at Jules. "Jules, Dan, Harpal, and Bridget." He didn't mention the Carsons-senior. "Please, Colin. We will not embarrass you or cause you any problems. We just need a hint about why and where he took our friend."

Silence answered, lingering for several seconds with a light click-clacking in the background.

Colin came back on the line. "Valerio is, indeed, on a wild goose chase."

"Many wild geese have been chased to yield unexpected results, Colin. Which one is this?"

"That silly library rumor in Ecuador."

Bridget perked up, leaning in. "Library?"

Toby shook it off, a wave of his hand to dismiss the notion. "Do you mean the Tayos caves?"

"That seems to be the general area," Colin said.

Addressing the room, Toby elaborated. "One of those crazy lost gold stories. And it's been explored to death. There are some majestic caves, but it's more of a geological wonder than archaeological."

Dan mirrored Bridget's perking up. "Hey, wait, you don't mean the Neil Armstrong thing, do you?"

Xander now looked confused. "He is the moon guy? One of the actors who pretended to fly there?"

Dan tutted. "No, he didn't fake the moon landings. But he might have encountered aliens."

Jules smirked. "Aliens again? Really?"

"It's true," Dan insisted. "This is what the expedition was about. Armstrong needed proof to go public—"

Colin coughed for attention. "Okay, I believe I have divulged far more than I am obliged to. I will email over all we have on Mr. Conchin's whereabouts and progress, but you might be better reporting him to the Ecuadorian authorities. If he has kidnapped someone."

"Just one other thing," Toby said, a finger to his lips to shush Dan. "He may be traveling with a priest. Do you know anything about that?"

Colin again paused before answering, as if there were someone else there, directing what he could and could not say. "He might be a former cardinal from the Vatican who joined a sect that split from the core Roman Catholic Church. He goes by the name Father Emory Ballard. We have frustratingly little on him, so he is probably just one of Valerio's intermediaries. I have to go now. But, Toby?"

"Yes?"

"Chatter suggests Valerio is obsessed with some weapon. The one he thought he'd find in that damn tomb that fell on him in India. We also believe it was he who dispatched the female Striovian general and her mercenaries to Montrose *and* raided that repository in Kenya."

They knew all about Kenya, but it was the first Jules had heard of Valerio's involvement with the Striovians.

"He seems convinced there's some sort of sword or spear. Probably metaphorical, but you never know. General Yanovna was chasing a weapon, too."

"Might it be real?" Bridget asked.

"Who knows? He seems to have exhausted everything from the Sword of Damocles to Excalibur. And now this golden library. I expect it's left over from the conquistadors or some such fantasy thinking. Whatever it turns out to be, feel free to *not* cause an international incident. A postcard will suffice."

The line clicked dead without a goodbye.

Harpal sat up straight as if in surprise. "Well, he was surprisingly forthcoming."

Xander pointed at Dan. “But he knows more.”

All heads slowly turned Dan’s way.

Dan held up both hands in surrender. “I had time to read a lot of stuff, okay? This was one of the more interesting things.”

“Okay, so,” Toby said. “Might I suggest Dan explain what he knows about Valerio’s destination and, therefore, where Prihya may be? How about you lead the briefing for a change?”

“Me?”

“Can’t be worse than Toby,” Jules said.

Harpal laughed. “Just don’t be boring.”

CHAPTER FIVE

Dan Vincent didn't talk much, unless you counted "Freeze, asshole" and "Yes, please, another beer" as talk. He liked to act because the academic side of his primary job was less important, even though he knew if he dug deep enough, he'd find something that would blow his mind. So, while imprisoned in a French chateau for weeks that turned into months, he turned to books. The internet, as well. You can only work out, train, and clean your (legal) guns so many times a day.

On Bridget's advice, he relied only on scientifically credible sources instead of YouTube to learn about historical anomalies. He read books with highbrow names and qualifications about subjects that verged on fantasy, including one featuring one of Dan's heroes, Neil Armstrong. The first man on the moon had trekked through South American jungles with a famous historian in search of the greatest archaeological prize in history, a project not fully understood to this day.

But before he could enlighten his colleagues and friends, Roger Carson chose that moment to stamp his authority.

"No. This is ridiculous. The contract we agreed on spells out exactly what would happen if you discovered additional areas of interest. I need to bring more than a playground to our..."

Carson was at a loss for words. Dan mentally inserted, "Masters," but Bridget's father snagged his preferred term.

"*Clients.* Discovering what appears to be a grand residence from three centuries ago, not to mention the farming or mining operation that these landowners allegedly ran—"

Toby tentatively raised a hand. "We're speculating, Mr. Carson. Nothing suggests this is a Chinese Pompeii."

"And landslides don't work like that, Dad." Bridget sounded as irritated as Dan felt. "It's mud. Organic material. Anything edible or anyone buried here will be reduced to bone fragments. And that's assuming it wasn't swept over a mile away, which happens all the time. I wouldn't even expect a skeleton."

Audrey Carson joined him. "Surely, Bridget, you understand as well as anyone that the first step toward success is to try."

"Mom... at best, you might find some wall outlines, house foundations, farming or rudimentary digging tools. But nothing of significance."

"Or you might find a three-hundred-year-old snapshot of Chinese rural life," Roger added. "I'll ship in your ground radar."

Jules, who had been uncharacteristically quiet, spoke up now. "I'm leaving."

Roger gave him a venomous look. "You're doing what, now?"

"My friend's been abducted. I'm takin' Dan, and after hearing his story—hopefully in less detail than Toby's usual lectures—I'm gettin' her back."

Roger gave a fake chuckle. "Do you believe there aren't people better suited to handle an extraction?"

"Probably. But if Valerio's kidnapping people off the streets to find a tomb or stash or whatever around the Amazon, I wanna know what that thing is. You heard Colin. He's fixated on a weapon. If it's anythin' like we've found before, it ain't something a guy like him should get close to. Not a government either."

"What weapon?" Roger asked, as if a weapon were as daft a notion as a unicorn.

"It might not be a weapon," Toby said. "General Yanovna followed the Reaper clues to Montrose in search of a vast power source, resulting in her incarceration. She—and we—found a small corner of it. A sample. It was part of a worldwide network, its exact purpose of which remains a mystery to us."

Danger. Death. Threats.

Dan's department. "Can't let him get it. And Prihya being with him, that's just more incentive to do it carefully. Ecuadorian military or police spec ops execute a mass raid, they'll get her killed."

"We can negotiate, or we can take her," Harpal said. "Either way, hear us out."

Jules had advanced and stood directly in front of Roger. "When we get her back, she'll come here with us. We'll use Charlie's new ground penetratin' radar to investigate this wreck of a site, and you can spin whatever we find as enhancing China's greatness to your clients."

Roger made a mental calculation, engaged in silent conversation with his wife, and both Carsons took a step back.

Jules made a shallow bow toward Dan.

Dan nodded his thanks and cleared his throat. Weird, being more nervous about this than readying to breach a Taliban warehouse. "Yeah, this came from some of my downtime research. I got into it, but not the big dusty volumes you guys like."

Bridget's brow furrowed. She and Toby sat with their arms folded, tiny smiles on the corners of their mouths.

Were they... humoring him?

Fine. He'd out-Toby Toby on this one.

"I only looked at the interesting stuff. Like, suspicious accounts backed up with science. Stuff that regular history don't explain too well."

"Do you mean where aliens could be the explanation?" Toby spoke up.

Yeah, definitely humoring him.

"Let him talk," Harpal said. "It's impolite to interrupt."

"Thank you, Harps."

Harpal aimed a finger gun at Dan. "Don't forget, we still have a fifty dollar bet on that one."

Roger appeared to be about to break his promise to allow Dan to speak. "Aliens, now? Really? What does this have to do with the caves in Ecuador?"

"Right, so..." Rather than get riled up, Dan held his reaction in check. "In August 1976, Neil Armstrong leads a massive expedition into the rain forest. He's looking for a cave system known locally as Cueva de los Tayos."

"Tayos cave!" Xander said excitedly. He'd joined his daughter to let LORI and the Carsons negotiate, but now he butted in. "Yes, yes, I know of this, too."

"Yeah, well, it's my story, so sit quietly and play." Dan coughed another catch from his throat. "Over a hundred people involved. Big private funding. Ecuadorian soldiers, scientists, tour guides, and historians... When I first heard about it, I assumed Armstrong had fallen on hard times and needed the money, but he was still employed by the federal government. He made a decent living. It started with this British scientist, Scott Hall. Reputable. He got Armstrong hooked."

"On what, specifically?" Toby asked.

"An underground ancient library."

Bridget's face lit up once more. The group had discovered many wonders, from an ancient art repository to an archive of scrolls inside rotting cases designed to crack a vial of acid if not opened properly.

A library full of what they assumed were texts from the race they'd labeled the Witnesses...?

That would be mana from heaven for Bridget.

Jules, on the other hand, rolled his eyes as he did whenever Dan suggested aliens might be to blame. "Oh, I've heard of this. I remember now."

"Didn't you recognize it right away?" Bridget said. "I thought you had perfect recall."

"Only when I compartmentalize it. For crap that's already been disproven a dozen ways, I move it outta my brain to make room. This? I glanced at it when I was nineteen, thinkin' it'd be a hot payday. But I wrote it off. Origin is a daft book from a Swiss guy, Erich von Däniken. Says ETs visited Earth and left behind books made of metal. Carved in some mysterious language."

He waited a moment, as if considering whether to go on with his take-down of the story.

"Look, just because someone respectable like this Scott guy or Neil Armstrong believes it, don't make it less stupid. I mean, how would that be practical? Even the Witnesses needed a resin to preserve their books."

"Ridiculous," Dan said, holding his ground, "for humans."

Groans all round. Mutters of, "Aliens again."

Dan wasn't deterred. "A Hungarian guy called Juan-something found it years before von Däniken wrote his book. It's a fact."

"Juan Moricz," Jules said, plainly mining his mental recycle bin. "Yeah, he found it alright. Found it, went in, brought out no proof whatsoever, and when Neil Armstrong came callin', he couldn't find his way back."

"But think about it," Dan said, including Roger and Audrey in his appeal. "If LORI find this library of gold, it'd be conclusive proof that aliens had once visited Earth."

Toby remained suspiciously silent.

Harpal asked, "Why else would someone like Armstrong believe this?"

"Glad you asked," Dan said. "Was it perhaps sparked by a close encounter during the blackout in comms during the 1969 moon mission?"

"Blackout in comms?" Bridget said.

"A full two minutes of nothing. Men on the moon, cut off. Silence. A comms fault that had never happened before, and hasn't happened since."

Toby broke his silence. "And what do you think happened during these moments?"

"There are accounts of Armstrong switching his comms channel to the medical officer's. The public did not hear it, but he says, 'They're on the edge of the crater and they're watching us.'" Dan treated the comment like a mic-drop, but no one responded. "What, or who, was watching?"

After another lengthy spell of people staring at him, it was Jules who spoke up again. "It's stupid. There's no evidence of that."

"Ah, but Armstrong never discussed the two minutes of missing audio. Was he under orders? If it was nothing special, nothing worth hiding, why say nothing? Why not say, 'Yeah, it was just us trying to get comms back up'? And later, his behavior shows elements that we recognize today as PTSD." Dan was back in the flow, circling back the way Toby always did. "Plus, Armstrong just got on with his required duties when he returned to Earth. The only extraordinary thing he did after the moon mission was this expedition."

Xander had been nodding along. He was an avowed moon-landing-denier, but seemed to like what he was hearing. "It's true. The mission into the jungle. All true."

"And people are still looking for it," Dan added.

"What people?" Jules asked. "Apart from your new friend the kook here?"

"Who's looking for it, you ask?" Toby moved toward Dan and, if he'd been taller, would have stood shoulder to shoulder with him. "Valerio Conchin, for one. Amongst others."

They all focused on Toby now. The man had looked amused as Dan took his usual job from him, but now appeared as serious as any other day.

"You knew about Prihya," Jules said. "You knew about that cipher thing. And hid it from us. Now I'm guessin' you knew about Armstrong's expedition and the truth behind it."

"Not aliens, I assume," Harpal said.

Jules cocked his head, clearly put out. "Anything else you're hiding from us?"

Toby conceded, and indicated Dan could stand aside, his moment in the academic spotlight over. "There's more truth to this than you might have anticipated. I need a prop, though, if you'll indulge me for a few minutes more. Follow me."

CHAPTER SIX

THE SUPPLY TENT in the camp's far corner held replacement parts for the Carsons' airlifted industrial equipment. Toby also wanted a smaller tent for items excavated during the dig. A long table held pots, a sword hilt, and figurines. These were the first signs that this was not a royal tomb but a wealthy estate belonging to a family with at least one lucky child.

Lucky, that was, if they survived the landslide that buried the property.

As the group entered the storage tent lined with shelves for the cleaned and preserved items, Toby was glad of the break from this rather mundane project.

Toby said, "In 1984, more than three hundred pieces of interest were uncovered near La Maná, in Ecuador. Metal plates, a few stone tablets, etched with glyphs, including what some say are Illuminati symbols, a few even resembling the pyramid on US currency. Personally, I thought they had more in common with Egyptian art, but that's over eleven thousand kilometers away."

"Where are these items now?" Roger Carson asked.

"In a private collection. And the owner has made it clear he has no interest in sharing. But before then, I once enjoyed the privilege of studying some of them."

Toby crossed the tent to one of the four freestanding cabinets, each one in fact a safe the size of a bedroom chest of drawers, for any items of value emerging from the ground. There had been no bones, no cooking utensils or pottery, no jewelry, and none of the home comforts one would expect to find in such an environment. But Toby didn't leave the safes empty.

As he entered the code for one of them, he continued his tale.

"The tablets appeared to consist of a combined artistic makeup of Mayan and South-East Asian. Surprisingly, many tablets displayed writing similar to Sanskrit, a language from far away, and not quite as old as the items were."

Bridget said, "No people who wrote in Sanskrit had a major seafaring industry. Little more than fishing and essential travel between islands and bays."

Toby opened the heavy safe door. "Much of the art and written tablets are calcite rock which has special properties, revealing more markings under ultraviolet light. More graphics. As if a secret message were carved there. Plates with circles and spirals, constellations, ritual depictions. And a map."

Toby reached into the safe and started edging out a wooden box as large as his torso and about six times as heavy. He had to walk it inch-by-careful-inch.

"This map depicted the continents as they would have appeared in the pre-ice-age, pre-Younger-Dryas era. Like the ones we saw in Canada. These continental shapes are from long before the world-wide floods and other catastrophes written about in religious and scholarly texts. Huge landmasses that are now submerged. A massive island from the middle of the Atlantic to its eastern point. We believed at the time it might have been the start of the myth that led to Plato writing his accounts of Atlantis."

"Huh, we're into Atlantis now," Jules commented.

"There is also the image—when viewed under the right light—of a Pacific island." Toby concentrated on easing the carton to the edge so he could get his fingers underneath. "An almost continent-sized mass, south of what is now Japan. For a while, we thought it coincided with Yonaguni."

"Which is...?" Dan asked.

Xander was nodding again, his daughter disgruntled since he took the iPad from her during the walk. "It is more evidence of an ancient civilization that lived long before even the Hypogeum Hal Salfieni's architects. Atlantis is one city—"

Jules said, "The Yonaguni rocks are natural formations that look man-made. I dived the area once. Looks like steps. A pyramid wall. But they've never found artifacts there. No sign of humans. *Or* aliens. It's just that square-looking crack that rock does under pressure. Toby, you want a hand with that?"

"No. I have it, thank you." Toby got his fingers then his whole hand under, supporting the top with his other, and lifted it up, pushing to his feet as his knees creaked, and lay it on the cabinet's surface.

"Let's get to the point," Harpal said. "I get the feeling Toby could talk about this for hours."

Jules agreed. "We start down more stupid paths like Atlantis, we'll never get out. What's in the box?"

Toby held back a fake chuckle. It always made him sound nervous, so he set it aside. Except now Jules was looking at him oddly. Had he detected something wrong?

Toby laid a hand flat on the box's lid. "Many speculated it was these items the Armstrong party had been searching for, but in the wrong place. However, this isn't quite how things went. You see, one Professor Petrionion Jaramillo claimed to have seen the library when he was aged seventeen. In 1946. Via a map given to him by his uncle. And it wasn't tablets or etchings."

"Where is this map now?" Roger asked.

"Ah. That's the question, isn't it?" Toby took a small, flat screwdriver from one pocket and eased it into the box's sealed lid, prying a hair's breadth of a crack where it had been nailed shut. "What this boy found, he said, was thousands of volumes of metal books, each weighing forty pounds each—"

"Eighteen kilograms," Jules said.

"No one knows what a kilogram is," Dan replied.

"You do know the entire world is metric, don't you? Even the US military and space agencies are metric. It's only civilians that cling to that stupid imperial system."

"If you're American, you stick with pounds and ounces, miles and inches."

Jules waved him off. "Metric's more logical. I vote the Institute should go metric. Show of hands...?"

"Ahem," Toby interrupted. "Is no one interested in this book?"

Bridget raised her hand. "I am."

"Me, too," Katrina said, also raising her hand.

Xander beamed at the girl. "Yes, let us hear more about this gold library."

"Thank you." Toby had levered a gap all the way around the box. "Getting to Neil Armstrong's party, they followed Professor Jaramillo's information through dense jungle, fending off wild animals, risking viruses untouched by man—"

Jules said, "Getting a bit flowery with the prose there, Toby."

Toby sighed, disappointed he couldn't paint a more vivid scene. "They found what they thought were the caves outside Tayos. The descent is long and dark, but once there's light, many of the walls look like they cannot be natural."

"Except it can be," Bridget said. "Rock often corrodes or sheers off in straight-ish lines."

"Like Yonaguni," Jules added.

Toby used a larger screwdriver to widen the gap in the lid. "They found Cathedral-like chambers, dating back thousands of years. They claim they found a burial chamber... a seated skeleton from around 1500 BCE."

Xander wagged a finger, an *ah-ha* expression leading him. "This predates Tutankhamun. Before the siege of Troy."

"Yes," Toby said. "But In 1500 BCE, Ecuador was very advanced. Comparatively speaking. The entrance to the chamber saw the sun shine directly inside during the summer solstice, which is rarely accidental. Of the ten miles of caves, they believed many appeared to be man-made. Unfortunately, Armstrong had to abandon the search after weeks of looking. Supplies ran low, and so did money to replenish them. They found no library, produced no evidence, their only assertion being that there were many more miles of unexplored caves."

Toby removed the box's lid, and all were silent.

Dan took that as his cue to break in. "Why did they give up? They could have gotten more supplies and more money. Why did

Armstrong go in the first place? Why did he never talk publicly about his reasons for joining the expedition?"

"My guess," Xander said, "is that they found this library. And it gives us the answers about life on other planets, the secrets of our galaxy. But the authorities want to control that information. And keep it for themselves."

Jules said, "The real mysteries here are: first, why is Valerio following a failed trail? Second, why was Prihya being tailed if the caves' location is already known? What sent her to Malta? Because I doubt Toby dug it out of a book. And how is it all connected?"

Toby dipped his hands into the box, dug under the straw and bubble-wrap packing, and slid out the contraption he'd had shipped over, but had not expected to use so soon. Funny how it reminded him of a three-foot tall grandfather clock with the clock face missing. He held it out for all to see.

"The cipher disk our new friend brought us is the answer."

Xander grew excited again. "You see? This is why we must find Prihya... and take what Valerio has seeking."

"And how do you expect to do that?" Roger Carson asked.

Toby opened a flap on the front of the machine, revealing a network of cogs and gears, the motion of the hinges causing a platform to rise out of the top, bearing what looked like a merry-go-round populated by planets and stars. "Because Charlie's secret project is here. A real, updated version of the Antikythera Mechanism, derived through plans we deciphered from a scroll Prihya supplied."

"Something else you kept from us?" Jules said.

Toby ignored the barb. "This should take us to where Valerio was headed. And, hopefully, Prihya too."

"If she's still alive," Harpal said.

"Indeed." Toby fiddled with the disk, found the gap between two dials inside the machine, and slotted it in. Perfect fit. "Now, let's fire this up, shall we?"

"No," Jules said. "This stinks. I need a word. In private."

Bridget looked worried. "What... what's going on?"

"I wanna clear something up before you do your thing."

"What thing?" Toby asked.

"Where you talk too much. But you kept stuff from us, and I wanna be sure first. Between you and me. Before we go on."

Toby saw it was fruitless to refuse.

"You know what I'm talkin' about," Jules pressed.

"Very well," Toby said. "Follow me."

CHAPTER SEVEN

TAYOS EXPEDITION CAMP - ECUADOR

Moses and Muzaffer dragged Prihya into Valerio's dark, hot hut by her arms, and she cried out as they released her with a shove into the intense humidity. Secretly, she was relieved to arrive at the ratty militia camp after the journey in the adapted Land Rover from the airport and on a rotting boat that resembled a US Vietnam-era troop carrier had left her with so many aches she would have been happy to lie on the ground for a couple of hours.

She quickly got her bearings.

The bamboo hut was connected to the earth by deep, bald roots that smelled like decay and greenery. A counter on one side held several scrolls, while a hammock on the other suggested Valerio liked to sleep elevated. Currently, he lay in the hammock, wide awake, watching the trio before swinging his legs over the side.

"Good afternoon." Valerio landed in his boots. Wearing beige shorts and a blueprint Hawaiian shirt, he looked like a car salesman on vacation as he all but skipped across the floor to the desk with the mesh office chair behind it. The furniture reminded Prihya of colonial explorer chic; all Valerio needed was a pith helmet and an ornate cane. "Great to see you again, Prihya."

Prihya held herself straight, unwilling to show fear. "Didn't know bamboo grew here."

"Two thirds of all plant species grow here. And bamboo sprouts so fast, it's one of the most environmentally sustainable materials known to man."

"Great." Prihya exaggerated a sneer to show how not-scared she was. "I'm the victim of a green kidnapping."

"Victim?" Valerio forced a quick laugh. "You're not a victim. You're the plucky survivor of what might have been a murder if I'd been in one of my moods that day. So, let's call it a... very robust invitation."

"Invitations aren't usually forced."

Valerio glided around the desk without sitting. Unlike when they last met almost four years earlier, he appeared vivacious, almost spry. He'd recovered in a couple years thanks to the Tomb of the First Priest, the wreckage from which Prihya had dug him and Horse. She was told on the plane from Europe that saving his life was a debt, and was the only reason he was offering her the choice to help rather than torturing her.

"Come this way," he said, making for the door with a little skip halfway there. His smile suggested a man about to offer a tour of his new house to his first guests. "Gents, you can stay."

He opened the door and led Prihya to an encampment that reminded her of a faltering militia rebellion. As soon as the scholar-assassins brought her from the river into this stinking place, she sensed the tiredness and frustration meandering through the air. Local mercenaries could not replace loyal soldiers like the scholar-assassins. Or Father Emory Ballard, it seemed, who joined them in what was clearly a planned arrangement.

After touching down yesterday, a helicopter had whisked him away, while Prihya and camp supplies were loaded into a lorry. Emory had opted to keep his priest's outfit and showed not a drop of sweat.

"Rest assured, Prihya, I am not only seeking the golden books. I am Mr. Conchin's spiritual advisor. While I am here, no harm will come to you. Unless you threaten harm first. Then..." He spread his hands as if helpless. "Then, Mr. Conchin will do what he feels is right."

Valerio grinned in an affected way that Prihya read as him trying for *mischievous*, but hit her as *malevolent*. "Cool, huh? I got my own spiritual advisor."

"One that'll keep me safe?" Prihya asked.

"Of course," Valerio said. "I mean, within reason."

"Sure."

Prihya figured they were lying their butts off. Still, she had seen Valerio act in far more erratic ways than he was today. Today, he seemed positively calm. However, if it meant getting his hands on whatever he believed lurked within the caves, she had no doubt he would murder everyone within his field of view, including Prihya.

"We've been camped here for almost a month," Valerio told her, with the air of someone meeting a new customer at their donut shop. "It's really hot. And dirty. And *so many* creepy-crawlies. Did you know it's louder at night than in the daytime? Those damn monkeys... But there's plenty of sustenance. Have you ever eaten bushmeat?"

"Yes," Prihya said.

"It's very nice. The sizzle is much more pleasing to the ears than their howls keeping me awake at all hours. And tasty. Do you know what MREs are?"

"No need to mansplain 'meals ready to eat,' Valerio. I've been eating MREs for years."

Valerio paused and looked guilty for a moment, plainly reading her snipe at him. "Very good. You were always smart." In the same singsong conversational tone, he added, "Tell me where my cipher is."

She shook her head. "It wasn't where I thought it was going to be."

"Come, come, that's a dumb denial."

Valerio resumed the mini tour, skirting the edge of the camp, keeping her away from what looked like trenches and open-fronted workshops where weapons and excavation equipment were being maintained.

"Let me tell you something you perhaps don't know. Our friends Moses and Renata examined the same evidence you did. They believe Muzaffer and Hilla can reconstruct the machine detailed in that scroll, and that all four agree... a missing cog was hidden in that temple. Because that was where a young explorer travelled to in 1946.

A clever ruse. Hide something ancient and precious in a place that has been excavated to death, where no one will ever dig again. Only, you did dig, and my agents would have dug there too, had they ascertained the exact spot."

Prihya said nothing.

Father Emory asked, "Who sent you?"

"I discovered it on my own. I'd broken up with my boyfriend and I'd gotten bored."

"And yet," Valerio said, "you have many, many resources unavailable to most girls traveling the world solo. The only way you could get as far as you did is with the help of someone like my old buddy, Alfonse Luca. Which means Toby Smith and his really annoying band of 'freelance archaeologists' are probably involved, too."

"No," Prihya said sharply. "I haven't heard from Toby Smith since he left New Zealand."

Valerio smiled and threw a signal back to where Moses and Muzaffer were trailing. "You deny Smith's involvement. But not Alfonse."

Damn, she'd fallen for it.

Valerio glanced briefly—and a little smugly—at Father Emory. "That means she is, indeed, working for Alfonse Luca."

"*Funded* by," Prihya said. "I work alone."

Valerio mooched along, gesturing at a mountainous hill, green laden with gray chunks. Beyond that hill was the Amazon river, the channel they'd transported her down after the bone-jangling, four-hour transfer from a logging firm's private airstrip.

He said, "This camp is the precise location of one of Armstrong's groups. They explored miles of caverns. We've gone deeper and found a few signs of ancient habitation, but no X marking the spot. I think this cave is a distraction. A red herring."

Prihya was familiar with Neil Armstrong's expedition, and Professor Jaramillo's diary. Jaramillo only ever hinted at why he'd maintained the deception until his death, and Prihya needed to know for sure.

"You always knew when I lied to you," she said.

"Indeed."

"Am I lying now?" She halted and faced Valerio, staring at his nose. She couldn't stand to look him directly in the eye, but people can't pick up the difference when you focus on the nose. "I don't know where the cipher is. I can't help you more than I already have."

Valerio studied her in silence. The soldiers and mercenaries gave them a wide berth, their crunching underfoot and occasional clatter seeming louder all around. A muffled *thoom* in the distance indicated some group was exploring potential entrances to the cave system.

Valerio said, "She's telling the truth."

"Technically, probably," Emory added in his light Italian accent. "I think, though, a lady of this intellect and guile has hidden depths."

Valerio gave him a curious look.

The priest said, "While she might not know where it is at this moment, but we are certain she passed it to a friend. So, whom might this friend seek out?"

Valerio nodded and returned to her. "Is that true, Prihya? Are you dicking with me using semantics?"

Prihya got instantly annoyed at her body language as her teeth clenched together. A classic subconscious attempt to withhold information.

She turned to Father Emory. "If you're a priest, how come you're working with this maniac?"

Valerio smirked at the word *maniac*.

Emory said, "I will ensure he is gentle when he collects your friend. And his daughter. No unnecessary death or maiming."

"He's right," Valerio said. "But make me pry it out of you, and I'll kill everyone who has come into contact with my cipher."

"I caution you, Valerio." Father Emory circled the pair, hands clasped behind him. "There is no point in accomplishing a holy mission if you lose your soul in the process."

Valerio pursed his lips as if holding in an angry outburst.

Emory halted by Valerio's shoulder, focusing on Prihya. "Although the Vatican and I parted ways, I maintain my vows. I aim to accomplish worldwide enlightenment. But the Holy See's plodding patience is... unproductive. Even when people like Cardinal Valdez flirt with your employer, Mr. Luca, it is not a direct line to the ultimate answers."

"My employer?" Prihya said. "I work for myself."

"*Benefactor*, then. You were supplied with much help from Alfonse Luca's shell companies, including the fixer in Malta. Xander Madri. He left Malta with his daughter, but we are unsure where he travelled on to. You must help us with that."

"What if I can't?"

Emory began pacing again.

Prihya held herself still. It was as if either man could pounce at any moment. And she remained under the watchful gaze of Moses and Muzaffer, despite their distance.

Emory said, "My holy sect's vows include proactivity in the glory of God. To this end, the Anthropocene Epoch... that's the time period through which we are now living, named after humanity's impact on the world—"

Valerio coughed pointedly. "*Mansplaining.*" Another cough.

"If you say so." Emory stretched out a patient smile. "The Anthropocene Epoch must be a *good* thing. If we are to enter the kingdom of Heaven, we cannot stand by and allow the world to fester on its current course. We must reveal history's secrets. And prove the people need to overthrow the existing regimes and embrace new—"

Valerio suddenly burst with anger. "*Where is my cipher, you thieving little bitch?*"

He held a placating hand toward Father Emory, calming himself.

"I'm sorry, Father, really I am. You preach being proactive, but you seem intent on chatting through your whole back story. So, let's skip that bit. She has thirty seconds to tell me something useful or I'll have Horse drop her in a hole, bury her up to her neck and smear her face with honey. Then I'll *personally* poke the closest nest teeming with bullet-ants."

He rounded on her.

"Am *I* lying, Prihya?"

She breathed hard through her nose. "You speak of stolen property. You never owned the cipher."

"You found it *thanks* to my property."

"You mean the scrolls recovered from that African mountain?"

"The scrolls. Yes." His eyes gleamed with manic joy. "And don't forget the things our joint adversary said on that day. That the Witnesses still exist. Or rather, they did at the time the knowledge was planted under the mountain. So, they must have left more obvious traces of themselves, perhaps as early as the Sumerian civilizations, or the Egyptians, maybe even those pesky Greeks."

"Or whoever populated this region?"

Valerio dropped his voice to a whisper. "Bingo."

Both men waited. At some point, Moses and Muzaffer had closed the distance halfway, and Horse had appeared from one of the tents and wandered closer.

They expected her to run.

She said, "I don't have what you need."

"I know," Valerio said, beckoning Moses over.

Muzaffer held back, resting his hand on his belt near the oversized sidearm holstered there.

Valerio said to Moses, "She doesn't have it, doesn't know exactly where it is, but admits her fixer, Xander Madri, took it and has been working with Alfonse Luca. How does that jibe with your investigation?"

Moses scanned his phone and swiped through a couple of screens. "Even with her dishonesty in play, if we factor in certain assumptions... that she did find the missing part... passed it on... and her partner hasn't rendezvoused with any of Luca's contacts... we traced her route, her other contacts, and Renata plotted her likely behavior... only one person stands out. And that is Xander Madri... who has had contact with only one group of people. Admittedly, they don't like him. Won't meet him because he's a bit of a crank, but..."

"Who?" Valerio said, his voice straining to remain even.

"Your old pals. The Lost Origins Recovery Institute. Toby Smith and the rest."

Prihya's chest felt hollow, her stomach empty.

Valerio asked, "And where are they?"

"China."

Prihya said, "Fine, I'll help you. Please, just... don't hurt Xander. He has a daughter, he—"

"Oh, I'm afraid it's too late," Valerio said. "With Toby and Jules and those others involved, I can't take any chances."

"*Please...*"

Moses said, "I can get us there in fourteen hours."

"No, I want faster results." Valerio glanced at Emory, who didn't meet his eye, then at Moses, who poised himself to work the phone. "I know someone much closer." He narrowed his eyes at Prihya and the corners of his mouth turned up at her evident discomfort. "And I'm pretty sure they'll happily kill a bunch of annoying people for us."

CHAPTER EIGHT

WESTERN CHINA, EXACT LOCATION: CLASSIFIED

Jules and Toby adjourned to Toby's private tent, which he'd furnished with a wingback chair, a side table, and a minibar. That was one corner of a utilitarian living space, the rest consisting of an army-style folding bed, a collapsible wardrobe, and a writing desk made from logs and a crate lid.

"Well?" Toby said, posing imperiously by his wingback chair.

"Okay, if you're gonna do the upper-class jackass routine, you might wanna pour one of those."

Toby opened his little cabinet and withdrew a bottle of Ballantine's whisky. He poured two measures into glasses without ice and unscrewed a plastic bottle of mineral water. He added a drop to his drink and offered the same to Jules, who sniffed the whisky, then poured a drop of water. It was how they drank it in Scotland, each person preferring a different degree of flavor, and Jules was becoming quite the connoisseur. Ballantine's wasn't a single malt, but it was one of the smoothest blends he'd ever tasted. It warmed him today and gave the impression of conviviality that Jules hoped would loosen Toby's tight tongue.

"You've been runnin' around behind our backs."

Toby sipped his drink and gave an affirmative, *Hmmm*. "I didn't want to involve anyone else in case the Carsons saw it as a breach of contract."

"You used Alfonse as a sock puppet to send Prihya on a mission you'd normally use us for."

"He acted on my request, yes."

"Even though the seven previous trips got us zip?"

"I made a promise that this journey will shine a light on many holy missions of exploration. Ones he was familiar with."

Jules understood. "Because the Armstrong thing was documented, and probably got roots in the conquistadors. Which were Pope-led."

"Not Pope-led as such, no, but the Vatican had strong links with—"

"So, yes, then." Jules felt no guilt in being what was seen by most as rude, but what he thought of as efficient. "How'd Prihya get involved?"

"Alfonse employed her via an intermediary."

"Because you and Bridget found the blueprint to that machine out there. What is it?"

"I asked before what you know of ancient computers."

"They ain't computers. The Antikythera Mechanism was found on a ship, but no one can see what it did. Best theory is it's a navigation tool. Shows the planets, some key stars, that kinda thing."

Toby downed his remaining drink and shuddered. "What we found was a more complex version, which Charlie recreated through a 3D printer, and cobbled together over the course of six months. The measurements were intricate, as fine as any Swiss watchmaker's. We couldn't make it work."

"Charlie figured there was a missing part, right?"

"Correct. And it could be the size of a penny to something as wide as a fist."

"The construction is cushioned, like springs."

"Correct again."

Jules was savoring his whisky. "So you reconstructed this machine, spent months of Charlie's time on it, recruited Prihya to find the missing piece, and you're gambling all our future relationships with Alfonse on finding this non-existent site?"

"The Tayos Caves very much exist, Jules."

Jules pointed at him with the hand holding his glass. "That's not the site I mean, and you know it."

"Fine. *Non-existent,* as we have come to understand it. But, from what I've read, quite feasible."

Jules no longer wanted to finish his drink, but felt strangely obligated. Toby's manners must have been wearing off on him. "Don't tell the others what you're really looking for. It's ridiculous."

"But you'll help find the caves? The real ones?"

"If that contraption can send us to the place Armstrong was lookin' for? Sure. But remember—"

"I have zero intention of revealing *all* the details. As you said, I'll be ridiculed. But you're not backing off?"

"Because even when you don't turn up what you're hoping for, I guess there'll be *something* more to come. Why don't you convince me about that? Then I'll see if I back you up with the team."

"Okay," Toby said. "Then let's get into the reeds and talk about ancient computers."

With the team still gathered in the storage space, and the Carsons listening in too, Jules agreed to let Toby outline his pitch without criticizing the content. Roger Carson kept his arms folded while Audrey maintained her pinched expression; Toby had a lot of work to do to convince them.

"One of the most famous pieces of ancient technology is the Antikythera Mechanism—"

"Ancient tech?" Roger said. An almost immediate interruption.

A lot of convincing...

"Let him speak, Roger," Audrey urged.

Roger shrugged and sighed, gesturing for Toby to go on.

"When I say ancient technology, I do not mean televisions and smart phones. I mean items like the Iron Pillar of Delhi, which dates from approximately 400 BCE. A twenty-three-foot-high construction which should have rusted and all but disintegrated over the years, but it has not."

"A pole," Roger grumbled. "Great example."

Bridget frowned at her dad and said, "If you want something more local, the Zhang Heng is the Chinese Leonardo da Vinci. He designed tons of inventions, including a seismograph. Back then, they believed wind and air caused earthquakes, but this device had a crank and lever which responded to the earth's movement. Genius thing sent a steel ball in the direction the quake was coming from."

Roger looked at her with the skepticism of a father listening to a six-year-old wax lyrical about fairies taking the last cookie instead of his daughter.

Rather than shrinking away, Bridget pushed back harder. "They found the Voynich Manuscript in 1912. Full of odd languages or code. Drawings of zodiac symbols, medicinal herbs, and alien-looking plants."

"Alien?" both Dan and Xander said together.

"Or ancient, never fossilized," Jules suggested.

"Fine," Roger said. "Ancient tech—"

But Bridget was on a roll. "The best one? The Aeolipile. A sphere. With *directional vents*. Add water, heat it, make it spin with the steam. No obvious use for it at the time, but it looks awesome. Invented by an engineer called Heron. Look at it from a different angle, it could be an early attempt at an *engine*, eighteen-hundred years before the industrial revolution. And don't get me started on Babylon. We might never have found the Hanging Gardens, of course, but the city, the walls, it's all such a marvel that the gardens could be a possibility just waiting to—"

"The Antikythera Mechanism," Jules put in, firing an apologetic head-tilt at Bridget.

She seemed to understand she'd been going on a bit.

"Indeed," Toby said. "They found the Antikythera Mechanism in 1901. A shipwreck off the coast of the island of Antikythera."

"Hence the name," Harpal said.

"Yeah," Dan said. "Hence."

Toby was undeterred. "The ship gave up the usual statues, vases, et cetera, along with a hunk of corroded metal. In 1902 they discovered gear wheels inside it." He paused for effect and continued. "Ancient Greece shouldn't have had this tech. It spent two thousand years in the ocean, and nothing else from its time can rival it. No others have been found, and this suggests an 'other' origin. And no, Dan, not aliens. But it could have tracked the heavens—stars, planets, the moon. Like a computer today."

It seemed to have snagged Roger's interest. "How can this exist, though? A *computer*? Really?"

Toby gave it a few seconds' thought. "Okay, what if you have a basic calculator that does every program—addition, subtraction, division, multiplication, square roots? What if you give that calculator a new piece of software that makes it do only one thing?"

"Such as what?"

"I don't know. Say you want it to compute pi."

"Please explain."

"It gives you pi."

"Okay. A calculator that calculates the value of pi."

"Pi is the only thing it does. There is no other program it runs. No other calculation it will make. It does nothing but compute the value you're looking for. Well, the Antikythera Mechanism used bronze gear wheels to calculate the cycles of the cosmos—the sun, moon, planets, the stars. They would know exactly where the moon would be ten years from the moment they set it up, and every day in between."

"Why have it, then?" Harpal asked. "For navigation?"

"The prevailing theory is it was to prove astrological theories of their scientists. That predictions could be mechanized was beyond the imagination of many people of the day. In the 1970s, a team X-rayed the device, then in recent years a 3D MRI scan showed more gear wheels, with new inscriptions on the wheels. Now, with AI models, we know it would have predicted eclipses, and shows the solar system as a ring. Arthur C Clarke said if they'd fully understood this tech, they'd have reached the moon within three-hundred years. It's *that* advanced compared to the other engineering of the day."

Jules needed to get them back on the matter at hand. The *point* of the lecture. "And the scrolls and books you and Bridget translated got you a new one. More advanced, but similar to the Antikythera Mechanism. *Right?*"

"Yes, yes." Toby took the hint and turned to the 3D-printed model he'd presented earlier. "There's a gap for another cog.

Different shaped cogs would send the operator to different places, using the movement of heavenly bodies as a guide, providing you knew your starting point."

Now Roger was listening, one arm folded across his chest, his other propping up his chin. "Are you suggesting this is like an ancient GPS system?"

"We haven't tested it. But we were hoping to. With this." Again, Toby showed them the gold disc. "Alfonse Luca has the working model."

"Oh, wait," Jules said. "You mean we can't make this one work?"

"No, the material is wrong. It needs to be copper and gold. Otherwise, the teeth can't mesh." Toby twitched as if startled by a sudden revelation. "Oh, you thought this would send us out there like a treasure map?"

"But you can simulate it, surely?" Audrey said.

"I believe, if the traveler had a malleable bit of metal..." Again, the disk. "Then once they were at the correct spot, they activated the mechanism via this handle, like a clockwork jack-in-a-box, it would imprint... if you'll excuse the air quotes... 'coordinates' on the malleable gear. Then the gear was taken and duplicated exactly before being shipped to your counterpart, who would arrive forthwith."

Jules was getting frustrated at the eloquent storytelling. "Then, to find the location, you put it in an identical device, set your current position, and as it turns, it guides the traveler using the stars."

All waited, as if expecting a new revelation.

"This is the way back to the library in Ecuador," Bridget said. "As a child, Petrionion Jaramillo brought the disc all that way to hide it. Then he lied to Neil Armstrong about its location. That's why Valerio wanted Prihya. He had hundreds of these scrolls, probably has a similar machine, and references to the library's location. But nothing exact. The disk is the key."

She rushed over to her father, stopped short of dropping to her knees, but couldn't hide the pleading from her voice.

"Let us go to Ecuador. You *have* to."

Roger took in the group. All were motionless.

"Immediately?" Roger said. "The answer is no. We have to bring our clients something of note, otherwise we'll lose a lot more than a historical site."

Bridget said, "Daddy, please..."

Roger righted himself, stood tall beside his wife, who appeared to agree. "Finish this first. Excavate where the house would have stood. Bring us what you find."

Audrey placed her hands on Bridget's shoulders and gave them a loving squeeze. "In the meantime, we will use all our influence in South America. An operation to rescue your friend. We can have our own people drop in, secure the services of—"

"Mr. Carson?" The Nigerian security operative stepped inside the tent, concern etched on his face. "The police are here. They are demanding to speak with whoever is in charge."

CHAPTER NINE

Dan's instinct that something hairy was about to impose itself had kicked in, gripped him by the back of the neck, and wouldn't let go. He and the Nigerian security chief, whose name he quickly learned was Ziggy—short for something he didn't reveal—stowed their SMGs on their backs and ensured they presented no threat to the incoming law enforcement officers.

Like birds, the group followed the Carsons and Toby in a V-formation. The Chinese security guards, whose job was to patrol the perimeter and see off hikers, were handcuffed and facedown as six uniformed cops spread out. Like Dan and Ziggy, they carried submachine guns. Dan counted two QCW-05s, three other guns with a design he recognized but couldn't name, and the leader with a pistol in a holster.

Dan shifted closer to Jules. "What do you think?"

"Don't like it," Jules said.

"Me neither. Stay frosty."

"Frosty? Really?"

Dan heard the line's corniness. "Sorry, too many movies."

"Just be sensible," Jules said. "Keep 'em busy, just in case."

He drifted away as the two contingents met.

Dan now noticed the vehicles they used to traverse the wild trails: two dirt bikes, a narrow ATV similar to a dune buggy, and two quad bikes.

"I am Commander Jin," the lead cop announced, alternating between Toby and Roger. Ignoring Audrey. "We must search this project immediately."

"You got a warrant?" Roger asked.

The commander laughed in a fake, mustache-twirling villain manner. Dan had seen this act from border guards dropping broad hints about "additional tax", in private security black ops guys faced with a belligerent terrorist sympathizer, and a mugger who'd erroneously pegged Dan and a girlfriend as easy marks.

The commander said, "We need no warrant."

He signaled his men, and the two with QCW-05s stood at arms, the guns pointed at the sky but hands on the butts and stocks.

"We do not wish to use force."

"What are your reasons for the search?" Toby asked.

"We will search. Stand aside."

"Not yet." Roger Carson stood between the cop and Audrey. "I want to speak with our representative first. This cannot be right."

"It is." The commander leveled a dark stare at him.

As the pair spoke, Audrey took out her phone and dialed.

Ziggy made firm eye contact with Dan. Slowly, the security operative lifted one hand to his opposite shoulder and pointed to where epaulets sit. Then Ziggy drew his eyes toward the commander. Dan shifted his gaze that way and scanned the epaulets' insignias. Two flower-like crosses with a single line at the bottom.

Dan nodded slowly, as if he were on the same page, but he hadn't researched the ranks of Chinese police in some time. He shifted back toward Jules, who would have been watching all Dan had.

He side-mouthed, "Those three SMGs? You recognize 'em?"

"Korean army," Jules said with equal discretion. "*South* Korean. K7 SMG, nine-mil, thirty-round mag."

"Right. And the rank. That commander?"

"Commander isn't a rank in the Chinese police. That's a sergeant second class's marking."

"These ain't police."

"Yeah, you think? Keep 'em busy."

"No calls!" The so-called commander barged Roger aside and snatched Audrey's phone.

Audrey shrilled, "Hey!" and Roger puffed up his chest with a deeper, "Hey!" and Toby stepped in with, "Okay, let's not—" but one man with a Chinese SMG moved between Toby and his boss.

The leader—not a commander—barked orders in Mandarin and the five subordinates spread out, cajoling the group, shoving them into a circle that now contained the gate guards. They stripped the visible guns from Dan and Ziggy, although didn't search them, so Dan held on to the snub-nosed Baretta he kept at his ankle.

Once all calmed down from mild panic to simmering annoyance, the leader asked, "Where is the African one?"

Dan smiled, his hunch having come good.

Keep 'em busy, just in case...

Okay, kid, do your thing.

Jules ran, shoving Xander behind a tree that was hidden by several bushes. He assumed the pair had arrived illegally because of Xander's hesitancy and the way he held his daughter who'd wrapped her arms and legs around him. Jules expected these men had information implicating Xander, the institute, and its people. Even though they weren't police, they could be working for a group that resented westerners encroaching on what was potentially a significant cultural discovery, with the police turning a blind eye.

Whatever these men were, it wasn't good. And the timing was too precise.

Xander arrives, presumably on a false passport.

After an alert, his visa gets checked and these goons get sent out here.

Or... more likely... a competitor gets a tip off that he's coming...

Valerio?

Jules instructed Xander to move cautiously. He still saw the gathering, and they had just noticed one or more was missing, so they had to hurry. Jules advised Xander to circle around the entrance clearing instead of returning to the camp.

The woods were so dense that a fence around the perimeter wasn't necessary, and they didn't have the security to man it. There was only one official way in or out, and that offered Jules a means of escape.

Not directly, though, as Roger Carson was still negotiating with the police-imposters. From his position now at four-o'clock from his original post, Jules heard Carson appeal to let the women go, but the guy in charge said, "That is very sexist and will not be considered."

A man dispatched to search for Jules raced back to his boss, spoke rapidly, threw a salute, and retreated.

In English, the boss said, "We know one of your people travelled with a little girl under a false passport, smuggling contraband into the country. He must surrender it immediately. Where is he?"

Xander hissed at him. "They want the disc."

"Yeah," Jules said. "And I wanna get gone. So, you're gonna do exactly what I say. Understand?"

Xander cradled Kat's head into the soft spot between his neck and shoulder. She was terrified, holding in tears. He must have been desperate to bring her all the way here.

Jules led him past where the chain-link fence ended, into an area that threatened to give away their position if they snapped the wrong branch or shook the wrong bush.

Within twelve feet of the vehicles, Jules assessed the mechanics of each, in case they'd taken the keys. He had one multi-tool on him. His flashbangs and other gear were stashed in his living quarters, having been shelved weeks earlier.

He said, "It'll either be a quad bike or an ATV. And we need to move fast. Got it?"

"Got it," Xander said.

But then all pretense of the legality of this incursion slid away. The leader was shouting something, Americanisms he must have heard on TV. "Hey, freeze, wherever you are. Freeze or I shoot!"

Shoot at whom?

But Jules only had to finger aside a single frond to see back into the camp.

Bridget kneeled on the floor while an officer pointed a K7 submachine gun at her head and the others held Roger Carson back from... doing what, Jules couldn't guess, but they were pretty much saving his life.

He couldn't avoid the fact that things had gotten more complicated. They weren't going anywhere yet.

Roger Carson was not a man who heard "no" very often. When the word occasionally crept into his sphere of influence, he expected it only in response to questions like, "Are there any issues of concern?"

No, sir.

However, as soon as they mentioned the interloper and his "contraband," Bridget had set about cursing up a storm, endangering herself like a lunatic. Alongside Dan Vincent and Ziggy Mtundu, Roger had tried to calm her, but the Chinese had fought the men off and dragged his little girl away.

With the struggle over, guns pointed at the archaeological team, Roger shielded his wife and tried to look both tough and compliant before the police commander.

"Hey, freeze," the officer shouted at the unseen fleeing men. "Wherever you are. Freeze or I shoot!" He faced Roger and smirked at what must have looked like rage. "Give us what we need and we leave you to your digging. Mr. Xing need not learn of your betrayal."

Roger couldn't help himself. "What betrayal? It's you who—"

"Harboring a fugitive. Trading in illegal antiquities. Obstructing a police officer in the execution of his duties."

"I demand to speak with Mr. Xing. He will not tolerate—"

Commander Jin hesitated beside Bridget and stroked her hair. She pulled away from him, aiming a filthy look that drew nothing but a sneer. "Call him."

"Lines are jammed," Harpal said.

Dan concurred. "Satellite, cells, walkies."

Toby frowned. "How can you be sure?"

"Because I am." Dan looked at Jin. "Right?"

Commander Jin gave a mildly embarrassed laugh. "Yes, well, we cannot be too careful, can we? So..." He patted Bridget on the head. "The disc. And the illegal immigrant."

"I do not know where either is." Roger pointed at Toby. "*He* had the disc."

Toby extended his arms. "Please, sir, feel free to search me."

Meaning he no longer had it. Roger was certain Toby would hand it over for Bridget's life.

But the comms, the heavies, the hostage-taking.

"This isn't an arrest or security operation," Roger said. "It's a robbery."

"Right," Dan agreed.

From her kneeling position, Bridget said, "Trust my friends. Whatever happens, go with it. They have done this before."

"No more stalling." Commander Jin took out his pistol and pressed it against Bridget's head. "*Where are they?*"

"The dig site," Dan said loudly. When the Chinese cop stiffened and approach him, Dan added, "They'd need to restock. It's where I'd set things up before heading cross-country."

Jin appraised the man, then Roger who could barely contain his anger, his panic at Bridget sitting prone in the dirt.

"Very well," the cop said. "Lead the way. If they are not there..." He prodded Dan with the gun. "I shoot you first. Then the girl."

The man Prihya had told Xander all about was as calm as she had said he would be. *Jules.* A man who will seem selfish and sometimes rude, but almost psychotically driven to do the right thing. Especially as far as saving lives was concerned.

He'd given Xander the choice: stay, and hope they handled the fake cops; or run with Kat, and let him handle things. But that would prove unworkable. The Chinese would give chase. They would capture him. And all this would be for nothing if he lost Kat; he'd have nothing to lose ever again. He'd have lost his universe.

So he followed Jules, taking a path beaten out by a migrating or prowling beast. They'd heard the threat and understood the hint from LORI's man-at-arms, Daniel—the one who had threatened to disembowel Xander if he attempted to access their home base in France.

Now, with Kat secured in the main part of the camp, he and Jules watched the hostages, including the two Chinese guards, file into the clearing filled with animal statues. As the cops manhandled the women—Bridget and Audrey—and were taking a rougher approach with the men, Xander thought about his daughter, about her sweet face.

Not the disc.

Not himself.

God only knew what his wife would say. He had not spoken with her in so long, not even in his sleep, but he couldn't spend more time worrying about how she might scold him in the afterlife right now.

Kat. She required safety. And he knew how some Muslims were treated in China.

Jules had his backpack half-full, and had frozen as if caught. As if he hadn't expected this.

Bridget said, "Hey."

"Hey back at ya," Jules replied.

They seemed ridiculously relaxed. Were they *flirting*? Prihya had said they were an unusual bunch with unusual ways, but even Jules's plan seemed unlikely to be so foolproof that they could *chill out* this way.

"The disc," the commander said, marching forward.

Xander felt like the world was slipping away. His promise to Prihya—unspoken but implied—could only be broken if his or Kat's life was in danger. While it had felt that way as they ran through the jungle, caution now seemed more sensible.

Like they'd been stalling all this time.

For what?

Xander played along. "He calls it a disc, though. Not a cipher. He does not know what it is."

"Yeah, so hand it over," the big one called Dan insisted.

"He's right," Jules said. "This guy's just being used. He's a sap. Hand him the damn thing and we can figure it out later."

Jules and Dan locked eyes. Dan's tiny nod of the head filled Xander with both hope and dread.

He reached into his pocket and braced himself for whatever came next.

CHAPTER TEN

DAN HAD no idea if Xander was reaching for the cipher, for something Jules had given him, or if the pocket was empty of all but a dreg of lint. Jules's deadened stare gave him no clue, except to confirm they'd had enough time to set up something more than hiding a girl and burying a gold disc.

Dan needed to be ready.

Xander brought his hand out of his pocket and tossed the item to Jin. The operative caught it, opened his hand, and cursed in... *Korean*? Yeah, even in that microsecond of chaos, Dan heard Korean, not Mandarin, as the miniature flashbang—Jules's own recipe making it non-lethal even in close quarters—blew in Jin's hand, blinding him and sending him reeling.

The other men reared up to unleash their weapons, a series of explosions thundering through the jungle. Jules had come through with the hastily set charges. A ripple effect brought them closer—thoom, *thoom*, THOOM—and a section of jungle blew out behind Jules and Xander. Debris flew, Dan and Ziggy grabbed the nearest gunmen, Jules swept a low kick to knock another off his feet, and Harpal grappled with the fourth. Dan first winded his guy and—sure of their status as North Korean mercs—snapped his neck and swiped his SMG. Ziggy looked surprised at first, probably because he wasn't quite 100% on the imposter front, but trusting a fellow military man, he did the same.

By the time the bodies hit the floor, Jules had knocked his guy unconscious and Harpal was choking out the merc under him.

Dan aimed at Jin, who was on one knee, trying to blink away the effects, but also had a palm-sized walkie-talkie in his hand. And he was giving orders.

A roar sounded from the direction of the main gate.

Dan faced the group under his care and pointed the opposite way. "They got backup. Lots of it from the racket."

"Six more," Jules said.

The freak.

"No," he added. "Eight. Two more coming late. Ten."

But a useful freak.

"The hangar," Dan urged. "Go!"

"Hangar?" Robert said, annoyed at something being kept from him even as he fussed over his daughter.

Bridget patted him away and caught up to Jules. "Kat?"

Xander clapped them both on the back. "We will get her now, yes?"

"Right." Jules glanced at Dan. "Get them all to the gunship. I'll get Kat."

Dan, Harpal, and Ziggy flanked them, shepherding the civilians and the Chinese guards along, but Jules and Xander rounded the diggers and trench to a path through the trees. Dan's group snaked down a trail with a lean-to, the engines coming closer and closer, until a pair of metal barn doors appeared, seemingly growing out of the trees themselves.

"What's this?" Roger demanded.

Dan heaved open the steel doors and the lights inside flickered on.

Toby gave him a bashful shrug. "Well, our friend in Sicily also has a degree of influence in this part of the world and—"

"The Chinook," Dan said. "Fire her up. Don't touch anything."

Ziggy stepped back to admire the vehicle for a second before corralling the three Carsons onward, another phase toward safety. The Chinese guards were being bundled toward the doors, Harpal and Toby urging them on toward what they'd called Dan's "paranoia trip" a few months earlier.

Dan hit the button on the frame he had painstakingly erected under the cover of night his first week on the ground. The canopy net covered in vines and branches and man-made camo decals swung away, a series of pulleys and gears winding it down past prefab walls.

Not for the first time in his life, Dan thanked the Gods of US Military logistics, without which he'd never have attempted such a paranoia trip as shipping a decommissioned Chinook, intended for airlifting heavy artifacts, into Chinese territory.

"Go on, now. Get inside."

They filed across the improvised hangar, and Dan turned away from the Chinook to see Jules emerging from a lean-to, his utility belt and a backpack in hand, alongside Xander cradling little Kat in his arms.

Engines were tearing up the jungle, coming closer.

Dan checked the side door to the Chinook was open and the civilians were inside. Harpal was at the controls, cans on his ears, and the engines whined to life. His voice came over the radio, into the earbud Dan had inserted as the need for their scorched earth escape became inevitable.

"This helicopter. It's like something out of a Bond movie."

"Out of date and way past its prime," Jules added from in the cargo compartment where the civilians were scrabbling.

Dan wondered what he meant, his thought cut short as the jungle erupted with gunfire and smoke. They'd arrived. And prisoners were not a priority.

Xander and Robert started shouting, protective of their loved ones, while Jules ducked his head down and hunched out of the Chinook, scurrying toward Dan.

"You comin'?"

Dan unfolded the stock on his SMG. "Doesn't look like it."

He raised the gun and loosed off a burst of three six feet to the left of the last cloud of gun smoke. Someone cried out. More gunfire returned.

Jules said, "Come *on*."

"Takes a few minutes to get the bird going."

With perfect timing, the gigantic helicopter's rotors groaned to life.

Dan fired again, pinpointing the sound of vehicles and picturing the pincer movement of troops and fake cops converging on them.

Jules gripped a fistful of Dan's jacket. "Let me hold 'em. I'm a better shot."

"Nah, they need you for whatever's out there. And wounding 'em won't cut it. They want us *dead.*"

He read the conflict in Jules's face. Jules was right that he was a better shot, his photographic memory extending to his skill with weapons and fighting techniques, but a mental block had always prevented him from killing intentionally. He claimed it was his aikido teachings that cemented it, but Dan put it down to habit and PTSD brought on by watching his parents murdered in a pizza joint.

Automatic gunfire erupted, forcing Dan to pull one of the hangar doors closed for additional cover. Couldn't risk a stray slug blazing through some circuit on the helicopter.

Dan tried to get a shot off, but the banging and clanging of the assault kept him pinned.

"Lock it," Jules said. "Barricade us in."

"Calculate how long it'll take nine or ten mercenaries to figure out how to get in. Or lob a grenade over the top."

Jules glanced up at the sky. "Fine." He rummaged in his backpack and pulled out two full-sized flashbangs.

Dan was happy to accept them. "It'll help delay them."

Jules held his gaze, clearly searching for a way out, seeing none, and accepting his new responsibility. "Surrender when we're clear. Give them what they want to hear. I'll come back for you."

Dan clasped his hand, both men pumped their grips, and then broke, Dan accepting the grenades.

"Hey, you two. See what I found."

Ziggy rejoined them, hefting an old M60 machine-gun, trailing a belt of bullets into a box he'd strapped over his shoulder. It was the sort of heavy-duty gun GIs would fire in Vietnam movies, mounted on choppers as they swept the South Asian jungles. Jules and Dan gawked at him.

He said, "Found this bolted to a mount. Hope you don't mind."

Dan didn't think it'd be useful until they were in the air, but Ziggy carried it with engaged biceps while leaning back a little. "I was saving it for a rainy day, but if you can handle the recoil, be my guest."

With the rotors speeding up, Ziggy poked the barrel into the gap between the doors, Jules and Dan prepping to open them wider. With a nod from the Carsons' bodyguard, they pushed the door open.

The machine-gun opened up, unleashing a barrage of lead at the encroaching mercs. The trees and foliage shredded, the men prepping to breach the hangar fell in plumes of red.

Dan joined in, picking off stragglers as they fled. A cowboy from the golden age of Hollywood might object, but those same men wouldn't hesitate to turn around and kill Dan or any of his friends the first chance they got.

Dan had to put them down.

But as Ziggy eased off the trigger, leaving their ears ringing and a stinging mist of smoke, it was clear there were others to worry about. The trees moved, the bushes wavered, and rotor wash kicked up a dust storm. Grit pelted them from behind, clearing the layer of muck within seconds, swirling it into the air all around.

At least five mercs clustered between a couple of tree trunks. A spearhead movement, intended to power through their defense.

"That was more than ten," Jules said.

"Couldn't hear 'em on foot," Dan said.

Ziggy fired up the big gun again, but this group was better trained than the others.

The rotors were almost at take-off speed. Dan could see only shadows and movement through the grit and dust.

"Okay, get in!" Harpal called through comms. "Come on, get aboard!"

Ziggy fired into the mercs' position again, but even with the added oomph of the M60, there was no way to penetrate.

Dan offered Jules a flashbang. "Shall we?"

Jules offered a rare smile as he pulled the pin and Dan did likewise. "It'd be rude not to."

Both men loaded their arms like baseball pitchers and hurled the grenades toward the grouping. The ordnance exploded near the targets and sent them reeling. Ziggy was about to pick them off when a *whooosh* sounded.

With only a split-second to dive away, a rocket-propelled grenade slammed high into the hangar wall. The *blam* of the explosion triggered a shockwave that knocked all three off their feet and sent Dan dizzy. He recovered enough to roll to his belly, SMG to his shoulder, and fire at the place the rocket had launched from. Ziggy, too, was up, strafing the jungle in a wide arc, flushing out anyone hiding there or moving position.

Jules yelled, "Get in!"

They all ran and dived into the Chinook's open bay. No sooner did Dan shout, "Clear," than Harpal lifted the bird, and they were rising.

Ziggy set the M60 back on its mount. No time to bolt it in place, but it gave him a platform to lay down covering fire as soon as the vehicle's belly cleared the top of the hangar. He was sparing with the ammo, blasting into the area the five mercs had fallen.

Then Jin stepped out of the trees, the rocket launcher on his shoulder, and Dan took careful aim. The Chinook was steady enough, rising in a line to get clear of the trees for him to pull a bead.

He fired.

Missed.

Even at this distance, Dan saw Jin laugh.

The man adjusted his stance and his aim.

Dan amended his bead.

Bam bam bam. A burst of three.

The rocket fired.

But it launched as Jin fell back, two in his chest, one in his head. The contrail spiraled, the rocket shot wide, and the massive helicopter dipped its nose and sped across the treetop canopy.

They were safe from the incursion. Now they just needed to ensure the real Chinese army didn't shoot them down.

CHAPTER ELEVEN

After a forty-minute flight to a private airfield arranged via sat phone by Mr. Xing, they were met by the Chinese military, who politely confiscated all of their weapons and searched them. Following this, LORI were respectfully but firmly ordered onto a small coach and driven six hours to an American embassy, where they were given an hour to freshen up.

Jules was the first to be led to the plain, utilitarian meeting room, which was soon filled with everyone who'd fled the dig, the space smelling of soapy apples from various showers. The two guards, whose fate was unknown, and Xander, whom Jules suspected the Chinese had detained, were conspicuous by their absence. Other than Roger, who had found a new suit, they'd been issued clean clothes that resembled prison sweats.

Mr. Xing joined them. He was a slight man, his skin loose on his face and neck, and an ill-fitting suit seemed to swallow his frail frame. Roger stood beside him as if about to begin a marketing pitch.

Mr. Xing said, "I am thankful you are all safe."

"May I be permitted to update my colleagues?" Roger asked.

Mr. Xing nodded once, his hands clasped before him.

"I am grateful to have been briefed at the same time as Mr. Xing," Roger said. "I can confirm the Chinese authorities know nothing about a police raid. It was imposters."

"Was that in doubt?" Jules asked.

Roger narrowed his stare at Jules, and Bridget nudged him.

"Right." Jules gave a shallow bow and addressed Mr. Xing. "I apologize for interrupting. It won't happen again."

Probably, he added silently.

"I could not prevent them from taking Xander into custody," Roger said. "He is not an American, so the Americans could not extend their protection."

Bridget raised her hand. Roger nodded.

She said, "His daughter?"

"Xander insisted her mother is American. While our hosts investigate this, she will remain under our supervision. She's in the embassy staff daycare at the moment."

"I'm not American, either," Harpal said.

"You and Toby are working for an American company. That's good enough. Not that you've done anything wrong. Xander entered the country with a false passport and a visa arranged through a former gangster. I will plead extenuating circumstances, but if you haven't followed current affairs of late, that isn't always a great argument here."

"Your story is intriguing," Mr. Xing said. "I will make enquiries. If your friend poses no danger to the People's Republic, I may be able to have him expelled instead of jailed."

Toby said, "Thank you."

Roger waited for more questions. Since Jules only had comments to make, he stayed silent and let Roger pick up the briefing.

"I have received assurances that the attack is being investigated and the dig is going to be far more secure. Once it's been cleared."

Jules bit his tongue. If he spoke, it'd go badly. If he was reading the room right, which he usually did, all their hearts had sunk at once. He almost heard them hit the floor.

Mr. Xing said, "I have arranged for Chinese reserve troops to be dispatched to guard the project. No raiders will return. If they do..." Mr. Xing mimed firing a machine-gun.

"No," Bridget said. "That can't happen. No way I'm going back there."

Her father glared at her with eyes that growled, *Shut up*, while her mom extended a hand that seemed to say, *Please.*

Jules wanted to intervene but seeing Toby's warning glare, he held back. It was likely only Bridget could have any hope of getting away with shattering the strict etiquette expected of them.

"I'm sorry. And I'm sorry to Mr. Xing, really I am." She looked furious and anxious, her fists clenched, cheeks rosy. "But we have to follow Xander's map."

"She's right," Jules said.

"And rescue Prihya," Dan said.

Jules hooked a thumb Dan's way. "He's right, too."

It drew a sharp look from Mr. Xing.

Roger chafed out an apologetic *aah*, and placed his hands together. "My daughter... and her friends... they're all very passionate about what they do. But please let me put their minds at rest."

All perked up at this.

"In the past thirty minutes, I have dispatched a private security team. I reached out to Alfonse, who... if you'll excuse the timing, will join us in a few moments." Roger fiddled with his phone, making a video call, which was answered within two rings.

Roger placed the phone on a black plate with a wire snaking into the floor, then Alfonse Luca's fleshy face beamed out at them from a TV on the wall.

"Hello." He waved. "You can hear me, yes?"

Jules could not help but smile at seeing and hearing from the former mafioso. He couldn't call the man a friend, exactly, but there was something he liked about Alfonse. His enthusiasm, his trust in LORI. While he had undoubtedly perpetrated many criminal acts in his life, he had committed himself to righting those wrongs; in league with the institute, his aim was to buy forgiveness through the Roman Catholic Church.

He said, "You are speaking about our plan?"

"That's right," Roger said. He addressed the group. "Alfonse is organizing travel and logistics. I'm providing a specialist team. They will extract your friend, Prihya, and return her here, if she wishes to come."

That didn't appease Bridget, though. If anything, the lines on her forehead deepened. "What about the library?"

Roger steadied his gaze, firming it in her direction. "Any intel on this library will be disseminated and acted upon once the Chinese project is complete."

"No. You can't—"

"It is for the best," Alfonse said.

Bridget ground her teeth, waiting for more.

"Bridget, my dear, my beautiful young friend. It is with reluctance I must agree with your father. The priority must be Prihya and retrieving her alive. If they need her, it means they lack the knowledge needed. The library will still be there. Let your father's private security personnel do their jobs."

After a beat, Bridget asked, "Which security team?"

"Theta Team," Roger said.

Bridget seemed unimpressed. "Of course you sent *her*."

"It has to be us," Jules said, ignoring the subtle gestures from Toby and Harpal to stand down. "Whether we have troops or cops or a freaking dinosaur army patrolling the dig site, this is Valerio Conchin we're talkin' about. Prihya can only offer him a clue or two, so it's only a matter of time before he gets his hooks into someone with more influence than your Mr. Xing here."

Mr. Xing remained unmoved, which is to say, he appeared deeply insulted.

Roger said, "You seriously think you have a better chance than a military spec-ops-trained unit?

"Yes," Jules said, no longer caring how arrogant he sounded. Time to blow it all or get something in return. "Not better at the military aspect, no, but this ain't a military op. It's reaching back in time and ripping ancient hidden history into the present."

Silence as everyone gaped at him.

He was as surprised at himself as anyone was. Hadn't realized he felt this way, but it was clear now. This was what he had to do.

"I want it as well," Toby said timidly, "but I must urge caution. Patience."

"That's your old spy instincts keeping you in check." Jules was pacing now, observing how Alfonse was smiling, a glint of humor, a bigger hint of pride. "Do I need to go on about the transfer of information to Bridget during our trip to New Zealand? And my own experience—

"Neither of you remember it," Harpal said, siding with Toby

"We got enough to know that the Witnesses were wise as hell. Highly intelligent. But didn't invent much. They just figured it out and spread the word, keepin' humanity from extinction."

Bridget stepped back in. "We know from Prihya that Valerio can't read those scrolls well, but he must have achieved *some* progress. Getting into 'em is hard enough, but reading them is another matter. This library could be the Rosetta Stone we need to translate the books and documents we've found."

"It could be the answer to all this. Everything." Jules normally kept his emotions under control. Not buried or denied; he was aware of them, acknowledged them, but had tamed them. He didn't let them direct his actions. Whenever he charged in, contrary to social norms, it was with good reason. And he had an undeniable reason to risk insulting Mr. Xing here: everything, starting with the bangle his mom had died trying to protect, had led to this, and it might lead further.

It *would* lead further.

Not where Toby thought, but somewhere.

"This isn't up for debate," Jules said. "We can't go back to that dig. We gotta go on."

Mr. Xing had ceased staring at Jules and Bridget and lasered in on Roger, as if he were responsible for the pair.

"Oh, boy," Roger said.

In America, Roger could have threatened, yelled, and made everyone listen. He wouldn't have sweated or felt guilty corralling them all back to work. If Bridget hadn't been here, he would have flexed his leverage of Toby and his guys. But she was here.

As he listened to Jules recount their New Zealand discoveries, he wanted to let them go. It was complicated. But Mr. Xing invested in the dig site and risked losing party standing and money. If either evaporated, the Carson Corporation stood no chance of securing the contracts Roger and Audrey were chasing.

Then there was Bridget to consider.

He promised her a top-notch education at a prestigious institution in exchange for her friends' use of the chateau, which they'd turned into their treasure-hunting lair. Perhaps compromising with her was a mistake, installing her at the Université Paris to study archaeology when he'd favored a business or law-related field. Unfortunately, debunking finds was part of the institute's brief, and the Xing dig was disappointing. Roger needed a glimpse into China's glorious past to present to party members who wanted to boost Chinese prestige abroad.

"Oh boy," Roger said at the first gap in their attempts at persuasion. He'd have some ass kissing to do with Mr. Xing regarding their manners later, but he could take it. "I really want to let you go. But the truth is, I need to keep Bridget safe, and watch out for her future career." Lingering on his daughter for only a moment, he stood back to take in the room. "She chose this. I sent her to Paris to legitimize her hobby. Abandoning an incomplete project looks bad. And if we abandon the dig site, we could be in even more hot water with the Chinese. Think about it. We had an illegal immigrant with us, while North Korean agents infiltrated the territory."

"We can still go—" Bridget started, but Roger cut her off.

"No. The decision is made, and it's for your own good." He paced back and forth, a habit he had accepted would never change because it helped him time his speeches and impose himself in boardrooms. "They've arrested the guy with the fake passport. We'll let Alfonse and Security Team Theta dig Prihya from Valerio's clutches, and you will all go back to work, under the protection of the People's Liberation Army of the Republic of China. Stay legit. And I swear, you can head to South America when we're done here. Deal?"

No one answered right away, so Roger bore his gaze into Toby.

"Understood," Toby said. "You'll get no trouble from me."

Roger looked at Harpal, who said, "I'm with Toby."

Dan returned a nod, and Bridget stared back numbly, her jaw sticking out like some sort of angry dog. Her eyes teared up, and she looked away.

"Jules?" Roger had left him until last for obvious reasons; with the others agreeing, how could the lad refuse? "Jules?"

Only, as he shifted his head to look beyond Dan and Harpal, then turned to see if he'd moved closer to Mr. Xing, it was clear Julian Sibeko was no longer in the room. "Where'd he go?"

Harpal shrugged. "Bathroom?"

Roger wasn't impressed. "Where the hell has he gone?"

Someone was laughing.

Alfonse.

The big man on the screen killed the laughter and said, "I believe the young man has quit."

"He can't quit," Roger said. "We'll stop him from leaving."

"He won't be going out the front door," Dan said.

"Still..." Roger saw Mr. Xing's tight lips, pursed as if wishing to shout, but decorum kept him mute. "He can't go hunting for that damn library, surely."

"Oh, didn't anyone tell you?" Bridget said. "Xander gave the disc to Jules right before the army intercepted us."

Should have seen that coming.

Audrey said, "My dear, what is going on? Does he honestly think he can—"

"What?" Bridge said. "Escape from a secure embassy in China, one of the most heavily guarded countries in the world? Well, if he can, and he gets out of the country undetected, surely he can get Prihya back and return with the key to the Witnesses' secrets."

Audrey faced her husband and gave him a firm look. Roger knew what that expression meant: she'd made up her mind about something he hadn't grasped yet. In business, it was an intuition about how an economy might swing or if a client needed one more push. Today, it was about their daughter. And, possibly, their future relationship with their Chinese partners.

"Mr. Xing," Roger said. "I believe we can make this work."

It was Audrey who outlined the new compromise. "We will keep the personnel in place in Ecuador, if Alfonse arranges transport once Jules surfaces. We will release Toby and his friends for intel, should the need arise. Satellite comms will keep all in touch. But work on the dig must resume, and remain on course to prove or disprove the viability of what might be under the landslip."

"Once the site is secure," Toby said, "we will return and finish what we started."

"Bridget, in particular, must face no danger."

Bridget softened without quite breaking her icy demeanor. "Fine. I'll be good."

Dan Vincent heard Bridget's words and was glad they weren't pouring headlong into a hostile jungle to do battle with Valerio again. Not that he'd back down from that sort of fight, but he could do without the added pressure of watching out for the guys with little combat experience.

But then, as Bridget said she'd be good, he caught a flicker. A tick of her mouth in the corner which almost caused her to wink. She caught him looking, turned her head so her father couldn't see her face, and she stopped suppressing the smile. It widened into a conspiratorial grin.

"Oh boy," Dan said under his breath.

Nothing good will come of this.

PART TWO

CHAPTER TWELVE

ECUADOR

The plane was a rickety bucket of former long-haul nuts and bolts holding together a long metal sausage with wings. But the important thing was that it flew. Jules would be fine as long as it passed over Alfonse's coordinates.

Before meeting LORI in Prague, Jules had never entered a country without a backdoor exit in place. He now relied on Phil Locke and Harpal to coordinate transportation, IDs, and visas for Toby and the crew. Despite his best efforts, he couldn't trust Mr. Xing or, unfortunately, Bridget's parents. They prioritized their daughter, their business came in second, and everything and everyone else trailed a distant third. Toby's institute held the same status as the digging and drilling equipment that the Carsons seemed able to conjure up whenever and wherever in the world they chose.

That's why he'd established three routes out of China, three "courier companies" ready to go if he needed them.

After taking off in Chile, he braced himself in the cargo plane's bay for four hours, wearing a fur-lined flight suit because the hold was not heated, and kept his parachute attached the entire time. The plane was packed with farming equipment held in place by nets, and his only source of comfort was a couch pillow on which he sat for most of the flight, listening to an audiobook by the Swiss author who popularized the Tayos Gold myth. The story was riddled with so many holes, it was as if moths had edited it.

However, it took his mind off the biting cold.

In Spanish, the pilot's voice came over a crackly speaker, although Jules strained to hear it over the engines and rattling hull. "Time to jump, my friend." A red bulb over the side door lit up. "Open the door and wait for the green."

Jules rarely found skydiving exciting, the process as simple to execute as a recipe from a cookbook. It was a shame, because he saw how much enjoyment Harpal got out of adventure sports like this. The physics, however, was set in stone thanks to Jules's brain and muscle memory. Unless he fell into a flock of birds or a storm, his descent from plane to land was entirely predictable. And, thanks to the advance party of Security Team Theta, there weren't any trees to cause a problem.

He heaved himself to the door and gripped the lever with both hands.

"Wait again," the pilot said over the intercom. If it hadn't been for the squelch of static, Jules wouldn't have known to listen for what came next. "You have a new instruction."

"I don't have new instructions," Jules said, despite the speaker being one-way. He applied pressure to the lever to unseal the door.

Someone tapped his shoulder.

Jules spun, one hand up to parry a blow.

Bridget dodged back with an amused look of surprise.

"Bridget!"

"Hi," she said.

"How'd you get here?"

"I was already in the co-pilot's seat when you got on board." She laughed, her eyes full of excitement. "I snuck away from the camp and Alfonse got me out. I arrived in Chile the same day you did."

"Why didn't you tell me you were here?"

"I like surprises. And the pilot said it'd be real chilly back here. He insisted I sit up front." Her hands found her hips. She was kitted out much the same as Jules, with additional padding. The thing that made him most nervous was the parachute on her back. "Well?"

"You ain't coming," Jules said.

"Oh, I am."

Bridget pushed past Jules to grasp the same lever he had. It was stiff and she couldn't pull it open.

"Two minutes," the pilot's scratchy voice said.

Bridget sighed, squared herself off in front of Jules.

He said, "I'm already in trouble with your parents, but I gotta do this. Whatever started with those bangles when we first met, it's led here, and this place... it might be the key to all those answers."

"Jules, you're acting irrationally. You need someone to help you see things clearly. That's me."

"Really? Is that why you're here? My personal shrink?"

"Jules..." Bridget took Jules's gloved hands in hers. "When we met, you were obsessed with getting ahold of your mom's bangles. You were a child when she died protecting them, so it makes sense you'd obsess over them."

Jules said nothing. He'd been through all this. With himself and real shrinks.

"But when you got them, Valerio dug under your skin. Made you see it wasn't the objects, but the question that hung over them. Now you got the bangles—and I'm guessing you brought 'em along for this ride...?"

Jules confirmed by disengaging a hand and throwing a thumb toward the second pack strapped to his front.

Bridget resumed her two-handed grip. "It's all coming back, isn't it? That... *drive*? That feeling you had when nothing else mattered? And you—*you*, Jules, always *you*—have to be the one who finds the answer."

She was right, of course, but Jules chose not to interrogate the issue more. He needed to hop onto that forward momentum, and he was powerless to slow its approach.

"Thirty seconds," the pilot said over the screechy speaker.

Bridget squeezed Jules's hands tighter. "So stop being such a baby and *share* your adventure."

"This ain't an adventure, Bridge. It's a mission. Valerio doesn't mess around. He'll have us both killed in a heartbeat."

"I know. But as much as I can't stand my dad's choice in security teams, they're good. Real good."

"I can't risk anything happening to you."

"Why? 'Cos my mom and dad'll be mad at you?"

Jules needed a breath to calm a sudden sick feeling in his gut. "Is that what you really think? That I don't care about—"

The pilot's crackling voice blared. "Open up, friends. I will circle the area for one minute. If you are not out, you are coming all the way to Buenos Aires with me."

Jules felt the plane bank. "I gotta keep you safe."

Bridget let go of his hands and grasped the door lever. "I know it's hard for you big strong men to believe, you and Dan and Phil and Harpal, but I ain't the frail little flower you treat me as. I can skydive with the best of 'em. I can scuba dive, too. I shot guns since I was big enough to hold one."

She strained against the lever and Jules saw it budge slightly, a clunk of the door and a whistle of wind showing she'd cracked the seal.

"Oh," she added, "and let's not forget my actual field training—as a goddamn *archaeologist.* Might be useful when looking for ancient buildings, don't you think?"

Jules saw the logic but didn't like it.

He took hold of the lever and pulled. The door flew open on its sliding runner.

The wind battered them, so loud Jules could barely hear himself, let alone communicate to Bridget. He tried, though.

"Stay close. Do what your dad's team tells you. And don't make me come rescue you *and* Prihya. We good?"

Bridget popped her goggles on, winked, and jumped out.

Jules clambered on to the rail on the outside, gripping against the turbulence and heavy air slamming against him as he pulled the door closed.

He glanced down, pinpointing Bridget's trajectory and, seeing she was heading for what appeared to be their target clearing, he let go.

CHAPTER THIRTEEN

As usual, relocating from airplane to terra firma was uneventful. Jules saw Bridget deviate twice, but Harpal's lessons paid off. On the ground, Bridget greeted Jules with an exhilarated smile and double high fives, which he returned out of politeness rather than some adrenaline surge. After they wrapped their chutes, six gun-wielding operatives emerged from the trees, dressed like the US Army but without insignia.

Bridget and Jules raised their hands.

The camouflaged gunmen, M4 carbines at their shoulders, formed a crescent to cover the pair from all safe angles.

Jules said, "Hey."

One guy advanced beyond the crescent, squinted at Bridget, then at a photo taped to the gun at his shoulder, and lowered the barrel. He half-turned to the jungle, nodded, and raised the barrel again.

Jules noted all were aimed at him only. Not Bridget.

A woman emerged from the trees, drifting around the crescent of men. Dressed in the same army-surplus uniforms, her face smeared in camo paint, she held her M4 ready to fire but aimed up and to the side—at *port arms*, as Dan would call it, a phrase he had assumed everyone knew when drilling them on the Chateau Caché estate. She halted when she had a clear line of sight of Bridget and Jules.

"It's been a while." The woman was a little older than Bridget, maybe thirty at the most, and while she had a southern-US lilt to her accent, it carried the air of a Middle Eastern origin, as if English was not her first language but she spent most of her time speaking it.

"Rayyana." Bridget had stiffened, but not out of fear. "Didn't realize you'd be greeting us in person."

"This is Julian Sibeko?" The woman—Rayyana—tilted her head Jules's way.

"Yeah."

"You vouch for him completely? I don't have his file."

Bridget stomped forward like a toddler instructed to tidy her room or there'd be no dessert. "Yes, Rayyana, I vouch for him. And you better listen to him, 'cause he's way smart." She passed the woman in camo, drawing the nearest couple of men's eyes momentarily. "Can we get moving? Our friend is still in trouble."

"And she's nearby," Rayyana said, locking eyes with Jules. "Ready, big guy?"

"Ready," Jules said.

"Good. Do what I say at all times. When I need advice on your specialisms, I'll call. For now, this is my gig. Understood?"

"Yes, ma'am."

"Excellent. We're going to get on real well, you and I." With a flick of her chin, the men stood down and Rayyana extended a hand to Jules, which he shook. "Rayyana Clinton. Head of security for Theta Team. We have intel you need to see."

Bridget called back, "You coming, or do I gotta guess the way?"

Although Jules had never been great at sensing emotion—or caring much about it—he identified the cues of tension, but sensed it was mostly one way. Either Rayyana didn't feel the same hostility toward Bridget, or she was a consummate professional doing her job.

Whatever, it looked personal, some sort of grudge, and Jules had always viewed grudges as petty and pointless. Allowing personal differences to interfere made no sense, especially when you might be reliant on that person for your survival. He'd ask Bridget about it later.

For now, once he took off the stifling flight suit, leaving him in black combat pants and a hard-wearing shirt, he fell in with Theta Team and asked how far they were from base.

"Two klicks," Rayyana said. "Targets are ten klicks south, and we do not know if they're aware of our presence. Keep silent until I speak, please."

The procession continued, Rayyana keeping pace with Bridget, while Jules remained close. Throughout, Bridget barely glanced at Rayyana, and Theta's team leader cast the occasional half-smile at Jules as if to say, *What's with this one, eh?*

"Base" was bustling with two dozen agents, much like a US army base. There was a satellite dish, military equipment stores, sealed gun lockers, and a massive pile of four unopened crates. As soon as Rayyana arrived, she issued several commands, and the four guys she spoke with saluted and got right to work. She directed Jules and Bridget into a frame coated in mosquito nets, which turned out to be a sort of mess hall, open to the elements except for flying insects. Jules gravitated toward two little boxes by one table with a British Union flag painted on them.

"Okay, spill," Jules said. "What's with you and the action dudette?"

"Nothing."

The mess tent was empty, yet the air was thick with the tangy scent of cooking, of salt and pepper, the combined ghosts of dozens of simple meals. It made Jules hungry, but he would not let Bridget off easily.

"It's not nothing, Bridge."

She threw her fists down by her side. "Fine. She was an orphan that my parents took on as part of a deal with her Iraqi uncle. You know what her job was?"

Jules didn't and wasn't sure if it was a hypothetical question or not. "She's clearly some kinda a spy or assassin or black ops type."

"Yeah, and the fact my parents have a person like that on their payroll is bad enough, but..." Bridget choked up momentarily, as if struggling to speak through sadness. "I turned a blind eye to their activities for so long. What kind of corporation employs private security personnel like private armies?"

"A corporation that works in dangerous parts of the world?"

Bridget let out a teen-like growl of frustration. Clearly, that last question *had* been hypothetical.

Jules said, "Sorry. You were saying your parents adopted this soldier?"

"She wasn't a soldier," Bridget said, as if it was obvious. "Not at first. One minute she's a maid, sixteen years old and training with the household staff, acting like my *friend* when we got talking. The next minute, though, she's learned to shoot, and she becomes this super-soldier spec ops agent."

Was the pause Jules's cue to comment? And if so, should he ask a question or support her? He settled with, "Uh-huh."

Bridget showed no annoyance, so he must have got that right. "My dad clearly employed her to spy on me. Pretend to be a maid, earn my trust, and... I dunno, report back."

"Could she have been a bodyguard?" Jules asked.

Bridget mulled it over for a couple of seconds. "Does it matter? It was still dishonest. My parents deceived me and she was a part of it."

Jules guessed it would be counterproductive to play devil's advocate, so settled for a noncommittal. "Huh."

"Wait." Bridget paced a slow circle, watching his face. "You like her."

"She's competent, sure."

Bridget watched him some more.

He said, "What? What is it?"

Movement caught Jules's eye. He turned to see the net shifting to admit someone he recognized.

"Hello, Jules. Bridget," came the Welsh woman's greeting.

"Charlie!" Bridget screeched and ran to her.

Charlie Locke embraced Bridget right back, the pair holding onto one another as if one of them had returned from the dead. She'd donned sensible jungle boots and pants, her hair tied back. Jules would expect nothing less. Charlie was another person whose competence he admired. Although, he couldn't understand why she was here, or why she carried a computer tablet six inches bigger than an iPad.

As Bridget broke away, Jules opened his arms and shifted forward.

Charlie stood at an angle, surprised. "Well, this is new." She reciprocated, the pair hugging in a way Jules never would have bothered with two or three years ago. It still felt alien and pointless, but it was what people did.

"Yeah, I'm trying new things," he said.

As they parted, Charlie laughed. "Human emotions, eh? Looks good on you."

Jules shrugged it off, glad he'd made the effort. "So. Good to see you. Thought you couldn't travel 'cos of family commitments."

"Nice try at small talk, boyo. Then straight in with the loaded question."

"Yeah, but it still stands."

"Had to babysit my new toys."

She lifted one of the Union flagged crates onto the table and opened the lid to its straw-packed contents: rubber circles with glass fronts and a tiny bulb visible.

"This is the perfect field test for these. Powerful LED pods, you can wedge them in place or leave them on the floor, and you light up caves like it's midday."

She opened the next one: fist-sized units encased in polystyrene. They were metallic green, with a black mesh button and a little lever, similar to a hand grenade with extras.

"Directional smart charges. They focus the force of the blast along a particular vector, making it—"

"Making it easier to blow stuff up without damaging precious objects," Jules finished for her.

She pouted. "Sure, boyo. Want to play with them? Be polite."

"Sorry. Not everything's new with me."

Charlie stepped aside as Rayyana joined them and quipped, "You've had your Q moment? Okay, reunion over."

Cleansed of camo paint and unarmed, Rayyana cut a striking figure, Middle Eastern coloring as Jules had predicted. Her sodden black hair clung to her shoulders and forehead, framing a thin but defined nose. She wore a deep green tank top that doubled as a ballistic vest, black jeans and heavy boots.

"Well?" Rayyana asked. "Snacks are coming. But let's talk."

"Charlie never told us why she's here," Bridget said. "Naughty girl distracted us with shiny objects. And don't fob us off with that nonsense about field tests."

"The truth is," Charlie said as they adjourned to a table, "I do have my family, and I really couldn't spare the months in China. And don't forget, I'm only *attached* to the institute. I don't work for Toby."

Jules had always been hazy about her exact status, coming in and setting up elaborate tech facilities and accompanying them on certain jaunts, but never fully committed. He understood, since her fiancé (now husband) had ended up in a wheelchair on a job from before he met them, but it felt a bit slapdash.

He said, "I'm guessin' your new and improved LiDar is here, too."

Charlie nodded with a smile. "Another big field test. And please... it's not LiDar. That's a brand name. This tech is all mine. And it's way more powerful now I've added X-ray diffraction and infrared spectrophotometry. And fitted it to a drone. We've pinpointed *so* many anomalous subterranean gaps, which correspond with the Tayos cave expedition."

"But nothing beyond that?" Bridget asked.

"A gold-filled library?" Rayyana said. "No, not yet."

"But Charlie-Dar ain't the main reason for you being here, is it?" Jules said.

Charlie gave a short, polite laugh. "Charlie-Dar?"

"Char-Dar might be snappier."

"You are *not* hired as my branding manager. And you're right. That isn't the key reason. This is."

She fired up the e-tablet and the need for a larger-than-standard screen was obvious: it contained a computer simulation of the 3D-printed machine Toby had presented back in China.

"After I built that ancient star map contraption, we digitized it for the 3D printer. But I found I could simulate the coordinates, providing we knew the starting point, and the shape and dimensions of the missing cog. We now know the starting point is the Hypogeum Hal Salfieni in Malta. We just need the cipher."

Charlie held out a hand.

From a pocket inside his black shirt, Jules took the small gold disc with the serrated perimeter. "How you gonna slot this in to a computer graphic?"

"Like this." Charlie laid the cipher on the desk next to a ruler for scale and used the e-tablet's camera to snap a hi-def picture. She tapped the screen a few times and the device replicated the cipher's shape into its framework and slotted it amongst the clockwork parts. "When I knew what this was, what we were looking for, I couldn't stay behind. Phil is clued in and ready to assist."

"He's on board?" Jules said.

"After two years inside with me? Followed by some intricate projects that Toby knew I wouldn't be able to resist? Oh, yeah, he's ready."

Jules smiled, imagining how much tinkering Charlie must have done. "It works."

"Takes a while. I mean, this is a visual representation that Toby insisted on. The real work is done behind the digital tablecloth—"

"We get it, Charlie," Bridget said in that annoyed-friendly way only close buddies can get away with. "Thanks. This... I suppose it translates to a literal map?"

"You betcha."

Jules saw Rayyana watching the computer do its job and asked, "Okay, so what's the story? What next?"

Snacks arrived and snacks were eaten, a collection of MREs and some more solid confectionary, washed down with fruit juice. Throughout, Rayyana broke down what they faced.

"Valerio Conchin has a contingent of about twenty men. He is based ten klicks from here as the crow flies, but we'll travel by river. This will position us away from their landing zone, allowing for covert ingress and extraction."

Jules pictured the op in his mind and didn't like it. "That means killing a buncha people."

"Bad people, yes. Most recruited from militia contracted to drug cartels over the border."

Jules bristled internally. While he wouldn't kill with his own hands, he felt little grief for the loss of life taken by another. He'd killed once, and that was accidental, and it had cost him a year of his own life, spent in an odd sort of penance while he worked as a cop.

That hadn't lasted long.

"We have a second target?" Jules asked.

"The library?" Rayyana said.

"Our best bet," Charlie said, "is a couple of miles south of where our drones spied on Valerio. We fly them too high to see, but it means we can't get close enough to make out much detail. My surveys suggest anomalies in the subterranean strata, but nothing conclusive. We'll know more soon."

She displayed the e-tablet's screen where the 3D render turned and worked, its gears spinning as a representation of the computer's RAM working overtime.

Rayyana said, "We think your friend arrived two days ago. Valerio's kill squad brought her shortly after the priest arrived."

"What do we know about them?" Bridget asked.

"Your parents supplied us with what little intel there is on them. Moses and Renata are married, both highly qualified and respected in the art and antiquities world, with a sideline in special forces-level killing techniques. Renata appears to enjoy it more than her hubby—or at least, it bothers her less. Hilla is very capable, qualified in aerial archaeology as well as many military and civilian aircraft, and highly skilled with a sniper rifle. Muzaffer has the most combat experience, first in the Turkish army, then with a US private firm. Embedded with the Kurds for several years until they forced him out after an unspecified incident with a prisoner, where he turned to academia and was recruited into this... what does your friend Prihya call it?"

"The scholar-assassins," Jules said.

"Right, that." Rayyana gathered her thoughts. "We neutralize them first. The priest, we try to take alive. He has diplomatic connections that might make things sticky if he becomes a casualty."

Bridget had been listening with faintly disguised irritation. "So we rescue Prihya, then move on to the library. Right?"

"That isn't your parents' instruction."

"Then I'll go on my own and you can tell them you let me."

Jules moved forward minutely, a subtle intervention that didn't quite place himself between the two women, but on the edge of it. "Bridget, let's hear her out. She knows what she's doin' here."

"Oh?" Bridget stepped back, her face open in an insulted bearing. "You think she's got it all nailed down?"

"I'd prefer to do it differently, sure, but—"

"Different, how?" Rayyana asked.

Jules wished he hadn't spoken, but it was out there now. "I'd prefer to go in covertly and pull her out. But this is your op. I ain't gonna—"

"Go in, sneak her out, then what? Wait for them to come after us so we're on the back foot? That's assuming you don't get caught in the act and both of you end up executed... and then they come after us, so we're defending again."

"Like I said—"

"No, Jules," Bridget interrupted. "I'd like to hear your plan." She aimed a pointed, huffy look at Rayyana. "You see things no one else does."

Rayyana closed her eyes, exasperated but holding it together. "He just said he'd trust me."

Bridget huffed again and stood in front of Jules, making him look at her instead of Rayyana. "Jules, you need to be clear. She's capable, sure, but she knows I don't trust her. She knows *why* I don't, too. She also knows when I'm here, I speak for my father, so if you have a better idea, I want you to come to me over her. Clear?"

Jules had never seen Bridget like this. While he struggled with emotional intuition, it wasn't an enormous leap to see her lack of reason extended to more than a single incident.

He said, "I'll always trust you, Bridget. Over pretty much everyone else."

Rayyana marched past them, shoulder checking Jules as she did so. "Okay, let's cut that out. Charlie, is that thing done?"

Charlie was examining the screen. "Just overlaying my anomalies with the cipher's destination."

Jules and Bridget crowded round, too.

"It ain't exact?" Jules said.

"It's a twelve-thousand year-old artifact," Charlie answered without prying her eyes from the screen as she overlaid a different topographical map. "The land's moved, the stars are in a different place, and it's designed to guide a person while they're using the device. There's a lot to work out, but..."

Her original mapping from the drone radar adjusted for the new data, highlighting two blocks on a hillside.

Charlie said, "We were not far away. It's just south of where Valerio is camped. Armstrong and his original party were less than two miles out."

Jules recalled the expedition from Dan's story and felt a buzz of excitement.

Answers…

"So," he said. "We head downriver. Recce the place, see what's there, then have Rayyana's people spring Prihya."

"I've studied the terrain," Rayyana countered. "We'd need to travel the river past Valerio's position, then circle back. Which is risky. Given he might have scouts along the bank."

Bridget said, "We do it Jules's way. He knows about this kinda thing."

Rayyana waited, one hand on a hip, angled toward Jules. "Well, big guy?"

Jules looked at Bridget. She blinked a couple of times, folded her arms, and stared back.

"We try it the bloodless way first," Jules said. "If it doesn't work out, I'll hand over the reins to the boss here."

"Thank you," Bridget said.

Rayyana tutted and moved to leave. "How romantic. I'll see you lovebirds get a private tent."

"Nah, it's not like that," Jules said.

Rayyana ignored him. "Know that my men follow my orders. If I believe we can't be successful with the sneaky approach, I will be more aggressive." She headed for the exit. "We move out before first light. Sleep well, lovebirds."

When she was gone, the remaining three glanced at each other.

"Right," Bridget said. "What do we do the rest of the night?"

"Sleep," Jules said. "I'll take in all the intel first. But sleep. It's gonna be a tough day tomorrow."

CHAPTER FOURTEEN

THE SUN ROSE above the horizon, illuminating the Amazon in a golden light, while citrus and the remnants of the night's light rain lingered in the morning air—a cool wake-up call augmented by coffee and protein-rich MREs. The river was calm and still as the Carson-funded small army launched four boats loaded with firearms, clothing, and machetes.

Charlie's usual arsenal of communication devices was missing. She'd created relays that daisy-chained together, allowing contact from below ground to the surface, but she couldn't tune them in to the equipment provided. It was better to leave them behind and pack her newer toys, such as a "smart directional detonator" that focused the force of a blast along a specific vector, and Rayyana had insisted the "VIPs" split up to minimize exposure in the event of an attack. Jules chose to travel with Rayyana, while Charlie and Bridget took a different vessel.

The river churned with the breeze around the first bend, masking all sound except the waves, which were loud enough to conceal voices from anyone on the shore.

Bridget and Charlie had huddled together, lost in conversation. Jules noticed them looking his way, but the roar of the water drowned out their words. Even if all she did was demand his attention, he wanted to hear Bridget's voice.

Yet, if he couldn't eavesdrop on Bridget and Charlie, they couldn't hear him, either.

"Rayyana," he said. "I gotta ask. Who the hell are you? Bridge said you were a maid, something like that? What'd you do to make her so... tetchy with you?"

Rayyana had resumed her full soldier getup, from weapons to camo face paint. "You're switching sides?"

"We're *all* on the same side. I'm bein' subtle around the person with the most emotional issues."

That made Rayyana smile. "Emotional issues. That's one take. Another is, I deserve her scorn."

"Why?"

"Long story."

"Long boat trip."

The vessel rocked against the current, Jules's hand gripping the side, fingers digging into the wood as they found a cluster of painted-over splinters. He met Rayyana's stern gaze.

"I'm a highly trained military grunt," she said. "The Carsons brought me to America when my parents died, but I'd already done two years at a military school. They employed me as a maid until my visa came through."

"Because of your uncle."

"He was involved in the resistance against ISIS. He and my aunt hated to risk me in the line of fire, so in exchange for a big contract, the Carson Corporation sponsored my resettlement. Assisting the US has its perks."

"You misled Bridget, though?"

"Not really. Not intentionally, anyway."

A thunk and a hop sprayed them with water. It had a mineral taste, leaving a trace of tang on the tongue.

Rayyana said, "I was her friend. That was never a lie. But I wanted to keep up my training. Only... the Carsons' lawyers believed I should stick with the role until my permanent visa was confirmed. With ISIS and other groups in the region... people who look like me... they would be distrusting. Better I play the frail orphan girl on the run for her life while my relatives support the US cause. Once I no longer had to hide my ability, I could join the military properly."

Jules saw where it was going. "You thought it wasn't a big deal. Bridget disagreed."

Rayyana bowed her head. "My actions are my actions. She believes I betrayed her. I think I was following instructions."

Jules's analytical brain forced him to see it from Rayyana's perspective more than Bridget's, yet he understood how emotions could cloud a person's judgement. How it had lasted this long, he couldn't grasp.

"Sucks," he said. "But she ain't dumb. She'll come around."

Rayyana said nothing, eyes front, mouth closed.

Both banks were now rain-forested rock the color of rain clouds, with rapids driving through it that squeezed the water into frothing waves. The boats handled it despite the additional turbulence, their heavy hulls an advantage to both stability, and to Rayyana's reluctance about opening up. The increased pace came with more noise, so chitchat ended. When they emerged into a calmer stretch, they pushed on, slowing when they reached the outer edge of where they knew Valerio had pitched up. The boats killed their engines, allowing the current to take them, and silence was the order throughout.

The trees were thick, a wall of every shade of green against an impossibly blue sky, the rainforest a magnet for uncountable migrant species. Hundreds of macaws, toucans, and parrots flew above the forest, the tree tops alive with monkeys, capuchin, and smaller mammals keeping in touch with the world below with a chatter louder than any of the humans on the water. A breeze carried the smell of its shores, the mud and earth, of life and decay, and of the vegetation on its banks.

Jules wondered how close they were to Valerio Conchin and Prihya Sibal. Were they a short jog away, or a lengthy, arduous hike? Were Valerio's goons watching as they floated by?

Eventually, around a massive rock outcropping, which reminded Jules of an elephant's head, the leader in the point boat signaled clear. They fired up the motors again, spearing deeper into the Amazon, where Charlie's calculations said the library lay. Jules regulated his breaths, his heart rate ramping up until he got it under control. He was ready.

"Promise me something, Jules."

He snapped to attention, Rayyana's voice startling him. "Promise you what?"

"Charlie said you have a problem with people dying. Especially when you can stop it."

"Respect for life. I don't call it a problem."

"Whatever you call it..." Rayyana lay a heavy glance toward Bridget and drew it back to Jules. "There could come a moment in there when you need to act quickly. When it's life or death."

"Yeah, I had a few of those."

"In a split second, if it's a decision between us in Theta Team or Bridget... remember we signed up for this. If it's between us and Bridget, it's always her. Choose to save *her*. Okay?"

Jules made the calculations. Bridget was his friend, but could he value her over the lives of several others in a pinch? It wasn't something he could analyze right now, but said, "Sure. I promise."

"Good." Rayyana checked her M4, which signaled the others to do the same. She tapped her throat mic. "Get set. We're beyond enemy territory now."

"You gotta do something for me, too," Jules said. "I don't wanna say it, but there's too much at stake. It's a precaution I gotta take."

"Name it."

He did. She didn't like it either. But she said yes, anyway.

CHAPTER
FIFTEEN

VALERIO CONCHIN HAD NEVER BEEN sure where his mind might wander off to next. So-called "experts" had diagnosed him variously with high-functioning autism spectrum disorder, ADHD, and a few even explained that *psychopath* could be a compliment. He felt no guilt or regret when destroying an adversary—literally or figuratively—but that didn't mean he felt nothing, ever.

For example, as he and Father Emory assessed the latest cavern, he was awestruck by its geometric shapes, long slabs cut at right angles whose shadows defined the hard lines in impossible-to-deny tooled blocks.

"Who do you think made this?" he asked.

Emory looked up from his e-tablet, seeming to contemplate the question. "Only the Maker truly knows."

"I think the makers are gone."

"I don't know why you'd come to that conclusion."

"I mean, look at this." Valerio rested his hand on the nearest wall. "Who can do this and then just vanish?"

The cavern was floodlit from below, ten massive bulbs illuminating it as a group of men, trained in death rather than archaeology, strolled around looking for something to do. But Valerio had already dispatched his experts.

Emory said, "It seems the makers' intent was that they would never be forgotten."

"That's what I was hoping for," Valerio said, snapping his fingers. "Look at this place! We must be on the right track."

"You need to calm down. We have no idea what's in there."

"An exit," Valerio said. "An entrance. A dead end filled with wonder. I don't care. I just want *something* that shows us the way."

"Maybe. You can't expect miracles. But you can be ready to act upon them, should the true maker see fit to bless us."

Valerio was unquestionably frustrated, but Emory was right. He forgot himself at times. He even denied the consequences of his actions, not just for himself, but for everyone else.

Prihya, whom he'd almost forgotten, walked to the cavern's center, where the shadows were the longest. Valerio could see the wonder in the young woman's eyes as she looked up, the walls towering above her. "It's beautiful, isn't it?"

"It is. But that's not the point." Valerio paced a tight circle. "It's also a labyrinth."

"A what?" Prihya asked.

"A labyrinth. You know, the Minotaur and all that. Armstrong wrote he could've got lost for years without resupply."

"You're saying that to scare me."

Valerio laughed. "Me, scare you? No, no, no. I'm here to protect."

Emory put a hand on each of their shoulders and looked sidelong at Valerio. "Ah, the impetuousness of the impatient."

Valerio flashed a look of irritation. "I'm not impetuous, Father."

"No, but you are, quite literally, a child at heart. A toddler who wants his dessert now, now, now!"

"I—"

Prihya got in with a short, sharp giggle. Unusual for a prisoner to be so forthright, so relaxed. "It's all very interesting. And I agree it appears man-made. But with no actual artifacts like pots or statues, it seems unlikely this is anything more than a natural formation. I explained this to you back when I wasn't being kidnapped and shipped around the world, but listen carefully again: rocks often buckle horizontally under pressure. It's fooled many a would-be game-changing archaeologist."

"And yet here we are," came Moses's reply as he emerged from the larger of two cavernous passages. He'd said the air had felt damp down the smaller of the two, so he and Muzaffer had taken the laser-mounted drones through the drier one. "We've worked out that it's geometrically exact. This chamber and the corridor, and the room at the end."

"Another room?" Valerio sensed his nostrils flare and his excitement rise to the surface. "What's there?"

"Not much. It's like a throne room or altar. Somewhere people gathered for a show. But the digital measurements show a uniformity that can't be random."

Prihya seemed to shrink back, edging toward Father Emory, the man who was making this expedition appear legit, hoping for a conclusion that matched a legend laid out in his Catholic sect's teaching. It seemed farfetched to Valerio, who ceased wondering about that and focused on Prihya.

Was she messing with them intentionally?

That stuff about rocks cracking in straight lines rang a bell with him, something people had been using to debunk the idea of random geological formations being ancient gathering places for years. He wasn't sure if it had been Prihya or someone else. He'd been heavily medicated for years, but the remedy from the First Priest's tomb combined with years of rehab had relaunched him. Rebooted him.

He was Valerio 2.0 these days.

"I recognize that look, Valerio," Father Emory cautioned.

"What look?"

"The one where you're thinking about killing someone or not. Prihya was not intentionally misleading us. She was using her eyes, not our friend's computer modeling and laser measurements."

Emory raised his e-tablet, which Moses had keyed in to the drone as it fed data through, although Valerio doubted the priest comprehended its meaning.

"Truly the Anthropocene Epoch is upon us," Emory said. "We are now stretching back into history in a way we never considered. We built great things even without robots and lasers, while modern humanity's impact on the world is one of destruction. Is it any wonder we seek reason in nature?"

Valerio reluctantly saw the light, but he was now thinking about a different target than Prihya. He wondered if the priest had served his purpose yet, and what use the crazy idiot would serve once they found the library.

It was times like this he wished his old friend Horse was here. Horse's new persona was more akin to that of a Doberman—loyal and useful, fierce and obedient. Which was nice. But even the most intelligent dog couldn't advise Valerio on strategy any longer.

Valerio reflected on the reasons he had initially allowed Father Emory to accompany him on the trip. Recognized that short-term legitimacy was useful but unnecessary and recalled how much the priest knew about the prize. Surprisingly, almost as much as Valerio.

More in some ways.

More...

Yes, Emory became more useful as time went on. If they couldn't trust Prihya yet, he had to keep Emory happy by not killing or maiming her. Besides, Valerio did not know who his backers were, only that he had once held a senior position at the Vatican, which made him a little too high profile to kill simply for being annoying.

"Thank you, as ever, for your counsel," Valerio said without an ounce of sarcasm. At least, he hoped so. He deferred to Moses and Muzaffer. "Anything else in here?"

"Nothing useful," Moses said.

"Okay, then. Next!"

Valerio skipped off toward the exit, a concealed fissure they'd blasted a couple of days ago, then waited while they checked the stability of the place before entering. Another frustrating delay.

As they neared the outside world, Moses's phone beeped at the same time as Muzaffer's. Both checked their screens.

"As we expected," Moses said.

"What?" Valerio asked.

"We have incoming. What would you like us to do about it, boss?"

CHAPTER
SIXTEEN

EASTERN CHINA, ARCHAEOLOGICAL DIG

AFTER FLYING BACK to the dig and spending a restless night in a new luxury tent (no bullet holes), Toby reviewed the new security personnel and the crew needed for a large-scale excavation, then dragged his heels across the warm sandy soil and leaned toward the fenced-off area around the new pit, bathed in the deep orange glow of a sunset. Dan held a phone to his ear while pacing a few feet along the yellowing linoleum strip that once led to a fuel dump. Preparing for the heavy machinery to take over, the Chinese workers gouged a guide line in the soil, piling dirt against the fencing, which pushed through and crept over like a colony of black ants.

LORI could be aboard a flight to Quito in an hour, ending the Carsons' hopes of being honored in Chinese culture. And yet, they were here, playing catch up to fulfill a dying goal.

Why hadn't the Carsons noticed Bridget's deception? Did they really not know their own daughter? Or had she hidden this impetuous, hard-headed side from them for years, only revealing it to Toby and the Institute because it was safe—even enticing—to do so?

"Dan?"

Dan held up a finger, listening to whoever he'd gotten through to.

Roger Carson emerged from a hastily built mess hall, hanging up a call of his own. It was one of two prefab structures they'd helicoptered in at twenty-four hours' notice, the other being a dorm room with bunks for the dozen workers they needed to complete what Toby still saw as two parts fool's errand and one part contractual obligation.

Roger gave a deep, heavy sigh. "Nothing."

Toby still didn't understand why Roger was here. He'd swapped his suit for swish hiking gear, but that seemed to be his only accommodation to the elements. As soon as they'd landed, Bridget had retreated to her tent to, what her dad called, *spend some quality time with the sulk princess*—as if she were a thirteen-year-old who'd been told she can't go to the mall with her friends after dark. Toby guessed she had been up to something, but the extreme of sneaking out of camp, then somehow ghosting herself out of the country, hadn't occurred to him.

"She's more resourceful than any of us guessed," Toby said to Roger.

It was supposed to be reassuring. But Roger didn't see it that way.

"I blame you, Smith. She never would have done this if not for you and that... boy she's chasing."

"She's not chasing a boy," Toby said. "She's merely headed in the same direction. And they are both adults."

"Twenty-five is barely out of the teens." Roger's face crumpled as if about to cry, but he steeled himself and tapped Dan on the shoulder. "Anything?"

Dan held the phone tighter to his ear and shook his head, turning away to signal the interruption was unwelcome. Bridget Carson was his friend. Dan had to find her... somewhere on the planet between here and the rainforests of Ecuador.

Roger turned to Toby, about to speak, when Dan hung up. "She's gone."

"Gone?" Roger said with mild panic. "What do you mean, gone?"

Harpal sauntered along, glancing at the dig, then standing before them, hands in pockets. "She's fine, you know."

Toby had clung to that thought since they realized she was missing.

Dan said, "At eight p.m. last night, Bridget made contact with one of Alfonse's intermediaries and demanded transport from mainland China to Ecuador. Once the guy stopped laughing, and she convinced him she was serious, the contact went and confirmed the request with the big kahuna himself."

"Alfonse did this?" Toby said.

Roger looked ashen. "The gangster spirited my daughter away?"

"No," Dan said. "She waited until everyone was in bed, snuck one of the dirt bikes from stores, and freewheeled it until she got a half mile away, then rode to the next village. I'm not clear on her next steps, but she made her own way to a town called Atajam where she was met by what Alfonse calls a 'specialist courier'."

Harpal said, "Oh, he likes his specialist couriers."

With a quick glare from Roger, Harpal quietened and Dan resumed.

"Long story short, she made it to Ecuador and onto the same transport plane as Jules. Since then, it's been radio silence. They have sat-phones but only for emergencies and six-hourly check-ins."

All digested the information.

At least she was safe the last anyone heard.

Toby almost voiced the platitude, but it would have fallen on hostile ears.

Roger's brows knitted together as he fumed. "Why would Alfonse Luca *do* that?"

"He's got a real soft spot for Bridget," Harpal said. "She's got him wrapped around her finger."

"We had an agreement."

Harpal waggled his little finger. "Unless that agreement specifically said he won't help Bridget get to the archaeological find of her dreams, Alfonse is going to back Bridget. Every time."

Dan gave a humorless laugh. "How come it's the 'action dudes' who are sitting on their butts doing a day job in the jungle?"

Harpal, who seemed to have appointed himself morale marshal, slapped Dan on the back. "Looks like you're the big brain on this one. Bridget can be Rambo for a change."

Roger Carson's face reddened. "That's my goddamn *daughter*

you're joking about. Do you have any idea how precious she is? Do you have any idea what I would do to keep her safe? I'll send in four teams the equivalent of Theta, bomb every city in that country if I have to."

"Sir," Toby said.

"No, before you say a damn thing, I will not calm down. I will move heaven and earth to find her—"

"Sir, *if I may...?*"

Roger's mouth hung open, but noise ceased coming out of it. In Toby's experience, calling men *sir* and women *madam* at moments of intense stress had a mild but effective influence on their mood—as if being listened to like a customer gave them a morsel of sanity to cling on to.

"*Sir*. It has been almost forty hours since she went AWOL. We have made progress in tracing her and we now know she *was* in the hands of people who are very experienced in relocating clients covertly and astonishingly quickly around the globe. She is with Jules, a very capable young man who has kept her safe—and she him—on many occasions. They also intend to meet with your Theta Team who, by your account, is your best infiltration and protection unit under your employ. Correct?"

Roger nodded reluctantly but firmly.

"Good. We also have on the ground Charlie Locke who has built a computer model of the machine destroyed by the Korean mercenaries. It will lead them to the location hidden on the cipher. From there, if they haven't already, they will recover Prihya Sibal and all will return home."

Roger chewed it over, still red in the face, but the tension had ebbed a fraction. "If the expedition is successful, they'll have to call in the authorities."

"Not necessarily," Harpal said.

Roger looked at Dan, who looked at Toby.

Toby said, "If Colin Waterson is wrong about the so-called 'nonsense' of Neil Armstrong's mission, then there's something very powerful out there. And if it's related to the Witnesses' technology that we've found to date, it needs to be analyzed and kept out of the hands of people like Valerio. Or the agents who might use it."

"Agents?" Roger said. "From which countries?"

"We already came up against Zimina Yanovna of Striovia."

"That's that tiny little country near Russia..."

"Who live in constant fear of annexation, yes."

Dan chipped in. "If Russia didn't have bigger objectives at the moment, it might have happened already. She wanted something powerful and because she has the same gift as Jules, she figured it'd be her big secret weapon."

"What sort of a weapon?" Now Roger sounded interested, curious, as if an opportunity were presenting itself. "What exactly do you think is out there?"

Toby considered a long list of possibilities, but took the advice of the men who frequently asked him to keep it succinct. "No one fully understands it. A power source is one use. But utilized with DNA transmitters, it could launch a plague. Or it can protect, if used correctly. There must be North Korean agents still hankering for the shield technology that they lost since they are working with Valerio Conchin."

"A powerful energy source," Roger mused. "Hostile nations know about it, and will kill to get it." He surveyed the camp, a lingering look on staring workers sending them back to their tasks. "Something like that needs to be controlled by a... *benevolent* power. Not ideologues and paranoid countries."

"Exactly," Toby said. Roger's brows knitted together as he fumed.

"And Bridget is in expert hands?"

"The best she can be, given the circumstances."

"Very well. Keep me updated." With that, Roger left them, calling back, "It's almost sundown. Make sure the crews quit for the day and get a good meal."

Toby, Dan, and Harpal gathered together.

"I don't like that," Dan said.

Toby's brow furrowed. "Why not? I thought I handled him well."

"For an ex-spy, you're pretty crappy at reading people who're planning on shafting you."

"I don't know what you're—"

"Yeah, we know," Harpal said. "You can't confirm-or-deny your past. But what we can confirm-or-deny is Roger isn't thinking about charity and good deeds when his little girl and security team find a hole full of powerful artifacts."

Toby was about to push back on the idea he was being naïve when Dan's phone pinged.

He checked the screen. "That's an alert. Damn. Looks like Valerio is on the move. And it isn't good news for our guys."

CHAPTER SEVENTEEN

ECUADOR

THE STEEP, uneven, thorny ascent from the river proved arduous. The rainforest's discordant orchestra of sounds rang all around, and the cool, moist air kept them from sweating. As they walked single file, Jules checked the computer model with Charlie every few minutes. It wasn't as precise as satellite navigation in a car, but it had an end point, which they mapped over a 3D render of the terrain.

They rested after two hours and Rayyana conferred with Montes, a local merc hired primarily for his wilderness knowledge. Although Jules spoke fluent Spanish, he missed some of the conversation because Montes spoke Amazonic Spanish, which was equivalent to a German speaker overhearing two Austrians in a coffee shop. He'd caught enough to infer that Montes had detected a problem.

Rayyana noticed Jules staring and gathered him along with Charlie and Bridget while Montes briefed the unit's other eight men. "We have access to surveillance satellites. Not quite CIA standard, but enough to see Valerio's group is on the move."

"This way?" Jules asked.

"This way, yes. We've also picked up that he's using low-grade drones, and it looks like they are sweeping the area before his company advances. Montes sent our own up. They're more advanced, fly higher, so Valerio's people are unlikely to detect them."

Charlie looked up, scanned the sky, and returned to Rayyana, who had taken a paperback book-sized e-tablet from her uniform. The tablet displayed miles of topographical representation, a series of pictures stitched together to form a coherent image of the land.

Rayyana said, "We have realview from the satellite and infra-red scans from the drones, pinpointing everyone's location. This is us. This is Valerio's people."

She indicated the two groups, Jules and company closer to the destination, with the incoming bodies spreading out in a pincer movement.

"We'll beat them there," Jules said. "They can't make up that mileage before we hit the big X."

"But what then?" Bridget asked. "This isn't some race where the losers turn around and go home with a participation medal. We have to defend the place."

"Chances are," Charlie said, "they're using *their* drones to track *us*. They got a rough location from Prihya, but they need us to find it for them."

"And these." Rayyana tapped the screen, zooming in on one of eight blurry patches. "Some odd heat signatures keep cropping up. They are probably small animals, large birds, or flocks of them."

"All different sizes," Jules said. "Lots of animals out here."

Charlie turned the pad around to see and zoomed in, then out. "So what you're saying is, be careful we don't step on a black panther or something."

"Wait a minute." Jules took the pad and stepped back so he could view the hillside up ahead. He craned to see between two trees, then scurried aside and clambered up a series of low branches. Looking back at the e-tablet, he called back, "Hey, can we get that 3D model of the landscape again?"

"Sure." Rayyana whisper-shouted which screen he needed to swipe to. "What's the problem?"

Jules lifted the tablet so the camera pointed to the terrain ahead, sweeping it around, like VR without the goggles, his memory having triggered a computer-like logic error but didn't see exactly what the issue was until now. He climbed back down and asked, "How old is the data?"

Charlie accepted the pad. "The original satellite download is from forty-eight hours ago. My Char-Dar drone mapped the contours about forty hours ago so we could overlay it on—"

"They blasted a section of mountain." Jules pointed at the screen, then up at the hill. "That bit's missing."

Charlie wheeled the computer pad around to find the right spot as everyone switched between the land ahead and the computer pad. When Jules compared the landscape to the photographed rendering on the screen, a knuckle of gray rock was missing.

"It's an odd angle," Rayyana said. "Easily solved by moving a half-klick south. We'd see it then."

"I accounted for that," Jules said. "You didn't hear anything?"

"The hills *could* have muffled the sound." Rayyana still didn't look convinced. "It'd have been like thunder or the more common blasting they've been attempting, so... maybe..."

"There's no maybe with Jules," Bridget said. "I've never known him to be wrong about something like this."

Rayyana looked around for Montes. Jules sensed increased tension in the Theta contingent, who were now checking the slides and ammo on their weapons. Montes approached Rayyana and spoke with her. Jules picked up enough and, judging by the concern in her face, Bridget had already translated the uncommon Spanish dialect.

"Bogeys incoming," Rayyana said. "They've doubled their speed. We have to counter that. Or turn back."

"They've been blasting at random." Jules's mind ticked off thirty tactics and explanations for the troop movements and settled on the most logical. "That outcrop was a guess, but now we're headed that way, they've figured they got it right. If we turn back, they got a clear run."

"You can't know that." Rayyana looked again at Montes, dismissing Jules.

"He's good at this," Bridget said.

"I get you like your boy-toy," Rayyana said, "and I get that you hate me for reasons I don't think I'll ever understand. But this is *big girl* time. Stand over there and let me do my job."

Bridget swallowed what was plainly going to be something loud and riddled with expletives, but she reined it in and touched

Rayyana's arm before speaking. "This isn't like other missions for my parents. You're not evicting civilians or fighting off bandits or defending a convoy. You're hunting an ancient repository in a race with a psychopathic billionaire. Jules has the measure of that guy."

Rayyana turned back to Montes, then pivoted to Jules. "You got more intel than we do?"

"Imagine my dad," Bridget said, "but insane. Imagine if my dad had no scruples and wanted a bunch of troublesome local residents dead or chased off, and he didn't care who died, as long as he got what he wanted... and then throw in a huge bonus for the desperate mercenaries he's employed."

"You've met people like that," Jules said, a statement not a question. "*That's* who's out there."

Rayyana held on Bridget a moment, waiting for more. Waiting, Jules suspected, for Bridget to show frustration or annoyance. Nothing came.

"You really mean this, huh?" Rayyana said.

"I've been... annoyed with you in the past," Bridget said. "I accept it can come across as a bit... petty. Sometimes. But not this. Jules has a way of connecting logic dots that most of us miss. Trust his instinct."

"Ain't instinct," Jules said. "It's a calculation."

"Fine." Rayyana stood back, shoulder-to-shoulder with Montes. "If you're the best at this sort of thing, what do we do about the incoming bogeys?"

"Never said I was in charge. I ain't a soldier."

"No one is a soldier," Rayyana said, "until they are obligated to make a decision like this."

Rayyana flicked the screen back to strategic positioning, the scale pinched out to show the red dots representing Valerio's people and the blue dots corresponding to their own location. Jules felt sick, numb in his hands and feet, and his brain became his own worst enemy. It froze, unable to accept that his next words could condemn a dozen men to death.

"You have to choose, Jules," Rayyana said. "Retreat and regroup, or do we take out the bad guys?"

CHAPTER EIGHTEEN

THE MAIN REASON Jules worked alone was that he preferred to rely solely on himself. Others dithered. A close second—or, to be technical, a branching reason related to the first—was that group decisions had consequences beyond his own fate. He'd never wanted to hold someone's life in his hands, nor place his in theirs.

"Can we put 'em off without deadly force?"

"Probably not," Rayyana said.

Jules looked at Charlie, a veteran of the British Royal Signals who'd experienced combat both on and off the battlefield. She wasn't on Dan's level, but few people were. Still, she was always direct and to the point. "I wish I could disagree."

A swift glance at Bridget confirmed she agreed with them.

Jules said, "In that case, if it's my orders you're followin', then no."

"No?" Rayyana said.

"No deadly force. Movin' quick is a better option."

Jules removed the machete from its straps and slung the pack on his back, the weight of the bangles reminding him that there was always another way. It struck him, even as he ignored the protestations from Charlie and Rayyana, that before meeting LORI, he'd divided his life in two—the before and after halves of his parents' deaths. His mother's, especially. As much as it troubled him, it was her face he saw clearly, and his father's was the one fading—troubling for a man with a supposedly eidetic memory.

There was before she died, and after.

Now his life was split into the years leading up to meeting the Lost Origins Recovery Institute, and the years since. It felt like more than four, but he didn't mind that. They had opened his eyes to a world beyond the known. A door cracked, and a wedge of light shone upon him, and he was grateful.

Today, he was determined to widen that door. More history. More of the legacy his mother had strived to protect... at the cost of her life.

"You coming, or what?" he said as he headed in the direction he'd memorized from the maps.

Rayyana called for him to wait, but this was a race now—the security team backing Jules up versus Valerio's mercenaries.

Jules heard orders in Amazonic Spanish, picking up enough to know Rayyana was instructing the team to spread but maintain visual contact, to check their satellite feeds, and to only engage if they had absolutely no choice.

Weird how orders work.

Weird how they were following his lead even though they disagreed with it, all because of Bridget's instruction to trust him.

"Good choice," Jules told Rayyana.

"Can we be sure we'll get up to the tomb?" Bridget asked. "Or whatever's buried up there?"

"Rayyana's got her assets in place." Jules sped up to a jog. "In case there's no other choice." He emphasized the last few words. "How's your cardio fitness these days?"

"Tip top," Charlie said.

"You know it's good," Bridget said.

Rayyana gave him an *of course I'm fine* look.

"Then let's double time it." Jules increased his speed.

They were deep in the forest now, the canopy thick above them, and the ground carpeted by undergrowth so thick it slowed their progress. Higher, the ground became rocky, and not all that wide, the incline steep, more of a face than a slope. The hidden drone above them gave Jules a moment's pause as he jumped over a fallen tree.

Bridget was breathing hard. Charlie sounded okay, but labored. Rayyana kept pace.

"How's the intel?" he called to Rayyana.

She was consulting the e-tablet. "Closing. But still at a distance. I'm getting clusters of activity, so they're gearing up to change tactics." She lowered the computer. "Jules, we should engage silently. Take on the point men and neutralize them."

Jules said, "Wait, what was it Valerio's men were wearing?"

"They're not wearing any special gear as far as we know," Charlie said.

"Why would they need to?" Bridget said.

"Sure. Unless..." He had a thought. "I bet they have—"

In that instant, his fear came true. The bushes came alive, and a huge body shot out, slamming Jules hard from the side.

Jules needed a tenth of a second to calculate the angle, the force, the surrounding obstacles—instantaneous to anyone watching—then he twisted, dropped into a wide, low stance, and pivoted as he brought his leading arm around the attacker's back. The man in camo gear and trailing a heat-masking thermal sheet spun in midair and landed in a heap.

The attacker righted himself, sprang to his feet, and snarled like a feral animal.

"Horse," Jules said.

Despite learning from Prihya what had happened to him, Jules couldn't subdue his shock at the man's appearance. Jules had broken the man's leg prior to Valerio dragging him into the tomb where they'd expected to find some sort of mighty, legendary weapon, where his boss had taken him before half a mountain collapsed around them. Seeing Horse on two legs was a miracle in itself.

Jules signaled the women to arc around him, handing off his machete and the pack containing his bangles. "Carry on, I'll catch up."

Rayyana aimed her gun at Horse. "I can drop him right there."

"It's okay. I've taken this guy out before. Now he's..." Jules struggled to find the words to describe what had once been a brutish-looking man with fierce intelligence oozing from within, who was now little more than a rage-focused creature, literally drooling. "He's my responsibility. Go. Now."

The two circled the flat ground, Horse like a hulking sumo wrestler, low and wide, arms and shoulders spread in an animalistic instinct to make oneself look bigger to an opponent. Jules had long eradicated formal fighting stances, but followed basic good sense: elbows in, hands at torso height, one a little extended, his legs planted at shoulder-width and his weight on the balls of his feet.

"Remember last time?" Jules tried. "Come on, you can't beat me."

It looked as if Horse was trying to speak, but a physical obstruction in his throat prevented it.

Jules had bested the beast when he was a shrewd fighter with an expert soldier's brain. This poor, angry creature before him shouldn't pose much of a problem. Jules simply needed to wait him out. Counter whatever came his way.

"Okay, then," Jules said. "When I get done here, I'll find your boss, tell him I whupped your ass, then I'll beat down on his."

Horse's features creased in even deeper anger, the snarl so inhuman Jules would not have been shocked to see the man turn green. The ex-special-ops soldier charged forward with a roar.

Jules sidestepped him but was unable to gain a grip or leverage; Horse moved faster than expected. The sledgehammer backhand almost caught Jules off guard, like a mousetrap triggered by a rodent. He ducked it, swept his foot around Horse's ankle, and tripped the big guy.

Horse landed hard, but showed no sign of embarrassment or pain as he flipped over and pushed up to his feet, launching into a sprint without missing a beat. Jules didn't have time to shift aside this time, so he rolled forward, tripping Horse as if he'd run into a barrel.

The hulking assassin sprang up and resumed his attack.

When Jules was fighting, time didn't slow down so much as he perceived each attack in an enhanced state, which he described to others as a slow-motion visual. In reality, it was more like how birds react to cars in mid-flight, or bats readjusting to catch an insect. A shoulder shift or a knee easing in a specific way telegraphed each move to Jules.

Horse didn't have any of that. He'd somehow retained his hand-to-hand combat training without even thinking about it. There was no thought process, no plan of attack, just an instinctive desire to destroy.

Jules had to adapt.

Instead of evading his attacker until he could subdue him, Jules switched to counterattack mode. He followed a hard block with a series of rail punches to Horse's ribs, more krav maga and wing chun than aikido.

The man stumbled, but he swung another of those spring-loaded backfists. This one caught Jules in the arm, sending shockwaves through his body as he fell sideways.

He, like Horse, jumped back up and landed solidly.

Horse was on him so fast that he barely had time to adjust, forcing him to the back foot. He could not block every incoming punch, their speed and power unpredictable as the technique resembled a playground brawl rather than two experienced individuals.

Jules had to attempt something out-of-the-box.

He squealed at the highest volume he could muster. It gave Horse pause, long enough for Jules to pivot, draw back one leg, and drive his heel backwards with the force needed to kick down a door—right into Horse's groin.

Horse grunted, jerked his hips back, and fell to the ground.

But only for a fraction of a second.

Horse had been stunned by a blow that would have floored the average man, including someone wearing a groin guard, but the pain appeared to fade as quickly as a glancing blow to his thick forehead. And Jules hadn't factored that in.

He'd assumed the fight was over as soon as heel met junk, and that all he'd need to do was hit a pressure point in Horse's neck to knock him out.

It made him sloppy.

Horse grabbed Jules by the neck, his strength and speed far too powerful and unpredictable. No matter where Jules hit him, no matter which nerve or joint he tried to manipulate, Horse stood firm—a statue carved in place with Jules's neck as decoration.

Clearly, either the spinal injury or the brain damage had dulled

Horse's pain receptors, which Jules chastised himself for overlooking in his calculations.

Horse squeezed, cutting off Jules's blood flow as simply as any choke hold.

Jules was blacking out, the world closing in around him with a gray haze, when he heard Horse tap a node that activated his throat mic. In a gravelly, forced monotone, he said, "Got him boss. Want me to kill him?"

CHAPTER NINETEEN

Valerio experienced so few moments of pure joy these days that he had to take what he could get.

Got him, boss.

The words washed over him like a lukewarm shower after weeks of sweaty humidity and filthy sleeping conditions. They were among a group of South American mercenaries—mostly veterans of drug cartels dispersed by government operations—mooching through dense undergrowth toward an unconfirmed target location.

However, given the subjects' track records, it was highly likely.

Want me to kill him?

Yes, absolutely.

But *want* and *need* were diametrically opposed concepts in this case. Not only might Valerio require assistance from the lad's special touch, he also had to keep the priest sweet. He'd already agreed to ensure Prihya remained unharmed by bringing her along under supervision rather than throwing her in a hole.

Father Emory was keeping an eye on Valerio, as if he was about to raid the former Vatican man's candy. Not that they had candy out here. However, candy would be nice. And a boost to the men's morale. Yes, as soon as he could summon a resupply shipment, he'd demand a slew of candy to go with the MREs, clothing, medicine, and whatever else was required.

Want was sometimes more powerful than *need.*

Emory's expectant expression reminded Valerio that they were all connected to the same communications system. He could snap Jules Sibeko's neck with a single command. And given the trouble the lad had caused, it wouldn't be entirely unjustified.

But no.

Valerio replied to Horse, "Use only the necessary force to keep him compliant. Broken is fine if needed. Not dead."

The priest nodded approval and resumed his mini conference with Moses, Renata, and Muzaffer, the trio increasingly deferring to Emory Ballard as they had twigged that Valerio did little without the priest's approval. Prihya stood off to the side, two mercs flanking her but not manhandling her unless she veered from the path Valerio ordered. Valerio joined them.

"Such a shame we all have eyes in the sky these days," he said.

A question came through Moses's squint, an iPad in his hands.

"Ruins any surprises," Valerio elaborated. "Not like the old days, eh?"

"The old days," Emory said. "When you had to wipe out dozens of lives indiscriminately?"

Valerio was annoyed at the man's barb, but didn't care that he was right. He had analyzed the other group's movements, the general direction, and confirmed the target. They'd been close earlier in the week, but must have missed it by some yet-to-be-determined distance. "We push on. We get there. We take out these annoying dots."

"They're not dots," Prihya said, as if she could see the screen. Which she couldn't. She wasn't allowed. "They're people."

"Collateral damage. Even Father Emory agrees. Don't you, eh?" Valerio slapped Emory on the arm like a teammate in some field sport. Not that Valerio had ever been sporty. He'd always been too sick. Until the healing pool confirmed the existence of magic in the world. Or... y'know, science that didn't have a name yet.

Emory bristled and shifted in between Moses and Muzaffer. "The boy who found the place in 1946 described the terrain, but it didn't match where we blasted. Are you sure that's where they are headed?"

"One of my gifts has always been prediction," Valerio said. "My father seeded me my money but disapproved of my investments. But I know people. I know their goals, their motivation, their endgame. And it's all the same. That's why I'm a real, honest-to-God billionaire, whereas my father died with barely ten million dollars to his name."

"Pauper," Prihya said.

"Yes, among my kind, he was a peasant gazing up at us through jealous eyes." Valerio switched gears. "Jules Sibeko just doesn't realize how damaged he is. That makes him achingly, almost boringly, predictable. Like you, my dear." He turned to Prihya, holding back from stroking her lovely smooth skin. That wasn't right. And he wasn't that sort of creep. "And you. You still resist the notion that you're on our side. You scoff at the suggestion."

She did, indeed, scoff. And turn away. But the frown betrayed her discomfort.

"Yes, you're on my side. Just like Jules will be when he realizes he needs me. Even though you haven't admitted it to yourself, you still feel that curiosity. Still want to get there, to see what knowledge will be granted or what danger will befall us. What fun!"

"Danger is fun now?" Muzaffer said.

"You have to treat danger as fun. Because it always comes around. For everyone. This time, though, there's a surprise in store."

"Yes," Father Emory said, meeting Prihya's returning glare. "A big one."

Horse's hand tightened around Jules' throat, causing him to gag. The towering monster laughed with a wet yukking hack, dead eyes penetrating beyond Jules's. His vision became blurry and gray, and he lost all strength in his arms. He hadn't heard Valerio's reply, but he could see Horse's disappointment in his down-turned mouth. But that turned to amusement as he teased Jules like a dog would toy with a stuffed animal before digging into its stuffing for the squeaker.

The gray flashed white, then orange, and the grip loosened.

Jules's eyes opened just in time to see a glowing, spitting ball spin into Horse's head, sparking in a shower of fire as he slapped it away. Jules fell to the ground, his legs cushioning but not supporting his weight, and recognized the object as a flare. He collapsed to the forest floor, as if his knees had turned to wet cardboard.

Horse swatted, spun in a circle, repeatedly hitting himself in the head, mewling in a high-pitched keening cry.

Jules mustered the strength to shuffle back, his blood flow returning to normal, orienting himself enough to see Charlie Locke darting out of the trees, the spent flare gun in one hand, a Sig-Sauer 9mm in the other. She aimed the Sig squarely at the man's head from five feet away.

"No," Jules said, an arm out toward her.

"That whole taking orders thing," she replied. "It doesn't work for me when I might end up dead."

"Look at him. He's a child."

Horse was slapping the smoldering skin, the singed hair, tears streaming down his face, now doubled over and cowering, fear replacing his aggression.

Like a playground bully with the tables turned.

"I'm partly responsible for him being like this." Jules found his feet, his legs and arms still a touch shaky. "Please. Let's find another way to beat them. He needs help, not a bullet."

Charlie bit her lip, studying the big Australian mercenary. Something plainly clicked behind her soldier's mask as she lowered the Sig to 45-degrees. Not aiming at Horse, but ready to return to firing position if he threatened them.

"You okay to run?" she asked.

"Yeah, let's do it."

Jules took off at a reduced pace, his mobility limited, while Charlie backed away, keeping Horse in sight until she no longer could. Then they ran.

"Hope we don't regret that," Charlie said.

"We've stopped the immediate threat," Jules said, his body recovering more with every step. "Time to go direct. Now it's just a race—"

"Sorry, no." Charlie kept pace, not a single step faltering as she delivered the verdict. "You were out of it. Incapacitated, you might say. While I pulled your arse out of the fire, Rayyana had to act. She made the decision."

Jules almost paused mid-run. "*What* decision?"

In the tight, man-made clearing, alongside Rayyana and Montes, the chain of command wasn't crystal clear, but Bridget had guessed this much: Rayyana's standing orders were to keep her safe and to escort them all to the destination, but the Carson name still carried authority. The witch had to do as instructed, regardless of how she felt. As long as it didn't threaten their lives, Bridget could demand pretty much anything of her and Theta Team. So, instructing her to defer to Jules meant Jules was in charge.

But Jules had come off worse against his old enemy, and the jungle was teeming with men coming their way. If Bridget didn't want to get caught in the worst fight of her life, she'd needed someone who could give orders. Rayyana was the right person.

The air felt heavy with dread, and she could hear the buzzing from the best solution available. Her left hand balled into a fist, but she couldn't tell how long it would take, or if Charlie had been successful in rescuing Jules.

Rayyana angled her head up, following the buzzing noise as her finger stabbed at the e-tablet. "Ah, finally."

With a rush of breaking foliage, Jules speared into the clearing, the tight knot of people here ready to defend themselves.

While Bridget had long admired Jules's commitment to preserving life, and Bridget herself was far from a bloodthirsty killer, she agreed with Dan: Jules's resistance to killing bad people, when those bad people would happily see them all perish, was obviously some sort of mental block, a trauma that needed addressing. Especially in their line of work. Holding over some DC or Marvel superhero code of honor was not normal, no matter how well-intentioned.

Jules had a wild look. "What's going on? Are we ready to move?" He was disoriented, out of breath, the kind of adrenaline spike Bridget rarely saw affect him.

Rayyana's eyes flicked up to Jules, her long lashes ludicrous on someone in full face paint. "We're going nowhere if we're dead."

"Let's pause a second," Bridget said. "Jules, what do we do?"

Rayyana's finger froze on the screen, one eyebrow cocked. "Well?"

Jules turned a full circle, head bobbing, switching side to side as if he might see through the thick tree cover. "Trust her."

Bridget's chest fluttered and her throat felt like someone had punched it. "Her?"

Charlie said, "Oh, grow up, Bridget."

Bridget's mouth fell open, but she managed not to pout.

Fine. *Trust her.*

"Right," Rayyana said, resuming her finger-path. "Watch. And relax."

Prihya had gotten lost. Not in the sense that she'd escaped and run blindly into the rainforest, unfortunately; she had no idea where she was. Even if she broke free of the muscle heads Valerio had assigned, she'd have no way to reach safety—not the camp, not the library, not to Jules.

She saw no way out until they came into contact with LORI and the people helping them. Valerio had indicated they were part of Bridget's parents' company, but that didn't seem likely. Weren't they oil execs?

Then there were the scholar-assassins, Renata in particular having held a grudge about Prihya abandoning Valerio's side. She had no doubt they would kill her as soon as she was of no use.

And what use, exactly, was she?

It was a question she'd asked the priest on the private jet out of Malta where she'd been uncuffed once in the air: *why do you need me if the cipher is already gone?*

"Because, child," the priest had answered with a patronizing air, "you know more than you realize."

"I know about the things you do. I know the pyramids have geometric designs millennia ahead of the supposed builders, that the Nazca lines have more significance than showing off to gods, that

Atlantis isn't what Plato thought it was, and that almost every government on the planet has historical secrets it's hiding from the population but won't say why. I know Stonehenge was once located in Wales and moved wholesale to Salisbury, and that Excalibur was a historical object and King Arthur was a real person but got mythologized when—"

"Have you finished?" Father Emory said.

"Not even close," Prihya replied with more confidence than she felt. "How much of these anomalies concern the Witnesses? I don't know and can't say. But I don't think any of it has anything to do with the Tayos gold or the cipher."

"Oh, my dear." Emory had patted her thigh then. Not in a creepy way, just a reassuring touch. "You have no idea how much help you are going to be."

Now, in the Amazon rainforest, Prihya had seen Valerio salivate over Jules's capture, then shoulder his way in to observe the feeds from their drones.

Seems everyone has drones these days.

Except, his smug celebratory mood soured almost right away, and then he couldn't get a reply from Horse on the radio. The scholar-assassins opened their own channels, speaking Arabic and Turkish, before reporting in that they had to move.

"Pull back," Muzaffer told Valerio. Then to Emory, "We must pull our men back. And find cover ourselves."

"Why would I do that?" Valerio demanded.

"Because..." Moses started, but cocked an ear to the sky. "Because of that."

A whining sounded overhead, the land playing with the noise so it was off to the side. Then an explosion shook the ground.

All turned their attention that way, before another explosion on the opposite side drew them that way.

Valerio's face erupted in shock and anger. "What the *hell*?"

Emory likewise rounded on Moses. "What is that?"

"They're bombing us, Father," Moses said simply. "The Carsons' personnel have armed drones."

Prihya's stomach churned with a mixture of fear and delight, hopeful only that they'd know her location.

Valerio hopped up onto a rock as if trying to see over the trees. He stomped his foot and yelled, “That’s so unfair!”

And it was.

Yet, even as the ordnance buried the forest beneath a cloud of soil, dust and a cacophony of booms and crashes, Prihya couldn’t help a smile behind her hands shielding her face. Perhaps Valerio wouldn’t emerge on top after all.

CHAPTER TWENTY

THEY DRAGGED themselves over the cliff that Jules insisted was their only option. Most people would not see what Jules saw as a near-certainty, but his vision had accepted the formation from a distance and only strengthened as they got closer.

At the edge of a boulder that jutted out from the blasted line of the rainforest, Jules ran his hand over the fissure—a jagged pseudo-triangle sixteen-point-six feet tall that normal eyes would have written off as a result of the blast that had sheered vegetation and the outer layer of rock and soil. Rayyana had established a perimeter around the vast plateau, the bombing run having killed some—but not all—of Valerio's men. She had allowed for a retreat while keeping her eyes on the sky for incursions on their position.

The remaining trees were bent over from their own foliage, providing shade from the hot sun. The four stood in a line at the stony rim, watching Theta Team form a defensive line.

"And Prihya?" Bridget asked. "What do we do about her?"

"We get access," Jules answered. "We get what we need. Then we bargain."

"Bargain?" Rayyana said. "With what?"

"With whatever useless crap we find that looks cool." Jules pressed his palms against the two sides of the fissure, as if bracing them open. It was pitch black inside, but the scant light from the sun illuminated enough of a passage to confirm Jules had been correct. "This has to be it. They unlocked it for us and didn't even realize."

"Are you sure it's not a trap?" Charlie asked, her attention on the drones' tablet.

Jules slipped the tablet running the cipher's computer model from Charlie's pack, more to reassure the women than himself. He set the graphic to start at Malta, ran the program again, and the trail spun into a blur of stars and continents, before settling on a point in South America. Their position. He zoomed in, ticking off the features on his thumb and fingers.

"The Amazon river, the contours of the land, and these small peaks. We're on number four. Here." He tapped the screen where the green land zoomed in again. "This is a wide margin of error. No way for a machine like that to be pinpoint accurate. But it falls in this area. And the way the explosives shaped this part of the rainforest... the angle these wedges are sticking out at... and this crack in the face... it's all pointing at something unnatural under our feet."

Silence.

"Well?" Jules said.

"Okay," Charlie said. "I'm convinced."

Rayyana turned on her heel and said, "Yeah, me too," then resumed giving orders to the men charged with protecting this zone.

Bridget was grinning, staring into the dark fissure.

If this is it, she'll be so happy. A library of gold books, maybe a history of the Witness, their culture, their—

Bridget caught him looking. "What?"

Jules said nothing. He couldn't. Which was odd.

Charlie said, "I need to go... do stuff."

"What do you need to do?" Jules asked.

She patted him on the arm and winked as she passed by him. "I'll think of something."

When she was gone, Bridget was still watching him. She turned back to the cave but was smiling, a red tint to her cheeks.

Right... stuff.

Jules parked himself beside her. "Hey."

"Hey."

"You okay?"

"Coming down from the adrenaline rush. You?"

"Same." Jules was actually battling with the idea his actions had resulted in men dying in the forest, but he pushed it aside; the order came from someone else. It was a mistake he didn't intend to repeat.

Bridget looked at him again. Her eyes had always been a rare blue color, the flecks in her iris appearing to sparkle in the right light, reminding him of the way his bangles lit up when he touched them.

She said, "Are you ready for this, Jules?"

They'd been dancing around these lingering glances for far too long. Life had always been too complicated to consider potential romance. He'd been hesitant to commit to friendship, let alone anything more serious. There'd been life-threatening chases around the world, a paranoid nation looking for a power source to end an external threat, the real danger of a global plague, and a project born of protection that turned deadly, and... being confined to a single location for months on end had also felt wrong.

His fault.

His quirks, his... *trauma*, if Dan was correct about him.

But he now shared her enthusiasm for unearthing old artifacts, particularly in relation to the mystery of the Witnesses. Some might say it had grown into an obsession that rivaled Bridget's and Toby's.

"I ain't so good at small talk," Jules said.

"I know." Bridget leaned against him, rested her head on his shoulder. "We don't need to."

"Good. Because I don't want to be a jerk or misread anything that might be goin' on between us. I ain't misreading it, am I?"

"No."

She leaned more heavily, as if snuggling into someone on a cozy couch. Now was probably a good time to put an arm around her, but Jules felt a stirring he didn't need. He had to concentrate. Park this for later. It could be a dangerous distraction.

"We need to explore this," he said.

"I agree."

"Just me and you. We'll be honest with each other. Figure out if we can make it work."

Bridget pointed at the fissure. "I meant I agree we need to explore this cave."

Jules stood stiffly away from her and said, "Oh, man, sorry. I mean, I, I don't know. Sorry, I—"

Bridget laughed, loud and full. Pulled him back to her and rested both hands on his chest, which roused that stirring again as their faces came close together.

She said, "If that's your way of asking me on a date when we return to civilization, then, yes. Let's do that."

Charlie returned, Rayyana backing her up, both carrying a bunch of kit.

"If you kids are ready...?" Charlie said. "These are my LED pods." She handed a small canvass sack to Jules, inside which were dozens of the rubber knobs with glass fronts he'd seen at the camp. "Lay 'em on the floor or jam into crevasses. They'll do a job for ten hours. Brighter than most flashlights."

Jules accepted the gift and broke away with Bridget, Jules dropping straight into business mode and assessing the array of handheld and head mounted flashlights, tools, and electronics. He still had the small pack containing the Ruby Rock and Aradia bangles, and now added the kit they might need underground. There were no comms past a certain point, and Charlie's relays they'd used on previous expeditions didn't work with the radios supplied by Theta Team. With the next phase of answers almost in reach, no one wanted to come back up for supplies.

"You coming?" Jules asked.

"No, I'll run external comms here," Charlie answered. "And I'll come save you from the dragon or whatever's waiting to eat you up."

CHAPTER TWENTY-ONE

Their steps echoed and reechoed down the rock passageways. Jules twisted one of the LED pods on the floor to activate the rechargeable battery, which emitted stunning lamp light to illuminate an area larger than ten feet cubed.

The external fissure was diagonal, but once they passed through the cave-like entrance, the angle shifted, revealing hairline cracks where the main mass had yielded under millennia of massive pressure. The walls and air were cool and musty, reminiscent of the river they'd travelled down. They had to walk single file and even duck where the ceiling closed in on one side, although it was wide enough to stand three abreast in places.

Its downward bend assured Jules that they had found the right spot—or, at the very least, an unusual feature. It had a buckling effect all the way down, but the walls at the base were straight. More strategically placed LED pods boosted their flashlight beams, revealing that nature and tectonic evolution had encroached on man's efforts and reshaped the fracture. Underfoot, however, was solid bedrock that only canted unevenly when the ceiling appeared to be intact.

Years before in Montrose, they had trekked in similar patterns, and Jules had intuited they were moving in a near-perfect Fibonacci spiral—the ratio found in nature, from sunflowers to nautilus shells. His theory was that they intended the symbolism to communicate with anyone advanced enough to interpret the ratio, acting as a test of newcomers' comprehension.

Showing off, Dan had suggested.

Jules had a more ominous explanation: it was a warning. Anyone who didn't understand the Witnesses' access passages was usually in serious danger before reaching the bounty.

"Are you sure this is man-made?" Bridget asked after fifteen minutes of blank walls.

"Could be older than what we found before," Jules said. "It's been tunneled out. The shape. The angles. It's not like square-edged wedges this time. It's intentional."

"So, it just wasn't maintained. Or they never decorated these walls."

Rayyana said nothing. She sporadically doubled back to check on the group of guys she said were shadowing them, but Jules wanted more to remain outside. Rayyana insisted it was a more defensible position if they had assets in the corridor.

Maybe Jules shouldn't have tried to hijack her command earlier. Sure, it had come from a Carson who had overall control, but there was no shame in deferring to someone with more experience. Or there shouldn't be.

"Guess they'd need a village guarding the pictures," Jules said. "Someone to repaint them like they had in India."

"Or etched in metal."

If there were gold or books or both waiting, and the people who put this here had the technology LORI had witnessed to date, why not plate the corridors with it?

"It's older," he said. "Look at the way the walls slope in. Tectonic plates, continents moving, volcanic activity a few hundred miles away. It all adds to the pressure of anything underground like this."

Rayyana rejoined them. "Are you saying it's unsafe?"

Jules shook his head.

Bridget answered, "We have to move quickly." She illuminated Rayyana's face with her head-mounted lamp. "Another ten-thousand years, and it might be closed entirely."

Rayyana took it in, then brightened. "We're here in the nick of time, then."

Jules said, "Geologically speaking, that's not far away."

For the next seven minutes, they trudged through the messed-up passages, which Rayyana described as "wobbly," coming across eleven tunnels branching off. Those tunnels became dead-ends within yards of commencing, although there seemed to have been efforts to illustrate the walls. It reminded Jules of the approach to the First Priest's tomb, which featured murals of natural disasters, of warriors wielding mighty weapons, holding back floods, repelling raiders, and more stories resembling modern legends than Jules had time to count. Here, nothing was readable or even discernible as an image. Everything had given over to nature and decay.

Until they came to their own dead end, where a wall loomed, spanning the corridor, embedded into the roof and floor.

They shucked off their packs, set out a series of LED pods to burn as bright as day without dazzling them, and used stiff brushes to dislodge dirt from the crease, revealing the wall rested in a groove. Making it, technically, a door.

Rayyana said, "Okay, this is academic territory. Unless you want me to blow it up."

"It'll be too thick," Jules said. "Any explosive powerful enough'll bring the whole place down."

Bridget made a show of tracing the outline, which was about as wide and tall as a school bus. "Feels solid. No markings."

Jules rolled up his sleeves, although he did not know why; it just felt right.

"What are you going to do?" Rayyana asked. "Massage it?"

"Saw somethin' like this before. I got a magic touch."

"Only," Bridget added playfully, "not quite *magic*-magic."

Jules sensed the smile come to him, then placed his bare palms on the stone door's surface. It felt rough, but there were definite grooves, so he focused on those. He could feel the markings, deep and precise, hidden by a layer of crud, which he didn't want to think about as it flaked off in dry, leafy layers. There were no scurrying creatures that they'd seen or heard, but that didn't mean there were no insect colonies or something else that might have layered this door with filth.

Rayyana glanced at her watch, shifted position to check the

passage they'd come down, then back to Jules. "Are you... communing with it or something?"

"No." Jules was creating a picture in his head, mapping the symbols and letters, seeing them as clearly as if he'd written them down, but could make no sense of them. They were unlike the markings they'd found on previous barriers and walls.

After a few minutes, he gave up and moved to the section of rock where the door vanished into the earth. Or the wall. Or someplace Jules hadn't thought of yet.

Recalling the last time he encountered a slab like this, he was expecting to find a keyhole like a figure eight, but after trying both sides, he accepted it wasn't there.

"The same people didn't build this," he said.

"Or they built it for a different purpose," Bridget added.

"Which was what?" Rayyana asked.

"We think the first one we found was supposed to repelling rising seawater."

Rayyana was visibly confused. They were hundreds of miles from the ocean, so why would it do the same thing?

Jules said, "Just another test."

He rummaged in his bag and removed the two bangles that had resided in the chateau's secure vault for the past couple of years. He took them out occasionally to look at them and wonder how much his mom knew about the Aradia bangle's origins, its function, its legacy. Those times he'd handled them as he mused about a past he'd never learn, the flecks inside the stone objects lit up, as if an electrical current were passing through. One red, one green.

As they did now.

Rayyana's eyes widened. "Are you doing that?"

"Yes," Jules said. "But I don't know if this'll work."

"You're throwing spaghetti at the wall, I get it."

Jules couldn't tell if that was sarcasm, an insult, or her way of understanding events as they unfolded. He didn't care, either, so slotted the two bangles together.

Both were circular, with gaps cut about an inch wide. The red-flecked Ruby Rock bangle's ends were cut in the opposite angle to the green-infused Aradia one, and when the opposite-cut sides met, they snapped together in a strong magnetic seal.

But they were not decorative. They were not jewelry at all.

Jules held them in one hand, placed his other against the barrier to complete a circuit of sorts, then pressed the figure-eight of the bangles on a section he'd cleared of crud.

Almost immediately, the symbols and grooves lit up in eerie green, spanning the wall. Both women retreated to take in the entire view. Jules had mapped it in his head, but as clear as that had been, he hadn't traced every groove, every depression. While his angle was tighter than the women, he still made out the concentric circles, formed of what modern humans might describe as morse code dashes. Some were longer than others, some curled in at the end, but it was definitely a series of circles, like a maze seen from above.

Then the vibrations came. Tiny, almost tickling his hands. Then they built to where a deep rumble and creak resonated from one side of the door.

The grinding came next.

In previous finds, the doors were mounted on chiseled stone hinges or maneuvered by magnets or magnetically influenced cogs. No rope or anything that would rot.

But here, with the tectonic shifts, the pressure from millennia of tiny movements, it seemed to have jammed. The door slid only a couple of feet before the grinding increased in pitch and the door shook like a car struggling in cold weather.

Jules released his contact.

"You okay?" Rayyana asked.

Jules examined the gap between the wall and door. "Fine. Just gotta breathe in."

"What's that? A two-foot gap?"

"Seventy-one centimeters. About two-point-three feet."

"Huh." Rayyana seemed bemused. "You got a tape measure there?"

"Nah, I just pay attention." Jules separated the bangles and slipped one on each wrist. "Come on."

He pointed his headlamp into the gap, grabbed his handheld flashlight, and shouldered his pack. He slipped through the door, which was over a foot thick and, as expected, too solid to blast through.

He emerged into a damp cavern not much larger than the previous corridor's width. The only sound was a faint trickle of water, interspersed with the occasional drip. In his artificial light, water in a raised pond rippled and eddied in a receptacle the size of a child's paddling pool. It took him nearly eight seconds to realize the movement wasn't a trick of the beams aimed into it, but the water's flow.

"Ugh, what's that smell?" Bridget said as she joined him.

Rayyana, too, added her light.

Jules offered his best guess. "It's sat stagnant for thousands of years before we opened that door. Nowhere for it to evaporate. I'm guessing what it's sat in is treated so the rock can't absorb it."

"And you... what?" Rayyana said. "Started it flowing like a river?"

Jules walked the room, needing only one LED pod to ascertain its shape. And it felt like that—a room. Not a passage or linking section, but a purpose-built room, designed to last beyond the civilization who built it.

"This is it, then?" Rayyana said. "We went through all that to visit a moldy spa?"

Bridget mimicked Jules's path, touching the wet walls, running fingers over the smooth surface. She sniffed her fingertip. "Salty."

Jules halted in place, turned on his heel, and returned to the pool. He dipped his finger in and touched the tip with his tongue. "It's more than salty."

He yanked the bangles off his wrists so quickly he nearly fumbled them both.

"What's going on?" Rayyana asked. "We need to swim under there. Don't we?"

"You don't wanna go swimming in briny water," Jules said, snapping the bangles together again. "These rocks, the elements in them, they're designed to repel seawater. The saltier the better. This tech, the underlyin' science, it links on a quantum level. My touch, the neutrons flowing through the planet, all of it. But then it has a bigger effect, a... a *macro* impulse. Stick these two babies together, add saltwater, it's like a violent chemical reaction on an epic scale."

Rayyana seemed to get it. "And brine..."

"Is even less pure than seawater," Bridget said.

Jules hesitated a moment. "You think?"

"I think..." Bridget had a manic gleam in her eyes, hands clapping in an excited-little-girl way. "If it goes wrong, we get wet."

"Or the cavern floods," Jules said.

Bridget thought for a second, then shrugged. "Go big or go home, right?"

"Go big or go home."

"Wait." Rayyana reached for him. "We're just gambling here?"

He didn't wait.

He plunged the two bangles into the pool and almost immediately the water fizzed, intensifying to bubble and boil around his hand.

Although it looked hot, Jules felt remarkably little—a vibration similar to when he first held them. The effect had not lessened over time, but he had grown desensitized to it. Until now.

Now, he felt more power than ever before. Sensed energy building and building, as if an explosion were imminent.

Then something new happened.

The water around the bangle spread out, away from the objects. There was air between Jules's skin and the swirling water, as if at the center of a whirlpool.

He laughed, giddy at the possibility. "Oh, *hell,* yeah."

Rayyana let out a similarly impressed laugh. "What on earth am I seeing here?"

"Like opposite poles," Jules said. "It's pushing it away."

He bent over the rim and pressed the bangles to the basin's floor. The water spread wider. When Jules touched the bottom with his free hand, it was dry.

"Come on. Let's see what's on the other side."

CHAPTER TWENTY-TWO

Poking at the console, Charlie watched Valerio's beads of light swarming across the monitor, his movement translated by the patrolling drone so she didn't have to squint at the vague outlines of men. Circling back, he appeared to be up to something.

Using her earbud—a subvocal bone-conducting piece of kit that she'd developed and improved over the years—she patched through to her husband, Phil, who was manning their station in their renovated garage back in Greenwich, London. She pictured him in his wheelchair, having "paced" for the hours she'd remained dark on comms, watching the same scene in silence.

"Charlie," came the man's relieved voice. "Are you okay?"

"Yes, babe." She was watching the remaining men shifting away from their previous approach and into what appeared to be more of a linear route. "I can't tell who's who, but if the earlier scouts are right, the cluster off to the south—"

"Enough of the commentary, honey. Are you *okay*?"

Charlie gave herself a mental slap, refreshing her brain to remind it that Phil knew nothing except the mirrored feed she set up. They'd had no comms since before they set out that morning.

She said, "Sorry, yes, I'm fine, babe. We've got a good post, highly defensible with ten expert guys with big ol' guns spread out watching my back." She could only see six of them, the others establishing more covert positions to serve as an early warning system should someone else slip through as Horse had. "We're good here."

"I thought it was an expedition, Charlie. Not a war zone."

"It isn't a war zone."

"Looked like one from where I was sitting."

Charlie figured he meant the bombing run. "Yeah, babe, it looked bad, but it was just chasing them back."

Phil sighed, clearly not liking the explanation. "Okay, fill me in."

"I think the cluster to the south of that lineup is Valerio himself. I'd expect Prihya is with them."

"Not back at the camp?"

"He'd want her nearby in case she's got something in her head that he needs."

"Will she tell him?"

"Gun to that head of hers? Probably. She's a civilian. A conspiracy theorist who's seen behind the curtain and found the questions she's asked all her life have answers that aren't what she thought. She's driven, but not a soldier. Not an agent. No matter what brief training she benefited from dating that Kiwi spy for a while."

Phil was pondering the explanation, and Charlie knew he'd be pinching his lip as he watched for something either of them might have missed. "What about Jules and Bridget? If you've set up camp, am I right in thinking they're underground already?"

"Yeah, they found it. Or think they have." She filled him in on the plan, but not what Rayyana was doing down there.

"There's more movement," Phil said. "Ten meters to your left."

Charlie checked the monitor, zooming in to their position on the ground. "What are you looking at?"

"The faded heat. Too big to be a human, but still... You checked it out?"

Ever-cautious, Phil had picked up on a vague hint of an anomaly.

Charlie said, "Rayyana Clinton identified that as animals. Her scouts had investigated before and saw one was a flock of birds."

Again, the pause. Again, Charlie could imagine Phil studying the screen, pinching his bottom lip, the light reflecting on his eyes. She wished she could put an arm around him, reassure him he wasn't about to become a single dad.

She held up the Benelli shotgun Rayyana had left her with and racked the slide near her head where the bone conducting tech would pick it up. "If some panther comes by, don't worry yourself, I'll handle it."

"They're endangered. Just scare it."

"Sure thing, babe. I'll be gentle."

"So, what's for dinner? You cooking a nice roast...?" But the casual, reassuringly normal conversation attempt cut off. "Charlie?"

"Yeah?" She was seeing what had set him off cold. "That's not normal."

"Never seen birds move like that."

Four of the grayish half-warm smudges were moving. Approaching from different directions.

Phil said, "Alert your men and get the hell out of there!"

Charlie shouted the alert in Spanish, and Montes—who appeared to be Rayyana's de facto second-in-command—got straight on the radio. The men in view all dropped into shooting couches, taking cover as Charlie rushed to Montes and showed him the encroaching blobs. Montes gave more orders, and the men sprang into action.

"They're sneaking around us," Charlie said, watching, listening for Phil. "They're multiplying. How is that..."

"He planned this all along," Phil said. "They've been waiting. Get out there!"

But it was far too late. The amorphous gray patches of warmth resolved into human heat signatures, and gunfire blasted into the Theta's men at the periphery. Four fell right away. Others returned fire.

Charlie and Montes dove for cover in time for the trunk beside them to splinter and shred. Behind the boulder, she kept watching the images from above. Twelve... fourteen men, converging on the clearing.

In the real world, two more Theta guys fell, dead, and the first of the attackers speared out from the trees. He was in deep camo gear, replete with moss and native leaves, his face hidden beneath a layer of paint. He covered the remaining pair of Theta men holding the line and spoke in what Charlie recognized as Korean.

"We have to surrender," Charlie said.

In her ear, Phil said, "Do what you have to. Just stay alive. I'll contact your other pe—"

The comms promptly cut out. Intentional damping, no question.

Then multiple troops streamed from the bushes, out of the trees. They must have used heat-dampening material incorporated into their gear, enough to mask them as human but insufficient to obscure them completely. They brought no prisoners with them, meaning the early warning lookouts were likely dead, too. That left two survivors, plus Charlie and Montes.

Charlie stood slowly, hands raised, and Montes did likewise, their weapons left on the ground. She assumed the invaders were all Korean by their appearance and the occasional snippet of language as one fired a question, followed by another. The man in charge replied gruffly, and his team used hand-waving sign language to disarm their new prisoners.

Within seconds, Charlie, Montes, and the two surviving men were bunched together on their knees, hands on heads, and no idea what to do next.

"Mr. Conchin, this is Son," the man said in clear English, touching his throat. He listened. "Yes, sir. We have secured the target. It is safe to approach."

CHAPTER TWENTY-THREE

Jules crawled into the pool's slick bed by bending a leg over the rim. The water walls receded farther as he entered. He was suspended between two wedges of water, as if behind glass, while gravity, or some sort of pump, gave it a roiling current—an animal caged and angry at its keeper.

Rayyana said, "Did your boyfriend just turn into Moses?"

"He's not my boyfriend," Bridget said which poked Jules in the throat, an emotion he quashed as soon as it reared its head. This was a mission, and he guessed Bridget was on the same wavelength. "And it's advanced physics. Not godly powers."

Rayyana adopted a playful tone. "Do you mean that? Or do you just not want him getting too bigheaded?"

"I don't think anything could inflate his head much more."

"Ladies?" Jules said, having progressed far enough that there was nothing but rock over his head. "You on a play date, or are you coming?"

The pair made a strange *hmm* noise, like friends about to giggle at a source of amusement, but they soon remembered their relationship didn't work like that and clambered in after him. Crouch-walking, Rayyana said she'd bring up their six, and advised they space out a bit.

"Keep your bearings," Jules warned. "If the water runs back in, you'll have to swim out."

Bridget sluiced a finger through the water. "How far does this go?"

"Dunno."

The electrical lights diluted the red-green glow from the bangles, but that still set the walls of water ablaze with fairyland beauty, as if neon were running through the fluid.

Within ten feet, Jules found a raised oval, like an upturned pot, but it had a figure-eight groove set into it.

Here goes nothing...

He wedged the bangles in.

Perfect fit.

A rushing noise got louder and the two sides of water stabilized. The animal had been fed and subdued. There was an oppressive weight to the air, too, which Jules attributed to the force emitted by the bangles that tamed the thousands of gallons around them.

"How far?" Rayyana asked.

The combined power of all six lights didn't reveal an end point, but that might have been a change in the floor's angle.

Jules said, "We've gone ten feet. If this is halfway, we got another ten. We'll start going up soon."

The surface was less slippery now that the bangles had been in place for a while, and it did take them upward. Jules's spatial awareness calculated it wasn't exactly halfway, placing him another ten feet from the oval receptacle that appeared to enhance the shield keeping them dry before they began rising again.

After a total of twenty-eight feet—which his brain couldn't help translating to 8.5 meters and change—they could stand in what would have been a shallow pool, had it been full, and came to a rim identical to the one they left behind. Someone with enough strength could swim that distance, but the current would have made it impossible without specialized equipment. It would have dragged even the most experienced free diver to wherever this channel flowed.

He was still thinking about how it could work, imagining a fairground ride of underground rapids powered by magnetism and whatever caused the bangles to react with impure water, when Bridget let out a squeal and Rayyana said, "Oh, my god."

That was when he noticed the sunlike hue to this chamber. He followed Bridget's eyes to the far wall and nearly whooped for joy himself.

Nearly.

This part of the mission still needed a calm head. It might not be what everyone thought it was, so celebrations were premature. If Toby's theory was even halfway accurate—that far-out, impossible nonsense he'd admitted to Jules back in China—everyone was in for a rude awakening.

But as they set out the LED pods that cast the chamber in a brilliant light, it was soon clear a different awakening was imminent. And it was far ruder than anything Toby had in store.

"We're too late," Bridget said. "It's gone."

CHAPTER TWENTY-FOUR

After confiscating her weapons, the Koreans allowed Charlie to stand, while Montes and the two remaining Theta Team guys, whose names she hadn't learned, kneeled in the soil. As well as the dozen-plus Korean troops and eight local mercenaries, the whole bad guy team was here: Horse, Valerio, the so-called scholar-assassins, the priest Charlie had heard about, and Prihya...

Prihya, looking unharmed, but certainly here under protest, since she warranted her own detail. But not so much protest that they had to manhandle her around. In fact, she could hardly keep her eyes off the fissure which led into the cave system where Jules and company had ventured, with no way to warn them.

Horse was singed, a cooling bandage on the side of his head where Charlie's flare had burned him, but as he surveyed the scene and landed on Charlie, he barely twitched in recognition. It was true, and curiously saddening, that the man who had once commanded all Valerio's murderous field operations should end up this way. As if the waste of a brain was shameful, despite it belonging to a sociopath.

Father Emory consulted with the two male scholar-assassins, the women absent, and Valerio paced back and forth with his hands clasped behind his back. He looked well, his hair full and blond, his body gym-toned despite his frame being a bit on the dweeby side, and he made the occasional skip as he awaited his people's verdict on what to do next.

The Koreans were what worried Charlie the most, though. They had been lurking in the undergrowth all along, generating the signals, the "smudges", no one could fully identify. Charlie was sure they must have utilized a new material, disguising warm bodies as flocks of birds or large mammal groups. It didn't take a mastermind to see where Valerio drummed them up from, either.

Charlie considered two possibilities: survivors from the facility destroyed when Jules, Dan, and Harpal stopped the North Korean separatists from activating ancient shields that would have destroyed more than they protected; or Valerio had partnered with the North Korean military and borrowed these men for a mission where he must have promised power or riches or both. Charlie wasn't qualified to question the strutting peacock on his latest power trip, but it didn't matter.

Valerio consulted with Emory and the two men who seemed to be debating the best approach, watching Charlie as he paced heavily around them.

"Did you really think it would put us off?" he said to her.

"Wasn't my call," Charlie replied, forcing herself to remain in place and not slap the smug prick.

"I know, I know, cliché alert!" Valerio held his hands up, a foppish, almost camp jig as he hopped around her. "The villain wants to be beaten. Only, I'm not beaten. And FYI, I'm not the villain either."

"Valerio," the priest said, looking up from what seemed to be a hand-drawn sketch of the area. "You know I find gloating unseemly."

Valerio pouted. "Is it a sin?"

"Not specifically, but knowing God and Jesus like I do, I am certain they would frown on it."

Valerio puffed up his chest. "I can take a frown from the Big Guy."

Emory rolled his eyes and went back to work. From what they'd gathered, Father Emory Ballard was an influential figure in a Vatican sub-sect, whose members sought to push for proof of the divine—proof that even the faithless could not deny. If he'd studied hard enough, explored enough avenues that led him to the Witnesses, he might consider this his goal. Undeniable divinity, albeit not precisely as laid out in the Bible.

Valerio was speaking again. "*I'm* the one trying to stop the villains, don't you know? Worse villains than me, I promise you. Really, you don't want them getting hold of the sword."

"*Valerio.*" The priest's warning came deeper this time.

Valerio waved the priest off. "It's fine. They'll come around. They'll understand. They just don't like my methods." He walked with straight legs, like some parody of a slow march, head-on to Charlie, where he stopped. "It's some culty bunch of assholes who want what I want. Father Emory was sensible enough to extract himself from their brood before they could do too much damage. But they want to be in charge when the..." He twisted toward Emory. "What did they call it? That end of the world thing?"

"The Rapture," Emory said.

"Right, right." Valerio returned to Charlie. "An apocalyptic vision where God wipes the world clean and the righteous rise." He spread his arms, his eyes wide. "And I am going to stop them."

Although she could not deny she'd been terrified since the moment they sprang their surprise counterattack, Charlie didn't back down from bullies. "And you're not a fan of Rapture junkies, no?"

"He'd be a fan if they shared," Prihya said.

Her keepers shifted their weight, as if readying to grab her should she dare advance on their dear leader.

Charlie said, "Yeah, he'd cozy up to anyone if it meant he got to touch this sword."

"It is not a literal sword," one of the scholar-assassins said. Moses, the clever one.

Valerio tutted and rolled his eyes. "They never are. And maybe you ladies are right. If this rapture cult stepped out of the shadows and made me an offer, who knows? I'm not beyond partnering with evil people if it benefits the world at large."

Charlie recalled the doctor who'd tried to unleash a plague through the Witnesses' volcanic network, but felt no need to remind anyone of it. "You're a hero walking a gray path, are you?"

"Edging toward the angels rather than the demons," Valerio said. "But yes, if the angels let me down, I'll have no choice but to tame a few demons."

To which Horse grunted and shifted his feet, looking antsy and in need of doing something.

"If they knew where the entrance was all along," Charlie said, "why not just come in?"

"Oh, we didn't know *exactly*." Valerio glanced at his big, damaged friend with what appeared to be genuine concern.

Emory had finished his confab with Moses and Muzaffer and joined Valerio and Charlie. "But even if we did know, Valerio admits his touch isn't powerful enough."

"Performance issues, huh?" Charlie said.

Prihya smirked.

Valerio's face turned gray, like a storm about to descend. "The items forged by our ancient friends need someone *born* to it. No one would be... virile enough to gain access. Especially not a man whose body is constantly knitting itself back together, thanks to the First Priest's tomb."

Charlie said, "Either Jules or Prihya's old friend, General Yanovna."

Prihya took half a step toward them. "Friend? She *used* me. You know that."

Valerio raised a finger. "But since the British authorities imprisoned her, it had to be Jules and the gang. Don't you understand? This is how it has to be."

"Why do you need Prihya?" Charlie asked.

Valerio seemed to recognize that she was hoping to draw more information, a wide, toothy grin forming. "Our advance party has had long enough, don't you think, Father?"

Emory turned to the fissure, its claw-shaped black entrance craggy and high. "While I remain unimpressed by your gloating, you are correct. Julian and Bridget are probably reading our books as we speak. Send in your people."

Valerio fist-pumped the air. "Yes!"

"But Valerio..." The priest lay a firm hand on Valerio's arm. "Do not start killing people for fun. Or for vengeance. We must secure the items before mankind's enemies do. That is the only goal. Are we clear?"

"Crystal."

CHAPTER TWENTY-FIVE

Bridget's chest tightened and she struggled to maintain her breath as her joy faded. What was clearly once a magnificent room, like a foyer, was now a wrecked dome of stinking damp subsidence.

"We're too late," Bridget said. "It's gone."

The massive geological pressure had been too much for this place (again; God, she was sick of thinking about geological time and pressure and effects), not to mention the disasters that had befallen the earth over the previous ten thousand years. All that remained was a small section, and it was difficult to tell how much of the gold embedded in the walls came from the library described by young Petrionion Jaramillo. Only the very tip of what had to be the Witnesses' cache was visible, and the golden books (maybe they were books) had been crushed.

"Guess it didn't *have* to be me, after all."

Jules's voice dripped with dread, with the same disappointment Bridget was wrestling with. All this was for nothing. The anticipated find of the century was compacted beyond any use, beyond anyone's grasp.

"Am I missing something?" Rayyana asked.

"It's gone." Bridget felt as much as heard the hard edge to her words. "There's nothing left."

Jules crossed the stone floor—once flat but now buckled—and stopped an arm's length before the curved walls that had collapsed upon themselves. He moved as if he were gradually transforming into rubber. His eyes, normally alive with a compulsion to solve the puzzle, were dull with acceptance.

It was over.

"It's not like it's over," Rayyana said.

Bridget was so tired she almost didn't move her head to look at the team leader, but her manners overrode any fatigue. "How do you figure?"

"Your mom and dad can ship an entire drilling rig pretty much anywhere in the world within forty-eight hours. We clear out Valerio and company, use the Carsons' diplomatic clout to schmooze the permits double-time, and fly in what we need to—"

"We ain't strip-mining the Amazon," Jules said.

Rayyana paused and frowned. She'd been caught up in the moment, an awakening of excitement at accomplishing their mission.

Except it wasn't accomplished. And never would be.

"Jules?" Bridget said.

He gave only the merest nod of acknowledgment before standing on tiptoes to touch the fragment of gold wedged in the wall. It appeared cold and solid, but Bridget had no desire to reach out to something she could never hold.

"It's pancaked tight," Jules said. "Layers of rock, thousands of years old. Ain't digging that out."

All stood in silence, the tiny LEDs from Charlie's pods giving movement to their shadows.

Bridget was missing something here. They all were. She couldn't see what, but there was definitely something.

"Y'know, after all we've seen, all we know about these people..." She was hoping someone would fill in the blanks, but Jules stared ahead, as if this was his fault for not arriving thousands of years earlier. "They predicted rising sea levels. They knew the ice caps would melt. They prepared their other repositories for disaster. But they didn't know about tectonic subsidence?"

"Yeah, Bridge," Jules said. "They can see waters risin' over decades. Pass on the measurements through generations. Make predictions, watch what happens when stuff like the Toba catastrophe goes down. But anything happening this slowly, they couldn't see it'd bury their—"

Jules cut himself off.

"Jaramillo."

"Petrionion Jaramillo," Bridget said. "The boy who said he found this place? He—"

Her turn to drop a sentence unfinished.

Jules's eyes widened, his breathing hesitant, waiting for her to say something. Bridget's heart beat faster, and she felt a rush of warmth as she said, "He found it."

"What?" Rayyana said.

Bridget felt her excitement rise. "The cipher led us right where he said he went. Even with the rocks having shifted. He knew where to go."

"She's right," Jules said. He'd seen it, too. "If the kid wasn't lying, there's gotta be more."

"So," Rayyana said. "We still got it. We just need a way to get in."

Jules stepped back, stopping when his foot tapped against a nub sticking out of the floor. He reached down and dug with his hand, pulling up a fistful of dust. When he opened his fingers, he was holding a small piece of gold: a coin about five centimeters in diameter, twice the size of the cipher.

"This ain't right."

Rayyana slapped the wall as if testing its integrity. "We could still dig through if we finish off the competition."

Jules shook his head and stretched his leg in a single step. "Wouldn't matter if we had a hundred weeks. There'll be contingencies." He scuffed his boot around, stopping at a click.

"You said you had to find it," Rayyana said, her voice rising. "And picking up trinkets and coins won't satisfy the Carsons."

Before Bridget could question that comment, Jules took a deep breath, crouched, and unearthed another gold disc. "Yeah. But these coins ain't coins."

Rayyana deflated, and Bridget felt her own breath coming fast. She knew what Jules was saying, but she didn't want to believe it.

"These were embedded in the floor. *Part* of it. Just time that's made 'em easy to pick out. Damp atmosphere."

Bridget overtook him and found the next one. It didn't slip out immediately, needing a tap with her boot to shift it. "I know what this is."

Jules bypassed the next and the one after, and did his computer-like calculations to shortcut his way to the conclusion. "Here."

Bridget and Rayyana joined him at a blank wall.

"That kid, the one who took the cipher to Malta? He saw more than this. No way did a solid, unbroken rock move that much in less than a hundred years. No signs of an earthquake, either. That'd leave cracks that hadn't healed."

Bridget said, "Yeah, I think we've all worked that out, Jules."

She pressed against the wall and her hand melted into it. Okay, not *melted*. There was resistance, but that was what it felt like. Buried to her wrist, it was dry, as if they'd shaved flakes of stone and compressed them into a semisolid state.

"Feel anything?" Jules asked.

"Maybe it needs magic," Rayyana suggested. "Why don't you give it a go?"

Bridget hoped her sigh and hooded eyes didn't come across as jealousy at what she perceived as Rayyana's flirting. "Let's try something a little less sci-fi."

She yanked her arm out, and the shavings slid off. They appeared to multiply as they fell out of the small hole. They were as light as wood chips, streaming out like a swarm of agitated beetles defending their nest, pushing the three humans back a few steps. As the swarm settled into a pile, they left a shaped depression eerily similar to the external entrance; a sharp fissure in the shape of a jagged triangle.

Jules seemed to have spotted the same thing. "Not the exact same shape as outside." He studied it some more. "It's smaller, lopsided by about ten degrees."

"What is—" Rayyana started.

"Leave him," Bridget said. "He's got a God-given freaky ability here..."

Jules looked at her with a softness she hadn't seen in him before. "Freaky when it suits you, hey?" Then he snapped right back to business. "I think this used to be the same as the outer door. They built it to look as if the land had crushed this section.

But it really has moved a bit, like enough to make it half its original size. Now we gotta clear out these stones and squeeze through."

"I have a folding spade." Rayyana moved to retrieve her pack.

Bridget was already peering through the newly formed tiny tunnel, her flashlight beam spotting the hard edge of an exit point beyond the beetle-rocks.

When she turned to tell them, Jules had also moved to grab tools.

How dare they? When her joy was like a balloon filling up inside her chest? Did they not realize there might be a library on the other side? A treasure? A weapon?

If she squeezed through, might she somehow end up buried?

What would Jules do in this situation?

He'd grunt, tell everyone to catch up, and then dive through.

Bridget didn't think she'd get far if she declared her intentions, so she planted her hands on the pile of rock shavings and tested her weight to make sure she wouldn't cut her hands through her gloves. The shifting surface was as rough as stony soil, with some patches crumbling beneath her. Knees came next, and the same thing happened—uncomfortable but bearable.

She began to crawl.

Her hands and knees burrowed in, and she sped up as she ducked under the eave. Her movement pinged little shavings and pebbles side to side, up and down, irritating her hands as they dipped over the edges of her gloves. The farther she crawled, however, the brighter the other side became.

Her flashlight beam reflected back at her.

"Bridge?" came Jules's call. "Bridge, what the hell are you doing?"

"I'm gonna be first through this time." She could literally hear her heartbeat over the rustle-crunch-swish of the surface, breathing in the dry, musty atmosphere from beyond. "Sorry, but I couldn't wait!"

"We don't know it's safe."

She was so close now, the entrance mere feet away. It was less than a six-foot scrabble from start to finish, and— "I'm almost there."

"Bridge, I'm coming in."

The scrape and shuck of shoveling echoed from behind, but she didn't care. The golden light up ahead was too much, too tempting, drawing her in, crushing her resistance, her good sense, when—

The floor gave way.

She sunk up to her shoulders as if leaning into a thick, grainy swimming pool. Her feet flipped into the air and her face hit the mass of rock shavings. She went under. As gravity and the stones' weight dragged her down, she had no control, delving, spinning, as if a wave had caught her.

Then, as she thought her lungs would burst from holding such a short breath, she halted. A sprinkle of stones continued, but she was at a standstill. Upside-down with her legs splayed comically in the air, but the ride had ended.

Leaning her body to the left dislodged the stones and sent a swarm trickling down her neck. She toppled over into a sitting position, with dust floating all around, her headlamp having fallen off and becoming partially buried.

First, she coughed. Then she wiped her face, feeling her sweat mingle with the dirt and grime that coated her skin.

"Bridge? Bridget?"

Jules's voice again. It was faint, but she could tell he had taken several steps into the short, narrow tunnel.

She called back to him, "I'm okay!"

Finally, she dug in and grabbed the headlight and swung it around. When she saw it, in all its wonder, she was stunned into silence. It was incredible.

CHAPTER TWENTY-SIX

"It's incredible!"

Bridget's shout came through as an echo, as if she were shooting it through a mic with poor feedback. Almost mechanical. Yet, with his head and shoulders in the unstable passageway, Jules could not deny he was annoyed at something more than her placing herself in danger.

I'm gonna be first through this time.

Had he really grown so petty? There was a time he saw these excursions as little more than a means to an end. They could have uncovered the Ark of the Covenant or exhumed the body of Alexander the Great, and he'd have said, "Cool. What's next?"

But this had struck a nerve he wasn't aware he possessed. It was more than an exclusive, incredible find. It was a gateway to what he'd started to see as the endgame. The key to a long-debunked legend that Toby apparently hoped would rise into reality, and what Jules hoped would answer questions he thought ceased dogging him long ago.

What was that bangle for? And why had his mother thought dying in front of him was preferable to letting crooks take it without a fight?

"I'm coming through," Jules said.

"No, you're not," Rayyana said, tugging his belt.

He pulled himself out and accepted the spade she handed him. "Get shoveling, champ. Then we can go see."

Jules pushed back the squidgy sensation he now identified as jealousy and set to work clearing enough space to crouch-walk through unaided. It was pointless, and he would never have felt this way if he hadn't hooked up with LORI. They'd softened him, shaped him into a more conventional person rather than the machine he'd had to become when working alone.

It wasn't all bad, though. He'd often worried that something was wrong with him, that he'd turned into a high-functioning sociopath. He was now on the verge of a date with a remarkable woman, on the cusp of one of history's greatest discoveries, and nearing the end of a trail of questions that had begun when he was fourteen years old.

It felt like a reward.

The Tayos Library was much smaller than Bridget had expected. Only three features dominated: a boxy stone cube that reminded Bridget of an altar; a circular moat of that briny water; and the back of a slab of rock, leaning toward her and supported by a block so she couldn't see what was on the other side.

It wasn't pitch black, though. A wan beam of daylight filtered through a shaft not much bigger than a manhole cover, landing on the slanted bed of tooled stone where it reflected a pattern like that created by a disco ball. The room was taller than it was wide and more bulbous at the bottom than the roof, tapering above her like a six-story-sized egg.

As she waded ankle deep through the soupy water, a damp coolness surrounded her, like leaving a tent on a misty spring morning, while a hint of grass and leaves filled the air. A current rippled around her feet, although nothing like the powerful stream that denied most from gaining access. She stepped out of the water, her heart beating fast with anticipation as she rounded what proved to be a giant shelf.

The slab started on a dais, then rose to a height a couple of feet over Bridget's head, and held twenty-four tomes of age-dulled gold in four rows of six.

Gold didn't tarnish, didn't react well with other elements. It was one reason it was so highly prized, aside from its rarity. These items had lain untouched for a long, long time, yet light shone on them like a lens flare in a movie, and a lump in Bridget's chest ran up her throat until she could barely contain herself.

But, contain herself she did, focusing on the situation, the task. She was an archaeologist, and needed to analyze rather than celebrate.

The shelf itself had carved notches supporting the books, which may have been in some sort of order that Bridget immediately tried to work out. The notion of the Witnesses having a Dewey-Decimal system amused her. However, the markings were not consistent.

Her fingers fluttered over the ones she could see in the beam of sunlight, angling her head torch to enhance the letters and pictures carved into the surface of each one.

She didn't dare pick one up yet. She needed to take it in, absorb it. The closest she got was swiping her fingertips over the third from the left, leaving a bright, gleaming trail as the dust adhered to her glove and revealed the book's true color and a series of symbols.

Through years of study, and with only rudimentary touchpoints—no Rosetta Stone to aid her—she'd established a rough approximation of the Witnesses' key phrases and what she'd dubbed "signposts"; symbols they used to denote categories such as "instructions" or "directions" or "warnings". Their tenses changed through melding two or more symbols, and their verbs shifted meaning depending on the slant of the lettering, like the "you" form being italicized and the past-tense of the "you" form merging with the "we".

The symbols she'd cleaned with one swipe of her hand today meant something along the lines of "salvation country". An odd phrase to the layperson.

Her gift for languages, though, for deciphering codes and symbolism with minimal input, was what first drew her to Toby's attention. Much of this skill extended beyond literal translation and boiled down to educated guesswork based on the culture being studied. Here, the literal meaning of "salvation country" translated to a phrase well-known over the past few centuries.

Promised land.

She moved on, still too nervous to pick one up, but knew she had to. She lingered on the book in the bottom right corner.

They were a uniform size, about twice that of the average hardback novel. She stood over her chosen tome and extended her hands.

Electricity coursed through her, like static prickling against a balloon. Her mouth was dry.

She was the first person to see this, let alone touch it, since modern humans were little more than cave-dwelling hunter-gatherers. Except, possibly, for a young lad who may or may not have gotten this far.

Bridget's fingers and thumbs curled around the four-inch-thick book. Lifted it. As expected, it was far heavier than a regular hardback, too, but not like solid gold. It smelled like a metal workshop. She weighed it in her two hands, and it would require her to hug it tight to take it out of there.

She laid it back down and opened the cover.

The motion made it creak like old wood, but felt as smooth as an oiled hinge. The pages within were much thicker than premium notebook paper. In four inches of content, there must have been thirty pages. *Gold leaf* had been her first thought, but it was stronger than that. The forging or mixing of some other metal or substance to keep the gold's fundamental properties while adding flexibility.

And they were perfect.

Etched letters, representing a language she knew at its most basic ABC level. These, if she could study them fully, might make her fluent.

She closed the book. There was work to be done.

After setting the two powerful LED pods to add to the natural light, Bridget checked every shadow for more passages or storage hidden by dirt or land subsidence, then realized she hadn't checked in with Jules or Rayyana for a while.

How long?

Minutes?

An hour?

"Hey, Jules, you coming?"

"Yeah," he called with a backdrop of scraping. "It's a tight fit.

These things make it tough for anyone bigger than a kid to get through."

"Well, thanks a bunch, honey."

Did she just call him *honey*? Oh, crap on a bike, that was embarrassing. And now he hadn't thrown a quip back, which was unlike him.

Business.

Get back to *business.*

She raced around the gold leaf tomes, still bewildered beyond words. She wiped every surface she could reach—all but the topmost row—and pinpointed all of those with markings she recognized, even if she couldn't read them. There were other symbols, too, one similar to the concentric circles that marked the outer door. She'd have to ask Jules whether it was identical or not.

The thought of leaving a single one behind made her ache all over. This was months, possibly years of work. And she could not wait to get stuck in.

She snapped a raft of photos of the books in-situ, then selected the first one, held it to her body, and waded back through the shallow briny moat, clung to it on her knees as she used one free hand to struggle through the passage, and came face-to-face with Jules at the halfway point.

He appeared dirty but impassive, as unemotional as when he was figuring out a puzzle or ingesting new information. "Hey."

She urged him backward and he complied.

Out in the original anteroom, she pushed to her feet, revealing the book, and Jules's expression changed. His eyes danced and his mouth was animated. He reached nervously toward her, and she relinquished the book.

"It's real, huh," he said, trying to sound cool. He failed, but somehow succeeded too.

Rayyana gawped over his shoulder as he opened the cover. "Oh, wow. That must be worth… I dunno what it's worth. A lot."

"It's priceless," Bridget said. "No way to place a value on it."

Jules turned the first gold-infused page, seeing what Bridget had seen, easing it over to the next. Then the next, scanning the contents, before moving on.

"Get me the holdall," Bridget said.

Rayyana paused, captivated by the golden book, only snapping out of it when Bridget gave a pointed cough. She whipped the folded holdall from the smaller backpack and flapped it open. Plenty of room for several books, but the weight would be a problem.

Bridget took the bag and was headed back to the library when Jules stopped her with, "Hey, Bridge?"

"Yeah?" She turned to him, only now aware she was out of breath from her efforts.

"What's this about?" He meant the book. "Simplified maps, diagrams, a couple pages of writing. Then more drawings."

"I don't have an exact translation," Bridget said. "The gist of it is what we always thought. And it isn't a title like we'd know it, more of a category or listing—"

"Details, Bridge. What's the bottom line?"

"If you wanna skip the interesting stuff, sure. It basically refers to something they called 'the Great Migration.' Or something similar. The pages showing maps and charts and diagrams, they look kinda familiar, but I can't place them right now."

"It's what Toby was holding back in China," Jules said, slowly closing the last page.

"There are other markings I've never seen before." She laughed. "Maybe Dan's alien languages."

"Toby's theory might be as nuts as Dan's. But let's get all we can outta here. We can work out the rest later."

"Right," Rayyana agreed. "Then let's move faster. This isn't a sightseeing museum."

Bridget said, "I'll carry what I can," and headed back inside.

After Bridget made three more sweaty trips, heaving out three books in the holdall each time, Jules and Rayyana broke through to the other side, where Jules quickly assessed the so-called library as another repository. It differed greatly from the others.

He'd thought it would be stacked like the library at Chateau

Caché, albeit in the place of dusty old volumes would be gold leaf backed items.

That the covers were sheets of gold was surprising, too. It wasn't purely the color, but the physical construction. He agreed with Bridget that it had been used to preserve the books' lives, meaning they were always intended for future use, not simply preservation as the resin-coated artifacts they'd found in other places had been.

As they carted out the rest of them, forming a short human chain, Jules estimated they'd been underground for less than one hour. Amazing how much life can change in such a brief span of time.

As Bridget set about documenting the place with more photos than she'd taken earlier, Jules selected the books one at a time before repacking them into more holdalls that they'd carried in flat, although he hadn't expected all the books to fit into the half-dozen bags with room to spare. Six in each was plenty, despite their weight, and with the wheels on the holdalls' undersides, they would pull them like suitcases at an airport over the rough ground.

Before packing each book, Jules flipped through every page, committing what he saw to memory. Although it was not an *exact* science, and an eidetic memory didn't facilitate 100% flawless recall, it was as close to a scanner as they'd get in this light; a phone camera would miss vital etchings or marks, lost in the glare of the LED lamps or the phone's own camera flash.

"Do you have to do that?" Rayyana asked at one point.

"Yeah," he said. "I do. Someone like Colin comes to lay a claim to 'em, or the Ecuadorian authorities, I can reproduce most of the content."

"From what?"

He tapped his head but didn't go into detail. He almost said, *snap-shots in my mind*, but that sounded pretentious and would elicit more questions that he didn't care to answer.

When done, and he was ready to go topside, he calculated it had been eighty-six minutes since they entered the cave mouth. He left Rayyana to check back up the corridor, then ducked through the passage into the library, and found Bridget sweeping her phone around, making a video which she narrated in real time.

"It looks like a vent here, with sunlight coming through, but it's narrow, and I can't see the actual opening. We've seen this kinda thing in Montrose, with a bunch a' mirrors redirecting the light in here."

She moved on to the cuboid rectangular slab.

"This is a bit bigger than a sarcophagus, but it doesn't have any markings that I can see. They might've worn off since the atmosphere isn't airtight. I'd guess at some sort of ceremonial function. Let's hope it wasn't human sacrifice. But who knows?"

"I think they had more intelligence than that," Jules commented.

Bridget kept filming, bringing it round to him. "And here we have the illustrious Julian Sibeko. Expert irritant of academia, but smart as a whip. I highlighted this weird moat thing. Perhaps Mr. Sibeko can offer a theory."

Jules had checked it over when he first entered, but it hadn't struck him as important.

He said, "It's a weak flow, but it ain't going round and round on itself. There's other channels heading off, so it's probably linked somehow to the main body out there." He gestured to the passage, meaning the heavier water barrier held at bay by the bangles. "My guess is, you can relieve the pressure out there by having this tributary end up here, and—"

Bridget lowered the phone, laughing. "It's okay. I stopped filming a while ago. Just wanted to see how long you'd go on for."

Jules failed to get the joke. "Right. Okay. You think we should head topside? Update the others?"

"Sure."

Jules indicated Bridget should go first, half-bowing like a gentleman, and followed. He heard her delighted coo and the name, "Charlie!" as Bridget reached the other side, but then she lowered her tone with, "Oh, no."

Jules was too close to go back, so pushed on out, finding Charlie stood in the center of the room alongside Rayyana and Montes. Flanking them, guns pointed at their heads, Muzaffer and Moses stood guard, while the women Jules knew as Renata and Hilla greeted them.

Jules and Bridget raised their hands to show they were unarmed.

Charlie bowed her head, then lifted it. "Sorry, guys. I'll explain later. If we get out of here."

Jules recognized Father Emory from his description.

Valerio came from the other direction, positively skipping with delight. "Hello, Jules. Nice to see you again. This is all brilliant, but I'm afraid it's time to give it all up."

"Please cooperate," Father Emory said. "I do not think even my influence can calm him at this point."

Jules saw how manic Valerio was acting, had seen him like this before, just before a pyramidal tomb collapsed all around them. There was no reasoning with him then, and he doubted there was now. "Lemme guess. We all get along. There's no need for bloodshed. We can all be friends?"

Valerio cackled, as if he were high on cocaine. "You know me so well. How about we go look-see how much else is through there, hm?"

Jules was powerless at this range. The scholar-assassins had them neutralized. He could tackle one, but the others would drop their hostages, and more than likely turn on Jules. It'd be pointless.

He replayed what he'd said earlier and felt foolish.

They unlocked it for us and didn't even realize...

No, they *did* realize it was here. But all they'd done was locate the door. They just didn't have the key for the lock.

Jules, plowing on in, *was* the key.

And now no one could prevent them from helping themselves.

CHAPTER TWENTY-SEVEN

Outside, Prihya felt sick as Valerio emerged with an even more arrogant swagger than when he'd entered. He headed straight for Horse. The silent sentry had stood awaiting his master's return like a dog—attentive but yearning for that familiar figure. Valerio said something Prihya didn't hear, and Horse sniggered. Again, the dog analogy held sway as he reminded her of Muttley from the old Wacky Races cartoons.

They had held her there under the gun, told her to wait quietly if she didn't want to get hurt, and when they brought out the prize, she would be privy to its teachings.

Did that mean they truly needed her as more than a hostage?

Regardless of their motives for keeping her alive, there was nothing she could do, no outside help to be called upon, so she sat and waited. Biding her time until Jules came up with some overblown stunt or crafty deception.

If he was still alive.

If they all were.

She didn't know how much time had passed, but eventually Moses trudged out, dragging a heavy bag on wheels with one hand, a huge pistol with an extended magazine in the other. Pulling an identical holdall, Jules followed.

For the first time in hours, Prihya relaxed.

Charlie, the woman team leader, and Bridget came next, urged on by Father Emory with yet another bag, and Muzaffer with a fourth and a similar machine pistol to Moses shoring up the rear. They arranged the bags less than ten yards from Prihya and her handlers. Three Korean mercs filtered out afterward.

"Okay, then!" Valerio clapped his hands together, rubbing them as if about to commence a particularly bullish board meeting. "Do we execute them now?"

"No, Valerio, we do not." Father Emory sounded like a put-out nursery school teacher as the naughty kid made another poop joke for all the class to hear. "We are on the side of God and the wonderful future of mankind."

Valerio crossed his arms as if leaning on something and tapped his foot. "Fine, Father. If we must save our souls at every turn, take the risk. But I know this one." He pointed at Jules. Then at Bridget. "And she's pretty sneaky, too."

"I'll trust in my judgement." Emory signaled Prihya's handlers to escort her over, and one of them did so.

All had gathered—or *been* gathered—a few yards from the cave entrance, the four bags nearby. The core contingent made for an interesting group, almost mingling as they were with their prisoners. Excluded were the Carsons' team stragglers who slumped to the side with their hands cable-tied to sturdy, low branches.

"Do you understand what we have here?" Emory asked. It took Prihya a moment to realise he was addressing her.

"We're at a significant location for these ancient people," Prihya said. "This is the place they outlined their plans for future generations. To go out and guide the protohumans."

"To observe them," Bridget corrected. "They didn't need to guide them. But education came next, in small areas. That was the repository we found in India. Their accomplishments in educating different cultures."

"My tomb," Valerio said, and Horse flinched. Perhaps there was more going on behind the mask than a beast in a man's body awaiting the next instruction to kill.

"Sure," Jules said. "Just a big journal. 'Dear Diary, today we set out to colonize the world. Here's where we went.'"

Emory unzipped the bag he'd been dragging and Prihya glimpsed something that had fascinated her for over a decade. Since she first learned of Neil Armstrong's expedition, of the evidence of civilizations far older than the natives chronicled and massacred by European Conquistadors, and the prospect of a higher intelligence, she'd written about the possibilities, the hidden agenda of those who sought to silence those explorers: golden books, piled in like sportswear after a racquetball game. The priest shifted two heavy books out of the way as casually as sifting through a collection of Harry Potter novels, and selected a specific volume. He eased himself upward, its weight apparent in the way he hinged his knees straight.

"This is why we wanted you, Prihya." Emory held it to his chest, the markings against his robes.

Prihya glanced at Jules, who gave a near-imperceptible shake of his head. She drew her gaze over Bridget and Charlie, the team leader who was supposed to defeat Valerio and—hopefully—release Prihya. But Jules was trying to say something without words.

Don't cooperate?

Don't hold back?

Don't fall for their tricks?

What was Father Emory hiding? What did he mean about this being the reason for needing her?

She settled on him with a hard-set mouth and harder eyes. "Well?"

"Men," Emory said. "Wicked men, particularly."

"Oh, I've heard this speech," Valerio said.

"Then listen again. And maybe try to understand it instead of tramping around like a spoiled brat."

Valerio huffed and held himself stiffly. "I'm still in charge. Remember that."

Father Emory made a shallow bow toward Moses and said, "I will remember our dynamic, of course. But please, hold to your own promise. This is a mission for the good of mankind, yes?"

"Fine." Valerio waved it off. "Try to persuade them."

Moses repositioned himself between Emory and Valerio as the priest resumed.

"Men—people, these days—with power... run this world. It is no secret. Our sect within the Catholic Church sought to advise the powerful how to redistribute the path of destiny to give more control to the average... 'man-in-the-street' is the phrase we liked to use. A Britishism, I think. But did the Church listen?

"No. They preached goodwill to all men, peace and prosperity to the world, but not at the cost of losing their influence. It is why we broke away. Why we decided to use the artifacts hidden by the Vatican to reveal what lay behind the curtain. Aided, in part, by items secured by the Lost Origins Recovery Institute, and by way of our mutual Sicilian friend. They expelled us, of course, which was no surprise."

"Who's 'we'?" Jules asked.

"Rapture monkeys," Valerio replied.

"The Church of the Forefathers," Emory said. "You call them Witnesses. We call them Forefathers. The *True* Forefathers, to be exact, but Valerio's scrolls were the first time we saw physical evidence of their existence."

"Why the Rapture obsession?" Prihya asked.

"It is no obsession. It is inevitable. The Toba catastrophe killed off the stupider humans and left the most intelligent to survive and to pass on that learning to generation after generation, building things like the navigation device that brought your friends here, like the contraption I have only heard about where Valerio found his scrolls, and even sent Mr. Armstrong to the moon and... here. The end of the Younger Dryas saw mass deaths, and what may well have been a comet triggered other catastrophes. But still humanity survived. And each time, we saw a leap in intelligence and wellbeing."

Jules blew out his cheeks and held up his hands as Muzaffer squared his shoulders off. Jules said, "Sounds a lot like you're preaching evolution, Father."

"What God seeded, and how He chose to nurture what sprouted is not for us to question. But to observe. And understand. And accept the truth. Whatever that truth is. And what's coming is another extinction event. All because those in charge refuse to prepare."

"Gotcha," Jules said. "A rapture."

"Only some of us call it that. The Church of the Forefathers merely wants to ensure the bad men with too much power, money, and control over misinformation do not keep a grip on the new world. They cannot, must never, own the knowledge now sitting at our feet."

Charlie and Bridget let out the same noise—a single laugh of disbelief. A double, "Ha!" without a hint of humor.

Charlie said, "Sorry, but I've seen a 'bad man with too much power and money' kill dozens to secure his own survival."

Bridget said, "And he ain't standing too far away from us."

"Yes, yes. Valerio and his killing machine lackey are such people. They provided much needed manpower and logistics, which my small breakaway movement lacked." Emory met the eyes of Moses, Muzaffer, Renata, and Hilla in turn. "You all worked for Mr. Conchin for a long time. You command the local operatives and those from Korea, correct?"

"We hold the purse strings," Renata confirmed.

"*My* money," Valerio said. "A slush fund that can't be traced to me, or the good father. Do we have to hear all this again?"

"No," Emory said. "I will forego the history of my organization and accept your gift."

"Gift?"

"The money we need for our continued security and transport." Emory nodded firmly toward Moses. "You see, these were never *your* people, Valerio. They always were, and remain, followers of the True Forefathers."

Moses pointed his gun at Valerio. Muzaffer covered Horse. While Hilla stripped him of his weapons, Horse's face creased into one deep frown, and Valerio's skin reddened at the neck, crimson creeping upward until his entire head seemed to glow.

"You can't..."

"Please," Emory said. "Save your indignation. You are the worst of men."

Renata searched Valerio and removed a small pistol from an ankle holster.

With Valerio and Horse disarmed, and Prihya's former guards strolling over with cable ties, Emory spread his arms.

"You see? My work would be far easier with this man on my side. I am gambling that the account he has given over to his—

sorry, *my*—agents is sufficient to locate and secure our ultimate goal."

"You wanna follow the Witnesses to where they went next?" Jules said.

"This is too remote to have influenced the Eurasian and African prehistoric humans. Yes, they have more—much more—the bulk of their knowledge and technology... elsewhere." Emory turned the book in his hands around so Prihya could see the front of it. "Well? Are you going to help us, Prihya?"

Prihya's breath caught. Her chest fluttered and she couldn't help but glide forward. She felt like she was floating. No one accosted her, no one shot her. In fact, Emory's smile seemed to welcome her as she examined the markings on the sheet of gold before her.

"It can't be."

"It is, child. And it is the main reason we wanted *you* here. To help us shepherd the Anthropocene Epoch onto a path of benevolent peace and harmony. This..." He tapped the book, his finger close to the outermost line of five carved concentric circles.

Prihya was scared and excited and happy and sad all at the same time. She didn't know which way to turn, so took in everyone surrounding her, from Emory to Bridget through Valerio and Horse, and ending on Jules. Her brain churned, seeing too many possibilities. Good, bad, hope, tragedy. No gray areas. Only the extremes of humanity's soul.

Hoping Jules would understand, if not now, then when the right time came, she addressed him directly. "You are always right. It's in the dirt. Trust your instinct."

"Huh, thanks," Jules replied.

His words relayed confusion, not getting what she was trying to convey, but a quick wink suggested he'd got it. Got the message. If he didn't, there'd be no chance of stopping these crazy people.

To Emory, she said, "This is... the answer?"

Emory nodded, sage and wise, confident in his commitment. "Humanity's impact on the world is so strong... the dominant force superseding nature and God... that we must be more responsible. Not just in the current trends of global heating and plastic waste and globalized politics subjecting masses of innocent people to subservience and poverty, but of how we evolve. How we live, breathe. It all must change. And we can only do that by altering our perceptions. That may require force. But I *intend* it to come about through inspiration."

"We all need some ambitious life goals, but that one sucks." The woman who led the other strike team had been silent until now, and her outburst took everyone by surprise.

Including Bridget. "Huh? What are you doing?"

"Have you heard enough, Jules?"

Jules looked at Prihya, cast his eyes down, and said, "Yeah. I think we heard all we need."

The scholar-assassins had picked up on the change in energy, instinctively setting their feet and gripping their firearms. Even the guys about to zip-tie Valerio and Horse froze.

"You're as crazy as any other megalomaniac," Jules said. "Rayyana, what've you got for us?"

"Oh, you're going to love this." Rayyana raised her voice. "Echo, Delta, Theta. Control."

Moses dived on Emory, tackling him to the ground as the others raised their weapons. The Koreans, too, reacted, but too late.

Rayyana shouted, "Action!"

Four simultaneous explosions ripped through the clearing, wood splintering, and several trees collapsed, scattering the unit of armed men.

Prihya didn't know exactly what they had planned, but was glad to be a part of it.

CHAPTER TWENTY-EIGHT

IT WENT to hell pretty fast.

Although Charlie hadn't briefed Jules fully on her directional charges, he'd deduced that the black mesh was either a microphone or a speaker. He'd taken a chance on it being a mic because an output device on a detonator was pointless.

The four voice-activated explosions blew in unison, taking in the "corners" of the clearing and obliterating three of the guards like matchsticks. Others dodged and ducked, running in all directions, plainly unsure of the severity of the attack.

Jules landed a sidekick in Muzaffer's kidney, followed by a knee to the head, knocking him to the ground before grabbing his gun and throwing it to Rayyana. She sprayed cover fire, driving back the two female scholar-assassins, while Charlie ushered Bridget aside, essentially chucking her behind a boulder.

Jules looked at the two Koreans who had been guarding Valerio and Horse but couldn't see the pair of prisoners. They'd fled as soon as the bombs went off.

Which left these two.

Fine.

Jules ducked left as their guns came up, using one as a shield and parrying that weapon aside. Then he dragged the soldier forward, avoided an impressive front kick that would have floored him if he hadn't predicted it from the soldier's hip movement, and swept the standing foot while landing a ridge hand strike to the neck. He went down hard.

The other guy had already raised his gun, but Jules was quicker, extending his leg to snap it aside before going in low with a groin punch. The soldier was wearing a cup, so his pain was minimal. But there was still pain. Enough to stun. Enough for Jules to land a rising elbow to the man's jaw, followed by a round elbow to send him to the land of nod.

As the man collapsed, Jules grabbed the SMG, spun, and dropped into a crouch before firing in a direction he knew none of his colleagues or friends had fled. The three-shot burst struck one man in the leg and drove two more in the opposite direction.

But Jules was out in the open, and he hadn't yet identified every adversary.

As the panicked guards got their act together and fired on him, he dived behind a cluster of boulders for cover.

More automatic gunfire rang out from the ledge next to the cave's fissure opening. Charlie had acquired a firearm and holed up with Rayyana.

Jules raised his head to take a mental snapshot of the situation: Four unwounded Koreans still in the fight; Muzaffer recovered and prowling the opposite edge with an acquired AK-47; Hilla and Renata only shimmering phantoms, having regrouped in the undergrowth; Moses bodyguarding Emory eight yards from Jules, nothing but his eyes visible between rocky cover, but protecting his boss held priority over attacking Jules. It would've been a simple shot in the fractions of a second when he exposed more of his head. Right between the eyes. But Moses's brow furrowed with a knowing grin, and Jules refused to take a headshot. Would never kill intentionally.

And that was the problem here.

Rayyana's next volley hit a Korean in the neck, and Charlie picked off a soldier who had broken away from the group.

"There more coming?" Jules called.

"Undoubtedly," Rayyana replied.

Two options: go scorched earth and try to lose them in the rainforest, and hope they pierced through the incoming teams, or bottleneck themselves into the cave and give the reinforcements, which were surely coming, a chance to catch up.

"Okay," Jules shouted, "let's go."

He popped up, threw several shots into the fray, wounding one incoming operative in the shoulder, then firing at where he last saw Muzaffer before slipping into the cave.

They'd lost their flashlights along with the rest of their gear, which left only the LED pods deposited earlier. It was plenty to see by for now, but Jules hoped they wouldn't have to hold out long enough to see if Charlie was right about their shelf life.

Ten yards into the passage, at the first mutation of the structure that gave him a shooting nest, he crouched behind and aimed the gun, set to single shots; no need to blow more of his eardrum than necessary in this tight space. He aimed past the incoming women, who filed in against the angled side to give him a clear view. When past him, he said, "Cover your ears."

He fired once, deterring an inquisitive body at the narrow gash of daylight. It hurt, but it was necessary.

"Where's Prihya?" he asked, taking off after them.

They were jogging, glancing back, Rayyana falling behind to the rear as a matter of duty.

"I thought Prihya was with you," Charlie said.

"Why would she be with me?" Jules replied. "I was taking out the guys with guns."

"She was closer to you, and you were making faces at each other. I assumed you had a plan."

"I didn't have a plan. She had a plan. *You* had a plan with Rayyana. I didn't plan anything."

Bridget rounded on them. "Would you quit it? We'll get her back. You heard the priest. She's not gonna die."

"Not on purpose," Jules said. "Hey, Rayyana, you ain't got some dive bombers or kamikaze drone strikes comin' do you?"

"Nothing like that." Rayyana paused by one of the LED pods, then carried on. "The camp will be aware we are in trouble and will establish an extraction plan."

"How long?"

"However long it takes to not die in the process."

"Great."

They kept going, their attention on the rear.

Approaching the parted underground river, Jules said, "They left the bangles in place. We can take 'em out and slow 'em right down."

"Then we don't have a clue what's going on topside, or in here," Charlie pointed out.

Rayyana agreed, "It is tactically poor."

Bridget said, "Tell me you got a backup, Jules."

"Only a fifty-fifty shot," he said.

"Fifty-fifty?"

They reached the water's edge and paused for breath, Rayyana holding the line at the wedged-open door.

"We have guns, but no spare ammo," Rayyana said. "No back door. No cavalry for some time."

"Okay," Jules said. "Fifty-fifty might be optimistic."

"Contact." Rayyana stiffened, gun stock to her shoulder. "He's got a white flag. Like, a real actual white flag."

"Who does?" Bridget asked.

"Me," came Moses's voice. "I am unarmed. We really are chasing peace. I am alone. And I just wish to talk."

There was a discussion. Brief, direct, and, if they were honest with each other, inevitable. Jules joined Rayyana at the tight space between the jammed door and the wall in which it was set, an easy position to defend in a gunfight, but impossible if they used explosives. Which they almost certainly would.

"Yeah?"

"Jules Sibeko," Moses said. "Are you in charge? Or should Miss Carson be out here?"

He literally waved a white flag. A handkerchief to be precise, tied to a twig.

"I'll do for now." One offshoot of Jules's eidetic memory was the ability to take in everything in his field of view at once and digest it as a regular person would when focusing on specific points. Here, there were faint sounds, Moses's backup no doubt, and a stillness to the air that felt like a portent of violence to come. "Whadaya want?"

"As I said, peace."

Rayyana edged farther out, using an outcrop of buckled wall to shield from the incoming passage while keeping Moses in her sights.

Jules said, "You got the books. You got Prihya, and you seem to think she knows more than us, so... why you chasin' us down here?"

Moses lowered the twig, placed his hands together, and shifted his weight. "In all honesty, we thought about sealing you in and leaving. But that is not how the Church of the Forefathers wishes to start our mission."

"You're a true believer, huh? Peace and prosperity for all?"

"Yes. I promise you—"

"Just so long as we do it your way, by your rules. I think I've heard this crap before. Like, a lot."

Moses dipped his chin, gathering himself. "You know the Forefathers occupied this region, long before our European and African ancestors could even rear livestock, sow seeds, form communities much bigger than an extended family group. They saw rising sea levels, the catastrophes imminent, and that they spread beyond their borders to establish an empire."

"Empire, right." Jules needed to get out of this alive, but Moses had tried to kill him before. If he argued too hard or threatened retaliation, he might never find out what this man truly wanted. "Historically, I ain't a fan of empires, but go on."

"Our past conflict, yours and mine, was based on our working for Valerio Conchin. We followed his orders because the Church was ill-equipped for such work. Now we have grown, and we have what we need. We control enough money and men and resources to follow this great race and unearth the knowledge that is our birthright. So, we extend you this opportunity. Come with us, in the footsteps of the Forefathers, to unearth their greatest secret."

"I've seen the symbols and maps," Jules said. "I ain't convinced."

"Well, we are. This path is the key to controlling the orbs. And controlling the orbs may dictate the future of humanity itself. You can be part of it. Or you can... choose differently."

Jules considered it, but he had too much history with the people on this trip. He couldn't ask Charlie, Bridget, or Rayyana to follow him blindly; they'd make their own choices.

"How about Prihya?" Jules said. "She get to choose differently?"

"Ah, our old friend." Moses clicked his fingers. "She is a pot of contradictions, that girl."

From the bend in the passage, Renata brought Prihya out, a knife in one hand, Prihya's arm in the other. The two stood there with LED pods behind and in front, shadows falling across both faces.

Renata said, "Tell them."

"Emory is partly right." Prihya had the voice of a victim speaking up to a bully, starting timidly then growing stronger with every word. "I can't verify everything. No one could, not without lab equipment, research, weeks if not months of—"

Renata squeezed Prihya's arm and moved the blade closer to her face.

"But... *but...* the mass migration, the expansion of the Witnesses, you must have seen what I saw. The headlines."

"Headlines, sure," Jules said. "But you know how these things can snowball. The modern world gives it a name or writes some legend about it, then any hint of it drops some crappy film on YouTube and the flat Earthers and conspiracy nuts are all over it. You want to throw in with these people over that?"

Prihya watched the knife as it withdrew, then winced as it poked into the small of her back. "If it means the answer to one of legend's greatest mysteries... Even if it isn't quite what we thought... isn't it worth it? Jules, with Valerio being hunted through the rainforest by his own men, we have better partners. People who've done bad things, but who hasn't? You were a criminal yourself. And here we are, with a chance to find—"

"Ah-ah," Renata said, again firming her grip. "No spoilers at this point."

"Correct." Moses adopted his beatific peacemaker pose, hands before him, pleasant smile. "They have to trust us. Join us willingly."

"Like Prihya is?" Jules said.

"She is still fifty-fifty."

"Fifty-fifty." Rayyana moved sideways toward the inner chamber. "Like your play here, Jules."

Charlie cut off Rayyana's movement, emerging from where she'd been eavesdropping, Bridget coming up behind but not stepping out. "Counteroffer."

"Negotiation," Moses said. "I can haggle."

"Back out. Let us go, let Prihya go. Then we can all have a good chat and think about it. Together. Any of us want to hop along with you for a ride, we go. And yeah, it'll be willingly if it means that much to you."

"Moses, do it," Prihya said.

"We cannot stay that long," Moses said. "We must act before the Carsons' reinforcements gather. You have two minutes."

"Can't do that." Jules had felt a moment of hope, that talking this out might work. "We need to contact home. To be sure you guys are on the level. This Church of the Forefathers, I never heard of it. You can't expect us to—"

"Then, sadly, trust has broken down."

Jules snagged Prihya's attention and she drilled her stare into him as she had outside when she told him to trust his instincts. A glance at Bridget and back via Charlie and Rayyana told him they were in agreement.

He said, "I'm sorry, but no."

Prihya let go of a breath she'd been holding, upset at the outcome.

Moses said, "Then I am sorry, too."

He said nothing more. Simply turned and walked away, Renata guiding Prihya after him.

Rayyana aimed at them, but Jules touching her shoulder was enough to prevent her shooting them in the back. He didn't believe she would have, but the temptation was there. They were negotiating, and if Jules wished to remain one of the good guys, he couldn't drop a death sentence on people like that.

They withdrew inside to where the dank, moist air surrounded the watery tunnel to what must have been a holy place for the Witnesses or Forefathers, or whatever name they'd given themselves. Rayyana kept an eye out as they gathered, but had nothing to say.

They'd rejected an offer that might have saved them, or might have walked them out into their own execution. No way could they trust people who'd assassinated the competition, betrayed their own subcontractors, and openly stated they were pursuing power. Regardless of how much they preached about peace.

Bridget broke the silence. "What now?"

"Are they gone?" came a man's voice from the parted underground river.

Charlie and Jules aimed their guns that way, while Rayyana shored up her position at the door.

Valerio Conchin crouch-walked out, his hands extended to show they were empty, a grin like a person meeting an old friend in a bar. "Hi. Yeah, I didn't run through the jungle."

"It's a rainforest," Jules said.

"Okay. But listen up. Why don't you come this way? I think you'll like what I've found."

CHAPTER TWENTY-NINE

JULES AND BRIDGET followed Valerio and his mute henchman under the bedrock, leaving the seasoned fighters to repel an attack from outside. Before parting ways, Rayyana had caught up to him and said, "If this goes badly, remember our agreement back on the river."

"We ain't there yet," Jules told her.

"Let's hope it stays that way. But keep your promise."

"I will."

Charlie had given him a suspicious look, but said nothing, preparing what little weaponry they had. The narrow aperture into the pool's entry point would prove difficult to breach for anyone wanting to take their quarry alive, the bottleneck working to the defenders' advantage.

There was no need to come in, though. Siege tactics of starving them out would work, and Jules didn't want to get started on when bathroom breaks reared their heads.

Bathroom breaks?

You're behind two of the vilest human beings you've ever met and you're worried about bathroom breaks?

Maybe he was getting jaded. He made a mental note to meditate on that later. If he got out.

They were soon on the other side together in the oversaturated glare of Charlie's LED pods.

Valerio again acted like a used car salesman—the open arms, a thousand-watt fake smile, extrovert body language. "Exciting, isn't it? I mean, who'd have thought it? Us... teaming up against a common enemy!"

Jules said, "We ain't teaming up."

"We sure as hell ain't teaming up," Bridget agreed. "You expect protection?"

"Protection?" Valerio heaved a big belly laugh and backhanded Horse playfully on the gut. "She thinks we want protecting."

Horse grunted and lifted his shoulders twice, emulating laughter.

"No, my dear, we don't need protection. At least, no more than you do. I mean, it'd have been suicide to run into the trees, so we came down here. Neither of us got fortunate enough to pick up a gun, but Horse has other qualities. And now here *you* are. Ready to *team up* with your nemesis."

"First," Jules said, "you ain't important enough to be anyone's nemesis. Second, this ain't some team up. You tell us some advantage, we use it. If it means you live as a result, it's a coincidence, not intent."

Valerio rubbed his chin theatrically. "It'll do for now. But believe me, you're soon going to want to team up. This way!" He darted aside, toward the expanded gash of an entrance to the main repository.

"No."

Valerio rounded on Jules, a ferocious face that snapped into fake geniality as fast as blinking. "Yes? What's the problem?"

The problem was, Jules wanted to go nuclear on this pair. He wanted to pound Horse into the ground—he wouldn't underestimate him a second time—and then pummel Valerio's face with a rock until he was no longer a threat to another living soul. This was a man who would kill whoever stood in his way, destroy whatever he deemed necessary, and do whatever it took to achieve his goals.

"Rayyana and Charlie can't hold off your assassins forever," Jules said.

"No, wait," Bridget said. "Not *his* assassins. They never were. Always working for Father Emory's church, stringing you along. Must've hurt."

Valerio blanched and his fists closed. Horse picked up on the man's anger and reacted with more intensity, his own fists balling, and he shifted into a short fighting stance.

"Easy, my friend," Valerio said, adjusting his demeanor, which calmed Horse down. "It's understandable they'd be skeptical. But when I explain myself, they'll go get their friends and remove the bangles from that nifty magnetized shield, and let the water protect us."

"Poetic." Bridget crossed her arms. "We can't trust you. I'd be more inclined to throw in with the priest. But since he's being a rude asshole, making demands without letting us confirm his stories, we'd rather not trust him, either."

"What's your plan, then?" Jules asked.

"Look at all this." Valerio pointed to the slanting walls, the almost-caved-in entrance. "The geo-subsidence is intentional. They built this library to withstand it."

"Or a crappy job."

"Oh, Jules, you need to have a little faith. If the Witnesses predicted flooding, the end of the ice age, and many other things, surely they knew a chamber like this would be subject to geological shifts. No, this—or at least most of it—is intentional. Otherwise, that water-based booby trap would not have worked. Speaking of which, maybe you should go get your other women and collect the bangles."

Bridget took offence. "Did you just say 'his' other women?"

"Water, my dear." Valerio gestured to the shielded pool. "Focus on that, not my language faux pas."

"Water...?"

Jules said, "What does he mean, Bridge?"

Bridget focused on the jagged way through to the looted library. "The floor was a pattern. Flooded, remember?"

"Puddles," Jules said. "And it looked like a pattern on the floor, sure."

"Think about it, Jules, and you'll get it," Valerio said. "You're almost as smart as me."

A muffled *whumpf*, then a *bang* resonated through the chambers. Two explosions, different ordnance. Dulled by the rock and water between here and there.

A flashbang followed by a grenade seemed most likely.

Jules rushed toward the pool, hopping in to a frustrated cry of, "Oh, not now," from Valerio. He descended the sloping bed, finding Charlie and Rayyana staggering toward him ahead of a cloud of smoke and dust.

"RPGs," Rayyana said. "Couldn't stop them."

Jules ran headlong into the smoke, nose and mouth buried in the crook of his elbow as he passed them coming the other way.

"Where are you going?" Charlie cried. "They can't get through yet. It's too dense."

He fought the stinging in his eyes, the heaviness in his lungs, until he came to the spot he needed. The bangles were still here, humming, vibrating gently in their slot. He grasped them in the middle where they met and yanked them free.

Although he could see nothing now, the water all around bubbled and groaned, the invisible shield weakened by him disrupting what must have been some sort of circuit. He heard sloshing nearer the source of the explosions, the water flooding back in now the bangles' influence had lessened. He was safe, here in a strange ball of magnetic static, but the smoke remained unaffected.

Sprinting back toward the library, the bangles keeping him dry, but the water far behind him resumed its flow, pushing more of the trapped smoke and airborne dust toward him. He upped his pace, racing now, up to the lip of the pool and out, as if it were flames on his heels. Rolling over the lip, removing the bangles from the briny water's domain, the smoke belched out around him, and the two fluid sides collapsed, clapping together in a whirl of conflicting currents.

"And now we can't get out?" Charlie said.

"Au contraire," Valerio said, flashing a smile. "I think the young genius worked it out."

"Yeah." Jules gave his most reassuring look to the others. "There *is* a back door. We just have to find it."

CHAPTER THIRTY

"So, we're safe for now?" Bridget said.

"More accurate to say pinned down," Charlie answered, still obviously disgruntled at Jules removing the bangles.

"It will slow them down," Valerio said. "But they have scuba gear."

Jules assessed the room: a flowing body of water between him and them, those chasing him far better equipped than expected, limited ammunition on this side, and a fifty-fifty gamble.

"Let's go." Jules led the way to the library passage, the bangles glowing red and green in his hands.

Rayyana accompanied them through, but cautioned, "If they have to prep tanks and secure bolts as they go, they could need a couple of hours."

Valerio made a noise like a half-laugh, half-*hmm*. A *ha-ummmm* of sorts. "And if the tanks are state-of-the-art rebreathers that require less than ten minutes of setup...? And the bolt guns and cables were designed to traverse undersea currents stronger than the one behind us? Hypothetically speaking, of course."

"Then our odds just changed from fifty-fifty to seventy-thirty," Jules replied.

"In our favor?" Bridget asked.

"What do you think?"

No one replied as they emerged into the egg-shaped chamber, the faint funnel of light from the shaft landing on the empty shelves.

Bridget lingered on there a long moment, her throat bobbing at the memory, as Jules regretted their rash actions. They should have waited. Rescued Prihya as a priority, then let Rayyana clear the area, regardless of who got hurt or killed. It wouldn't have been Jules's hands taking the lives, so why would he worry?

Because he'd have endorsed it.

Whenever LORI were forced to kill, it had been either self-defense or proactively taking down people who would destroy them around the next corner. Jules wished they were more skilled, level-headed the way he was, so maybe they wouldn't have to resort to those methods. But he'd long resigned himself to acting like an introverted vegan in a world of meat eaters: *you go ahead, but it isn't for me*.

Perhaps he should act more like those activist vegans; lecturing, demanding another way to sustain oneself, demonstrating another way. While he still felt guilt over an accidental life he'd ended, he'd never intended to kill anyone, and he was still alive.

Or should he accept that sometimes—rarely, but *sometimes*—killing might be justified?

"I can't blow the charges," Rayyana said.

Bridget snapped out of whatever she was thinking. "What charges?"

"The ones I set in the tunnels." Rayyana showed her a small pad strapped to her arm, hidden when they searched her. "Must be too far away, and now the water's back."

"Why not blow them sooner?" Valerio asked.

"Didn't know there was a back door." Charlie cocked a hip and placed her hand on it, a pointed look toward Jules. "Well? There *is* a back door, isn't there?"

"It's an underground repository," Jules said. "It was built by people more intelligent than modern humans, who'd have reached the moon if they'd given a crap about that sort of thing. It'd be dumb not to have a way out."

"I have others in the room out there," Rayyana said. "But they will not blow if I am outside."

"Meaning they can follow us," Charlie said. "If they get through."

"They will." Valerio wasn't where he'd been a few seconds ago. He'd climbed up on the six-point-five-foot cuboid altar at the edge of the room. "They'll be here in about fifteen minutes. And please don't think you can counterattack by picking them off as they climb out of the water. They'll have thought of a counter-counter for that kind of counterattack." He frowned. "That's a lot of countering. Anyhoo, take a look at this."

Jules tucked away his urge to snatch Charlie's gun and shoot the man in the gut, and hopped over the raised sections of floor, wading through the final depression that was too wide to jump, then waved off Horse's cupped hands that offered to bump him up. He climbed up under his own steam and joined Valerio on the altar, the surface of which was large enough to butcher a cow.

"What am I lookin' for?"

Valerio pointed at the cavern floor, where concentric circles branched off into channels, focusing on a single point like a bullseye.

Jules had partially mapped the pattern already, having walked much of it, but the visual was incomplete. Now, he saw what appeared to be a maze, reminding him of the sequence of walls and traps he'd traversed under the North Sea. This was nothing like it in terms of the shape, but he was starting to see the Witnesses as puzzlers, testing the intelligence of anyone wanting to crack open their heritage.

"It's not a maze," he said aloud. "It's a map."

"No, no, no." Valerio snaked an arm around Jules's waist, pulled him tight, and directed him to the middle. "All the raised sections look like paths, like the diagrams on a few of those books. And I know, I know, they're the reason they wanted Prihya. A segment of her expertise. But I'm sure you and your Toby Smith have just as much knowledge about what that means, don't you?"

"Difference is," Jules said, slipping out of his hug rather than break the arm, "Prihya's our friend. And we don't gauge our friendships based on transactions or what benefit they bring."

"Really? That's *so* weird. But okay. Look at what you're searching for, the real goal here, and ask why they built it like this. *This* one. *Here*. Not the maps, not the legends, but this building. Right now."

Jules's brain usually snapped into place, a computer calculating simple sums and commands. Today it was sluggish, which he blamed on lack of input. It also embarrassed him that Valerio saw something he couldn't.

But then it arrived. Like an owl snatching a mouse, one moment it was running free, the next he had it in his grasp.

"Jules?" Rayyana called. "Time's ticking."

Jules sat on the edge of the altar. "How long can you guys hold your breath?"

"Flood the chamber?" Rayyana said.

Bridget gestured to the passage leading to the pool. "With that gross water?"

"It won't be that stuff," Jules said, having rejoined them at ground level. "The cubic meters needed would mean a whole reservoir. Must've built some sorta channel from the Amazon or another underground source we ain't mapped."

"The fresh water will dilute the old," Valerio said, sauntering with Horse lumbering alongside. Lumbering, yet light on his feet, as if ready to pounce should anyone show a hint of aggression. "Look at the shape of this place."

"The middle is a funnel," Jules said. "Water's trickling out, so slow it's hard to see from here, but from up on that dais, with the shaft of light, it's clear."

Bridget said, "It's flowing *from* somewhere."

"And 'cause the level stays the same, it has to *drain* somewhere. It's using gravity or some mechanism."

"Like an Archimedes screw," Charlie said with an air of wonder.

"A what?" Rayyana said.

"An ancient mechanism. Never been found, just plans and diagrams for it. A long pole with a screw-like pattern set in a water-tight tube. Starts in a river or lake, and turns, scooping water up the screw's plates, and out the top. It's theorized for irrigation, but—"

"But, but, but," Valerio said. "The details are unimportant. What *is* important is it's been almost ten minutes since we got in here, which makes it imperative we start flooding the chamber now so it can fend off our new common enemy." He came alongside Jules and put his arm around him again. "*Teammates.*"

Jules thrust an elbow back into Valerio's stomach, doubling him over and triggering Horse's lunge. Having been ready for it, Jules sidestepped and used the big man's momentum to throw him flat on his face, slapping the water and splashing salty brine water onto Jules's bottom lip. It truly tasted horrendous.

"Wait," Valerio managed with a wheeze.

Horse, having flipped over and propped himself up on the watery bed to attack again, looked up at Valerio, confused.

"I deserved that."

Bridget was smiling, as was Charlie.

Jules trotted over the raised sections toward the center, just away from the slanted slab that had served as the library's shelves.

"Charlie, I need a second opinion."

Charlie hurried over and hunkered beside him, examining what had ostensibly been a very low-pressure fountain, recycling the water like a faulty pond filter. It resembled a small boulder set into the floor —the bullseye Jules saw from up high.

When Charlie rapped on it with her knuckles, it sounded hollow. "Right, so you want to crack this open, yeah?"

"I don't know," Jules said. "That's the second opinion I need."

"You're sure about the diagram?"

"Focusing energy or force on a central point. Here."

"Then if you activate whatever comes through, it'll need something to push against."

Bridget and Rayyana had gathered, Valerio closer but keeping his distance alongside the dripping wet Horse.

"The walls?" Jules said. "This cavern is shaped just right. Wide base, narrowing at the top, to push us through some kind of chimney."

Bridget craned her neck, staring upward. "I don't see a chimney, Jules."

"It's there. Remember India? How the fire funneled that air out?"

"This ain't India."

"No, but when I was up on that block, there was airflow. Wasn't just the small shaft, neither. There's a second exit. And there's only one place it'll be."

Rayyana said, "That's stupid."

"There were probably other routes back when they built it," Jules said. "Ladders, walkways that've fallen away, something. The flooding'd just be a means to drown people robbing the place. Like lettin' your dog bite a burglar while you run out the back and call the cops."

Charlie had finished her analysis and pointed the way Bridget was gazing. "Up there. If it isn't blocked."

"If it is, the pressure'll release it."

"Before or after we all drown?" Bridget asked.

"Dunno." Jules shrugged. "But Emory's assassin dudes are coming."

"Yes." Rayyana's voice rose over the others. All faced her. "And we have another problem." She was showing them the detonator on her arm. "I still can't connect to the bombs."

"You don't need to," Bridget said. "We're getting out."

Charlie's lips tightened and Jules didn't want to say it.

Bridget whipped between them, though. "What's happening? Why can't we—"

"There's not enough time," Charlie said. "If the asshole-in-chief is right about the equipment, Moses and co are already in the water, clamping bolts to the ground, and pulling themselves through."

"And I'm always right," Valerio said.

"Shut up. The point is, the water needs to press against something. Right now, it's going to trickle out through that hole into the other room. That part needs to fill up too, or there won't be any way to fill this place and generate the force needed."

Bridget's head fell, then scooped up to take in Rayyana. "Meaning we can't reach the backdoor."

"Unless we block off the hole," Rayyana said. "And I can't do it from here."

CHAPTER THIRTY-ONE

Bridget seemed weirdly distraught. "You can do it from inside the passage."

"The charges are set," Rayyana said, unsure why Bridget was so upset. "I can do it verbally, or when the radio signals can reach the detonators."

Bridget whirled toward Charlie, and Jules was about to hold her back as it seemed she might throw a punch. She settled for baring her teeth at the Welsh engineer. "How could you build bombs like that without a timer?"

"This is a field test, a beta." Charlie kept herself calm, but the steel in her tone brooked no nonsense. This couldn't be a debate. "The timer was planned, but I'm still developing it. The delay commands kept getting mixed up with the immediate execution. And the directional nature means minimal risk to the person setting it off. But I can go through it all with you later. Right now, we need to focus."

When Bridget pulled away, her eyes were moist. She gravitated to Jules, of course, but the lad saw what Rayyana did. He just hadn't admitted it yet.

Rayyana said, "Jules, this is the only way. And time's wasting. They could be out there already."

"Hold 'em off," Jules said. "The water's gonna flood their chamber. Push 'em back and make 'em retreat."

Rayyana kind of liked the innocence on display, but it was frustrating for someone who needed to act decisively, not least because of the reality of their impending deaths. It was run-of-the-mill annoying, too.

"If I can do it and come back, I will."

"What do you mean, 'if'?" Bridget demanded. "Sit in the tunnel and press the go button."

"That's the plan."

"Then why are you acting like I'll never see you again?"

Rayyana understood, then. The deep-seated resentment that had boiled inside Bridget for over a decade, and the truth behind it. The real reason for her anger and now her fury at Rayyana leaving them.

"When you and I first met, Bridget, it was off the back of your parents signing a deal with my uncle. My guardian. His wife had never cared for my company, and believed the best way to save me from my father's enemies in ISIS was to send me to Europe on one of those dangerous boats. They would assure my asylum once they saw the scope of the danger I faced.

"But your parents took me in. Gave me a job. You and I… our friendship… was never a job. Never my reason for being there. Yes, I was a makeweight in a deal, but your parents treated me well. And once they knew I could handle weapons, they asked me to train as a security guard.

"I was pleased. I didn't enjoy being a maid or gardener. I wanted to do my duty.

"You saw me move on, training, going deeper with the company's special forces units. By that point, your parents let me find my own way. They didn't see me as some plaything for you, and nor did I. This was my journey for my life. And I never understood why you hated me until later."

Bridget was crying now. Her hands lay on Rayyana's shoulders, and Rayyana touched her waist, as if about to dance. Their foreheads came together.

"Betrayal is the hardest thing to overcome. But really, I just did not communicate effectively with you. And then—"

"Then I wouldn't listen," Bridget said, a sob deep in her throat. "I heard it, but I didn't believe it. Thought everyone was lying to me because they didn't want to hurt my feelings."

"You had few friends. And I abandoned you. I understand."

"Don't go." Bridget wrapped herself around Rayyana and held tight.

Had she been an enemy operative, Rayyana could have broken the grip one of six ways, five of which would require hospital treatment. The sixth was still rough, though, so she hugged Bridget back while appealing to Jules through her eyes.

He shook his head.

Rayyana said, "You made me a promise. If it is between risking Bridget's life and mine, you pick her. No questions. No hesitation. I am the soldier here. She is more important than either of us."

After another moment of deliberation, Jules came forward, took Bridget's wrists in his hands and applied a little pressure. She looked up at him and he nodded. A whimper rose from Bridget, and reality set in.

She said, "I'm sorry. I'm so sorry..."

Rayyana wanted longer. She wanted to say it was her own fault for concealing her true nature in their early days, for not being forthcoming with her. But while all that was technically true, it was merely a personality flaw, a fear that the southern belle princess might dump tomboy Rayyana, who knew how to fight, to shoot, to do all the things boys did. After, though, when Rayyana revealed her other self, she was still the same person, the friend, the almost-sister.

"I don't want it to be this way," Jules said, hugging Bridget tight. "I don't wanna risk her. Or leave Prihya behind, either. But we need to regroup."

"We could surrender," Bridget said.

"They're zealots," Rayyana said. "If there's one thing I know about, it's religious zealots who put their mission above all else."

A deafening gunshot echoed through the cavern.

Charlie had taken up a position by the entrance and fired through. "They're here!"

Gunfire returned, scattering all. Jules spun Bridget around and half-carried her behind the bookshelf, while Horse shielded Valerio. Rayyana skipped over the shaped floor, backing up Charlie.

At the passage mouth, she tried the detonators again. Nothing.

She looked back to see Bridget watching closely, but Rayyana's lack of reaction tipped her over again, and it was clear in her face. She knew.

As Rayyana knew.

It had to be this way, and it had to be fast.

"What do we have?" she asked Charlie.

"About ten rounds." Charlie had set the SMG to single shots. "No more explosives, though."

A clatter of bullets pinged through from the other side. Moses calling, "Give it up and you live."

Charlie shouted, "How about you give it up and let us alone?"

"We cannot risk this. You can still corrupt our mission. Please, do not make us finish you this way. Join us. Or surrender and let our destiny play out."

Charlie gave a *maybe* shrug. "What do you think? Do we trust them?"

Rayyana flicked her setting to bursts of three. "Are you really asking?"

"In a sarcastic but firmly sentimental way," Charlie answered. "Unless you want me to set off the charges."

Rayyana had liked Charlotte Locke from the moment they met. Direct, intelligent, with a sparkling accent she couldn't get enough of. But she was also a mother, a wife, and an essential member of the team Bridget worked with. There was never a question of inviting her to close the door behind them.

She shouted, "Jules, hit it now!"

Jules released Bridget, crouched by the burbling cone, and placed the bangles against the flowing water. The fizz and pop and crackle of green and red electricity zigged and zagged through the ornate floor pattern, blasting a radius around him clear of fluid. It was also vibrating the cone, a miniature volcano. The floor trembled, and all fell silent.

Renata's voice was next. "You got three seconds before I send in an RPG—"

The ground lurched once. Settled. Complete silence.

Then a thunderous roar built up from below, and the cone

exploded like a shaken soda bottle. Water blew up and over them, hundreds of gallons in a matter of seconds. The floor's pattern was hidden first, then it was up to their ankles.

Valerio opened his arms and whooped with delight, as if welcoming the first rain following a drought.

"As close to full auto as you can," Rayyana told Charlie.

"I'll burn through the ammo."

"I know. Give them the impression we have more than we do. It'll make them hesitate long enough to get me into the passage. Then I'll do the same. Drive them back. It'll give me time."

"Time?"

"To get in range, blow the charges on their side, and..." Rayyana's voice caught. It wasn't like she hadn't known this was a possibility. In a way, this was better than dying in the service of an oil deal or defending a platinum mine. In another way...

No, it wasn't good at all.

But protecting Bridget—something she'd have done even if it wasn't her sworn duty—was as good a reason as any.

"Now," she said.

Charlie lay down three bursts of three in quick succession, deafening Rayyana in one ear, then a final two-shot before the slide clicked open.

Rayyana didn't look back. No time for a final, lingering stare or salute or wave. She dived into the tunnel, which was already three-to-four inches deep in cold, fresh water, and crouch-ran as fast as she could.

She heard Muzaffer call, "What's happening? Where is this water coming from?"

Then she let loose with her SMG, destroying her eardrums to the point where she didn't even hear the gun click empty.

It did the trick, though. She got to the end of the passage and encountered no resistance. Peering out, she discovered that she'd pushed them back farther than expected—all three of them in wetsuits, Moses, Renata, and Muzaffer—but not far enough to neutralize them.

She didn't hear what Moses said, but she noticed the gun coming up.

She raised her arm, pressed the detonation button, and ducked back inside. Nothing happened.

She felt rather than heard three slugs hit the opposite wall, and a ricochet bit her shoulder. The bullet lodged in her muscle, and she knew they were closing in on her.

Rather than retreat, she lay flat on the stream from next door, aiming her empty SMG as if about to unleash a barrage on the approaching scholar-assassins. It gave them enough to think about changing course, but nothing more.

Their return fire sounded muffled, but the effect was powerful, pelting her face with debris. At least three ricochets broke through her skin, two in her back and one in her leg.

No more time.

Never enough time.

Her words sounded garbled, as if fed through an electronic voice changer, but she had to state them loud and clear. "Victor. Nasty. Direction. Volley."

From what she saw through the smoke, the assassins realized what she was doing, and ceased firing. No need for an order. They turned and dashed toward the pool, where their miniature air tanks awaited them.

She considered letting them run, assuming the threat of death would keep them at bay while the chamber filled.

But it was only a second's hesitation.

The likelihood of them returning to the library was too great. They'd attempted to murder her. And they *had* killed many of her men, people she'd known for a long time.

She didn't *want* to let them live.

"Execute."

The bombs *cracked* and then emitted a deeper *thoom*. The directional force rent a block, then the others flashed off too.

The three assassins were still on their feet when the roof gave way and crashed down upon them.

Rayyana pushed backwards, scrambling to save herself, but a massive weight dug into her thighs. Glancing back, she found the way barred. One ricochet must have done more damage than she realized, as she didn't feel any pain.

She was sad more than angry. In some deep part of her soul, she'd thought maybe she would survive this, that it wouldn't be a sacrifice.

As the rest of the cave collapsed and her world turned black and numb, she was satisfied that she'd done all she could. Her debt to the Carsons was now repaid, and Bridget had a chance of living.

In her final seconds, that made her happy.

CHAPTER THIRTY-TWO

Jules focused on one thing after the cone blew its top: assessing every tremor and shift in the chamber. It was over a minute before he realized Rayyana had departed.

This filled him with terrible guilt, which he didn't feel often. He'd hoped there was another way, that she and Charlie could devise a plan to trigger the charges from here.

But the explosion and the powerful groundswell confirmed her demise. Grime and dust billowed from the passage, threatening to suffocate them before catching the through-breeze and dissipating upward. An updraft forming a vortex. As the floor fell three feet, churning the knee-deep water into waist-high waves, everyone screamed. It was cold, but it smelled fresh, diluting the brine as expected.

Charlie had gathered with him and Bridget, while Valerio and Horse edged closer. They were still gambling here.

The light beam chimney's angle, barely wide enough for a human man, had shone on the golden books lying at a 45-degree angle. A marker with a brighter light source, perhaps. It could even have been the flammable liquid used to light the massive repository in India. If the hidden shaft at the top worked the same way, it made sense for it to function as both a chimney and an escape hatch.

Jules remained close to Bridget. She firmed herself up, what Toby would call a stiff upper lip, deflecting her grief at the loss of what had once been a close friend and would almost certainly have been again had she lived. Jules avoided overanalyzing it. He avoided all conversation. He was shivering in the cold water, as were those around him, including Horse, whose nerve centers had been dulled by his accident.

As the water reached their chests, Valerio asked, "How long do we have to tolerate this?"

"Another twelve minutes," Jules said.

"Your brain really is remarkable. I'm glad you're on my side."

"Ain't on your side. Just won't let you die. Unless I have to choose."

Jules's words sounded as ominous as a death threat, and he meant it. If he could let Rayyana go, he'd let Valerio drown over Bridget or Charlie. It wouldn't take much to engineer an accident.

No. They weren't at that point yet. There was still a chance to take him in and hand him over to the authorities. It wasn't like there was no evidence of his crimes. In Ecuador alone, they were legion. If Jules dumped him on the police's doorstep, gift wrapped with proof, he expected the Carsons' influence would trump Valerio's money.

They started to float.

"Okay, so we're treading water now," Valerio commented.

Horse bobbed close by, but Valerio indicated he was fine.

Jules was acting the same way toward Bridget, but was less obvious about it. Or so he hoped. They'd agreed to try out being more than friends once this was over, but he knew she'd object to any excessive display of chivalry.

She cast a half smile his way. "Still fancy our odds?"

"Eighty-twenty," Jules said, but his attempt at gallows humor went unremarked upon.

Five minutes passed in silence. Silence but for the chattering of teeth. All knew to preserve energy by reducing all movement, including vocal cords.

As soon as the water level passed the light shaft, illumination dipped to a predawn hue, a shimmering of artificial LED pods alongside the narrow beam of sunlight. It made for a spa-like ambience.

Except much, much colder.

In another two minutes, they were close to the roof, the aperture coming into view, though still difficult to view thanks to the dying light. Only, now they were here, a few feet from salvation, it was clear the chute's angle wasn't the reason no light was getting through.

Some light dappled on the rising surface, but it was weak, threading in needle-thin rays.

"Hang on," Jules said. "That ain't right."

"Oh dear," Valerio said, spotting the same as Jules.

Charlie forced her teeth to stop chattering long enough to say, "Damn it, Jules. Eighty-twenty?"

"Yeah, odds are droppin' again." Jules squinted, trying to make out a path though the roots and fallen branches that barred their escape as solidly as any prison. "We'd need a chainsaw to get through."

"And an hour of free time."

Jules took every bit of data, every morsel of visual input he'd gleaned from the chamber, and processed it through a dozen scenarios. Usually, the results were as fast as a computer. This time it took a few seconds.

"We gotta dive."

"Dive?" Valerio said. "I do not dive. I barely swim."

"I don't care. Bridge, Charlie? We got about five meters till we hit the light vent."

Bridget said, "What's that in regular numbers?"

"Sixteen feet," Charlie answered. "You can do this."

"*You* can. I *might*."

"I'll be right with you," Jules said.

Valerio slapped the water as if launching into a tantrum. "What about me? What about Horse? He can't fit through there."

Jules might have said something crass or dismissive, but he'd gone through every option already. Up, through a dense pocket of vegetation that would fill with water long before anyone could break through, or down, and risk the narrow tube of mirrored metal.

"I didn't plan this. And I'm real sorry. I'd help if I could. You might get through, but..." Jules still felt a deep regret and even a weird, reluctant sadness over what had befallen Horse. "Your pal here... you'll have to leave him to—"

"Fine, fine." Valerio got closer to Horse. "My friend, I need a hand getting back to that little hole in the wall." He pointed at the ever-darkening shaft. "Then you'll need to do your best to get out... up there."

Horse looked up. Nodded.

Valerio said, "We're good."

"Just like that, huh?" Jules was more sure than ever that if he one day chose to kill someone, it would be a person who doubled as a moral vacuum, who would send his supposed friend to drown if it meant saving himself. "Hold your breath once we're in. We'll rise."

As the strongest swimmer, Charlie went first, leading the way, followed by Bridget, then Jules. Valerio would follow with Horse's help, but Jules found himself half-hoping the man would meet with another obstacle that sealed his fate. He didn't want to be the one to kill Valerio, but he wouldn't mourn his death.

Wonder what that says about you. It'd be a bummer if Dan was right all along.

Down, through the numbing cold, the golden sunbeam was a beacon. Jules could open his eyes, as did Charlie and Bridget, so they could navigate to some degree, although it was far murkier than he'd hoped. River water, debris within the cave, millennia of accumulated dust.

Charlie reached the hole first and waited. Bridget came next, but Charlie held her hand, keeping her aside. Questions in Bridget's face verged on panic, but she held it together.

When Jules got there, Charlie gestured to the bangles on Jules's wrists.

Of course.

If they encountered an obstruction, he might have to open it using his special touch.

Jules accepted and pulled himself toward the entrance, when a hand grabbed his ankle. It yanked him backwards, where he tumbled and took almost five seconds to right himself and let the murk clear.

Horse had pulled him aside and was holding off Bridget and Charlie, while he stuffed his boss into the escape tunnel. He then tried to squeeze in himself, but his shoulders were too wide. He pulled out and glared at Jules, as if daring him to fight here and now.

But they weren't mermen.

Horse swam upwards, away, and Jules heaved his strokes forward.

His lungs were turning on him, demanding he breathe, so he dared not waste another second.

Inside the shaft was cramped, and he was glad he'd extended his arms over his head to help guide himself. The track curved sharply like a hockey stick, then leveled out into a straight vertical run.

Kicking, pulling, rising, he sensed the pressure lessening. The world grew brighter with each kick, every yard gained. The biggest anxiety for Jules concerned what he could not see—Charlie and Bridget. Hopefully, they were right behind him.

Then the angle veered off again. The passage was still flooded, but now he was swimming almost horizontally, needing more effort to get through the water, until—

Thump.

He came up against Valerio who was, in turn, trapped.

Neither could speak, but the problem was obvious: like the other chimney, nature had encroached, but not as severely. Here, two roots had penetrated a seam in the metal tube, blocking the way.

Then two bodies hit Jules from below, and the nearest one began clawing at him. Bridget, from the size of her.

But Jules couldn't spare the time to try communicating or reassuring her through hand signals. He saw past Valerio and noted the man in front had his eyes closed. He was pulling and pushing the root, but it wouldn't budge.

It was too strong to break without additional power.

And there was none to be had. No tool, no weapon.

As he always did, Jules fed himself every morsel of information he could summon. His oxygen-starved brain worked more slowly than ever, but he came to a possible solution.

The pressure from below...

The resistance in front...

The fate of the man before him...

Jules got up closer to Valerio, curling his knees to his chest. He wedged himself into the small gap between Valerio and the shaft's wall, and felt the man thrash around in the inches he could. Jules stuck out a hand and jabbed the man's trachea, then guided his head so his body bent sideways.

The swell from below intensified.

It pushed Jules up harder, albeit slowly, his body and Valerio's combining to form an imperfect seal. It was leaky as hell, but it was working.

The pressure of what must have been thousands if not millions of tons of water rising from below, now far higher than the shaft, forced them hard against the offending roots. Valerio's resistance gave, as he took the brunt of the pain, releasing an underwater scream that would surely doom him.

Jules had to save his friends, though. If the price was Valero Conchin, so be it. He had to do this.

A creak sounded, then intensified.

Then a snap.

Then more snaps, wet and deep, but Jules was moving again.

Suddenly, he broke through, shooting horizontally, then they rose again. Not vertically, but an incline.

Up.

Until sunlight burst into a gigantic, all-encompassing screen. They were airborne, flying out of the widening shaft like champagne corks.

Jules oriented himself in midair, redressed his bodyweight according to gravity's pull, and plummeted down, down, thankful Charlie and Bridget were close behind and screaming—meaning they were alive. It was twenty feet and change to the Amazon river, and he'd never been so relieved to land in a fast-moving body of water in his life.

PART THREE

CHAPTER THIRTY-THREE

Emory's people were seething, so it didn't take a genius to conclude Prihya's friends, and probably Valerio and Horse, had escaped. Prihya knew they had no choice but to leave her, yet the decision stung in a way she hadn't expected. A small comfort was the injuries suffered by Valerio's—no, not his—*Father Emory's* scholar-assassins. They'd been working for this *Church of the True Forefathers* all along.

Muzaffer and Moses half-carried Renata out of the entrance with her arms over their shoulders to relieve pressure on her injured legs and what appeared to be part of her torso. Muzaffer, too, was bleeding from his head and arm, while Moses appeared unscathed.

The guards forced Prihya to stay back, amid what had now become a familiar-looking base camp of tents and cooking stations. She wanted to open the hay-lined crate in which the scholar-assassins had stowed the golden books, but she was forbidden to approach.

Guess we're bedding down for a while.

They laid Renata on a cot carried out from a newly erected tent, and a medic was called, while Moses and Muzaffer reported in to Emory.

"They blew the library and flooded it," Moses said.

Prihya literally gasped, like a bad soap opera actress learning her husband had cheated with her sister. She had no idea where the expulsion of air came from, but it drifted to the ears of those disseminating events.

Muzaffer marched toward her. "*Her*. She is one of them. We gut her alive and send them the video of her screaming. Let them watch as life fades from her in the pain of—"

"Now is not the time for vengeance," Emory counseled, although all it did was freeze the big man in place. "Prihya was not party to their actions. Were you, my dear?"

Prihya didn't like the idea of sucking up to her captors, but she liked the idea of being disembowelled in the age of TikTok even less. "No. And... I am surprised."

Moses masked his anger better than Muzaffer, but it was no less potent. "Surprised at them trying to kill me and my wife?"

"At them flooding the library. Bridget, especially, would have objected."

"I notice you focus on the cavern. Not my wife."

Renata lay still, peaceful, as if meditating. Morphine injection. Two Korean troops—one a medic—examined her wounds. From what Prihya could see, some were gashes, others scorches; she'd been caught in some sort of explosion, although not severe enough for any sort of savage IED.

"They didn't intend to kill," Prihya said with confidence. "Unless Valerio took control somehow, Jules wouldn't allow it."

"Maybe he has changed his mind," Muzaffer said.

"Not Jules. I don't think he can."

All took a moment to decompress, to stave off the primal urge to lash out.

Emory said, "The chamber was empty of useful items. The altar remained, but the artifacts we were hoping would be there were not. The Forefathers took their wares with them."

"What items?" Prihya asked. "You have the books."

"Do not tell her," Moses said.

Emory considered the advice, glancing around the camp, conflict evident. "You are curious about this, yes? You have seen the map and the diagrams. You know what we seek. Beyond the Tayos caves, I mean."

"You think the Witnesses, or Forefathers, whatever you want to call them... you think they had weapons? Something you can use to expand your cult."

"Our *church*." A flash of anger, quickly suppressed. "We are still God's children."

"Wait. You still consider yourselves Christians? You seem to worship these Forefathers."

"We revere them, but Christ is our ultimate savior. His proximity to the relics shows our church and the fate of the Forefathers is intertwined. Why, the bangles your friend commands... one was worn by Christ's mother, was it not? The other secured and cared for by Saint Thomas himself before founding his own church in your native country."

"You're still Christians, but you've elevated unknown people above Christ."

"Elevated? No. Do Christians who believe in Moses's feats decry Jesus? No. What about Noah? Adam and Eve? The Forefathers are part of history. Just because they were not written of in the modern Bible doesn't mean they never were. It doesn't mean they were not once part of the faith. The gospels are heavily edited accounts that suited the men of the day, so what if Noah is an analogy for your repository in India? Not an ark for animals, but for knowledge? What if Cain and Able were brothers disagreeing about the course of mankind, and Abraham a priest of old?"

"They still kicked you out of the Vatican, though," Prihya said.

"Enjoy your chitchat," Moses said, moving away with Muzaffer. "We are leaving."

"We can camp the night," Emory said.

"No. We leave now. I have told Hilla to evac. No more waiting. We go. Now."

"You work for me."

Moses rounded on him. "Do I? Or do I work *through* you? For the Church? For the true master?"

Emory remained silent.

"I thought so." Moses departed to be with his wife.

Emory called after him, "You are assigned to me. You advise me. But, through the Church, you obey my orders, as you would a general on the battlefield."

Moses's head bowed, reminding Prihya of any husband at the bedside of an ailing wife.

"But I value your advice," Emory said. "We will, indeed, leave as soon as we are able."

"Thank you, Father."

A moment passed where Muzaffer first held his puffed-up tough-guy pose, then broke off to dig out a sat-phone.

Emory barked several orders in Korean, and clockwork efficiency took over. The tents started coming down, kit packed in various sacks and crates.

Emory returned to Prihya. "Where were we?"

"You getting kicked out of the Catholic Church for heresy?"

"Yes, yes. We had planned for it, though. And, on our own, we thrived under the banner of good. Of the quest for ultimate knowledge. We saw evidence of a higher intelligence guiding our pre-Biblical ancestors. But it was not until we found Valerio Conchin, and examined the Lost Origins Institute's discoveries more closely, that we saw the evidence was unequivocal. But, the Vatican..." He gave a cringy sort of shrug. "They are not too fond of evidence when it defies the accepted narrative."

"And you just lead these people now?"

"It was not without bumps along the way. Within our own ranks, the disease of control took root. We fought for the very soul of our movement, and now we have a clear line."

"Obey or die?"

Again, that angry flare crossed Emory's face, something he clearly worked on hiding behind a priest's stoicism. "Death to enemies is a last resort. We prefer to convert them."

"Are you trying to convert me?"

"You saw what was on those books, what we seek. You have wanted the truth for years, have you not? And your research is going to help us more than you can realize."

Prihya wasn't sure if she was more annoyed at the man's condescension or that he may have been right. She wanted to see this through, but would prefer to be with Jules and Bridget, not this religious zealot. For now, she would play along. After all, if she was to be carted around looking for where the Witnesses built their mini empire, it was reasonable to assume LORI's path would intersect with hers along the way.

Father Emory smiled. "I see we have an accommodation."

Before Prihya could deny it, a helicopter's rotors thundered in the distance, a heavy bird coming in.

"Hilla is five minutes out," Muzaffer reported. "She wants to know the cargo."

Emory assessed Prihya and then the crate of books. "We will take Renata and one medic, the three of us, and Prihya. And the books, of course. The rest will leave on the other helicopters." He locked eyes with Moses and the pair exchanged respectful nods, their earlier conflict buried. "We must be on our way. In the footsteps of our True Forefathers."

CHAPTER THIRTY-FOUR

Jules strode over the hardscrabble ground cleared of trees by industrial means, a middle figure in the line of four survivors. The sensation was not unlike slow motion, but he determined it was nothing more than the effect of his feet traversing unmoving land after hours on the river.

Valerio's emergency exfil site was a bustling tent city, filled with the chatter of Slavic voices, the clanging of pots and pans, the whirring of generators and other machinery. The pungent stench of smoke and cooking fires drifted on the air, overlapping the acrid tang of gunpowder. As much as Jules dreaded the thought of accepting an iota of hospitality from him, it was the most logical approach in terms of surviving the next twenty-four hours.

Although outfitted like an army barracks from a Vietnam war movie, Jules saw no weapons more powerful than an AR-15. Lots of AR-15s. He counted twenty-four people, with many more in the surrounding forest. And plenty of tech: satellite dishes, monitoring stations, a helicopter pad, a runway with a Boeing cargo plane at the back end.

"This was our supply chain," Valerio explained as he led them through. "Emory knows about it, of course, but he also knows how well-equipped we are. Meaning he won't try anything direct."

"You sure?" Jules said.

"As sure as I can be."

Jules checked back on Charlie and Bridget, both bedraggled and exhausted. Charlie had suggested they don't follow Valerio to his stronghold, while Bridget had offered no opinion, suggesting she'd follow whatever Jules and Charlie decided. In the end, Jules made the point that the Carsons' backup group was several miles away, and were operating in the country under strict rules, so they followed Valerio here and would take off home as soon as they could.

Jules faced forward. "Yet you had no clue Emory was going to drop you like a hot brick as soon as he could."

Valerio pulled up, rounding on Jules with a lizard-like grin. "Perhaps you'd like to try your chances with Emory and our Korean friends."

"Nah. Just show me to a sat phone and we'll get outta your hair."

"Right, yes, of course. This way. It's the least I can do after your save back there."

As they crossed into the camp proper, it was clear the operatives were all Caucasian and the man in charge spoke English with an Eastern European accent. "Sir, the arrangements are in place."

"Very good," Valerio said without stopping. "Wheels up in fifteen minutes, yes?"

"Of course, sir." He was about to leave, but said, "Sir, are you aware of the arrival an hour ago?"

Valerio stopped. "Who?"

"Your bodyguard, sir. Horse is here."

Valerio's face lit up like an actual human being hearing delightful news. "He's here?"

"Infirmary, sir. This way."

Valerio followed the man and Jules, Bridget, and Charlie tagged along, all breaking into a jog as they approached a heavy-duty tent with an improvised white cross on a red background. Valerio whipped the flap open, and all entered through a waft of alcohol and stale sweat, finding Horse on a bed, wearing nothing but shorts with lines coming out of him.

The Russian-sounding doctor said, "Sedated. He was covered in cuts and lacerations. Like he pulled himself through a field of barbed wire."

Horse had red gashes over much of his body, the worst on his forearms, shoulders and chest, with angry welts and cuts across his face. Some wounds had been stitched, others needing only butterfly strips. Even with his scorched skin, courtesy of Charlie's flare, he looked peaceful, but Jules imagined him clawing and slashing through the tough roots and branches like a desperate animal, whatever it took to free himself.

"We have pumped him full of antibiotics, too, sir. He was very dirty, so I cannot see any way he did not get infected during his journey."

Valerio bent over Horse and stroked the man's hair. "My old friend. You never were one to give up, were you?"

The doctors gave the pair space, leaving the LORI trio standing in the silence.

Charlie coughed to draw Valerio's attention. "So, you're using Russians?"

"Striovians," Bridget said, her ear more finely tuned for accents than Charlie's.

"Correct," Valerio said. "Striovian refugees, to be precise. They swore loyalty to Zimina Yanovna before her arrest and incarceration as an international terrorist. Those who supported her could not go home. Those who declared her a hero and swore to fight in her name were declared criminals. I offered them sanctuary."

"In that Indian town you pretty much own?" Jules said.

"Where I recuperated, yes. They are loyal to Zimina and their country, not the highest bidder. Because I am making enquiries and funding campaigns to negotiate the General's release, they pledged themselves to me. My cause is her cause, you see."

"You want to release Zimina Yanovna?" Charlie said. "She's insane."

"She is highly motivated to protect her country from Russian aggression and western interference. Her solution is unconventional—"

"She wants to obtain a power source she can't control."

"Like I said, unconventional. But you understand unconventional, don't you, *Jules*? She has the same genes that flow through you. She controls the bangles and the elements, and whatever security measure the Forefathers—sorry, force of habit around Emory Ballard—whatever measure the *Witnesses* put in place. It is unfair to label her insane, simply because she, like I, operates on a higher plane of intelligence."

"But you're insane, too," Jules said.

"Again, only by some measures. By my own, I am a colossal narcissist with sociopathic yet charming tendencies." He flashed another of his smiles that told everyone that he knew what he was saying was crap, but didn't care. "Let's go find you that sat phone."

Valerio made for the exit, pushing back the flap.

Jules played the gentleman and held the way for Bridget and Charlie to step through into a semicircle of Striovian soldiers, every second man aiming a gun at them.

"What is this?" Jules said. "We had a deal."

"Yeah, but you know..." Valerio shrugged, hands in his pockets. "There are deals and there are *deals*."

"My father will have figured out where we are," Bridget said.

"And that's a very scary prospect, my dear, I assure you. But for now, let me assume your daddy doesn't command a legion of nationalists willing to die in service of their country who have procured weapons and satellite access from a great number of capitalism's enemies."

Bridget swallowed and wet her bottom lip. "He has resources."

"Thought not." Valerio rocked on his heels. "Allow me to make a brief assumption. You were in that cavern a long time, pulling those heavy books together. A certain chap with a photographic memory might well have had time to review all—or most—of what they contained."

Jules said nothing. Charlie and Bridget stared.

"Thought so." Another grin. "So, here's my offer. Share everything with me and I'll allow you to contact your people to arrange pickup. *Or*... and I think you'll like my *or*..."

"Or what?" Jules said.

"Or, you and I go where that turncoat Emory is going. Help me take the prize from him and his religious crazies, and ascend to our rightful place on top of the world." Valerio reverted to a plain speech pattern, as if suddenly realizing he was grandstanding. "I mean, you're going there, anyway. Why not go together?"

The guns never wavered, and Valerio demonstrated uncharacteristic patience. Charlie was tensed, ready to fight if it came to it, and Bridget held firm, showing not an ounce of fear.

"Let us discuss it," Jules said. "Me and them."

Valerio gestured with one hand that he would allow it.

The three huddled together, stepping back from the men with guns.

Jules said, "He's half right. We're goin' as soon as we're out of here. And I don't think Toby'll be allowed to join us."

"Why?" Charlie asked.

"My dad." Bridget appeared downcast. "He'll stop it."

"He won't want to follow this up?"

"Nah, he only wants that contract," Jules said.

"It's true," Bridget said.

"So, to catch up with Prihya and Emory, we gotta fall in with Valerio?"

"I'm not doing that," Charlie said.

"He's a mass murderer," Bridget agreed. "No matter how much we want to go, we can't. Not with him."

"Okay. Decision made." Jules broke up the meeting and approached Valerio, who was waiting not-quite-as-patiently.

"Great, so... you've come to an agreement?"

"I'll go with you," Jules said. "But the girls ain't."

Charlie spun him roughly around. "What?"

Bridget said, "Jules, you can't."

"We need answers," Jules replied. "The Witnesses were *here*. It's where they lived for generations. Then they migrated out. Where to? Where did they take this weapon, or whatever it is you think you're gonna find?"

Jules disengaged and faced Valerio again.

"I'm in. But Bridge and Charlie? They walk. And I only cooperate when they're safe. I'll help find what you're looking for. Then I take Prihya home and you help me stop the religious fanatics gettin' their hands on the Witnesses' stuff."

Valerio made a theatrical, "Hmmm," and rubbed his chin in an exaggerated *thinking about it* manner.

Jules said, "What?"

"Oh, nothing. Except, at every opportunity, you were at great pains to insist you had no interest in a team-up." He pointed at the women, too. "All of you said extremely mean things about me and implied you could never trust me. So, no, Jules, I'm sorry. This *isn't* a team-up. I'll just kill you all if you refuse. I'll start by chopping off this one's feet." He dropped a nod toward Charlie. "At least this way, you get *something* out of it."

"Come on." Jules stepped forward, a little too closely for the two armed men flanking Valerio, who leaned in protectively. Jules held up his hands and said, "Just let them go. I'll—"

"Nope." Valerio pulled back his shoulders to straighten his back, his chin up and chest out, showing off for his men. "I'm in charge here. No deals. Either you're all in or you will all make a splendid meal for whatever scavengers roam this rainforest at night." He turned to the women, nice as pie, and said, "Well? What's it to be? Join me and share the end of the line and end up showered in glory? Or die, oblivious to the wonders of time?"

CHAPTER THIRTY-FIVE

ARCHAEOLOGICAL DIG, WESTERN CHINA

THE SUN ROSE between two peaks, rising at a distance beyond the forested hills which Toby Smith could not determine. Five or ten miles? Fifty? Toby would never understand how Jules assessed such things without flinching. It should have lifted his spirits, which were currently swimming in the gutter, as he made his way to the communications station near the newly built helipad, the odor of dry soil and human sweat heavy in the air, and the occasional waft of gasoline and engine fumes ghosting by.

The encampment was now teeming with workers, twenty shipped in from various impoverished villages in the region, working hard for minimal reward. At Toby's objection to the exploitative labor, Roger Carson vowed to add a significant bonus to whatever remuneration the local government had forced them to accept. They'd uncovered much of the landscaped gardens surrounding the children's statues, which gave those funding the dig a smattering of good news: ornately constructed walls, a maze, and a summerhouse filled with rotten furniture and what Toby identified as an artist's stash of paintbrushes and canvasses. Unfortunately, there was no actual art.

Toby's consternation was not caused by the workers' amicable banter as they prepared for their meager breakfast rations, but at Dan waking him with news of Jules, Bridget, and Charlie.

They were alive, had escaped serious injury, but were in the hands of Valerio Conchin. Despite having—incredibly—discovered the Tayos Gold, Valerio's partners had betrayed him, fleeing with the artifacts and Prihya. Since then, emails had poured in, hand-drawn renderings of what Jules had memorized and shared with Valerio's permission. Toby did not know why this was happening.

Dan and Harpal were already on edge when he entered the communications station—a prefab unit housing satellite feeds, several computers, and a couple of large ultra-high-definition screens—with Roger Carson leaning against a tall stool. Valerio was front and center on one of these high-definition screens, with Jules, Bridget, and Charlie standing submissively behind him in a tent similar to the one LORI slept in for the China dig.

"We're all here?" Valerio said in his boardroom voice. "Good. You'll have received the material by now."

Toby had distributed the images to the team's e-tablets. "Everyone has been briefed. Now, why are you holding our people?"

"I'd like an answer to that, too," Roger Carson said, hands gripping the stool seat so hard it could leave an imprint forever. "I have teams in the area, ready to deploy if you so much as—"

"Daddy, Rayyana's dead," Bridget said.

Roger's mouth hung open, and he jumped as if startled. His eyes took on a sheen as his skin paled. "Dead…? How?"

"She was saving us." Bridget's voice strained, holding herself together after a loss. "She was a real hero, Daddy."

And… *Daddy?* What was that? Bridget was in her mid-twenties, and Toby had only ever heard her call Roger *Daddy* when being sarcastic or trying to manipulate him in a knowing, somewhat meta way. Was it a code, perhaps?

"Touch any of them, you die," Dan said.

"Oh, it's macho posturing time, is it?" Valerio jammed his hands into his pockets. "Okay, I'll play. How about this for a rejoinder: as if you haven't tried and failed plenty of times already."

"We always had other priorities," Harpal said. "Like not dying ourselves when buildings are falling down around us."

"Sure, you keep telling yourselves that. Okay!" Valerio clapped his hands and smiled. "Are we done puffing up our chests, or should we arm wrestle? If that's even possible digitally?"

"Talk," Toby said. "Let's hear your threats."

"No, no, Toby, you misunderstand. After much back and forth, a bit of negotiating and stalling, we are now as one."

"As one?" Dan said. "Is that asshat language for 'asshat'?"

"No, it is an erudite way of saying a team-up. But these folks don't like the idea of working together, so we're going to do it under the threat of *death*. I hope that's okay with you."

The four men adopted equally perplexed frowns. If they were anything like Toby, they were considering how to respond to someone asking permission to keep their friends hostage.

"You need something from us," Toby said.

"Pool our knowledge, agree a destination, and uncover the greatest archaeological find of the past three thousand years. Oh, and Mr. Carson might lend us some equipment if needed. I'm a little short right now."

Roger stood from his stool and held himself straight and stiff. "I'll do no such thing."

"Huh." Valerio reached off screen and returned with a large, silver Smith and Wesson .45 caliber revolver. "I get bored easily, especially repeating implicit outcomes on hypothetical scenarios. Let me summarize. Gun. Daughter. Boom." He mimed blood pouring out of his head.

Roger said nothing more.

"Good." Valerio replaced the gun wherever it came from. "As a gesture of goodwill, let me start. The Witnesses lived here, and in various places around the region, in the centuries before the European descendants of those intrepid African explorers migrated across the Bering Strait and populated the Americas... millennia before Columbus 'found' the land mass."

Valerio's exaggerated bunny quotes seemed to be aimed at the Americans present, although Toby thought Valerio was American too, so the man's point was unclear.

"They evolved along their own genetic route, perhaps with a long-lost common ancestor, or perhaps humanoid form is the pinnacle of the natural world over hundreds of thousands of years."

"Maybe they're not from around here," Dan said too quietly for the mics to pick up.

"We'll never know for sure," Valerio went on. "What we do know is, they thrived until the Younger Dryas period, where ice melt changed the world's shape forever, and other theorized catastrophes occurred. But that is when their influence petered out. Do I have this correct so far?"

"With some glaring omissions, yes," Toby said.

Valerio smirked. "I'm sorry, Toby, was that the intellectual equivalent of macho posturing? An academic burn? If so, color me impressed."

"Factual statement," Toby said. "To give the scale of the Witnesses' scope. We have found evidence of intelligent manufacture dating back to pre-Toba times. When the super volcano erupted and almost wiped out human life, a sudden surge in intelligence allowed small numbers to survive. Scientists estimate around ten thousand human souls were alive before this great leap forward, and we believe it needed an outside influence to push it so quickly."

Dan pointed upward.

Harpal rolled his eyes.

Toby said, "It's an important point. The Younger Dryas ended around thirteen thousand years ago. Toba was seventy-four thousand years ago. The gap between the two is astronomical in terms of human evolution, and if the Witnesses' civilization spanned that time, it was remarkable that they communicated with descendants and continued on their path."

"Probably a long way before Toba," Jules said from over Valerio's shoulder. "I mean, they can't just appear, right?"

"Correct," Toby said. "They had a thriving if small civilization, either living alongside the protohumans who survived Toba, or living isolated in a hitherto-unknown location."

"But probably this one," Valerio said. "South America is now mostly rainforest, mountains, deserts, or has been built over by newer peoples. Inca, conquistadors, the twentieth century 'progress'." More bunny ear finger quotes. "My goal here, though, is to find where they migrated to. What was it, thirteen thousand years ago, that drove them out? Thanks to young Jules's remarkable brain, we might answer that."

Toby glanced down at his e-tablet, an instinct followed by the others in the room.

Valerio stood aside and gestured for Jules to take center stage. He invited Bridget alongside, as if this were a rehearsed student presentation.

Jules said, "Yeah, I sent on all the sketches and words and symbols, best I could. A lot of it just looks kinda familiar if you know much about the history of certain areas. Check out number four."

They all did so, finding a structure like a blocky pyramid.

"I know, and I'm guessin' you all figure the same. Ancient building techniques mean a pyramid is just the easiest, most secure way of stacking somethin' really high. And you're right. But we got other stuff, too, like how to support a big-ass statue..."

He slowed to allow people to flip through the pictures.

"There's this thing that Charlie called an Archimedes Screw for bringing water up to the surface from underwater wells and low-lying rivers."

Toby found the diagram Jules meant. It was a quickly-sketched rendering, but he saw what it was supposed to be. "Yes, an ingenious method of irrigation. This other design, with plants and crops, has certain similarities to accounts of the Hanging Gardens of Babylon, which is theorized to have used such a machine, but—"

"Are you stalling?" Valerio said, butting his way into the center of the screen. "It feels like you're stalling."

"Nope," Jules said. "This is just Toby." He waited for Valerio to slink back. "And I hate to side with the psychopath, but he's right. Let's motor on this. Toby, you've been holding somethin' back for a while, and I understand why. But now we know more, it's time to come clean."

The three men in the comms station looked Toby's way, Dan and Harpal less pleased than Roger.

"It's not anything I could speak about," Toby said. "It might even make Dan's ideas about aliens seem sane."

"Hey," Dan said.

"That's fair," Harpal said.

"Okay, I've had enough." Jules had been through the wringer the past couple of days, and now his frustration at keeping secrets from the team was evident. "I can't keep covering for you, Toby. This is what you were hidin' all along. What you refused to tell the others."

"You knew?" Bridget said.

"He's right that it's crackpot. That's the only reason I played along. Now, we got some hint that there's a grain of truth to it. Not the high fantasy myth, but something. So come on, Toby. You wanna tell 'em or should I do it?"

Toby had both hoped for this day to come and for Jules to quash any idea of it being true. Because now he had to make his case, based on flimsy legend and flimsier modern evidence.

"Well?" Bridget said.

"Yeah," Dan added. "Well?"

"Okay, fine." Toby lay his e-tablet down and held his chin high. "I *have* been hiding something from you. Nothing more than a theory. Well, not even a theory. More of a hypothesis, because a theory isn't necessarily—"

"Cut the waffle," Harpal said. "Out with it."

Toby needed a breath to gather himself. "Even with what we have learned of the past, and the Witnesses' hidden pocket of history... this is a tremendous leap for serious scholars. Let me outline the possibilities, and we can see if you conclude the same as me."

CHAPTER THIRTY-SIX

EXFIL CAMP - ECUADOR

In the musty, hot tent, Jules was visibly frustrated at the additional words about to be spent, but Bridget voted to hear Toby out. She wanted to be sure she understood, because having had two of her closest friends lie to her, she needed a path to forgiveness.

"Let us start with ancient machines," Toby said. "Not electronic or digital, but devices with moving parts performing a task. The evidence is undeniable, even without Charlie's computer simulation of the design found in the Witnesses' texts. The Antikythera Mechanism, of course, is the most famous. Years ahead of its time, which I put to you, may well have been based on that of the design the Witnesses used."

"That's way more advanced," Charlie said. "But they'd have needed a bunch of other components to interpret the directions. It's not much more than a fancy compass that you have to adjust when navigating. We have computer modeling and GPS to do the heavy lifting, so it was much easier for us."

"True. But that doesn't make it any less remarkable. If the Greeks had developed the Antikythera Mechanism themselves, not inherited it, they would have evolved and grown their knowledge to the point of powered flight, even space travel, by the time Queen Victoria sat on the throne."

"You said that already," Jules pointed out.

"Did I? When?"

"Five days ago. Move along. It's old news. Or I drop the big spoiler for you."

"Fine, fine." Toby gathered himself. "We have multiple diagrams in our library—"

"Me too," Valerio said. "I have lots, too. But this one stood out. Impressive we both saw the same potential, don't you think?"

"Can we stop?" Harpal said. "If we have to be civil to the psycho billionaire, can we please stay on track?"

"Very well." Again, Toby seemed shaken even through the screen. "The diagrams for the Witnesses' navigation machine are often accompanied by pictorial representations and what appear to be written accounts dating to twelve thousand years ago."

"The Younger Dryas," Bridget said.

"Correct. They denote slow, geological events spanning many decades, which match the great melting at the end of the Ice Age."

"Ooh, ooh. Sir, sir!" Valerio had his hand in the air, plainly mocking Toby. "My theory. Can I say my theory?"

Toby grunted and sighed.

"I think the Witnesses lived longer than homo sapiens. They saw time differently than we do, so had more insight into the changing world."

"Something we've considered," Bridget said.

Jules added his sigh to Toby's. "But ain't a shred of evidence. Can we move on?"

Valerio closed his mouth with an invisible zip and threw away the key.

Toby said, "There is evidence, both physical and in these later accounts, of a cosmic event either during the great melting or soon after. Soon, in geological terms, I mean. It triggered disasters around the world—"

"For the uninitiated," Bridget's dad interrupted, "what might a 'cosmic event' entail?"

"A meteor strike," Bridget said. "We think it was a meteor or comet that crashed into Canada hundreds of thousands of years ago which brought the unusual elemental properties that work the Aradia and Ruby Rock bangles."

Charlie nodded, pinching her lip with thumb and forefinger. "And either carried some unknown radiation or quantum-entangled particle. The Witnesses' ancestors used it to develop the orbs with huge potential in terms of the power they generate. Well, not *generate*, not literally, but somehow command it and manipulate it. And—"

"And we don't know," Jules said. "Move on. We're nearly at Toby's point."

"Oh, grouchy," Valerio said.

Toby hit some keys on his e-tablet and offered it to Harpal. "Can you make this appear on there?"

"Might not have been their direct ancestors," Dan pointed out.

Harpal coughed pointedly. Dan shrugged but said no more. Harpal took Toby's device, pressed the surface twice, and a picture of an old sketch scanned from paper appeared on the screen in Ecuador. It showed a comet entering the atmosphere above a landscape.

"This is from the writings of the Greek philosopher, Plato," Toby said. "He received a historical account from a man named Solon and recited this in his work. Anyone remember the names of Plato's texts?"

No answer except in the form of folded arms and tired stares.

"Very well. Plato wrote *Timaeus* and *Critias*, circa 360 BCE, detailing a great natural disaster. The effects correspond to the archaeological evidence of a comet strike around that time, which wrought much destruction across the northern hemisphere."

"We know that for a fact?" Dan asked.

"Yes. In thousands of places, geologists have found—"

"Nope, not going there," Jules said. "But since we're onto Plato, and since I read both those books a while ago, I can see we're ready to start saying stuff like, 'it's impossible' and 'that's just a myth' before we get into it big time. So, come on, Toby. You want to tell the others what was in Critias?"

Bridget was already there, and she understood their reasons for holding back, although it was not quite as unbelievable as it would have been a few years earlier.

"It's a myth," Valerio said, breaking the silence. "A story."

"A *parable*," Bridget corrected. "Plato made it up to highlight the fate of rich, hypocritical powerful people who set themselves above regular folk. Or so the thinking goes."

"*Must* it be a myth?" Toby asked. "People thought Troy was a myth for years, but the Turkish site of Troya proves myth and history can meet. Historical fiction can inform the present."

Jules hit his own set of keys, replacing Toby's screen's image both there and in China: two pictures, each showing a series of concentric circles. One that he replicated himself, copied from his memory of several of the golden books, and a hand drawn scan from a textbook similar to the sketch of the comet. "Anyone recognize this?"

One by one, the penny dropped. First Charlie's mouth formed an "O" as her eyebrows knitted together, which made Valerio chuckle because he was obviously already on the same page as Toby, then on the screen both Harpal and Dan lifted fingers to point at their tablets as they processed the images.

"Nah," Harpal said. "You're pulling my leg."

Only Bridget's father hadn't recognized the drawing of one of the most famous cities in the world of myth and legend.

"It's Atlantis," Bridget said. "We're talking about Atlantis."

CHAPTER THIRTY-SEVEN

WITH THE WORD *Atlantis* out in the open, Jules experienced the mental equivalent of loosening a belt after eating too much. Not that Jules could ever bring himself to gorge on junk food, but he'd eaten a huge Christmas meal when LORI was confined to the chateau, and experienced serious bloating.

Valerio, too, seemed happy. "Finally. Now the fun really begins."

"We don't know the location, though," Dan said.

Harpal joined him, fully in agreement for a change. "We can't just ask Google Earth. How do we find it?"

"Wrong question," Valerio said.

"What's the right question?" Bridget asked.

"The trouble," Valerio said with a wink, "is we only have one set of books, only one account of the Witnesses' migration. Father Emory has them all, along with my research that will be needed to cross-reference everything. He'll be free to find the city and exploit whatever he finds."

"Your weapon?" Jules said.

"It's there. Myth and reality combine. Don't you see?"

Roger Carson barged into view, centering himself on the screen, peering into it as if searching for some camouflaged marine animal in an aquarium. "Am I the only sane one here? You're talking about a children's story."

"Not at all." Toby ushered Roger aside, a placating hand patting his shoulder. "Plato's account was taken from thousands of years before his own time, recounted to him by someone called Solon around 360 BCE. The events took place over nine thousand years before then. It's unclear where Solon received his intel."

"Myths and legends were oral traditions," Bridget said. "We see it all over. Noah's flood is the Christian and Jewish account of the same story in almost every culture and religion in the world. And you mentioned another earlier today—while Babylon was a real place along the Euphrates River, and the walls are there to see, there are only stories about the gardens. Paintings that look different, stories that say different things. This is where Atlantis comes from. Stories across time. Plato made it his own as a cautionary tale."

"Fine," Roger said. "What does Plato tell us?"

"Still the wrong question," Valerio said.

Jules sensed his frustration rising. Instead of poking people to prompt a question, why not answer it? He wouldn't give Valerio the satisfaction, though, so kept it inside.

Besides, Toby was already engaged in more waffle. "Atlantis was a city made of concentric circles, located within view of the Pillars of Heracles. Despite its minor importance in Plato's work, the Atlantis story has had a considerable impact on literature. Including children's stories and popular movies. But now we think it's possible... at least *I* think it's possible... that the Witnesses spread from their base to aid fledgling homo sapiens in their accelerated learning."

Jules could not hold back anymore. He needed to step in. "Listen up. This is all you need to know about Plato's version. He called it 'technologically advanced.' The people lived on islands made up of circles like the Witnesses designed before migratin' outta here. The Atlanteans supposedly lost a war with Athens, and ended up wiped out. Internal fighting, plus a bunch of natural disasters. That's 9600 BCE. I miss anything, Toby?"

"A little detail, yes—"

"Anything *relevant*?"

Valerio said, "Just the tsunami."

"Sure," Jules said. "Probably a tsunami that finished off the city."

"Let me bring science into it, since I spent an absolute fortune on this." Valerio waggled his fingers and grinned—a magician about to deliver the big twist in his trick. "Roughly 12,900 years ago, massive global cooling kicked in, which was the end of the line for around thirty mammal species, including the mammoth. More significantly, it spelled curtains for the so-called Clovis culture of prehistoric North Americans." He paused, an eyebrow cocked. "Am I sounding like Toby Smith?"

"A bit, yeah," Jules said. "But go on. I think I see why."

"Okay, cool. I've funded many excavations, searching for more of that funky rock in the bangles. Know what I found? *Nano-diamonds.* In the sediments from this time period. Six sites—six!—across North America alone. Murray Springs, Bull Creek, Gainey, Topper, Lake Hind, and Chobot in Alberta. Such teensy-tiny diamonds, you wouldn't think were special. But they only occur in sediment exposed to extreme temperatures and pressures. Such as...?" He presented a flat hand toward Jules.

"Like in an explosion or massive impact."

"Bingo! Combine that with evidence aplenty of a wall of water spreading across the globe in under three hours, and we have a winner. Continental flooding, tsunamis, everything, matching up—very roughly—to Plato's writing on Atlantis."

Toby was thinking it through. Jules could have given him the answer, but he let the older man work it out. "A fragmented comet bursting in the atmosphere and raining down on the oceans... the melting at the end of the Younger Dryas was interrupted, was it not?"

"Sure," Jules said to get him to the next sentence without going off on a tangent.

"I funded searches further afield, too," Valerio said. "Europe, Asia, here in South America. All turned up similar minerals and elements of the same age. Massive burn-off, followed by erosion and a total change in the flora."

Toby again considered the science. "A fragmentary body breaking up and multiple surface impacts above the ice sheet or offshore in the ocean... It explains why there'd be no single impact crater. But it would mark the size of the comet as a cousin to the asteroid that wiped out the dinosaurs."

"And like that impact, this also happened in a single day. The Witnesses must have built Atlantis as a base to expand their knowledge. But even a race able to observe and predict age ices can't see a comet heading our way. No wonder—*boom*—it wiped out the nation state."

He was monologuing again, which Jules found irritating, but let it pass because it seemed relevant.

"I assume this is the end, then?" Jules said. "Like, it ain't gonna point the way? We got a few sketches from the cave, a rough direction, and some old writing that might have been passed down through oral stories for ten thousand years? Great."

"What's the question?" Charlie asked.

Jules turned her way and Bridget gave her a quizzical look.

"Valerio kept saying we were asking the wrong question earlier. Before his fascinating geology lesson."

Valerio smiled her way, wagging a finger. "Very good, my feisty Welsh bunny. Yes, the question we should be asking. Well, *you* should be, since I already know the answer."

Jules didn't want to follow his winding tale, but no one else seemed to have worked out the cryptic meandering.

He said, "Why did they want Prihya? Why wasn't she fighting harder to get away?"

Valerio touched his nose and pointed at Jules. "Bingo. Don't you remember? I recruited her because of her enquiring mind, her determination to get to the truth, and something more specific. Her many, many articles on pop culture's legendary stories. Where do you think I got all the knowledge I just babbled out? Where do you think I got the hints about where to dig? It was her. *Prihya*. She knows all this, and now she knows more, thanks to the Tayos library. Academics rubbished her. But not me. And now it's time for her and her friend Xander to shine."

"Xander?" Dan said. "Hey, I'd forgotten all about him."

"Perhaps, Bridget, you might petition daddy-dearest to urge his paymasters to grant clemency for the poor chap?"

Roger looked into the screen. Bridget gave a firm nod. Roger slipped away, phone in hand.

"So." Harpal clasped his hands and rubbed them together. "For hundreds of years, the finest academic minds throughout history have been trying to crack this Atlantis enigma. Let's work it out this afternoon, shall we?"

CHAPTER THIRTY-EIGHT

AIRBORNE—LOCATION UNKNOWN

IT ALL MADE sense to Prihya. In many ways, she had been correct about Atlantis for many years, ever since she began learning about the historical record. But, after hearing Father Emory's account of Valerio's comet theory, combined with the unmistakable illustrations from the Witnesses' migration tomes, she realized she had been wrong as well. Worse, now that she was seated in comfort onboard a Gulfstream jet, with the offer of wine, Prosecco, and soft drinks only a raised finger away, she was beginning to appreciate the resources at her disposal.

Appreciate?

Uh-oh, no. A far more malevolent feeling made her feet want to dance, her fingers dig imaginary holes, and her mind race: *excitement*.

Having written off ever learning the truth about the city state of Plato's mythical writings, the smoldering wreck of frustration now blazed with potential. Yet, the man in the luxurious chair opposite her had kidnapped and threatened her, and may have killed her friends. Not outright, she knew, but because he had sealed them far underground, rescuers would only have a small window to access the caved-in areas and haul them out.

She'd also inquired about the captured soldiers, which Muzaffer stated they'd handed over to local mercenaries on the ground to trade for ransom now that the Church's business in Ecuador had concluded.

As a result, she vowed to remain silent.

But the allure of Atlantis, which she'd tried to convey to Jules to trust what he was seeing, proved too much. She limited her responses to short, tight sentences and monosyllabic answers. Her efforts were successful until Emory presented her with evidence of the coalescing geological record, the timeline of the Witnesses' planned migration, and stories espoused by Plato and others.

Although Emory kept calling them the *Forefathers*, or *True Forefathers*, Prihya had called them *the Witnesses* for so long that it was difficult to shake; an appropriate name considering their efforts to preserve prehistorical art and written works—items never imagined by those who wrote history's official accounts.

No, sir, there were no writings before Sumerian scholars committed them to clay. Anyone who claims otherwise is a kooky, tin-foil-hat-wearing conspiracy theorist... regardless of how much conspiracy theory *becomes conspiracy* fact *right in front of your eyes.*

"So," Emory said, sitting forward in anticipation. "That is where we stand. You can either keep obstructing me for no good reason... or you can be a part of the greatest discovery of all time."

"You know where it is?"

They were the only ones in the cabin, except for a mute Arabic-looking young man dressed in a waistcoat, a clean white shirt, and pressed trousers. Moses remained by Renata's side in a separate cabin that they had hurriedly converted into a field hospital. Renata's wounds were no longer life-threatening, but she was so diminished, Moses wanted her sedated to prevent her from attempting to reclaim her place in the field. Despite obvious signs of psychological damage—the pair were psychopaths, sociopaths, or something-paths; Prihya couldn't tell the difference—their love for one another seemed genuine enough.

Meanwhile, Muzaffer, and Hilla had boarded the bare-bones plane that had transported Prihya to Ecuador in far less comfort than she now enjoyed. They were preparing for the landing, briefing the soldiers with no nation, and making plans to defend it if anyone tried to intervene.

"I think we have a location," Emory said. "But it is wise to have an expert in that field on hand."

"If you know I'm an expert, you have my theories. You don't need me. It's all out there. I'm not holding back some secret clue."

"I know." Emory raised a finger and the lad tending to them brought a fresh class of red wine, the smaller size that people drink outside cafes in France and Italy. "Prihya?"

"A Coke, please. Diet."

The young man gave a shallow bow and all remained silent until he returned, popped the cap on the tall, thin can, and poured a small measure, before leaving it to settle on the table between Prihya and Emory. He retreated, and Prihya had more questions.

"When you get to Atlantis, what do you think you'll find there?"

Emory sipped his wine. "Valerio is a corrupt, greedy man. He craves power. So, what we will find there is power. Of a sort. We are not sure of its exact nature, but we know of the orbs that change state depending on the correct interaction, and we understand approximately—is that the right word? We have some basic understanding, anyway. The orbs are magnetically charged and focused on molecular entanglement at the quantum level. They allow neutrons to carry information, then translate it into matter. They interact with one another yet remain independent. So, it stands to reason there will be other items, other uses not yet discovered. Would you agree?"

"The quantum stuff always sounded like sci-fi, but I think we have the same understanding."

"Good, good. Because how do you think a race like the Forefathers would be greeted, trying to force education on the ape people around Europe?" Emory placed the glass down and held up a hand as if in apology. "I am perhaps being uncharitable. There were many, many branches of humanity alive during that time, but only homo sapiens survived to the modern day. I think because it was these ancestors who pushed through from the Toba eruption. Their intelligence won out."

"As if they were chosen?"

"Chosen by natural selection. And yes, yes, I am aware that many

Christians will recoil from that phrase. But, honestly, how can it be anything else? God plants the seed, tends to the earth, and watches His children grow into what you see today: a disappointing mix of greed, ignorance, and violent reactionary vitriol."

"Except you."

"Except *us*." Emory's eyes got wider. "I wish Jules and Toby and the rest would see sense, because I think they, too, are among the chosen. Those who will be saved, once we wield the power of the True Forefathers. And you, Prihya... you will be instrumental in keeping that power out of the hands of men like Valerio Conchin."

Prihya had to admit that, although Emory was an extremist on the same level as Valerio, she saw Valerio as more malicious and dangerous than her captor. But it was one thing rejecting the devil she knew in favor of the one she had only just met, it was another to actively side with that devil.

As if reading her mind, Emory said, "Jules and his women, and Valerio and Horse... they are stuck, not dead. I wanted them to survive, but I cannot risk them interfering in this discovery. Contingency plans were made, and more contingencies are in place. So, please, Prihya. Trust me. This is your chance to not only uncover history, but to *make* history."

She'd heard a similar offer before. The man she assumed was buried in a library made her a similar offer. This time, though, it felt less risky, like the endgame was worth the bad stuff.

"You kill no one else," Prihya said. "You order no more assassinations. And you obey international law."

Emory lifted his wine to his lips, sat back as he drank, and sighed with a smile. "I will order no deaths unless our own lives are threatened. I can only promise I will *try* to obey international laws."

"And in return I help you find the exact location?"

"But if you obstruct me with lies, Prihya..." He replaced the wine, laid his palms flat on the table, and lowered his voice almost to a growl. "You will be the first to see me break the no-killing promise."

She knew better. Knew she shouldn't agree to work under these conditions. But they would go after it regardless, wouldn't they? If she said no, they'd kill her and drop her out of the plane over the ocean.

And this was her chance. Her dream come true. It just fell under less-than-optimal circumstances.

She said, “Fine.”

“Good.” Emory brightened, his shoulders relaxing as he reached for his drink and raised a toast. “We have the books, the brains, and years of evidence. Let’s get to it.”

CHAPTER THIRTY-NINE

ARCHAEOLOGICAL DIG - WESTERN CHINA

Toby would be lying if he said he didn't enjoy researching history and relating it to modern-day discoveries or evidence, but he promised Dan and Harpal, and—by a serious look through the screen from Ecuador—Jules, that he'd be brief. Or as short as possible.

Which may not be particularly brief. But he'd give it a shot.

In addition, he had an assistant join them just before reestablishing contact with Valerio.

"Xander, welcome back." Toby had shaken the man's hand, while Harpal and Dan greeted him with macho nods and fist-pumps—at odds with the way they'd all greeted him previously. "Are you well?"

"I am unharmed." Xander put a brave face on it, but he'd spent three nights in a Chinese jail with no idea that his daughter was being cared for in an American embassy, paid for through the Carson Corporation. On the transport here, he spent a while on the Chinese version of FaceTime, which was the best Roger could manage after lying that the man was essential to the dig's progress.

With Bridget under threat, there was no telling what Roger Carson might risk.

His contract? Surely yes.

His company? Again, what father wouldn't sacrifice all the money in the world for his daughter?

They reconnected with Valerio's group and Toby took center stage.

"Myth and reality. Often opposing concepts. But in this case, two sides of the same coin."

Harpal raised his hand. "Objection, your honour. Cliché alert and veering from the point within five seconds."

"Sustained," Jules said. "Toby, skip the intro, please."

"Very well." Toby accepted the charge and dug into his mental reserves. "Let's look at the most detailed written account of Atlantis. Plato. This is his written account from 960 BCE."

He switched to a preprepared slide of the pages. Rather than narrating, he summarised, quoting sparingly.

"This says that the State—Athens and, more broadly, Greece—stayed the course of attacks from a point in the Atlantic ocean. The notion was that the Atlanteans would invade Europe on the way to Asia. The island was 'in front of the mouth which you Greeks call "the pillars of Heracles," there lay an island which was larger than Libya and Asia together.' It was possible to cross from that island to others because the continent encompasses that 'veritable ocean'."

"That's pretty big," Dan said.

"Remember, we're reading three-thousand-year-old writing," Bridget said. "And it's a translation, too, so things could be lost or deliberately changed."

"Indeed." Toby had thought he was doing okay, and the interruption threw him a little. "And also bear in mind, this is what a man called Solon *told* him about the island Plato was viewing. Not that Plato knew for sure that all this was true."

No more comments meant Toby could continue.

"He goes on to describe a narrow entrance in a real ocean, and 'the land surrounding it may most rightly be called a continent'. Which is a bit of a contradiction. The nation isn't a continent but is *surrounded* by one. It goes into more detail, then. The island of Atlantis had a confederation of kings, of 'great and marvellous power, which held sway over all the island,' and spread far and wide."

"Marvellous power," Valerio echoed. If he'd drooled, Toby would not have been surprised.

"After the war followed violent earthquakes and floods. In 'a single day and night of misfortune' the city and its warlike inhabitants sank into the earth, and Atlantis disappeared into the depths of the sea. The site became 'impassable and impenetrable,' because the disaster left a shoal of mud caused by the island's subsidence."

Jules said, "An earthquake, followed by a massive wave. Makes sense. But then, didn't some islands around Greece have similar experiences? Couldn't that be the same way the great worldwide flood stories get mixed into folklore?"

"It's a theory, yes. But let's focus on the matter at hand, shall we?"

Toby indulged himself with rare pleasure at being the one to demand focus.

"This has led to many candidates being identified as Atlantis. A great civilization that built a city on a landmass either in the sea or close to it. Ancient in the true sense of the word, it was destroyed by water and sunk beneath the waves. Meaning it is impossible for the remains to be as obvious as the Great Pyramids of Giza or as intact as the Hypogeum Hal Salfieni."

"Candidates?" Roger Carson asked.

"Let me open the floor to our expert."

"Yes, yes." Xander was shaky, but clearly eager to contribute. He was here because of his in-depth knowledge of the multiple theories surrounding Atlantis and, in particular, Prihya's shared digital experiences of the search. "Let us start with Yonaguni off the south coast of Japan."

"No, let's ditch that one," Jules said. He had spent the intervening hours reviewing Prihya's theories about Atlantis's location, his ability to ingest large amounts of information far stronger than the rest of them combined.

"Why? It is a long way away, yes, in the East China Sea. Perilous water of sharks, currents, and typhoons. Very difficult to dive to. But, it has terraced steps like Machu Pichu, the size of five football fields, with steps climbing eight stories. Every side is regular, and it predates the pyramids."

"I know about Yonaguni." Jules counted off his reasoning. "The monument's form is broken up, not blocks built from the ground up. And sure, looks like regular shapes, kinda looks carved."

Charlie had been nodding and added, "It's geological fact that sandstone fractures under pressure in near-straight lines. Flowing water, currents, the weight of the water above... all would have smoothed it further."

"Ain't any tool marks, either," Jules said. "No other objects found, which you'd see if it had been occupied. It's all a big coincidence."

"Very good," Toby said. "Next?"

"Let us skip those that are not old enough," Xander said. "Like Knossos and Alikanos Bay. And look at the region most supposed experts agree on. The Straits of Gibraltar."

Toby knew this one. "Geophysicists suggest it is a good punt. Plato mentioned the Pillars of Heracles. Many think this is the Strait of Gibraltar, the maritime boundary of the ancient Greek world."

Toby added a map to the screen focused on the southern tip of Spain and the northern point of Morocco at the mouth of the Mediterranean ocean.

"Yes, yes." Xander sounded enthused, his turbulent experience in custody fading. "About fifteen kilometers off the Gibraltar coast is a sandbank. It would have been above sea level at one time. It lies under a shipping lane. Very difficult to map. Scans show the bank resembles an island. Imagine, with lower seawater. And consider please, Plato says Atlantis was lost in one day and night. This island sits on a..." Xander paused, recalling the phrase. "It falls between two tectonic plates. An earthquake, followed by a tsunami..."

Toby highlighted the spot on the map being described. "It would be well positioned for a seafaring race to explore the world. A sensible base in the Mediterranean."

"No man-made lines or structures," Jules said. "There's more evidence on land nearby, stone-age people makin' huge progress. Farming land, raisin' livestock, more advanced buildings. But rising sea levels just pushed people back inland."

"Donana National Park," Xander said.

"Yeah, it's a good choice," Jules said. "Scientists identified geological patterns kinda similar to Plato's measurements. But there's also a rectangle matchin' Poseidon's temple, which Toby didn't mention. It's a key feature of Atlantis, and I reckon it's one of those things that'd settle the evidence. This is all on land, though. Deep under the mudflats."

"Donana was one of Prihya's favorite locations. It defies some of the original scientific theories."

Harpal said, "There's science to this?"

"Not the time." Toby levelled a narrow-eyed stare his way. "Xander, continue."

"Donana Park was a wide, shallow bay at the time of Atlantis. Plato mentions Atlantis faced Kadir, which is the ancient name for modern Cadiz. This city is north of the modern area. If there was once a mighty city there, it now lies beneath the mud flats, untouched for thousands of years."

Jules was the quiet one, the one whose face appeared most serious. "It's on a fault, like that sandbank island. Inside the subduction zone, making it vulnerable to tsunamis after a quake."

"And there are many years of evidence showing tsunamis hit that coast," Xander added. "Sea rocks spread far, far inland."

Charlie bristled as she shouldered past Valerio, but she soon turned to the matter at hand. "Tsunamis also take evidence *out* as well as smashing it *in*land. It could have pulled a lot of evidence out to sea. Has anyone mapped Donana Park in detail? Ground penetrating radar?"

"Yes," Toby said. "There are many human-scale underground layers scanned and mapped, evidence of it being populated. But no excavations of great significance. There is much speculation it is what the Bible referred to as Tashish, a city revered by scholars for centuries. Much like Babylon in the Syrian region and Ubar in Iran, it has been the subject of speculation and madcap theories for as long as its existence has been known."

Dan had his hand in the air, waiting for attention. When it fell upon him, he said, "Remember how I did a bunch of reading?"

"Yup," Harpal said. "Searching for aliens in books and YouTube videos."

"Not just aliens, man. I don't have an addiction. I came across Atlantis. Some of Prihya's stuff. Some others, too."

Jules said, "Great, let's hear your favorite."

"If you head back to Knossos on the Greek island Crete, that place has its very own megastructure. Advanced building techniques, like *super* straight lines. Doesn't *all* match Plato's description, but who's to say the guy didn't embellish? After all, Troy isn't as the Iliad describes."

"This is getting scary," Harpal said. "The guy sounds like he's making sense."

"And bulls!" Dan added.

"Bulls?"

Toby decided to back Dan up, impressed he'd kind-of remembered all this. "They *were* a powerful symbol back then. Bulls were highly respected and roamed the streets of Atlantis."

"Okay, let's get down to it," Jules said, that thread of irritation Toby had come to know well making his words curt, his tone strained. "Santorini was a volcano during Minoan times, but the explosion was three and a half thousand years ago. Could be the original Atlantis had Knossos built on top of its ruins. Could be multiple destructions, and maybe it got destroyed more than once. But Atlantis ain't any of those. None of these we've mentioned."

Valerio, who had been uncharacteristically silent, let out a hoot of a laugh. "Oh, about time. Let's finish up, shall we?"

"Why can it not be one of those?" Xander said. "There are few options left."

"Because of Prihya, you foolish little man." Valerio posed with one hand on his hip and a cheeky smile. "She had a preferred option. One not many scientists agree with, and geologists laugh at her in the comments section on that YouTube film. If Father Emory protected Prihya, and went to all that trouble to keep her alive and bury us, it's because she is *right*."

Jules nodded. Clearly, he concurred. "Follow her lead. Monitor the activity in that area, and when we confirm she got it right, we move."

"I can't agree to that," Roger Carson said. "I won't willingly endanger my daughter."

"I'm going," Bridget said. "With or without your blessing, I'll be in there. So you can send what we need, or let me fend for myself."

All stood in place, waiting for Roger to make the next move. Toby couldn't read the man. It was as if he were waiting for Bridget to back down, which she wouldn't. She couldn't. Valerio would kill her. Even so, Toby suspected she'd be going anyway.

"Where?" Roger asked.

"North-eastern Africa," Jules said. "The Eye of the Sahara."

After confirming the details needed to back up his daughter, Roger Carson had departed the tent to issue the necessary orders, leaving Toby to end the call and assure Valerio he would play ball. It was impossible to see how Jules might turn this in their favor, but Toby would never bet against some tweak to the promised plan.

He excused himself, trotted after Roger Carson, and waited while he finished his phone call in the clearing where they had uncovered the animal statues.

"Yes?" Roger said.

"A request."

"What kind of request?"

"The kind that will facilitate Bridget's homecoming more efficiently."

Roger stared. "Was that English?"

"Let me, Dan, and Harpal meet them in the desert. Jules is an able lad, but Dan and Harpal are professionally trained operatives. At the first opportunity, they will extract our people."

"Under the guise of backing up that lunatic's uncovering of Atlantis?"

"Exactly."

Roger scuffed his boot on the ground. "I saw my daughter's face when you were discussing this. She barely even glanced at Valerio. She looked at you and she looked at Jules. She *wants* to go."

"Then we take out Valerio, and *we* go. When it's safe. It's lain under the sand for millennia. If it's even there. It can wait a couple of weeks to—"

"And the religious lunatic? The fanatic who's got your other friend hostage?"

Toby saw the point. It was a race, of sorts, but Emory would find it more difficult to access the Eye of the Sahara than a team backed by a multinational corporation with financial and mineral contracts based in the region. They had a razor-thin edge. *If* they could take Valerio off the board.

"I will provide manpower," Roger said. "Once they locate the city, or prove it's nonsense, I'll ensure my daughter and the other two get handed over, per the deal we have struck."

Toby feared he would play it conservatively. Like any decent negotiation, he had a backup.

"Roger, it will take at least eight hours to reach their destination, another six-to-eight to travel overland. I have more resources in France. My team can monitor progress, mobilize faster, and offer support. I beg you, please. Let us return to the chateau."

Roger Carson had his hands in his pockets, casting his eyes over the dig.

Toby said, "There are ample staff here, and we will be back—all of us—to finalize things for your Chinese clients. Roger—"

"Fine," Roger said. "On one condition."

"Name it."

"You take my jet, not that piece of crap you people fly in."

Toby didn't wait around thanking him. He turned, walked, and only stopped when Roger called his name.

"Yes?"

"Toby, forgive my ignorance, but... what exactly *is* the Eye of the Sahara?"

THE RICHAT STRUCTURE, AKA THE EYE OF THE SAHARA, MAURITANIA, EAST AFRICA

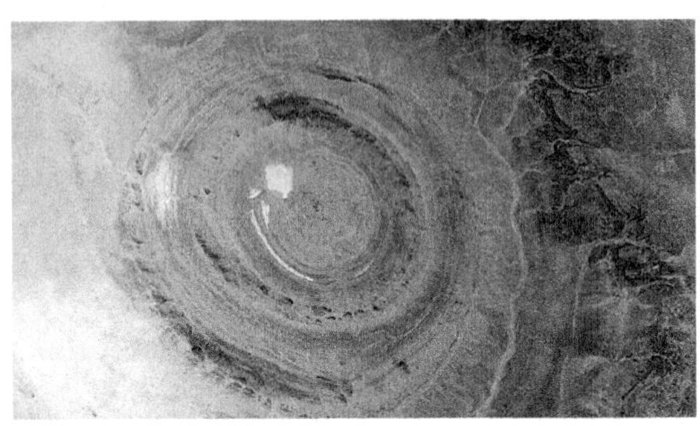

CHAPTER FORTY

BOEING BJJ 737 JET - MAURITANIAN AIRSPACE

Charlie Locke wanted them to be wrong. She hated conspiracy theories, crackpot explorers declaring definitive proof of hidden facts when it was nothing more than fairytale speculation. Yet, as they flew over the Richat Structure—nicknamed *the Eye of the Sahara*—she could understand why people gravitated toward this place as a source of mystery and wonder.

"Makes you wonder, doesn't it?" Valerio said, as if plucking the word *wonder* from her mind.

He was too close, leaning on the back of her chair to see out the window. She could smell him. Not sweat or lack of hygiene, just a general malfeasance, his corrupt soul seeping out through his pores. It was particularly annoying because they were secluded from the small army of Striovian troops in the other part of the small passenger jet, and forbidden from stepping out anywhere but the bathroom, making them Valerio's (literal) captive audience.

Charlie angled the lush chair away. "Makes you wonder about what?"

"Why no one thought to excavate here before."

Jules was lounging opposite her, clearly only pretending to sleep, so Valerio left him alone. Bridget sat beside him, going over the data, the hand-drawn sketches Jules had provided, and the symbols and words on separate papers. She had already deduced the Witnesses' intent to leave, to seed new civilizations throughout the world as tribes migrated from the north, and to establish a gleaming base from which to operate closer to the Eurasian continent. Of course, they didn't call it Atlantis, but the name was indecipherable, so they stuck with the legendary moniker, much to Charlie's chagrin.

"They *have* scanned it," Charlie said. "I know for certain because I came here on a research trip. One of my first jobs after leaving the Royal Signals."

"Oh?" Valerio said. "I didn't know that."

"No reason you would. It's just a geological landmark."

"And written off as an impact crater. Was that your doing, Mrs. Locke?"

Charlie took the use of *"Mrs."* as an implicit threat. A reminder she had more to risk than her life. "I was an unpaid intern researching the ground penetrating radar tech. I've since improved it. Shame you kidnapped us and forced us here under the threat of death. Otherwise, I might've pulled together a couple of passes before diving on in."

"I like diving on in."

"Yeah, so I've seen. Patience wouldn't be one of your strong points, would it?"

She glanced over at Horse in a seat angled at 45-degrees; stitched up, pumped full of painkillers, despite his dulled nerve receptors. He'd been released into Valerio's care, the billionaire asshole stating he didn't want the big fella to miss out on anything, but Jules said it was more likely he craved someone nearby who wouldn't think twice about sacrificing themselves to save him.

"Hey, are we there yet?" Jules stirred from what might have been heavy meditation. It was almost certainly not sleep.

Valerio skipped around to the other side of the table. "Jules, nice of you to join us." Behind the chair, he put both hands on Jules's shoulders and spun him to the window. "Easy to see why Prihya thinks this is the place. I can't wait to touch down."

"Then what?" Jules asked, watching the bullseye of igneous rock pass by beneath them.

"Then, we greet the Carsons' industrial machine with open arms and start digging."

GULFSTREAM JET - AIRBORNE

As they approached the destination, Prihya relaxed, possibly because of the time, sleep, or fatigue. She didn't feel like a victim.

Emory continued to imbue the cabin with the atmosphere of a cafe or bar rather than a race to the center of a lost empire. The Church's Ecuadorian government contacts confirmed Valerio's escape, but Jules, Bridget, and Charlie's status was unknown. Before Prihya slept, Emory switched from alcohol to water and now drank Italian-style short, strong coffee, its smooth roast filling the cabin. She also accepted one, which boosted her.

She thought nothing of indulging Emory when he asked, "What is the Eye made of? Why do you favor a place forty miles inland rather than something more coastal?"

"Coasts move," Prihya said. "As for the Eye, they call it a natural phenomenon, a geologic dome a hundred million years old. They said the circles we see were formed by wind, pushing sand and mud over the rocks. But anyone can see how strongly it resembles Atlantis. The rings, the timeline according to Plato, and all the other things people want to ignore."

"Okay, then, ignore my collar for one moment," Emory said. "And allow me to play devil's advocate. What matches a place like the Richat Structure to Plato's account?"

"Fine, I'll play." Again, Prihya's conscious mind chastised her for being so friendly and accommodating, but her instinct to expose lies, show herself to be right, or—more precisely—prove to naysayers she was no crackpot, sent her mouth into overdrive. "The geography of the Eye matches both the descriptions and artists' impressions of Atlantis. Geography *and* geology. There was a ton of upheaval around 11,500 years ago. Ancient maps show rivers in the middle of the Sahara, and the capital of Atlantis was made of concentric circles. Two of water, three of land, with the Temple of Apollo in the middle. That *matches* the Richat, the Eye, almost precisely."

"And the Pillars of Heracles? You did not think these could be the Straits of Gibraltar?"

"For a while, yes, of course. But look at the Eye's landscape. Two mountains to the north could be interpreted over time as mighty pillars. From the air, it's easy to see the sweeps of white waves over the land. Classic tsunami aftermath. The white blemishes on the landscape are *salt*. Where else would this come from but the sea? And the only way for the ocean to flow that far inland is from the world-wide cataclysm of, say, a comet striking."

"This is not the only place with such evidence, surely?"

Prihya thrived on conversations like these. They energized her, regardless of her sparring partner. "The Eye is surrounded by a large plain. It comprises black, red, and white stones. Elephants are plentiful in Plato's accounts, which aren't exactly common in Europe. An abundance of exotic fruit and vegetables, which you only get in this region with some serious tech to make the soil fertile. Only cultures that know how to tap deep wells had such growth, even a few thousand years ago... Ubar, Tashish, Babylon, the Jews Moses lived with in the desert for forty years. The Sahara may have been lush forest until around thirteen thousand years ago... same timeline as we're looking at... lots of iron, copper and gold. Mauritania is now a big exporter of all three."

Emory had cracked a smile and it showed no sign of healing over. He was enjoying this as much as Prihya. "Tell me more."

"Okay, sure." Prihya took a moment to savor the deep flavor of the coffee and reminded herself to keep drinking before it went cold. "You've heard of Atlas?"

"The titan of Greek myth?"

"Yes. A name Plato would have been familiar with. But Atlas is also the first king of Mauritania. And Atlantis is sometimes translated as 'the island of Atlas.' And we have the Atlas Mountains north of the country."

"Which incorporates the Pillars, you think."

"Herodotus was an independent cartographer, not a student of Plato and nor does he appear to have any sort of link. His most famous map shows Atlanteans on the North West of Africa, and also the region in the Eastern Mediterranean, around Assyria."

"Assyria? You mean modern Syria? The Middle East?"

"Or the 'cradle of civilization,' yes. Herodotus's circle, with Athens at its center, covered most of Europe, Africa above the equator and the Middle East."

Emory's smile grew wider. "And what of the physical studies that appear to debunk the idea of Richat being anything but a geological anomaly?"

Prihya didn't even need a sip-pause to compose an answer. "A classified study of geo-magnetic forces around the structure shows they are much stronger than usual. The Witnesses—your Forefathers—are known to utilize magnetism. And consider how much they link different sites via quantum entanglement. LiDar scans of the Eye even found a rectangular shape at its heart. This matches the description of the temple of Apollo."

"Although, obviously, Apollo is a Greek myth, not something the Forefathers would have named."

Prihya shrugged in the affirmative as she drank.

Emory said, "Isn't it too far above sea level? twelve hundred feet?"

"But there's so much evidence of flooding, of moving water. You can see with your own eyes the same patterns as Dry Falls National Park in Washington State... all accepted as part of the flooding at the end of the Younger Dryas. Easily risen through volcanic activity. The Atlas Mountains are active geologically, and the Eye is accepted as part of a recently active area too." Prihya had memorized little of Plato's exact text, but she knew this part. "'For which reason the sea in those parts is impassable and impenetrable, because there is a shoal of mud in the way; and the subsidence of the island caused this.' The new plains are those between sea and Eye... so when he calls Atlantis an island, it might not have been literal, not as we understand it. But, the concentric circles, the measurements, the size, the description, the geography... it all matches."

"And lo and behold, the Richat Structure is your conclusion."

Prihya finished her coffee. "Amen."

"I wonder," Emory said, "how our friend will arrive."

"You're going to cut him off?"

"Cut him off?" Emory chuckled. "I think I can be a little more creative than that."

MAURITANIA - RICHAT MISSION BASE CAMP

Jules saw Valerio's staging area for a helicopter transport to Atlantis as a prelude to war. Helicopters, soldiers, supplies, weapons, and—appropriately—the LORI contingent and Valerio in eye of the storm. An unfeasibly massive drill, two industrial-sized excavators, and numerous vehicles with exploratory permits were waiting on this private, desert-surrounded airstrip.

With Horse back on his feet, shakily pretending he was fine, the five of them watched the operation from a marquee surrounded by chicken wire and translucent polythene that shielded them from the dust but not the roar of engines and gears. To check progress, Bridget had to flip the polythene aside, which felt like probing a scab that wasn't ready to fall off.

"Mommy and Daddy came through," Valerio told Bridget. "They really do have impressive influence over corrupt officials and zoning."

Bridget said nothing at first, instead gaping in wonder at the sheer size of the operation her father had pulled together. That the Carsons had interests in most countries with rare earth metals wasn't surprising, but the speed with which they attained the necessary permissions was what had clearly thrown her. "I didn't realize they could bypass so many regulations so fast. What must they do to—"

"Just be glad they can," Charlie replied. "Otherwise those so-called inspectors Emory has on their way—AKA the Korean mercs—would have a clear shot at it."

Jules could tell Bridget was upset, maybe more. It was as if a curtain had been pulled aside and the scale of her parents' influence had shocked her. There was little to do. No choice.

Valerio had cornered them, and Emory—leading a church of fanatics—could be worse than Valerio. Jules would have involved Colin Waterstone, whose position as curator for the House of Windsor somehow granted him unfettered support from Interpol, but he found no chink in Valerio's invisible fence and almost no chance Toby Smith would consider Colin an ally.

"We have to head out there," Jules said. "But you don't."

"What's that?" Valerio said.

"Bridget ain't needed. She's dead weight on that helicopter. Leave her here. Bring her in if her skills are needed."

"Like hell," Bridget said. "I'm not gonna let something like my parents supplying..." She struggled for the words, so waved her hand around... "all this... keep me from seeing it with my own eyes."

"There might still be nothin' to see," Jules said. "Even if this *is* the place, there's a chance it's a dead mess of old bricks and mud."

"I don't care. I'm coming."

"No. Final answer."

"Jules, listen to me." She stood before him and pressed both hands onto his chest, bringing her mouth closer to his face so he could feel her breath on his skin. "You trust me to come, or forget any hint we were ever gonna be more than friends. Take this away from me and we won't even be that."

Jules controlled the turmoil in his gut by not pleading with her. He wanted her to be safe because he was afraid of taking her into a siege battle and wanted to do the right thing. He should never have allowed her to jump into the rainforest with him; she'd almost died.

Not this time. Not when the danger had ratcheted up so high.

When Bridget's eyes teared up and she pulled away, he felt something he'd only ever heard of before: his heart literally ached.

Valerio smirked and mimed cracking a whip. "You gonna let your lady dictate terms to you?"

Aside from his fear that Bridget was not exaggerating losing her as a friend, Jules had no ego in these matters, no interest in gender roles or taunting from the likes of Valerio. "Bridge, this is *not* your fight. If Valerio takes you, I ain't going, and he can shoot me in the head if he don't agree. Look around you. You think your folks're doin' this because of some *maybe* archaeological discovery? Nah. They're doin' it for you. And I'm doin' this for you." He faced Valerio. "She stays."

Valerio remained a statue, unmoving, for several seconds. Perhaps he calculated the benefit of calling Jules's bluff and the inconvenience of further delay. Eventually, he inclined his head toward Bridget.

"I'm sorry, your man here is correct." He spread his arms, indicating the activity all around. "You've served your purpose."

The same foreman who'd greeted them crunched the polythene tarp back and poked his dust-crusted face inside, lifting his goggles and pulling down his scarf. "Your transport is ready."

CHAPTER FORTY-ONE

THE RICHAT STRUCTURE - STAGING AREA

It was a dry, rugged place with sand, salted dirt, and—surprisingly—wildflowers and beetles. Military trucks carrying people and supplies climbed the hills from the plain. The local mission leaders trained the Striovians to operate the heavy lifting platforms, transport equipment across the fragile protected zone, and build scaffolding to prepare for drills that arrived by the same helicopters the Chinese used to move tanks and heavy trucks into remote locations.

Jules watched from the grounded helo in which they'd flown here, leaving Bridget behind, and which now served as mission control.

The Striovians secretly deployed a field hospital and several mobile units around Father Emory's ragtag Korean contingent's potential ingress routes, as if a proxy war between two nations were about to unfold. Jules informed Roger Carson via sat phone, keyed in to Valerio's headset, and received a bemused grunt and enough patient guidance to calm him.

"You've heard rumors about our mining operation?" Carson asked him. "We're not planning on leaving anything behind—least of all, whatever might exist underground. So there's no need to worry about logistics. It's necessary to cover your butts."

Jules shrugged uncomfortably. The mining equipment, the speed of the setup, regardless of the Carsons' company being in the region already, was stunning. And frightening. Valerio was virtually their partner at this stage.

"And, Jules," Roger Carson said.

"Yeah."

"Thank you for protecting Bridget. I know she can be stubborn, but it was the right decision."

They signed off, leaving the combination of Valerio's Striovian forces and the private security from the Carsons' copper operation to set up the gear.

"Jules?"

It was Bridget, who had remained on comms back in Valerio's private jet. It was another link in the chain, a job for her to perform, where she had objected at first, but Charlie convinced her it was important.

"I got the satellite feeds here," Bridget said. "The Striovians are setting a perimeter. My parents' men are all over the place. Some inside the Eye's border."

"That's right," Jules said, feeling Valerio's gaze on him. He glanced around to find the man studying him, as if daring Jules to go against him. "Charlie's supervising the excavation prep. Valerio's got enough firepower to keep any land-based attack away long enough for us to know if there's anything here."

"Jules..." She hesitated, a catch in her voice before letting the line die. It was only temporary, though. "Please remember, these are not like Theta Team. Rayyana, she..."

Again, her voice hitched, and Jules swallowed the same emotion; the woman had died so they could be here, now, on the edge of the Sahara.

Bridget returned to speak. "They are thugs and mercenaries. Taken from militia that might otherwise be working for terrorists. As soon as someone comes in with a better offer, they'll be gone."

"I guessed," Jules said. "Where are the Mauritanians in all this?"

Bridget paused again, showing perhaps further concern about her parents' shady business dealings.

Valerio made no secret of listening in, and when the radio silence lasted too long, he answered for her, as if it were obvious. "It's a poverty-stricken country. If Father Emory hasn't paid off the officials, law enforcement, and the like, the Carsons have. They want what's here."

"And what is here?" Jules asked. "What do you think is here? What's so important? Because it ain't curiosity about a lost city. And I don't think it's more orbs providing power for some quantum machine."

Valerio had no answer, but concealed his lack of knowledge with lame humor. "Let's not worry about the details. Let's just find out."

Through late morning and into a broiling afternoon, Jules observed the operation, absorbing every aspect and processing every scenario he could discern from the facts at hand. It made for miserable insight.

First, with the Carsons' vast resources and whatever tactics they employed to grease the wheels for what the permits documented as "non-invasive scientific exploration" of the Richat Structure, Valerio's group had beaten the Church of the Forefathers by several hours.

Second, though, was that it was *only* a few hours. Plainly, Emory—and whoever held sway over them from the shadows—possessed enough clout to keep the wheels turning, granting them access to the country, and allowing a sizeable movement of people and resources to compete with Valerio.

The third aspect that overrode almost everything else was the unbelievable skill and professionalism of the militia and workers that Roger Carson had sent with the equipment. He must have transported an entire mining company, along with the engineers and private security, to operate and defend it.

"Happy?" Valerio asked, returning from a recce with Horse, who waited outside the helo's bay.

"Not really, no," Jules replied.

"What's the problem?"

"Just a real psychopathic worry."

"Ooh, you're coming over to my side of the fence?"

"No. Difference is, I know it's wrong to feel like this."

"Aww, come on. Tell your Uncle Valerio. I won't laugh, I promise."

Jules curled his fingers around the chair's arm and leaned back. "Leaving Bridget behind might've been a mistake."

"You think so, too?" Valerio gestured with one hand. A nerve twitched under one eye. He didn't seem aware of it. "Intriguing. What's your reasoning?"

"With her tucked outta the way, the Carson Corporation's men might not be as careful where they point their guns. And Roger might try to extract Bridget before our agreement's done."

A nod from Valerio, slower and calmer than before. "Of course, I considered that. But I have other means of inspiring loyalty."

Jules didn't like where this was going, so he ran a hand over his short hair and said, "Gotta hope we get through the other side without testin' that."

CHATEAU CACHÉ – BRITTANY, FRANCE

Toby distrusted Roger Carson. Their original deal, which allowed Bridget to continue working with LORI and kept the institute in the chateau they had spent years adapting, had started out convivial enough. Toby would have *volunteered* to investigate a site that could rival the Terracotta Warriors in prestige, but they needed the money, so Roger Carson's offer—to cover him legally—was appealing.

After they determined the find was far younger and less interesting than China's most famous historical touchstone besides the Great Wall, Roger began acting less like a benefactor and more like a tycoon protecting his assets from tax authorities and his failings from a boss who would fire him. It strained but didn't break the relationship.

With their assets distributed around the globe, Toby had now stretched those resources further by retreating to the chateau, complete with Charlie's "Demon Server" and all its computational power, a vast library of first-hand literary texts, and links to dozens of online and dark web vaults no civilian should view. It helped that they were back in familiar territory.

The only speck of dirt in the well-oiled parts was Roger Carson himself. To ensure they kept their end of the deal, he accompanied them to France, but hadn't interfered since preparing for whatever

Jules brought out of the desert. He preferred to split his time between Bridget and the military-grade response to a fluid situation. He was no longer the benevolent archaeological enthusiast. His ruthless CEO persona pursuing a bigger deal was grounded. All that remained was a powerful father in danger of losing his daughter, with seemingly unlimited personnel, money, and willpower.

"Roger," Toby said, catching him at the hub of Charlie's operational lounge, which reminded Toby of a high tech CSI room from those US television shows. "Is there anything we need to know yet?"

He'd been watching for hours, the drills and excavators moving into place as if the scene was being streamed by a time-lapse filmmaker. He'd split this on a second screen with the base camp where Bridget was sequestered aboard Valerio's plane, one well-equipped with comms gear, and which Roger had surrounded with a small unit of men drafted in from his mining contingent without informing Bridget.

Or Toby. Until now.

"Nothing," Roger said. "But my men have the direct line here. If they strike anything of interest, I'll be the first to know."

Other feeds came from sketchy body cam footage, in which Toby kept spotting Charlie, dust-coated and looking very much within her element. What she didn't know, she was learning quickly, and was issuing instructions along the way, which was something he was sure Phil Locke back in Greenwich would be happy to see. Roger didn't know the entire episode was being piggybacked and recorded, and Toby saw no need to inform him—unless he attempted something untoward.

"How long until they begin?"

"At least an hour."

"And the incoming threat?"

Roger switched his view wider and flicked to a readout that his commander on the ground was sharing between the chateau and the Striovians. "Ninety minutes, give or take."

"There's going to be a fight."

Roger nodded. "One we aim to win."

THE RICHAT STRUCTURE - STAGING AREA

After three live-fire combat tours—one in Iraq, two in Afghanistan—Charlie was hard to impress. But erecting the kind of drill she had seen boring holes for oil or shale gas in under two hours was special. The men knew the device as well as Charlie did her homemade inventions. The teamwork required to bolt it together over uneven ground was perhaps even more inspiring than the British Army's achievement in bridging a gorge in a day to ship out hundreds of wounded civilians from a village in Helmand Province.

The fact this was teeming all around her, across the face of a World Heritage Site, would draw an avalanche of criticism in the future—and never would have happened in a country where Carsons and Conchins held less sway. It thrilled and nauseated her equally.

At the center of this forty-kilometer-wide plain—or forty klicks in her military brain—she felt as small as an ant. Even the massive industrial project around her was a toy compared to the view. Elevated ridges, dark rims toward the edge and within the concentric circles were, according to Prihya and her cohorts, the remnants of a city buried by a tsunami 13,000 years ago.

But if they found nothing except what the science said was here—igneous rock, salt, bedrock tectonically conveyed from a long-lost body of water—they would unforgivably destroy a remarkable landscape. She wondered how the people of Mauritania would react to a small cabal of government officials—not the government itself, she had learned—accepting bribes to allow two foreign groups to trample and foul on a source of national pride by boring a hole wide enough to drop a London double-decker bus through.

Riots and revolutions had rampaged over lesser crimes.

Charlie would have preferred to spend a couple of hours testing the drill, but intel had reached them that Emory was leading his men to the outer ridge, testing the Striovian-Carson coalition, but not attempting an incursion just yet. But it was coming. It left no time for health and safety concerns, which the foreman—a Senegalese man who emanated a gruff air of complete competence earned over decades of experience—waved off in an almost insulted manner.

"I know my drill," he said. "My men know their machines."

The other machines were secondary excavators, backhoe diggers, and a dozen men with equipment typically found wielded by road crews—only larger and more powerful.

Dull cracks floated on the air, garnished with the occasional crackle, a thump, then more dull cracks. Gunshots, cushioned by the rim surrounding this part of the massive plate of rings.

The bad guys were here.

Or were they already set up, about to desecrate one of the world's modern wonders?

Again annoyed at losing her bone-conducting subvocal comms, Charlie hit the button with her thumb and called Jules through the inferior throat mic. "What's happening?"

"They're twenty klicks out," Jules replied, using the military vernacular. "You gotta go now."

Charlie said, "Roger that," and gave the foreman her nod of approval.

Within five minutes, they broke ground over the Richat Structure.

CHAPTER FORTY-TWO

Even in violent situations, Jules always remained calm. He saw no difference between fistfights, gunfights, and legal challenges like chess and field sports. Analyze the situation, set a goal, and choose one of many options while calculating the odds.

Today was different.

Today, too many variables caused Jules's head to veer from one potential disaster to the next. He became dizzy in the heat of the helicopter's belly and couldn't determine a success rate. It wasn't even fifty-fifty. He didn't know the Striovian mercenaries' defensive capabilities, nor Carson's men's, and could not be certain of the enemy's offensive drive, so he couldn't even set a clock.

He could only compare the time it would take them to cross the twenty klicks from the outermost defenses, should the security personnel fall immediately, and a more leisurely exploration if the Korean fighters failed to advance. It was unacceptable, and the ground beneath them vibrating with the constant drumming of the drill gave Jules a headache.

"We're three hundred feet down," Valerio said excitedly.

Another dumb, incalculable situation. "That's great, but if there's another three hundred to go, we might be havin' guests to deal with before you replace the next drill bit."

"You're such a pessimist. I have Horse up top. He'll spot anything worrying. It's all small arms fire at the minute and we have the advantage of positioning. Don't fret. We'll be fine."

Jules watched the monitor, which split between live images of the drill pulverizing and extracting earth and hard-packed salt and sand, and a sickly green ground penetrating radar feed. As they dug deeper, the darker hues disintegrated, blending with the destruction.

The low noise of the drill had thrummed so constantly through the belly of the helicopter that Jules's ears rang when everything suddenly stopped.

The readout said 139.42 meters: around 450 feet.

"Are we there?" Valerio asked into the radio.

"Hold please," Charlie answered.

"Wow." Valerio sounded breathy, a damsel swooning at a knight's bravery. "That's... almost as tall as the Washington monument."

"Half the height of the Eiffel Tower." Jules's mouth was dry as he fought to keep his eyes locked on the monitor. "It's also one and a half Big Bens. What's your point?"

"That we're well below where any scan could penetrate. Everything here is new to mankind. Hidden for thirteen millennia."

"You're such a drama queen," Jules said.

"Got something," came Charlie's voice.

A new line opened, squelching into the satellite radio channel.

Bridget said, "What is it? I can't see."

The greenish monitor revealed a straight line, the readout figures suggesting a sudden change in texture.

"Silt," Charlie said. "Sand. Packed in, but not like rock."

Jules couldn't help pushing his calculations to the forefront. "If a tsunami swept through a city and the landscape stopped it dragging everything back out to sea... that'd cause this, wouldn't it?"

"Probably. I'm adjusting the settings. Stand by."

Charlie's fingers barely worked. They fiddled with the knobs, which if it had been her own tech would have been voice-activated or touchscreen, and the camera, which was mounted on a section of the drill that kept it safe from debris, lowered into the hole. Although it could be used as a camera, it was more of a lens for seeing into the past, with settings for penetrating hard stone, sand, water, and a variety of substances that often obscured history from view.

All she had to do was tweak it, and it would render the clouds of dust that marred her vision and coated her tongue insignificant.

Slowly, a shape coalesced.

"Oh my God," Charlie said. "Get the sluice in here."

The sluice functioned as a high-pressure water cannon. It had an in and out and was astronomically expensive to use in the desert where there was no ready water supply. One of the trucks that rushed out here was a tanker carrying 100,000 gallons, which was quickly hooked up to the sluice.

Normally, this type of equipment was used to pump water deep underground into shale reserves, dislodging the deposits and bringing them to the surface. It was what caused earthquakes in communities where people like the Carsons had no say in whether the material was extracted.

In this case, however, they took out the drill, inserted a ridiculously long hose, and set it to maximum. Then they lowered a second hose, equipped with its own genny and pump, to extract the gunk and runoff, providing a clearer picture of what they'd uncovered.

The scan revealed they had struck a crafted object. A freestanding unit, such as a pillbox or massive shed, rather than one of those naturally squared-off rocks embedded beneath others. As the water revealed more, Charlie took in the scene and relayed it to the team, despite the fact that they were also watching.

"The building has walls, there are steps, and... are they Greek colonnades?"

"Greece wasn't a country back then," Jules said.

"You know what I mean."

Bridget said, "They could have influenced later designs."

"If it isn't a plant," Charlie cautioned. "Wouldn't be the first hoax or mistake. China is still a pain in the arse for Toby, isn't it?"

They watched some more. The shapes grew sharper on the green screen, murky but somewhat clearer on the true vision camera that used a powerful lamp to highlight what the sluice was excavating.

"This is it," Valerio said. "This is the Temple of Apollo."

Jules said, "Could be a shepherd's hut for all we know."

Valerio was right about one thing: Jules was a pessimist.

"The soft layer is getting blasted away," Charlie said. "It supports the data. A massive cataclysm, sending sea bed and soft matter inland."

"I knew you'd come round to my way of thinking."

"Data isn't thinking, boyo. Don't mistake agreeing with you for making us friends."

Valerio said nothing in response, his silence welcome.

Charlie said, "The Witnesses might have seen the ice age and calculated the end of it, but as we've said before, they couldn't have predicted a meteor strike."

"Making 'em geologists, not astronomers," Jules said.

"Dan's gonna be sad."

Bridget said, "I want to come out there. I want to see."

Charlie had all but forgotten about the fighting in the hills coming their way, but Bridget's plea refocused her. "Not yet."

"Let's kit up," Jules said. "Time to see if this temple is the real deal."

FATHER EMORY'S GULFSTREAM JET

Although the plane had landed, the engines continued to run, filling the chilled, air-conditioned cabin with a strained whine, as if the craft begged to be let loose and shoot back into the sky. Renata was sedated next door, while Moses, Muzaffer, and Hilla had been dispatched to oversee troop movements in order to penetrate the fabled city before Valerio, Jules, and the others could obtain the artifact—or artifacts—that would give the Church of the True Forefathers the power to inspire the world to a better future.

"The Temple of Apollo," Emory mused. "What do you think this is? Really?"

Prihya had engaged with him to survive, then to make her experience more comfortable than if she'd scratched at his eyes and spat in his face, before deluding herself into thinking she was a guest—as if he wouldn't kill her the moment he decided she was no longer useful.

She asked, "Do you think they've found it?"

"Progress reports are not clear. But they stopped drilling and are sending people into the borehole."

"Sounds like they found it."

"My question remains. What do you think it is? This temple?"

Prihya had never fully explored it, but the question had come up before. "Plato only refers to it as a structure at the center of the middle circle. He says bulls roamed freely, as cows do in my country, but elephants and other exotic creatures were not uncommon. The temple? I'd only be guessing."

"Your guesses brought me to your door. They took you to the Lost Origins Recovery Institute. *They* took you to the key that landed you in Malta, and the cipher we needed to bring us, eventually, here. So, indulge me, Prihya. What do you suppose the Temple of Apollo is?"

"I think Plato called it a temple. Not the Wit— not the Forefathers."

Emory nodded along, as if he knew the answer and was testing Prihya.

"Could be anything," Prihya said. "A place to worship gods we haven't seen yet?"

"How many deities have you found mentioned by the Forefathers? How many idols can you theorize they prayed to?"

"Zero."

"They were either atheists or agnostics who wondered about the afterlife, about the origins of life, but did not invent scripture the way most ancient religions did. Unlike ourselves, who have documented proof of our deity, they built, they taught, they faced what they could hold in their hands, not in their imaginations."

"So it was like a corporate headquarters, then?"

Emory smiled. "Or a place of education. Somewhere to show their technological advances...?"

"The orbs we've found previously?"

"Or something similar. A weapon, perhaps, to prove their mightiness?" Emory posed like a bodybuilder for a second before lowering his arms. "We think of them as intelligent, correct?"

"Yes."

"And we equate intelligence with benevolence, do we not? Peaceful people."

"Right."

"But what of Plato's other details? That Atlantis fought against what they called Athens in his day? That the people of that continent fought back."

"How? Against the Forefathers' superior intelligence and—if you're right—the weapons they had?"

"That's the real question, isn't it? How did a primitive people repel the would-be saviors of their race, if those saviors weren't quite as altruistic as we assume? What if they were educating these early humans at the barrel of a gun? What if the humans didn't want what the Forefathers were offering?"

Emory dipped his chin, so his eyes turned up to keep Prihya in sight.

"What if the earliest explorers from South America came to Europe, not as an advance scouting expedition, but as exiles? As people who opposed their grand plan to expand?"

"Then the Temple of Apollo might be..." Prihya's gut tightened, causing a frown to crinkle as she pondered what Emory was getting at. "It might be a war room. Somewhere they stored or showed off their weapons."

"And if a tidal wave surprised them? Rushed over them at a hundred miles per hour?"

"They would never have hidden their weapons. They'll still be there, one way or another."

Emory sat back, crossed his legs, and steepled his fingers. "Now do you see why the temple is important?"

Prihya looked at him closely. "You already have something else up your sleeve, don't you? Another surprise for Valerio and the institute?"

He grinned. "Yes. Definitely."

CHAPTER FORTY-THREE

THEY ABSEILED down the angled borehole, the ground-out rock still warm from friction, only cool enough to touch because of the water pumped through earlier. Out of the sun's glare, it was at first hot and humid, then dried and cooled the deeper they climbed. Charlie went first, Valerio in the middle, with Jules bringing up the rear. Horse manned the topside, corralling the African security personnel and ensuring no one messed with the ropes. The same winch had already lowered a crate into the hole using spare lines.

"To carry up my new toys," Valerio had said, unnecessarily in Jules's opinion, but the man liked to talk. He'd even directed the mining contingent to move the drill a kilometer west to explore another promising section of land. "This whole basin is going to disappear," he'd said. "And we're the ones who get to keep what's here."

Coming down in the crate were portable arc lights, of the type often seen on movie sets, which took a while to set up on tripod mounts, angled for the best view. Then all Jules could do was stand back and bathe in the sight.

Observing the grainy, green-veiled shapes had felt surreal and detached. Being here for the first time and seeing what had been submerged for thirteen thousand years was a sensory overload: The building, which was still partially buried, resembled an acropolis but with harsher lines; the colonnades seen on the monitors now stood four stories high, holding aloft a slab of cracked and discolored roof; and the stairs were the pinnacle of a rising sweep of long blocks, most of which were hidden beneath the spongy mud and ancient deposits they now walked on.

Walked?

Staggered. Floated. Skipped.

Jules compared it to walking on the moon, but without the low-gravity bouncing.

Blasted silt and sand had stained the stonework reddish-brown over millennia and the structure was angled at between 20 and 26 degrees, not 45 degrees like a diagonally felled structure. The salty, damp haze of the excavation made Jules's face clammy.

As they neared, the symbols became clearer, faded slightly but still visible in relief across the top slab that served as the roof, while a pair of stone doors, similar to those found in aircraft hangars, towered in the square-cut brickwork. Drifts of dirt remained in places, but the industrial pumps had cleared the floor for the most part.

The solidity jolted as Jules placed one foot on the first of four visible stairs, all tilted and disappearing into the ground to his right. It felt strange, like stepping off a boat and onto dry land for the first time in several hours. The firmness jolted him into a new reality, where the awe faded and his brain settled into numb acceptance.

But he didn't want that.

He didn't want to think of it as a task or a calculation. He wanted to feel it like Valerio and Charlie did, with their mouths open and eyes fixed. They were astounded, as Jules had been, and as Bridget would have been if she had been present. He felt bad for her. Guilty for abandoning her, even though it was for her safety. Compelled to document everything and calculate his chances of success—

No.

Jules ascended the stairs. He cast his mind to the golden books, the multiple versions of imperfect plans for the city the Witnesses planned to build. As he lifted and planted one foot after the other, he realized he was at the center. One of many circles, now buried but once separated by water-filled canals, where people must have gathered, where the Witnesses dwelled, taught, and—

"Oh, my," Valerio said.

Despite the water blast residue, the temple floor was visible from the top step.

Most of the runoff had drained into the muck that covered the rest of the presumed city, implying that there were more pockets of space below for it to drain into. It left behind a mosaic, similar to that of many Roman villas, except that the tiny squares were glass or a glasslike material. However, it was still a mosaic. A violent artwork. *War*. Bulls—or bull-like creatures—rampaging through an army, guided by riders wielding swords, spears, glowing whips, tridents, accompanied by an elephant-mounted catapult, and more. Too many to see without developing the ability to fly.

Valerio must have been thinking the same thing. "I'll send a drone down for a clearer picture. Let's get that door open. I hope you brought your jewelry."

Jules had secured both bangles on his wrists before descending, although as he passed through colonnades under the roof's lip, a chill swept through him. A psychological trick, perhaps, as he crossed into shadow. But it was artificial light casting the shadow, not the sun. No reason for the temperature to drop.

No, this was something else.

Jules said, "The doors aren't locked."

Charlie progressed along the same line as Jules, hesitating in what Jules saw as a shiver, then joined him at the door. "You're right."

It was cracked and buckled, more like the way metal would, yet it was definitely some form of stone. Jules moved his head to take it in from different angles and found an undulating seam of green. Shifting further, the hue turned red.

Jules removed a glove and brushed the cold, wet surface. It was rough but not sharp, and flat except for the bent corner. A vibration hummed beneath his palm. The red and green seams closest to him then lit up, spreading and branching out, ink spreading through veins.

"This is like the door in India, where I had to plant the bangles in the hole and form a circuit. No need here."

"The tech is more advanced," Valerio said as he came level with them.

"That tomb was thirty thousand years old, so yeah. Imagine where we'll be in another fifteen thousand years."

Charlie shifted closer, so she was almost kissing the surface. "That door, and your bangles, they repel seawater, don't they?"

"Right."

"So, this didn't work, did it?"

Jules fanned his fingers, as if making a deeper connection might imbue him with some psychic vision. It didn't. He just got warmer, more aligned with the substance, the structure. It might have been a placebo effect, but he also gained a sense of closeness to the people who built it.

And why wouldn't he?

All evidence pointed to his genetic line meeting here. His mother, at least one grandparent, a great-grandparent... thousands of generations of unbroken heritage flowing through his fingers.

"How could this be here all this time? How could I not know? How could they hide it from me?"

"Jules," Charlie said, "no one hid anything. There are millions of tons of rock above us. Even the most advanced LiDar would never have—"

"*You* were here." Jules twisted his head toward Charlie. "You knew."

"Jules, are you okay?"

"I'm a long way from okay. My mom protected these bangles, knew there was somethin' different about us, but she died before she knew it all. If this was exposed when you were exploring the scans, the man-made lines, the—"

Charlie leaned closer to him. "This isn't a cover up. Modern scans *today* couldn't penetrate this deeply. Ten years ago, it couldn't see under the first six feet of soft soil, never mind the rock up top. Some fuzzy shadows aren't *evidence*."

"You should probably let go now," Valerio said.

To Jules, the idea of relinquishing his hold was ludicrous. "No."

"Seriously." Valerio backed off, unusually cautious. "Charlie, if you could be so good as to remove him from the big glowing door...?"

Charlie stepped back, scanned up and down, then Jules turned that way. The rock was glowing more brightly than before, ramping up the energy, like a nuclear reactor about to melt down. The floor hummed, too, the wet patches rippling.

Jules couldn't stop, though. The urge—no, the *need*—to see it through was too much. Like his life depended on hanging in, remaining here, at his post.

Although, that wasn't right, either.

It was like *all* their lives depended on it. All the lives in this city, needing him to spread the energy wave out, through the floor, through—

A mighty *thump* in his ribs tore Jules away, Charlie's shoulder planted in his torso as she barged into him. She wrapped her arms around his legs, lifting him and landing on him in a heap. The wind blew out of him, and his head swam.

The Welshwoman had apparently joined a rugby club since they last worked together.

She rolled off, got to one knee, but kept one hand pressed on Jules's chest. "You okay there?"

"The people," Jules managed to say. "They all died. They all died because I acted too late. I could have saved them."

CHAPTER
FORTY-FOUR

Jules quickly recovered, but Charlie insisted on a time-out while they drank water, although he suspected she wanted to see if he was faking his mental realignment. They agreed that Jules had tapped into some connection with the last person to activate these rocks, and that the energy had to spread underground, through passages or arteries to the outer walls. Basic quantum entanglement suggested that all points in the universe were linked, and some speculated that time could also be accessed. Just not in the TARDIS or DeLorean sense. But Jules had perceived it, the terror of a wall of water rushing toward them, and their helplessness in the face of certain death.

"And Atlantis fell," Valerio said.

"Let's go." Jules pushed to his feet, put his gloves on, and returned to the door. "Someone bring a light, eh?"

Because one corner of the door was so buckled, Jules and Charlie simply inserted their hands and pulled. What had been sealed through magnetism in previous structures was aided in its opening by the same power. The door swung open smoothly after an initial burst of force, revealing a dark chamber ahead of them, a wedge of light revealing only the base of another staircase.

"Looks like the seawater didn't get inside here," Charlie said. "Or drained away and dried up long ago."

Jules advanced, aiming his flashlight at the base of another staircase. "Buried the rest of the city. But I guess this part was saved."

Valerio, hustling like a proper worker, delivered one of the powerful lamps sent down ahead of them, and the illumination displayed the entire chamber. "Oh, my. This is turning into a very good day."

It was about the size of a typical European church, with a deceptive entryway due to the submerged structure. The stairs rose at least one story, topped by a block under a stone marquee-style construction, and surrounded by a sweeping bank lined with blocks that reminded Jules of stadium seating.

Jules imagined a ceremony or presentation in the center, attended by civilians or an audience of peers. This could have been their Congress or Parliament. Maybe they practiced a form of direct democracy, or debated, or put on plays, or—

Charlie froze. "What's that?"

Jules glanced all around, listened. Then he sensed what she did. "That's not me. I'm wearing gloves. Boots." He looked to Valerio. "You touch something?"

"Jules, Jules, Jules." Valerio joined him on the bottom step. "The gifts bestowed to me in the First Priest's Tomb are far weaker than your natural makeup. I can just about open their scroll boxes and make their artifacts glow. You don't really think I can cause an earthquake do you? Even one as puny as this?"

"It's the second drill," Charlie said. "They've broken through into another chamber. That's why it's echoing."

"Bingo." Valerio fired her a grin. "Looking at the plans Jules so artistically reproduced, we think there is an item of significance elsewhere."

"Why?" Jules asked.

"There was a glowy thing."

"Glowy thing?" Charlie said. "I'm glad we're keeping it sciency."

Jules had been in something of a neutral trance when he sketched the maps and symbols. That was how his memory worked—a compartmentalized mental library from which he selected relevant information in near-perfect detail. He recalled it now.

"The 'glowy thing' I drew was like an asterisk. A kinda basic star."

"Okay, enough chat." Valerio clapped his hands once. "Let's go see what that altar does."

Shirwac Gasal was kidnapped by men whose faces he could not remember at a young age, too young to remember his parents, what happened to them, or even where to search for his lineage. The 1980s Isaaq genocide in Somalia killed two hundred thousand people, an abomination of a war in which Shirwac killed his first man at eight years of age, or so he was told. He didn't remember much about it, and spent his teens in Rwanda amid the blood diamond trade. Despite gunfire and blood, he remembered little of that violence either. Shirwac demonstrated a calmness and proficiency that made war seem as mundane or everyday as baking, and was traded between armed groups like a footballer, never understanding the conflicts he fought and never resenting the occasional wound from an enemy whose name he never learned.

When the Americans came—during which war he had no clue—he was plucked out of that life, taught English, and found he could serve a new master without a gun. He was a go-between, a strategy advisor for incursions into enemy territory where religious zeal fueled an inexplicable bloodlust, and he trained volunteers to fight the enemies of freedom in his county. After the Americans achieved whatever goal brought them to his land, he rarely needed to fight, despite holding a prominent position in Somalia's war against pirates, smuggling, and terrorist groups.

After becoming a father at forty-five, he sought private work. Safer employment. The Carson Corporation was hiring, and his skills matched the vacancy: site security manager.

His experience protecting mines, cargo, people, and fighting in inhospitable climates prepared him to travel across African nations where the Carsons had a license to explore for minerals or oil. He missed his wife and three children, but his money kept them safe and his benefits would make them very wealthy if he died in the line of duty.

His only fear was that he would miss out on seeing Mia, Ducalle, and Aamino succeed in the new world without his experience and advice to guide them. He had seen so much, watched the world burn and grow, and seen the black hearts of men heal or die. Few men were sufficiently equipped to pass on his knowledge.

He was unsure how he ended up at the base of a three-hundred-foot borehole, viewing something he had never imagined. But here he was, under instruction from his boss's boss's boss, assured morally and financially that this was a wise assignment, and he was glad.

After the drill hit an air pocket, he'd turned off the machine and his men cooled the hole, then he descended on a winch like his subcontracted boss had used to enter the first opening.

This job, switched from a promising copper seam in northern Mauritania, was increasingly uncomfortable. The boss was a jerk, and his assistant was an almost-mute weirdo who looked at Shirwac like a dumb native from a Tarzan movie. Now they were desecrating a global protection site. However, Roger Carson, whom Shirwac had met and shaken his hand, gave the orders, and expected efficiency above all else.

For the first time since he had no choice in whom he served, Shirwac did not fully understand his assignment. He just followed his orders. After discovering the impossible, incredible room in the air pocket, he placed the call he had not expected to make.

Winched out, distancing himself from his shocked men, Shirwac called Roger Carson directly, using a satellite phone he wasn't allowed to show the temporary boss. As per the briefing, the line picked up with two clicks: one for Mr. Carson and one for his daughter, Bridget —*Miss* Carson.

"Captain," Mr. Carson said, although the title was honorary not military. "You have news for me?"

Having spoken English more often in the past thirty years than the two dialects of his youth, Shirwac was fluent, but he had to concentrate to settle his mind. "It is as you said, sir. Signs of intelligent design. People built what is there."

"And what is there?"

"It is like... a cradle, I think. With a ball in the middle."

"A ball?"

Miss Carson broke into the conversation, although Shirwac had been told she was only to listen in. "What color was it?"

"Color?"

"Bridget," Mr. Carson said. "You are here as a courtesy only."

"Dad, I have experience with these things," Bridget answered. "Let me hear it."

Mr. Carson went silent for a beat, then said, "Okay, Captain. What color was this ball?"

"It was black," Shirwac said. "Smooth. And even though everything else was crusted with dirt, this thing, this ball, was dark and clear. It was impossible."

"Was it hovering?" Miss Carson asked.

"No. It just lay there in the middle of a room made of metal."

"Metal." Miss Carson sounded like she had more to say but was reluctant. "Did you touch it?"

"No, ma'am."

"Captain," Mr. Carson said. "I want you to secure this item, the cradle too if you can—"

"No!" his daughter cried. "Don't *touch* it. That would be—"

A scratch sounded, like a needle pulled too quickly from a vinyl record, and Miss Carson fell silent.

Mr. Carson offered no explanation. "Captain, I want you to secure the item, this *ball*, and the cradle too if you can manage to dislodge it without endangering your men. You have to do so quickly. I do not want your men out there, defending the perimeter longer than necessary."

"Thank you, sir. May I ask one thing?"

"Of course."

"What was your daughter saying, please? She seemed like she had objections about—"

"Bridget always resists me breaking new ground. If even half what I've heard about these orbs is true, this could make anything China has to offer obsolete. Bring it up, Captain. As quickly as humanly possible."

CHAPTER FORTY-FIVE

Jules hadn't considered the block an altar, but it was possible. Religious ceremonies, sacrifices, weddings—all possible audience-facing events. Although, it didn't necessarily have to be for humans. It could have been a market.

They climbed steep stairs with high blocks, possibly designed for taller people. After thirty steps, they reached the summit, gloomy despite the powerful lamp, and arranged themselves around the block to spread their flashlights. The floor was colored mosaic glass, but the distribution bore no resemblance to anything real, just a pattern of solid colors, radiating out from the center.

From the sarcophagus.

"Who do you suppose this is?" Valerio said.

The man-shaped lid was seven feet long, the bald, robed carving preserved almost perfectly in smooth, white stone. He had five toes, uniform in size, but one was angled out like a semi-opposable thumb. His folded hands held a three-headed spear, not quite the trident depicted in Greek artwork of Poseidon or even DC's Aquaman character, but close. It lacked only the barbed ends.

"Atlas?" Valerio suggested in answer to his own question.

"Why Atlas?" Charlie asked.

"The king of Atlantis."

"This wasn't called Atlantis by the Witnesses," Jules said. "We have no modern reference. Could be a leader, a respected dude, a founder—"

"Let's check out his bones." Valerio put both gloved hands on the lid's edge and pushed. Nothing happened, except his feet scrabbled for purchase.

"Bones'll be long gone," Jules said.

Valerio's legs pistoned, his feet slipping. "Then whatever is in there. Gold, adornments, the weapon itself."

"You think this trident represents the weapon?" Charlie asked. "The thing you've been looking for?"

Valerio grunted, out of breath, and laid his face on the man's shoulder. "I don't know. I just know it is an item of great power that makes men bow before whoever wields it. I don't want religious fanatics getting access. Do you?"

"I don't see a gap here," Jules said, having checked around the whole sarcophagus. There was no seam, no break. "This ain't a lid. This is a complete piece. Unbroken."

"Okay, that makes me feel much better in terms of my manliness. Or lack thereof. I'll just lie here a little longer." Valerio squirmed, as if snuggling in tightly to the man for comfort.

Charlie ducked down and assessed the block, nodding to say she agreed with Jules.

Jules said, "Wait."

Valerio peeled his cheek from the stone man's shoulder. "What?"

"Go back, go back."

Charlie popped her head up. "Yes, Jules, what?"

"Keep the flashlight there." Jules lowered his own so it aimed at the floor, returning the horizontal statue to the dusk-like gloom as before. "Valerio, take your face off the guy."

Valerio did so.

Jules took off his gloves. "Get ready with that tackle again, Charlie. Only, less ribs this time."

Charlie frowned but kept watching.

Jules placed his hands on the statue. The trident in the man's hands lit up. Green flecks glowed, brightening the pyramidal structure's peak. "When Valerio had his face on it—skin-to-stone—I thought there was something there. A weak glow. Now I see it."

He reached for the trident itself.

Valerio slapped his hand away. "That's *mine*." He lunged and grabbed what had looked like a section of the artwork.

He jerked, grunted, and tightened his grip. The wan light remained, visible because the flashlights were averted, and a tendril of green electricity crackled around his hand.

Valerio strained but couldn't let go. "Err, help?"

Jules clapped a hand on his elbow, drawing him backwards, but in his haste he hadn't replaced his glove.

The lightning crackled, snaking in zigzags up Valerio's arm, encasing Jules, bonding him to Valerio. The static tingled, then prickled, then stabbed like needles. Both men cried out, and a thousand images coursed through Jules.

The film ran so fast he could make no sense of it. The pictures, like old colorized movies, zipped along in no order, someone else's dream remixed and mashed into a confusing pot of stories.

And someone was pulling him upward. If he let go of Valerio he'd fly up into the cavernous roof, unsure how to get down.

He dropped, fell back, landing in an undignified tangle of limbs. All three of them scrambled to disengage, Jules landing on his knees, searching for the flashlight. He was breathing hard, exhausted, as if the wind had been punched out of him.

"What *was* that?" Charlie said.

"Give me one minute and I'll tell ya." Jules wrote off the flashlight, stood, and found the trident had been dislodged from its mount but still lay on the block. "This is either gonna be amazing or the dumbest thing ever."

And Jules, without a barrier between him and the trident, snatched it up and pulled it out. The artifact glowed strongly, but the lightning—which he correctly assumed reacted to Valerio's hybrid genetics—burst painlessly up his arm. All around, the glow spread, and Jules held the trident over his head as if he was a warrior triumphing over a worthy foe.

The roof lit up. Symbols and pictographs, painted in green light, red light, some white like a florescent tube. They didn't change, didn't morph, didn't dance, but he knew what they meant. His connection to the past, bridged through whatever branch of physics covered a metal-infused spear and its previous incarnation, translated the symbols inside his brain.

And he was terrified.

"Oh, no..."

Charlie said, "What is it? What does this mean?"

"We're so stupid. It's obvious now."

"What?" Valerio shouted, cradling his injured forearm.

Jules gazed at the trident, holding it before him as if he wasn't sure it was real... as if all he'd thought was now in flux, and he could barely trust his own mind.

"This isn't Atlantis," he said. "We gotta leave. And *fast*!"

Shirwac was halfway back down the hole with three of his most trusted men at staggered distances when the call was patched through to his radio earpiece. He was surprised it reached this far down.

"This is Bridget Carson. Am I speaking with Captain Shirwac?"

It was Captain Gasal, but Shirwac did not feel it necessary to correct her. "Yes, ma'am. But I should not speak with you."

"I know. And I swear I have no intention of getting you in trouble, but I have a friend in London who managed to patch me through. You have to hear this."

"I must follow your father's orders."

"Orders that might get you killed? He doesn't know what he's asking."

Shirwac's feet were planted on the tilted ground, a faint echo tinny as it bounced from one slanted metal wall to another. "You understand this?"

She was breaking up, but he could hear her. "We've studied these artifacts firsthand, and we barely understand them. Just know if you set it off, it can release an unknown quantity of energy."

"An explosion?"

Shirwac moved aside for the three men following him with excavating and lifting equipment as they descended slowly.

"Not an explosion," Miss Carson said. "Not like you're used to. When the wrong people touch it, there's—"

"Bridget, get off the phone," Mr. Carson said, crashing into the open line.

"Dad... you might end up screwing this whole thing—"

But she was gone.

"Captain, back to work," Mr. Carson said. "And if my daughter reestablishes contact, you ignore her. Am I clear?"

"Perfectly, sir."

But Shirwac now moved slowly. There was a shake in his fingers, an icy line of fear coursing through him, like the first time he was sent to disarm a roadside bomb. He thought of the temporary boss, and his big boss on the phone, and decided which one he trusted more. The one who scattered his men around like pawns whose lot in life was to sacrifice themselves, or the one determined to evacuate everyone as soon as possible?

Not a difficult decision.

As soon as the engineers arrived—two Nigerians and a German—they set to work at a plan they'd formed before returning down here: blow out the stone fittings using micro charges, secure everything in clamps, and take the cradle and the ball it contained up into the sunshine.

"One thing," Shirwac said to the crew.

They faced him, disgruntled about being unable to set to work right away.

"Do not touch the ball with your hands," he warned. "Or that cradle. If it takes longer, so be it. But if experts are frightened of it, I will take no chances. And neither will you."

CHAPTER FORTY-SIX

WHAT JULES HAD HOPED WOULD BE a quick and easy scramble to the surface was anything but. He needed to persuade Valerio that they were in the wrong place, despite not knowing *how* he knew. The information was not delivered in the manner of a Ted Talk or a series of words inserted into his head. It wasn't even the path his consciousness had taken to observe the past—only *observe*, not interact—nor was he necessarily reading the runes etched into the domed roof.

They just made sense.

The symbols all around them glowed green from one angle and red from another, and while they did not convey a message left behind for worthy beings to comprehend, their pattern sent Jules's muscles cramping when he refused to run.

It was fear. A threat. A warning.

Jules said, "This isn't where the people leaving the golden library came."

"Then who built this place?" Valerio demanded, swinging his arms wide.

Jules could only swallow as it crashed upon him in waves. He needed to get out, get to safety, get away. A physical pain surged not just through him but *around* him.

"You stay if you want." Jules then pulled on his gloves one at a time, the trident's light dying as he swapped it from bare skin to tough cloth, and ran down the stairs. At the bottom he heard—and felt—a deep *pop*, which he identified as a faraway explosion. "Come on!"

He hadn't needed to worry about Charlie. She trusted him and was right on his heels, out of the open door, across the damp earth, and reached the access point at the same time as Jules. The sunlight shone hot from above which placed it right over the borehole, a stark contrast from the damp cold of what they'd thought was Atlantis. They were still kitting up for the extraction winch when Valerio jogged up beside them.

"What's going on? What is this? Why are you running?"

"We can't be here," Jules said. He unhooked a walkie from the pack they'd brought down and called for evac.

"But there's so much to explore!" Valerio said.

The structure, the ground, the very air around them... all of it trembled. A thick, meaty vibration, sonorous and penetrating.

Jules's harness pinched him tight and pulled him upwards.

Charlie keyed her walkie and was again only a few feet behind him.

Valerio cried out in sheer frustration before clanking and thumping around. Whatever the quake was, it had rattled the guy, slapped some sense into him.

The ride up was fast, swinging Jules into the walls a few times, which he cushioned with his feet, the air getting drier and hotter the higher he got. In less than a minute, his head came out onto a land that looked strikingly different than when he descended, with no men besides the guy operating their winch.

Around them, the land was a cloud of sand and dust, like water evaporating from a lake on a cold morning. He assumed it was because of the vibrations, the pulse, the blasting. Possibly the fighting, too.

"What the hell happened?" he asked Horse as he clambered out of the abseiling gear.

The huge, mute man had returned under Valerio's earlier order. He stared back, then lifted an arm to point at a new setup a hundred and forty meters away. Drill, crew, smoke. Another *pop* and more smoke plumed out of the hole.

Charlie arrived beside him and unhooked herself without unbuckling the harness. "They're blasting?"

"Yep," Jules said. "They want what we've been looking for. Daddy Carson does, anyway."

Jules hefted the trident, looking it over as if for the first time. Dull, with a matt grey finish in the daylight, Jules couldn't give it up. He thought about plunging it into Horse's chest, cutting Valerio's line, and hightailing it out of there. But he didn't kill. And he didn't use phrases like "hightailing" either, although that last point should have been far less significant than the former. It wasn't, though.

Valerio made it into the open, Horse helping him out of the apparatus. The 4x4 that Valerio had driven from their staging area to this central point was still in place, the route taken once a trough of tire tracks now obliterated in the wake of the pulses.

Jules jogged to the vehicle, calling back, "I gotta see what they're doing over there."

"We have time!" Valerio said, as Horse lumbered toward the driver's door.

Jules was about to object, when Horse held up the keys—actual keys, not an RFD fob—and gave a genuine guffaw. They would have to fight if Jules wanted to drive, so he gave it up and jumped in the back, laying the trident flat across his lap. Charlie got in beside him, Valerio in the front with Horse at wheel.

The engine growled to life and took off, bumping and thumping over the untamed ground, while Valerio held the walkie to his ear.

He lowered it, his skin sallow and grey. "They were using small detonations to free an item from its housing."

"And...?" Jules said. "They kept on doin' it?"

"Even after those bigger pulses?" Charlie added.

"No." Valerio twisted in his seat, his expression grave. "They stopped blasting ten minutes ago."

"Then what did we—?" Charlie started, but the answer was obvious.

"A defense mechanism," Jules said. "They set off a defense mechanism."

"Then we ride it out, surely?" Valerio said. "We get what we came for and—"

"It's not *here*." Jules was sick of trying to get through to him. Why could he see it when a guy who boasted about his intellect could not? Hubris? Denial? "Emory played us."

"Played us? What about the fighting? The incursion of troops?"

"It's not an incursion." Even as the 4x4 bounced, juddered, and skidded, Jules was simply too tired to shout or allow his frustration to manifest. His arms were limp, his chest hollow, the fight simply draining out of him. "It was a distraction all along."

FATHER EMORY'S PRIVATE JET, AIRBORNE

Prihya wasn't sure if she felt guilty or thrilled flying over the landmass where she believed Atlantis once stood. She never wanted to hurt LORI or Jules, but her goal from before she met them was to find Atlantis. Or proof of aliens. Or the hidden world hollowed out beneath our own. She even enjoyed her kidnapper's overly familiar gentleness, a priest who had just gone to the back of the cabin to take a call.

He now returned and settled before her.

"Good news?" she asked.

"I told you I had a surprise for them. Of course the greedy Carsons and narcissistic power-mad Valerio came to an understanding. And, of course, they will desecrate a glorious ancient city. If only half what I am hearing is true, the Richat is a far more intriguing place than we imagined."

"What's happening?"

He told her what his scouts had reported of the Eye's awakening, and she could not help but wonder if she had been right all along. Could Richat be Atlantis, and Emory was mistaken? A man who willingly sent twenty or more mercenaries to their likely deaths in order to sell a deception?

"Are you sure it's—"

"Quite sure," Emory said. "Richat must really have been a site of impressive power. But it is not Atlantis."

Prihya was amused, and that annoyed her. She shouldn't have been *amused*. *Hurt* that she'd been wrong, *embarrassed* that she'd spouted hours of incorrect evidence. Certainly not *amused.* Especially because it was far simpler than she'd thought possible.

She said, "The academics may have been right for a change. Atlantis, the capital, not some satellite city or lesser town... it was more obvious all along. Jules Sibeko told us so, and even he hadn't realised it."

"And now he's no longer needed, he'll be buried and forgotten. How do you feel about that?"

Prihya smiled outwardly, but inside she truly hoped Jules was not done yet. "I barely know the guy. But he was a good one. Decent. I wish he'd sided with you instead of Valerio."

She held her tongue for what felt like minutes, but was probably seconds.

"So... are we nearly there yet?"

"Be patient. Be cooperative. And I will show you a truth no one has dared imagine."

CHAPTER FORTY-SEVEN

Jules's brain would have fried without every morsel of available intel. Four sources of data helped him understand the fighting, the shifting land, and their position at the drilling site, the epicenter of these sonorific pulses that were increasing in frequency but not strength.

From a satellite Valerio claimed was an advanced prototype for GPS technology, he learned the column of men invading from the north was down from twenty-two to fourteen, fanned out in a pincer formation to spread the defenders. This was a unit trying to encircle their enemy, not penetrate it. Before his accident, Horse would have seen this and smelled the deception in a heartbeat.

From the spotters holding fast at the staging area on the lip of the structure, they streamed footage to the tablet Valerio reluctantly gave Jules: the gigantic eye in the desert was alive, the markings that had been confirmed as mineral deposits darkened with new ridges driving through the soil, all before being obscured by the swirling sand whipped up by the sonic waves.

"The build-up of rocks must have secured and grew over the original structure. Adding to it, until it looked nothing but natural."

"Got it," Charlie said. "But does it help us?"

It helped Jules. It popped a pressure valve and released a fraction of his stress. He needed more, though.

As they pulled up by the drill site, he processed more data from a third source: his own observations.

They found the trident and the strange markings that had frightened him at the center of the... okay, he was gonna call this what it was: a city. As shown in the Ecuadorian gold etchings, they entered a network of concentric circles and found the trident, which Jules believed connected the city's power and technology to the whoever was capable of wielding it.

He considered that for three seconds and added it to his growing library of what-the-hell-is-going-on.

Valerio opened his door. "Okay, out, let's go."

Jules, Charlie, and Horse disembarked and crossed the gritty fog to where four engineers were treating a man in the first aid recovery position. One of the Carsons' African contingent. As three big, muscular men tried to shield him with coats and the fourth rushed to one of the massive trucks parked ten meters away—ghostly in the thickening air—his nose bled, his eyes were open, and his fingers twitched.

Jules shouted, "What happened?"

Yeah, he was shouting. Why? The wind wasn't loud. No explosions, gunshots, nothing. So why shout?

His ears felt stuffed with cotton balls or water. His frown was mirrored in the faces around him, and when he indicated his ear, Charlie nodded that she was experiencing the same.

"Infra-sonic frequency," she called, and it plainly hurt, as it had Jules.

Human hearing ranges between twenty and twenty thousand hertz, so whatever pulse emitted the soundwaves assaulting them right now had to be lower than twenty hertz. If it were more than twenty thousand, their eardrums would have burst.

Jules chose to go with it. Eyewitnesses were his fourth source of data, and he needed it.

"What happened?"

The man in charge, the one Valerio had called Captain Gasal at the staging post, stood from the stricken man.

"We did as he told us. We followed her advice. We touch nothing with bare skin. But as soon as we move the ball's housing, we have an earthquake. Then Jake..." Gasal glanced at the man on the ground. "He saw the ball falling, so he steadied it. With gloves on. But then... *boof!* We are all thrown over." He raised his hands to his head but didn't touch it. "Is like nails in the brain. We see, we hear, just enough to escape..."

"A ball," Jules said, with Valerio and Horse crowding the man, too. "What color?"

"You all want the color. I do not know why. But was black. Then, when Jake touched it... was silver. Chrome. Metal."

"Lightning?"

"Static electricity."

Jules chided himself for insulting the man's intelligence. He was a highly experienced security expert, trained in engineering. "You left it?"

Captain Gasal stared back at him, then at Valerio.

Valerio's temper flared, grabbing Gasal by the shirt and getting in his face. "Tell me you replaced it."

Gasal had been a stoic, professional leader throughout the day. Seeing the panic blowing out of Valerio visibly spooked him, though, the uncertainty in his round, white eyes cleared as he pointed back through the fog.

"We accomplished our mission."

Jules blinked away the throbbing pain in his head. Shook off the sand eddying around him. His legs refused to move without conscious thought, and as he commanded them to carry him, he staggered alongside Charlie and Valerio.

An orb lay on the ground, surrounded by a shattered casing of smooth, white stone. A couple of years ago, one of these items rendered Jules unconscious for the better part of a day; another unleashed a plague; and a third powered a portal to the past, resurrecting a long-dead volcano's guts and drawing magma into the present where none had existed for eons. Charlie and Toby hypothesized that the two points in time had merged due to quantum entanglement, which neither the Witnesses nor modern humans could comprehend.

In other words, these were powerful, unknowable objects.

"It's mine!" Valerio said.

"No." Jules stepped in front of him. "You can't take that."

"I can do anything I want."

Two powerful hands landed in Jules's chest, propelling him backwards across the ground. He tumbled and righted himself, then jumped up to find Horse bearing down on him.

"Damn it."

Jules ducked low, rolled forward, and hit Horse in the shins. The big guy flew over him, landing hard and bouncing. He wouldn't stay down long.

Valerio snatched a radio and keyed it, shouting, "All units, this is Papa Jones, code purple-cassock-witness." He turned his head, smiling in a way Jules interpreted as cheeky, but was probably something else. "That means they come get me out of here, if you were wondering."

Jules and Charlie backed up to join Gasal and his guys, two factions forming inside the maelstrom. The infrasonic thrum deepened, making Jules's eyes water, his legs shiver, his stomach churn.

Through the gloom and the brown mist now billowing as far as he could see, shadows rose—those ridges observed earlier, now penetrating the surface, pushing upward.

The *whup-whup-whup* of a rotor overrode the pulsing, and the swirling patterns changed to a spiraling hurricane five hundred yards away.

Charlie yelled, "You can't land a helicopter in this."

"It's designed to fly through sandstorms around oil fields," Valerio said, as Horse rejoined him, now holding a gun. "I think it'll manage."

Horse chuckled with his big, dumb yukking laugh.

"You can't take that out of here," Charlie said, a hand cupped around her eyes. "We don't know what'll happen. You've seen what just moving it has done!"

"For all we know it could've been the trident doing it." Valerio gestured to the 4x4 they'd arrived here in. "Speaking of which, bring it to me."

"No way," Jules said. "Get it yourself."

"Jules, my young friend." Even in the middle of the tumult of certain destruction, Valerio found time to patronize him. He pointed at Charlie and Horse's gun followed the finger. "I understand she got shot a while ago. Looks fine now, but wounds are never really gone, are they?"

"Don't," Jules said.

Valerio was right—the body only had a finite amount of resilience.

"Not a fatal shot." Valerio gave the most reasonable smile in the world. "I only want you to obey me. Is that really too much to ask?"

"Don't shoot her." Jules sidestepped in a scuttling rush, palms out. "I'll get it."

The chopper descended, flinging sand like tiny grains of glass on the skin. Jules lowered his head, one hand over his eyes, and dashed toward the vehicle. Still wearing his gloves, he opened the back door and took out the trident.

He could barely see as he jogged back toward the standoff. Which meant they wouldn't see him.

He could not give up the trident, even if it wasn't the "ultimate weapon" Valerio and Emory seemed so determined to wield. No one knew what would happen if the orb were to leave the vicinity of its circuit. Because that was what the circles represented. They were points of power fused with geology and the molecules from which the universe was built, linked by magnetism and electrical fields and a whole subsection of science to which Jules had never committed the time. If he made it through, he promised himself it would be his next project.

For the time being, all he had was educated guesswork.

Emory isn't interested in this site.

Valerio is grasping at straws; he wants the orb simply so no one else gets it.

The land is rising, plates shifting deep underground.

They've all seen magma revived when it seemed impossible.

What if this is the prelude to an eruption of similar magnitude?

A caldera the size of the Richat Structure would wipe out the continent and spread ash across half the planet.

Only... No.

There was something else in the air. A tang he'd noticed at the temple, which had seemed impossible.

Yet, they were dealing with the impossible. *Impossible* was the new normal. If Jules could calculate all that in the time it took him to jog four paces, he allowed another second to assess the risk of his fresh inkling paying off.

It's worth it.

"Sorry Charlie."

Jules removed his right glove and clasped the trident in his hand. The glow bloomed, effervescent in the massive cloud. With the helicopter touching down, and a dozen Striovian men incoming, Jules had little choice.

CHAPTER FORTY-EIGHT

He hefted the weapon over his head, drew it back like a javelin, and as soon as Valerio's and Horse's silhouettes darkened into definitive shapes, he launched it. He'd made tiny adjustments thanks to the turbulence and the added resistance in the air, so it wasn't flying straight and true.

It hurtled toward Horse's head at first, skimming by him at the last second as the rotor wash of the still-unseen helicopter caught it —as Jules calculated it would. Beyond him, it flew onward, past the shocked engineers, and slammed home into the orb.

Its middle prong shattered, the black surface spiderwebbing a series of cracks around the impact point, the outer two gouging furrows at the diameter.

The soundless hum ceased.

The ground fell still.

The sand in the air slowed to a flurry, propelled only by the rotors of a helicopter that was now visible through the murk.

Valerio stared in shock at the trident, still glowing a deep green. His mouth was open. He blinked slowly, trying to take in what was, on the surface, the stupidest thing anyone had ever done.

Jules rejoined the group, all except Horse frozen in place. "Hey."

"Jules..." Charlie sounded as stunned as Valerio looked. "What. The. Hell?"

"Lucky guess," he said.

A mound twenty yards around them had risen, a stark, grey rock jutting five yards high. Over this, the Striovian men Valerio had recalled scrambled toward them.

"Lucky?" With both hands on his head, Valerio turned 360-degrees, and sighed as deeply as Jules had ever heard a man sigh. "You killed it."

"You don't know that," Jules said.

Valerio twitched his head toward Charlie. "Two in the gut."

Horse hefted the gun and pointed it Charlie's way.

Jules cried, "No!" and flung himself in front of her.

The gun went off.

But that wasn't the only defending bang.

The ridge behind them lurched, screeching and cracking rocks rising from their millennia-long resting spot. The sudden rupture threw Horse off his feet and the bullet went high, the gun tumbling from his hand.

The incoming soldiers disappeared behind a wall, pulverizing all in its way as it burst from beneath the sand. Jules grew heavy-footed, his ears thick, and the helicopter veered away. The massive drilling rig buckled, swayed, and collapsed, sweeping all heavy machinery into the earth.

The quake was the strongest and most widespread yet.

Charlie babbled about how impossible this was, but Jules ignored her. He mapped the land he could see, which wasn't much, but enough to see the millennia-old jagged rocks and deposits fall away, leaving smooth stone like poured concrete. There was surprisingly little dust, hurled high above them, and it would descend as soon as the shockwaves eased.

He remained calm. Blanked out questions of how, concepts of time, and any deeper meaning the event might reveal.

The pressure in my ears.

The shift in gravity.

The land—the entire Richat Structure—was rising.

It wasn't just blocks soaring on enormous gears and pulleys, magnetically charged rails, or whatever secured the city. Everything had fragmented, shifted, and now labored skyward.

Remembering Horse with a jolt of fear, Jules found the big guy cocooning Valerio. The engineers seemed to copy Jules, bunching together, their fallen colleague among them.

The ridge that had erupted and then loomed ahead of them, cutting off Valerio's Striovian backup, appeared to be sinking, but the pressure from below, like being in a slow elevator, showed it had simply ground to a halt.

Then Jules was rising.

Cracking, grinding, rending... every bass-laden growl of shifting land boomed around them, through them, freezing every person in place, the seismic reverberations oppressive from every angle.

Jules saw exactly what was happening.

"How...?" Charlie said again.

That he could hear her told Jules the earth-shattering transformation was easing.

He could also hear more than the booming and cracking that had filled the world. And he was suddenly aware of Horse standing nearby.

"Easy, big fella." Jules found himself down on one knee, a hand outstretched. "This ain't over yet."

"What do you mean, not over?" Valerio demanded.

He marched up behind Horse, who was now flexing his fingers into and out of fists. It was like a playground bullying scene.

"Listen."

Jules pointed into the air, although it wasn't coming from above.

A rushing, sloshing torrent announced the next phase. With a rhythmic slapping, fine moisture hit the air before the splashes sprayed over the edge of the new valleys—wet and salty, almost steam as it merged with the hot Saharan air.

Jules and Charlie crawled on their hands and knees to the lip of their outlook, their *wall*, and peered over. Valerio and the engineers crept one at a time, hesitant to risk their heads and shoulders over the edge. But when they plucked up the courage, every set of eyes widened. Every finger gripped tighter for purchase.

A broiling cauldron of water filled the space between the walls. Twenty-two feet down, even Jules could not fathom the volume. The newly formed canyon curved away, no end in sight, and the water continued to rise.

Nineteen feet down.

Shirwac Gasal stuttered a couple of times, then managed, "Where... did this..."

"Trapped," Valerio said. "All this time, held in stasis."

"Or it was never here," Charlie said. "Ancient magma was impossible when you were trying to infect a continent, but that helped stop you."

Valerio let out a disbelieving laugh. "You think this is time-traveling water?"

"Not time-traveling," Jules said. "Just existing in both times at once. There and here. But I don't care. I just want that helicopter to touch down before the dust cloud lands."

"What dust cloud?"

Jules pointed upward.

Above them, not quite blotting out the sun, a curtain of red and orange hung over them, blasted high by the power that pushed the city they'd mistaken for Atlantis from its grave. From afar, it must have resembled a dome.

"Ah, good call," Valerio said. "Horse, please do the honors."

Horse lumbered toward Jules, his hulking frame shadowed by what little sunlight penetrated the murk.

Jules leapt up, his fists clenched, and his heart racing with anticipation, even more than witnessing the rising water. It was a fight he didn't want, but he'd end it fast if needed—broken bones didn't work no matter how resilient the owner.

With the tang of ocean impossible on Jules's tongue, he expected Horse would move first, unable to contain his impatience and bloodlust, then he could counter—

"Ahem."

Charlie's voice might have been a distraction for many, but Jules didn't risk tearing his gaze from Horse.

"Umm, boys?" Valerio said.

Horse had no such qualms about breaking his concentration, twisting his head to his boss-slash-best-friend's comment.

Jules risked a glance.

Charlie held Valerio in a choke hold, while Shirwac rested a thick-bladed knife to his throat.

As the water reached the ground's level, waves rolling back and forth, spilling over with its movement, Valerio said, "I think we might have to work out a compromise."

The helicopter—a reconditioned Russian military vehicle—landed amid a shower of dirt and sand. Jules and Charlie loaded Valerio and Horse into the craft's belly having secured the men's hands with rope retrieved from the engineers' remaining gear, and the men employed by Roger Carson helped their injured friend on board before following. The pilot was also under the Carsons' employ, so there was no tedious standoff or posturing; he got them airborne in seconds.

As they flew upward, Jules ignored Valerio's prattling, his offers of riches and glory, and watched the circular construct define itself below.

Through the brown-orange fog, the lines were clear: concentric circles like the maps he'd memorized in the golden library, the books outlining plans for the Witnesses' migration; water filled the canals between the city's streets, still churning from the enormous movement needed to release it into this place; whether it had been trapped beneath the rocks that repelled seawater or kept within instead of protecting the city from the incoming tide, its release marked a huge shift in humanity's historical record. An Atlantean-like city's resurrection would be impossible to conceal.

And what benefit did such a secret truly bestow? Other than making the select few who know of this hidden past feel superior in their possession of the truth, what, really, was the point in hiding it?

Granted, the orbs were clearly dangerous, and how Jules had triggered what he was watching still didn't gel inside him fully, although he had plenty of ideas.

Would these discoveries fall into the hands of governments? Would wars be fought over the scientific research that might—*might*—lead to great advancements when applied to modern technology? Or would it be monetized in the hands of people like...

"Crap." Jules had to shout his request over the engines' whine. "Can you patch me through to the airplane?"

After a few seconds of back and forth, the pilot passed back a headset, and Bridget's voice came through staticky but legible.

"Jules, what's happening? The satellite feed is grainy, but it looks like... like... something is coming through the ground. Like..."

"Yeah, Bridge? It's not the Atlantis from Plato's writing. It's somethin' else. I'll explain later. Right now, I gotta ask you a real personal question."

"How personal?"

"You trust your dad?"

"My dad? He's probably listening right now."

"Don't matter if he's listening. Do you *trust* him? If the answer's no, he'll find out real quick—"

"It's no, Jules. Not after today." Her voice caught, then resumed. "I'm sorry, Dad, if you're here. But I tried to tell you. Your need to own this stuff, this power..."

"I understand." Jules tried to feel what she was feeling, to see how hard this must be, but all he saw was the need to do the next part right. "We're stuck. Backed into a corner. And we can't trust anyone else. It has to be us. The Lost Origins Institute. And I ain't handing Valerio over to just anyone."

Valerio cocked his head, eyebrows bobbing as if he was hearing all, despite the noise drowning out every word.

Jules turned away. "Get ahold of Colin Waterston over in Britain. He'll know what to do with his asshole."

"Then what?"

"Then..." Jules hadn't thought that far ahead.

At ground level, the men who'd been cut off—Valerio's people, the Carsons' security forces, and the Koreans sent by Emory to keep them busy—retreated along their own lines, columns of ants fleeing the rising tide. And, like a sad, crumbling empire, the first of the walls toppled over and crashed into the water. The waves consumed it, and the domino effect was immediate.

One after another, the towering pillars and platforms that had risen under the forces no one had yet explored, could no longer support themselves. Whatever had secured them eons ago, and pushed them into the light once more, faded and relented, sucking the city back beneath the surface.

There would be ruins to explore, Jules supposed. But if the authorities chose to conceal it—no matter their reasons—he expected they would succeed.

Which left only Bridget's question: *then what?*

"Then..." Jules said. "*Now*... we get serious. We find Prihya, stop Emory, and bury anything that might pose a threat to the world."

PART FOUR

CHAPTER FORTY-NINE

CHATEAU CACHÉ - BRITTANY, FRANCE

BRIDGET SPENT HALF the fifteen-hour flight from Mauritania to Doha negotiating with her father, the breaking point proving to be his self-preservation. He'd kept Audrey in the dark about the Richat Structure to "protect her from litigation and criminal charges if anything went wrong," so Bridget's mother's involvement was all it took for him to give in. The three-way video call from a Doha terminal showed why the Carson women were not mere spectators, berating Roger until he agreed to vouch for the aircraft, sponsor the foreign nationals' temporary visas, and house Valerio and Horse at the Chateau until Colin Waterston corralled his Interpol contacts into picking up the criminals.

Bridget wanted to take a bath, put on her pajamas, and hibernate after the past week's trials. She only had time for hugs from Dan, Harpal, and Toby, a shower, a change of clothes, and a meal with strong coffee before rejoining a team that felt more like family right now than her own father.

The hub was part upper-crust gentlemen's club with green leather wingback chairs and couch for breakout person-to-person tete-a-tetes (Toby's aesthetic) and part slick, state-of-the-art tech with a touch-screen table, a crisscrossed pair of clear screens that gave a near-perfect 3D-rendered holographic display, and a new 8k 60-inch screen as clear as a freshly installed window (Charlie's design). Dan and Harpal were playing a shoot-'em-up video game on Charlie's big screen, which she watched with the detached exhaustion of a mother discovering her children lying in a muddy puddle, resigned to the fact they could get no dirtier so might as well enjoy themselves. Bridget was surprised to find herself still mad at a cleaned-up Jules as he slept on the overstuffed green leather couch.

She expected her annoyance at him benching her to fade, but doubt still nagged—could she have saved the city if she had been present? Talked the engineers out of obeying her father if she was there in person instead of a voice on the phone?

As for her father, she'd barred him from what came next, despite him kindly hiring someone to fly their much older Learjet back from China. She wasn't sure if that was a compromise, an apology, or a sign he was ready to cut them loose should they choose to go their own way.

Xander Madri and his daughter, Kat, wandered into the hub, Toby having greeted them at the door as the car service dropped them off from the airport. Her father's influence with the Chinese allowed Xander's release on the condition that the Carsons paid for his removal and guaranteed he would never return without the ruling party's permission. Her dad made this out to be a massive humanitarian endeavor, but Bridget saw it as basic human decency.

She would thank her dad, as was proper, but would not gush about it.

"We're all here," Charlie said. "Boys, can we pause this?"

"I'm kicking an Australian kid's butt," Dan replied. "Give us two minutes."

"Okay, no problem." Charlie hit a button on the remote and the screen cut to black.

Harpal stood, controller in hand. "Hey. What was that?"

"We have guests," Toby said.

All eyes except Jules's turned to Xander, and the game was quickly forgotten as the group gathered to greet the friend of Prihya's who had contributed much during his release to the dig site.

"I am sorry," he now said with his head bowed. "Richat seemed the strongest contender."

Jules stirred, having clearly woken up as the voices rose around him. "It wasn't a contender. It was real." He sat up, stretching. It wasn't only the easing of kinks from a nap; he and Charlie were physically tested out there, so even a star athlete would feel the strain. "Just wasn't the place the mad priest is heading."

"And where's that?" Dan said. "I'm not warming the bench anymore. Time to get out there."

Bridget smiled inside that Dan had used the same terminology she'd thought of when Jules forced her to sit out the events at Richat.

Only Jules?

No, Charlie had agreed. Or at least, she hadn't objected.

Shouldn't Bridget be just as mad at her as she was at Jules? Or did the betrayal cut deeper because she and Jules had been on the verge of exploring their friendship in a new way? A new phase of their lives?

Could she go down that path with him now?

"Let's get into that," Toby said. "Charlie?"

Charlie switched attention to the 3D nest where she had lined up coverage gathered during the flight, and the day-long aftermath of the rise and near-instant collapse of the ancient city. As the team formed a crescent around the screens, a series of images flashed up, mostly jerky satellite captures.

"Let's go through it chronologically. Some of this is theory, some proven fact thanks to what Jules and I went through. But starting with the golden books."

Charlie paused, nodding for Bridget to take over.

"The books were a roadmap," Bridget said and, as if on cue, one of Jules's sketches popped up on the screen, showing a rudimentary map of the Ice Age's northern hemisphere. "They were a blueprint for the Witnesses, who had evolved in isolation and developed formidable intelligence long before the protohumans across the Atlantic became homo sapiens. They designed cities that would work in unison with the slowly rising waters, a place to live while they spread out, shared their knowledge, and helped humans evolve the way the original Witnesses saved even older humans from the effects of the Toba eruption another seventeen thousand years earlier."

"So, what do we think?" Harpal asked. "The Witnesses evolved, got cosy with humans to save them, then retreated to South America?"

Toby took that one. "We see their footprints throughout the world, having built small city states or tribes, and preserving their achievements, all of which was wiped out by super-volcano eruptions that changed the Earth's climate more than once, and perhaps meteor strikes to boot. We see nothing more of them in our discoveries until—as Bridget eluded—the Younger Dryas signaled a massive expansion of humanity. They had no choice but to engage once again."

Bridget picked up the narrative. "They expanded, built their cities. Their exact purpose, we still don't know, but there was more than one."

"More than one Atlantis?" Xander said. "So, maybe we are correct. About all those sites?"

"Nah," Jules answered, still a little bleary eyed. "Most ain't old enough. Might be two, might be three or four. Might even be more in the middle of oceans we'll never find. For now. Let's stick with Richat and wherever Emory's going."

Bridget waited to see if Jules had more, bristling at him talking over her. "The only Atlantis is the one Plato wrote about, and at this stage it doesn't matter if it's in Africa, Spain, or the Mesopotamian basin. What matters is, we figure out where Father Emory is going."

Dan punched a fist into his palm. "And kick his ass."

"No," Toby said. "We pass on the tip to Interpol and whatever country is responsible for the site and let the special forces and trained professionals do their jobs."

"Aww, that sucks."

Bridget said, "What we need to do is eliminate the impossible. We think the Richat city was either on the coast or was fed by a tributary. Right, Charlie?"

"I've watched every bit of footage I can," Charlie said. "Jules and I have discussed what we remember. Based on all that, I think the cities were built to work in unison with the rising floodwaters. In India we saw they could repel seawater, but that's *thousands* of years before the new Ice Age hit, taking away that need. Having advanced significantly, they now designed cities to *absorb* higher tides instead of fend off temporary flooding. Not only the deep channels between the circles they built, but wells for the run-off. Like a soakaway pit in a house. The circular constructs, I guess, would be linked so getting around wouldn't be a problem, and connected to the bedrock of wherever they were built."

"Cool," Jules said. "So, the water fills the channels between the land, and if floodwater gets too much it diverts underground to these wells."

"Except, when the comet that Valerio told us about broke into five or six chunks in the atmosphere and all hit the planet at terminal velocity, the surge was too much. It'd been designed for the meltwater, to prevent flooding, not shield against a tidal wave or massive groundswell."

"What I saw when I was connected to the trident in their temple..." Jules shuddered, unusually subdued when recalling his experience. "What I *felt*... they had a failsafe, a wall like the doors made of the same stuff as the bangles... but it wasn't enough. They didn't get to it in time."

"The catastrophe shifted the city," Toby said. "Split it from its moorings, destroyed the populace, and then settled back over the water."

"Right," Charlie said. "The barrier that was supposed to stop the seawater coming *in* prevented it from flowing back *out*. The city sank into that reservoir, and the desert swallowed it."

"Until we came along," Bridget said. "Reactivated the opposing magnetic poles that stopped it sinking under minor strain, then when Jules skewered it with that spear... I don't understand that."

"All we got is guesswork," Jules admitted. "I think moving the orb set off a chain reaction that never got going during the earthquakes and tidal waves. Like it suddenly woke up and tried to protect itself as a last resort."

Harpal let out a single note of a laugh. "Scorched earth evac."

Jules ignored the comment. "The trident... that seems to be like a lightning rod, or a circuit breaker. They might've used it to control or regulate the power, but when I stabbed the orb, it didn't kill it right away."

"It caused a surge," Charlie said. "Like cooking a spoon in the microwave. A load of extra, unwanted power blowing around the appliance, spreads to your home electrics, and blows every fuse in the house."

"So, it threw the city back up where it belonged," Jules added. "Let it bob around on the seawater that'd been trapped there, but didn't have the stability to control it."

Charlie indicated the 3D nest of screens where the satellite images showed the warped, cataract-infused aftermath of the scene. The circles were still present, but no longer concentric, no longer the wonder it had once been.

She said, "The sea water will be absorbed by the land around it, now it's been released. The structure is settling back into place. And the stories put out by the authorities are being believed by the media for now. But I doubt they'll hold."

"What stories?" Dan asked.

"Natural phenomena," Toby said. "Geological disturbances, an earthquake."

"Won't hold," Harpal said. "Evidence of human interference is all over the place." He pointed at the mangled point of a drilling rig. "They'll spin it as illegal exploration for minerals, I'm guessing, but they'll need a scapegoat."

Bridget said, "Luckily, we've got one in our basement."

The room quietened. They'd never held someone prisoner before, and the chateau wasn't really equipped for it. Since it wasn't a medieval castle, it didn't even have an old dungeon they could repurpose. The nearest secure unit they had—other than the room housing Charlie's supercomputer, the Demon Server—was the wine cellar. It was as secure as any prison cell, a condition insisted upon by the Carsons' insurers upon learning the value of the wine therein. No one expected Valerio to drink himself to death in there, so the only risk was he'd be petty enough to smash the bottles as revenge.

But he'd been confident when they forced him in there. He'd told them, "I know more than you. I know the secondary site Emory favored. And I'm not telling unless you let me out."

They'd expressed humor at his declaration, Dan and Harpal particularly happy to see Valerio and the exceedingly confused Horse behind bars, albeit ones intended to keep criminals *outside* the vault.

"We could always ask him," Jules said.

"No, absolutely not." Toby puffed up his chest and stared down his nose, the way he did when needed to stamp some authority. "We assured Colin and his law enforcement associates that we would hand over Valerio as soon as they arrive."

"Which is when? 'Cause I can chat to the guy until the Gestapo arrives, can't I?"

"Chat?" Dan said. "How about interrogate?"

Toby had a phone to his ear. "We have absolutely no authority, legal or moral, to subject someone to— Ah, Colin, yes. ETA?" Pause. "Of course..." He held the phone out to Charlie. "Perhaps so everyone can listen?"

Charlie placed the phone on the touchscreen tabletop, where the sensors detected the device and paired with it, sending a photo of an AI-painted cartoon stork-Colin hybrid to the screen above and patching the audio through to the wider hub. "Okay, we're all on speaker."

"Hello, everyone," Colin said. "What a wonderful, colossal mess you've blundered into. It was just what I needed. Mrs. Waterston is over the moon that we will no longer be glamping in the Cotswolds because I have to fly to the godforsaken desert to tidy up what should have been a quite splendid discovery."

"It's still a *splendid discovery*," Jules said. "Just gotta dig for it. Piece it together—"

"Ah, yes, young Jules. You'll be pleased to know you are officially a wanted man in Mauritania. Wanted for questioning at the very least. Perhaps you'd like to accompany me there after I collect my package from you in about two hours."

"Nah, I'm good. Add it to the list."

"Of course. That brings it to... six countries where you can no longer show your face. Is that correct?"

"Somethin' like that." Jules held up eight fingers and winked at Bridget.

Winked?

Jules never winked.

He said, "Look, Valerio's got intel. Think we can ask him some questions before you cart him off to whatever black site that don't exist?"

Colin snorted derisively. "Do you seriously think he'll give up one iota of information that doesn't benefit him?"

"No," Dan said. "But it'll be fun trying."

"Your leader already sent me photographs of both men's current physical states. Any additional bruising will be treated as criminal assault. Clear?"

"Wuss."

"Clear?"

"Yeah, clear." Dan scuffed his foot and edged toward the games controller. "Got better things to do anyway."

"Look, people." Colin's tone relented from the haughty telling-off manner. "Just hold him until we get there. I will arrive shortly before the Interpol prisoner transport so I can assess security needs. Do not mess this up."

"We won't," Toby said.

"Good. Because..." He sighed. "His Majesty has been briefed and is taking a more... personal interest than his predecessor did. I am to report twice daily."

"I get the impression you have more to say, Colin."

"He don't wanna," Jules said. "He might be annoyed with us, but I'm guessing his boss ain't."

Colin let out a breath and said, "His Majesty wishes to convey his admiration for your bravery and for bringing to justice a man we have long been interested in detaining. Should this escalate, or should other circumstances require it, he might even consider inviting you to become legitimate subcontractors in the future."

The team smiled as one, a smirk or two, plenty of raised eyebrows.

"Even I reluctantly concede this episode was not without merit. As long as you hand over Valerio and his henchman, we can wipe any other misdeeds from the official and, more importantly, the *un*official record."

"It's a deal," Toby said.

Bridget saw how happy it had made Toby and searched for Jules's reaction. Except she couldn't find it.

Jules was gone.

CHAPTER FIFTY

Jules backed silently out of the hub before Colin concluded because he saw where it was headed. Colin needed to present himself as superior, as if the British Empire still held authority over troublesome colonials, so Jules didn't need to hear it. While he had made great strides in meshing into a team, he still possessed a brain, and that brain couldn't help but send him in different directions when the team was wrong.

He speed-walked down the hallway leading to the kitchen and heard a soft clacking sound coming from a door near the end, which was usually locked. Toby stepped out with Dan and Bridget flanking him, their faces tight with tension.

A secret passage? Really?

"What?"

"You know what," Dan said.

Jules did know, but he wanted to hear it, remaining silent until Toby spoke up.

"Jules, the discovery at Richat is remarkable, but you and Charlie are fortunate to be alive. We are not in a position to recover Prihya from a religious fanatic flanked by a squad of armed, well-trained nationalist fanatics, no matter what Valerio Conchin shares with you."

Jules threw out his arms, losing patience. "I can't believe you're abandoning the trail when we're so close. All we've gotta do is figure out where they are. We'll find Prihya *and* the capital city. Bridge, you feel it, right?"

Bridget looked at the floor, an internal battle playing out on her face, then back up at Jules. "I *want* to go. I do. I was so angry at you leaving me out before, I *should* be with you on this, but... What if Colin is telling us the truth? What if we can work as contractors with him and other European nations instead of sneaking around and fighting them?"

Jules stared back, the gears in his head working and falling into place. "It's about your dad."

"My dad?"

"You wanna be free of his hold over you. Now you've seen it. When he sets his sights on a shiny object, you can't trust him. At all."

Bridge pursed her lips, jaw tensed.

"She is correct to feel that way," Toby said. "If we do what Colin asks, we all win."

"How can you say that?" Jules said. "Compromise never works with him. It's do as he says, or he'll find a way to screw us. When it comes to the institute, all he's ever wanted is to put one over on his old mentor."

"Yes, yes, but I think this time it's different. There are other parties involved, new management. Plus, they must all have been aware of the possibility of an older race, but nothing on this scale. We have so much more research, we have a savant with languages—" He gestured toward Bridget. "—and we have you. A man who links with the technology in a way you and Charlie are only just starting to understand."

"They got another conductor if they want her."

"I seriously doubt General Yanovna will cooperate with anyone she sees as a threat or as complicit in neglecting her country's security."

Jules didn't know Zimina Yanovna the way Toby did. He'd worked out they had a past from before Toby entered the archaeology field, which was clearly a position in British espionage circles, so he would defer to Toby's expertise on that. Still, it didn't mean he'd consider becoming an employee of the British Royal Family, given their history.

"Dan, you here to strong-arm me?"

Dan shrugged. "I don't know the first thing about what's going on, pal. Just that it'd be bad for you to get tempted by Valerio's answers. Last time it happened, you threw a massive goddamn wave at a yacht and took off on a Jet Ski."

That wasn't exactly how it played out, but Jules took the point.

"Fine, I'm outvoted." Jules was already packing his bags in his head. What to take, what to come back for later. "I'll be in my room."

He turned and walked away, stopping when Bridget called his name.

"Yeah?"

"When we're on solid footing," she said, "we can pick all this up later. When it's resolved."

Jules nodded and went on his way.

Up the wide staircase, heading for the first floor landing, Xander was waiting for him, arms folded, barring the way. But not like Dan had been.

"They are wrong," Xander said. "And you are the only one who sees it."

In Jules's room, Xander did the usual thing people do when they want to talk about forbidden subjects—stuffed his hands in his pockets and paced.

"Get to the point," Jules said. "I tolerate stalling and chitchat from the others, but you got things to say."

"Prihya." Xander ceased pacing and spoke with his hands close to his face. "She and I, we became close. Online. Or, at least, I thought we did. She asked her employer to use me on the island, because she knew I could be trusted and that bigger secrets waited for whoever—"

"Look, if you're writing a novel, this is cool backstory. But anythin' you wanna tell me about how you're such great friends and you trust her and you believe in hope or whatever, I either already know it or don't care. I'm sorry if that seems rude, but you're trying to convince me to go against the institute. And no matter how much they talk without sayin' much, they've been good to me. So gimme a reason, Xander. If that's why you're here and not just yappin'."

"I know where Atlantis is."

Jules let the cool breeze of Xander's sentence wash over him. "Keep talkin'. Convince me."

"She and I believe in many possibilities. We narrowed it down to three. Richat, a site near Syria, and the Mediterranean basin."

"Evidence?"

Xander spoke with eloquence. Only a couple of times did Jules have to remind him to move on from shared knowledge, mainly about Richat. He explained how the site in the Middle East was too remote, too far from the ocean back in the times they were discussing and landed on the coastal region in the Mediterranean.

"The Pillars of Heracles must be the Straits of Gibraltar. The site is perfect for war with Greece, and it matches the travels of Plato. It's possible there would have been people here who remembered the ruins, who passed on the stories. And what is more, the deep scans—like the Eye of the Sahara—hint at regular shaped objects, including a sizeable rectangle, and curved patterns."

"Curved," Jules said. "Not circular?"

"Like Richat, this is very deep. The sea was at a lower level and, as you saw with the city you brought out of the desert, the force of a tidal wave would crush or bury a city of forty kilometers with ease."

"So, where, exactly?"

Xander's passion for this site ebbed away, his hands falling limp and face softening. "That, I am sorry, I do not know. Not precisely. Prihya... she had her aim on Richat. The others, she felt, were less likely."

Jules rubbed both hands over his head. He'd run off before. He'd gone his own way plenty of times. But Bridget and Toby, and all the others, forgave him. Did not view it as a betrayal. He'd done things they were unable to, understanding the situation on a different level.

This wasn't the same.

All of them knew. All of them knew the facts, and all understood Valerio might hold the key.

"Show me," Jules said. "Show me the evidence, and we'll work it out."

Two hours of examining Prihya's videos, including a series of outtakes that Xander accessed on a private channel, gave Jules nothing more than they'd discussed over the video link while Toby was in China. A series of possible sites, but nothing that proved definitive. Heck, in one of the more bizarre outtakes, she seemed to be advocating for the plot of land in the Middle East, although why that didn't make it to the full version was obvious: it was a mishmash of more than one legend.

Still... it had made a certain sense.

"We concentrate on the Med," Jules said.

"We are running out of time." Xander had started talking with his hands again, the skin on his face and neck tight. "If they find it... if they have no more use for Prihya..."

Jules checked his watch and recalled Colin's ETA was about now. They needed to choose.

"Xander, where's your girl?"

"With Harpal and Dan. Playing Mario Cart."

"Okay, first things first. They might've been playing Mario Cart when you left 'em but they ain't now. I guarantee they're blowin' away zombies or nazis or nazi zombies. Second, I can't decide yet. I need to speak to *him*."

Jules had expected to find someone guarding the wine cellar, but there was no one. There was only a camera, but because he had hacked into the chateau's security system years before and had left his bot sleeping in case he needed it, he spent thirty seconds setting it to a loop of the motionless passageway and stairs before heading inside.

Jules told himself that he hadn't made up his mind yet. He might not have come down here if he hadn't persuaded himself that there were still factors to consider. He certainly wouldn't have sent Xander to keep the others talking and out of the way. The cellar featured 1940s-era wooden fittings, barrels, and tables polished to a high sheen that revealed their true age, the musty air intentional to enhance the olde world atmosphere. The arc of the pillars and beams resembled the foundations of a medieval castle, with rough concrete fascias leading to a redbrick tunnel that housed the valuables. The style of barred gate normally found in small-town jail cells was used to secure access. Only the bare bulb from Jules' side provided a wedge of light near the door, like a welcome mat.

"Hey."

Valerio huffed in the dark, shuffled behind a shelf, and wandered into the light, a wine bottle swinging at his side, held in two fingers. "Are you going to join me?"

The bottle appeared intact.

"Oh, this?" Valerio lifted the wine to his lips and took a swig. Lowered it. Smiled. "They left a corkscrew in here."

"Yeah?"

"Yeah. Once you've opened a bottle of pinot noir from vineyards of Chambertin Grand Cru, sip it directly from the neck, and agree every penny of those seven thousand dollars is *very* well spent, you get to bash hell out of the corkscrew." He lowered his voice to a stage whisper. "Makes a wonderful lock pick. *Right, Horse?*"

Two enormous hands grabbed Jules from behind. Before he could react, he was dragged backwards. Expecting a knee in the spine, he thrust both feet out behind him and connected with a solid block. The block gave only an inch or so, while Jules flew forward. He righted himself, landing on his feet, braced against the steel door. Horse framed himself to charge.

"Wait, wait, wait, I'm here to get you out."

Horse launched forward but pulled up—presumably at some signal from his boss.

Valerio said, "We got out of the prison cell, but the cellar door is sealed. So, if you're not here to taunt us or interrogate me..." He reverted to that breathy stage whisper again. "I'm listening."

"You and Emory had a plan," Jules said, still braced, still staring at the freight train that wanted to batter him. "After the Tayos Caves. Expecting something like the cipher Prihya found in Malta, weren't you?"

"Or a map. Or a diary. Something to send us straight there."

"But it was just the plans for the city. The vaguest directions. Should've realised they were settin' out to explore. They didn't know where they were gonna settle. Just what they'd do when they got there."

"You know their secret, don't you, Jules?"

"No." Jules nodded toward Horse. "We okay?"

"For a few minutes. I heard a car pull up, which I assume is someone I don't want to meet?"

Horse stood down.

Jules pushed to his feet. "We got two sites. One I'm more sure of."

"Tell me."

Jules bullet-pointed his discussion with Xander. "Just need the exact location for the Med site. And you said you knew."

"If I knew for sure, I wouldn't have packed my bags and headed to Brazil."

"Ecuador. But that's a fair point." Jules still had a use for him, though, perhaps more-so than if he'd simply dropped the location on him. "Then I don't need you."

Jules turned away, posing as if ready to fight Horse.

As hoped, Valerio intervened quickly. "I can track Emory."

"Oh?"

"We move in the same circles. Same corrupt officials to get us near-instant access to places most universities take months to allow anyone into."

"You sound real proud."

"I am. And you will be too. If you save your friend in time."

"I got some conditions."

"No." Valerio placed the bottle down, half-finished. "I have what you need. Not the other way around. So, here's my offer. I get to keep whatever is hidden in the true Atlantis. At the temple of Apollo."

"Another trident?"

"Oh, the real place we're looking for has much more than that."

"Whatever. What else you want?"

Valerio thought about it. "Actually, that's it. Oh, and your word you won't arrest me again."

"Done. But only if I get a promise from you. No killing. And Prihya is the priority over any artifact."

"Yes on the first—although only regular people. If I have a Korean gun pointed at me, Horse *will* save me. As for the second point... well, let's just say I won't stop you from prioritizing human life over my essential goal. Fair?"

It wasn't, but it was better than he'd expected. "Fine. You stick close, you—"

A door opened. Footsteps sounded.

Colin's annoying voice: "Yes, yes, Toby, I'll be fine. I need thirty minutes with the prisoner, then we'll be ready to depart."

Jules hid behind a pillar.

Horse slipped back inside the cell without locking it, as nimble as ever which was weird on a hulking monster like him.

Colin entered the anteroom. His wingtips clopped across the flagstone floor and halted in the center. "I know you all think Mrs. Locke is some sort of futurist genius, Jules, but we have been monitoring this place for ten years. Much like your intrusion into the system, we piggyback in now and again. So, when we spotted you sabotaging the feeds in here, I chose not to alert Toby."

Jules stepped out from his hiding spot. "Hey."

Colin pivoted his way. "I assume you have a plan."

"I do."

"Care to clue me in?"

Jules stepped toward him. "Not really, no."

CHAPTER FIFTY-ONE

TOBY DIDN'T THINK to check on Colin's interview with Valerio until the Interpol team arrived. They'd been talking for thirty minutes, which had passed slowly as he and the others rested or worked on scenarios in which Prihya led Emory to Plato's Atlantis. Except Dan, who complained about Harpal not wanting to play a violent computer game before letting Kat join him. Charlie threatened to cut him off unless he switched from gory zombies to a garish racing game.

Having expected a paramilitary-style mob of cops, Toby was surprised when Margarete Laurent, the chateau's live-in housekeeper, led in a smart-suited male detective named Detective Inspector Denis and his partner, a short woman named Detective Constable Sinha. They left a half-dozen similarly dressed men and one woman outside, all with bulges from sidearm holsters on hips or under arms.

The inspector asked to meet with Colin.

"Of course, right this way." Toby nodded his thanks to Margarete, who tutted and closed the door, then led them toward the kitchen where the passage to the cellar commenced. "I really hope you can extract enough information to effect a rescue. Our friend and colleague is in quite some trouble."

Denis, whose French accent was as thick and heavy as his eyebrows, replied with a curt, "Yes. Thank you for your assistance."

It sounded forced, as if someone had fed him the diplomatic

response. Toby sensed a tiny emphasis on *assistance*, too, hinting that the detective inspector was less than enamored to be here. No sense in pushing it or antagonizing the man.

Toby opened the heavy cellar door, and the two detectives descended the stairs with loud clops. At the bottom, they rushed forward, out of sight, triggering Toby to hasten too. At the bottom, he found Colin Waterston propped against a work bench's thick, wooden leg, the Interpol detectives fiddling behind him. A *snip* sent Denis back onto his haunches, having freed Colin from cable ties that had secured his wrists.

"About damn time," Colin said. "Now, arrest them all!"

Detective Inspector Denis arrested no one. His line, "I am under orders to assist in the transfer of Valerio Conchin, not follow your every order," gave Toby hope that things weren't as bad as they appeared, but then he added, "I will decide if a crime is worth arresting someone over." He had towered over Toby while Detective Constable Sinha stood behind to prevent him running. "Explain what has happened here."

Toby stuttered, sighed, stuttered some more.

Harpal and Dan hurried down to join them, both armed.

Denis and Sinha drew their sidearms and shifted position to reach cover, Denis shouting, "*Drop your weapons.*"

"They're my security," Toby said. "Don't shoot."

Dan and Harpal recognized law enforcement right away and placed their guns on the floor, then retreated with their hands raised.

"Charlie said the feeds were hacked," Harpal said. "Saw you go into the room, but no one came down the stairs."

While Denis covered the two men, Sinha gathered the two Sigs and backed away.

"Jules," Toby said. "Has to be Jules. Is he not in his room?"

"I'll check," Dan said.

"Freeze." Denis still had his weapon trained on the pair.

Dan relented and held position. "Come on, we gotta move."

"As much as I hate to back them up," Colin said, "this pair are, indeed, working for Toby Smith. They are licensed to carry those guns on private property, too."

Denis slowly lowered his weapon. "They may have them back when we leave. Now, where is our package?"

"Ask my jailer," Colin said.

He stood back and pointed in one of the corners by the empty makeshift cell. Xander walked forward, hands away from his body, palms forward.

"Do not shoot me either, please. I know where they are going."

"How do you know that?" Toby asked.

"Because I helped them."

Denis put his gun away and massaged his temples with his forefingers. "I was ordered here on my day off. I find our prisoner is missing, guards with guns, and now an accomplice ready to confess. This is not what I expected today, and it is giving me a headache." He lowered his hands and stepped away so he could take in the whole scene, Sinha joining him. "This is the dumbest, most... what is the word?"

"Inept, sir?" Sinha suggested.

"Yes, yes. Is the most *inept* operation I can think of. Incompetent." He glared at Colin. "You may hold influence, but this is my responsibility." To Xander, he said, "Why did you release a man who kills for fun?"

"Because I know all Prihya knows," Xander said. "I can think like her. She and I agree on this thing. And Valerio confirmed it. I will show you where to go, now he has a head start."

"A head start?" Toby echoed. "As in, they *want* us to go after them?"

"They can't have taken his plane," Harpal said. "It's impounded, right?"

"Correct," Toby said. "Colin arranged that as soon as we touched them down."

"So, they must have taken Roger's jet. I doubt we'd catch them anyway, but—"

Xander said, "It may all be over by the time we get there."

"*Goddamnit!*" It appeared Dan would have punched something had all the surfaces not been so solid. "This is just like India all over again. Only this time we don't have a homing beacon to track him with."

"Why did we stop using those again?" Harpal asked.

"Hadn't thought we needed 'em. Guess we need to start up again soon as we—"

"*Gentlemen*," Colin said. "Perhaps I can be of assistance. While I admit I got sucker-punched, and could do nothing to prevent the escape, I will, however, provide you with all the unofficial help I can muster—"

"Hold, hold, please," Denis said. "You are allowing these civilians to help retrieve the prisoner? My superiors will be more surprised than me. And take more convincing."

"We have one last chance to get Valerio Conchin." Colin spoke to Denis but was looking at Toby. "These people are well-placed. They are also more invested because they have friends at stake, as well as their freedom. If they do not give us their full cooperation—including roping in their extremely well-resourced former-mafioso friend—then you, Detective Inspector Denis, are more than welcome to charge them as accomplices in Valerio's escape."

CHAPTER FIFTY-TWO

After confirming the codes (and "car keys" as Valerio called them) from the chateau storage locker and retrieving his favorite belt of accessories—a handful of mini flashbangs, throwing knives, and two batons of his own design that extended into bungee cords with small grappling hooks—Jules stole LORI's aged Learjet easily. He was well-known to the airfield's security personnel (in a good way, for once), and Valerio trusted Horse to fly them out of the country, despite some passive-aggressive jibes about its distinct lack of luxury.

After taking off, they spoofed a transponder to piggyback a Barcelona-bound passenger plane into international airspace before their airwave scans detected any alerts. Jules stipulated "no chitchat" so he could focus on their destination and plan for every possible scenario.

He closed his eyes, recalling every line and symbol from the golden books. Cross-referencing this with Plato and Bridget's translations from scrolls and books that seemed related, he confirmed they were on the right track. He also considered that Prihya and Emory were well ahead, and that his analysis matched Valerio's underground channels' intel that a religious group was hiring drilling and mining crews, fast track carnés to transport equipment across borders, and black market sources who'd confirmed a shipment of C-4 to the region.

Their agreement to keep silent lasted until the third hour of the flight, when Valerio quit reading Critias—one of Plato's works in which he writes about Atlantis—and asked Jules to join him up front.

"Is it necessary?" Jules asked.

"I have been quiet all this way." Valerio waggled the book. "We're coming up to where we need to be. Indulge me. It might help add perspective to whatever is going around in that remarkable brain of yours."

Jules had done about as much predicting and hypothesizing as he could, leaving only thoughts about Bridget's reaction to him running off. Again. What Charlie thought, too. And then he'd started listing the people in the institute whose opinion he cared for, starting highest and working to the lowest, but that annoyed him because it wasn't something a decent person would do. He should care about what was right, not what others would think of him in the short term, and he was convinced this would benefit them all in the present and future. It wasn't scratching an itch, or his need to be the one to uncover the secrets. It wasn't even about his mom or dad or the bangles—which he'd brought along.

It was simply the most logical path to take.

As was acquiescing to Valerio's request to join him where he stood before the cockpit's open door. The man was an undeniable narcissist, so to deny him more chatter after so much silence would mean bottling it up longer, and a more annoying eruption of verbal diarrhea later.

Valerio said, "Richat was never the place the Plato learned about."

"Nope. Can I sit down now?"

"All verifiable evidence points to the Mediterranean, or close to it. Which means the best option is a long, long way from the Greek islands, or Mr. Plato would've been more specific."

"Yeah," Jules said, trying to sound interested but not really.

"Which leaves...?"

Jules peered out the cockpit window over Horse's shoulder, the deep blue ocean shimmering below, the sun in the southwest. They'd flown due south over France, skirted the Catalan coast and the Costas, then essentially turned right to fly west over the Med. To the left was a green and brown land mass, and to the right was a veined carpet of green with grey patches. At their altitude, they could see roads and beaches, small towns with white buildings, a church, and cars.

The Straits of Gibraltar. A British territory annexed on the far south of Spain, the residents 100% British yet—despite clear votes of self-determination—Spain still made occasional claims over the land.

Jules was possibly a wanted man there, too, albeit for a minor bit of burglary which he cut short because the item he was supposed to steal was clearly a fake.

Valerio said, "Geophysicists suggest this is a good punt, and I agree. The Pillars of Heracles, the maritime boundary of the ancient Greek world. Many think this is the place. About eight miles off the Gibraltar coast is a sandbank, which would have been above sea level at one time."

"We covered that," Jules said. "Under a major shipping lane, difficult to map. But they tried. And got nothing. Not one pot. I know you're not bringing us here. We're heading west. *Out* of the Med."

"Correct. Have *you* figured out what *I* figured out? The truth?"

"I think so."

"Regale me."

Jules went back to his seat. "In a real short span of time, people in southern Europe advanced a ridiculous amount. Farming agricultural land, raisin' livestock, buildin' more advanced stuff. But over fifteen thousand years it pushed folk farther back. Sea levels rose. No advanced race is puttin' up a city in the middle a rising sea."

"So...?"

Behind Valerio, and out of his window, Jules watched the land curve, the sea an immovable, constant force, both beautiful and deadly.

Jules said, "The Richat Atlanteans were the bad guys. They built their city with a goal of helping progress the people around Africa and Southern Europe, but sometime between construction and the time we're talkin' about—generations coming and going—they moved on to conquest. Slavery. Like the giants' remains we found. The guys back in Ecuador, they'd sent out scouts to map progress and what they'd become. The Ecuador guys, who hadn't lost their way, needed a base to work from. Their own Atlantis. They saw how the Europeans were advancing and the Richat dudes felt threatened. That's the fear I felt back there, in their temple. A risin' hatred that I couldn't speak about at the time. But I recognise it now. The Witnesses came along to this region—gateway to the Med—and built a similar city facing the Atlantic. Probably more than one, if the books were anything to go by. But this one, Plato's Atlantis, was a defensive measure. They helped the Greeks, the other Europeans, fight back against the Richat guys, driving 'em back to Mauritania to regroup."

"And then?" Valerio said.

"And then the comet hit. No one expected it. Totally unpredictable. Wipes out the Richat Atlantis, anything near the Mediterranean, and whatever else was built on the coasts around then."

Valerio stared at him with a smile that looked... *hungry*, weirdly, but Jules was probably misreading it. "Blasted walls of water all over the globe, set off earthquakes, and destroyed all that this race had built. All gone, because of one twist of fate." He continued staring. When Jules didn't engage, he added, "You know exactly where we're going now, don't you?"

"Yes."

"And do you think your Lost Origins tribe will catch up with us?"

"Not in time to stop Father Emory and his Forefathers church. And a lot depends on whether Colin does what I think he's gonna."

"Which is?"

Jules remained silent. He was aiming for "enigmatic" but expected he looked smug.

"Fine," Valerio said. "Then I hope you have a plan for gate-crashing Donana Park. Because I'm not sure we'll be able to put down anywhere safe."

Jules shrugged. "We'll work something out. They'll be expecting us from the south. Have Horse drop below radar now we're far enough east, and circle around north. Then we do what we need to do."

"How exciting," Valerio said, and headed off to help Horse plot a course.

They had to be right this time. They had to get there before

Emory dug into that temple. Because, if what Jules saw and felt in the Richat site was any indicator, no one—especially a religious fanatic—should ever access what the Witnesses left behind.

CHAPTER FIFTY-THREE

Colin provided the equipment, while Alfonse supplied the means. Dan, for one, was ecstatic at the prospect of finally being unleashed. The Action Dudes had returned to their rightful place as the tip of the LORI spear, driving into new territory on a beachhead.

That *could* be an exaggeration.

But, after months of toiling away in the Chinese jungle with a trowel and a small brush, getting out there felt good, if only in his gut. There was still a lot of trekking inland at dusk, as well as a lot of planning, before they could really let loose.

It was the first time Dan felt even a smidgeon of affection for the bird-faced British aristocrat. When he called whatever bigwig was running the Interpol op, who confirmed to Detective Inspector Denis that he and his people were to retreat to a secure location and await further orders, he and the entire LORI family were left to gather and listen to Xander as he revealed Jules's intent in detail.

Admittedly, all Dan heard was:

blah blah, freed Valerio because Jules is an asshat who thinks he knows better than everyone else...

...heading off to rescue Prihya because Interpol are moving too slow...

...blah...

...can't let the alien artifact fall into the wrong hands...

(although Dan *might* have inserted the "alien" part himself)

...Richat wasn't the Atlantis of Plato, but they're going there now...

...historical evidence, blah blah, not just one city...

...blah blah, it's over there, like, for real *this time...*

...come mop up Jules's mess when he's finished playing nice with the psycho-killer billionaire...

And they agreed. Colin agreed, Toby agreed, Bridget bit her lip and agreed. Dan and Harpal griped for a while, but Charlie took the neutral route that sold the team wholeheartedly.

"Sheep-headed idiot might get himself killed. But this is where we are. Colin can't mobilize an Interpol warrant that fast, am I right?"

"You are," Colin confirmed.

"So, he uses the Royal fleet or whatever to get us in position, sets us off, while he pulls his strings behind closed doors to convince the powers that be to send in the cavalry."

"Correct. You are the astute one, aren't you? No wonder you don't work with them full-time."

"And these guys," Harpal said, "they're just hanging out in a dark room watching on a satellite feed and not listening to reason until it's too late?"

"Er, no, our lawyers are in Brussels, and they are preparing paperwork for a judge to sign, and for three world leaders to classify as beyond top secret, before deploying an armed response unit that will help you and your friends—maybe—survive the next twenty-four hours. These things take time. But you can light the way, so to speak, give us a beacon to home in on."

"Pawns?" Toby said.

"Pathfinders," Dan said, eager to get to where he was right now. "Get them the intel. When the muscle is ready, it drops the hammer."

"I'm not sure what any of that means," Bridget said. "But if I get to slap Jules hard across the face, I'm in."

As soon as Dan's mouth opened to object, Bridget put a finger in his face, almost taking out an eye.

"And do not even think about benching me like Jules did. I'm your linguist. Your code breaker. You need me there, on the ground. Capeesh?"

No one moved.

Dan had frozen. "Did you just say *capeesh?*"

"Yeah, sorry," Bridget answered. "I'm not sure where that came from."

"Alfonse," Charlie said, bringing them back on track. "What do we need from Alfonse?"

What they needed from Alfonse was a smuggling route. Colin arranged for them to be flown into a British base in southern Europe on a plane with a call sign reserved for a royal whose offspring was 23rd in line to the throne, then transported them to a Royal Navy vessel not usually assigned to waters this far from dock. It blasted them along at full speed, meeting up with a motley crew of men who appeared to be fishermen, but whose boat was sturdier in the water, faster than the average fishing boat, and far cleaner, despite the tang of fish not quite overpowering the thick aroma of marijuana that surrounded every member of the crew.

When they were clear in international waters, Dan unsealed the smugglers' hidden compartment and chose Sigs and lightweight carbines for himself, Charlie, Harpal, and, after much cajoling and convincing she could handle it, Bridget. Toby made do with a Browning 9mm, which he examined with what Dan took as nostalgia. They were dressed in khaki, part Army surplus, part rugged hiking gear, which Jules had mockingly referred to as "archaeologist chic." Dan saw it as practical, and he was in charge of this stage, so everyone dressed appropriately and brought the right gear.

They checked their packs after landing on the deserted beach. Toby communicated with Colin via the biscuit-tin-sized transponder that fed into Toby's throat mic. He and Harpal were on comms duty to Brussels, while Charlie established contact with Phil in London, their children visiting Phil's parents so he could concentrate. He made it clear that he had been climbing the walls with worry during her dark period when Valerio had cut her off. It didn't help that the only access he'd gotten now was a one-way patch that he couldn't change or even advise on.

He couldn't use direct observation satellites, but he could bounce signals from several to sync with Charlie and Dan's body cams and let

Charlie, Dan, and Bridget talk to him. Only Xander was excluded from radio comms. Colin insisted on him coming, but Dan didn't trust him after siding with Jules, so Xander's most lethal weapon was a shovel.

Colin questioned the need for manual equipment like this when it was likely they'd be bringing up the rear after the donkey work, but Toby wanted to be prepared for delicate finesse.

Kit checked, illegal firearms in hand, they tramped up the sand, leaving the salty, seaweed-laden air, and hiked into the cool evening shade. The sun was setting, and the land was full of natural dangers, changeable geology, and groups who might oppose strangers trespassing on what many in this country considered untouchable land.

After thirty minutes of trekking, they met their guide, Omar, who led one such group—highly protective of their heritage and trustworthy only because Colin Waterston and the British had helped preserve the natural habitat, despite cod-scientists, adventurers, and Father Emory asking about excavations and deep drilling. Colin had vouched for him and the few guides driving the Land Rovers that idled in the reedy marshland.

Four men, four vehicles. Six passengers.

"Dan," Dan said, extending his hand.

Omar shook it, introduced himself and the three others—Theo, Paulo, and Brad—all dressed in black with headscarves similar to those Dan had seen terrorists wearing in hostage videos. While he knew—factually—this was simply practical gear to fend off dry and dusty conditions, it didn't sit well with him.

"Great," Dan said, looking around the vehicles. "I'm with Bridget and Charlie. Toby, you and Harpal take that one with Xander."

The journey inland was bumpy, the boats that brought them up the coast and into the estuary now long gone. Omar removed his head gear in the cab and wore a pained expression as he drove in silence. Dan was certain it was not an act. He was a tiny man, stocky, and what hair he had was a comb-over. The scars on his arms were old, and he had fingers that were knotted from years of hard labour.

To build camaraderie on what was likely to be hours in a confined space, Dan would normally ask his guide about his life, but he thought it likely Omar would either tell tales of great hardship or of military experience or rebellion that—since Colin Waterston recruited him through back channels—Dan might not appreciate. Instead, he kept an eye on their progress on the e-tablet Charlie had supplied. They were a red dot in an area of natural beauty, preserved by law and presided over by... well, people like Omar.

After a few broken conversations and Phil commentating to relieve tension, they reached a complex in the wilderness. It was an unexpected sight, lit by a series of small bonfires and built into the hillside with three-foot-thick wooden walls. Dan saw inside through large, square windows as they passed. If the geological equipment was any indication, there were ten or twelve people, men and women, using a stock of instrumentation from a lab or university field office.

No guards, no security, and no indication that it was anything other than an academic or naturalist complex. Except there was a perimeter fence.

While they may do good work out here, this was not exclusively an innocent scientific endeavor.

All of the passengers disembarked, and three women brought food out on platters that were pungent in a good way—full of spice and herby aromas—and placed it on a long table with a plastic tablecloth, where the drivers dug in. Omar, pulling his headgear back on for warmth, motioned for LORI to join them, and they all ate quietly. It was hot, and one of the veg-ball dumplings was far too spicy for Toby, who stuck to the meat and rice. Omar spoke up after washing it down with fruit juice.

"The destination is four hours that way." He pointed between two moonlit hills which appeared arid in the dark. "We will lead you as far as our GPS permits. Then we are ordered to let you go on your way. Alone."

"Thank you," Toby said, practically bowing. "Your assistance is very much appreciated."

Omar gave a respectful nod, his expression remaining grim. "You will do nothing to violate this land."

It wasn't a question, but Dan treated it like one. "If anything gets violated, it won't be us doing it."

"We leave in five minutes. You may use the bathrooms."

Omar left them alone to consult with his men.

Harpal said, "Anyone else nervous?"

"Be stupid if we weren't," Dan replied. "Question is, if Jules is doing more than going after Prihya and stopping Emory, do we treat him as hostile?"

"No!" Bridget said. "Whatever he's done, he's doing it because it makes sense."

"To him," Charlie said. "Don't get me wrong, I like the guy. I was proper suspicious of him for a long time, but I know he isn't malicious. He's just..." She pulled a pained face as she glanced at Bridget then past her to Toby. "I think he's damaged. Lets his obsessions control him."

"Agreed." Harpal squeezed Bridget's shoulder, plainly sensing she was about to argue. "It works out. Sometimes. But he isn't seeing the bigger picture. And I don't just mean the institute's future, or getting Colin off our backs, or getting away from relying on the Carsons' goodwill."

"Goodwill?" Bridget said. "You mean emotional blackmail."

"I mean, Jules is off on his own. Again. We won't do anything to hurt him, not intentionally, but we all know how his brain works. He's already calculated every option, given the data."

Dan shifted so he was facing them all. "We'll do our best to make sure he survives long enough to let Bridget kick his ass, but... Jules knows this might be a one-way trip for him."

They stood in silence, the night air thin, colder than they'd expected. A car door closing, followed by the clack of platters being removed brought them back to the present.

Toby said, "As unsavory as this is, Harpal and Dan are correct. Xander... Do you have anything to add now we're nearing the site?"

"Only that it is the right time to go dark," Xander said. "We cannot alert the people waiting for us."

"Which means...?" Charlie said.

"You know what it means," Dan answered.

Charlie nodded and reactivated her subvocal mic, the bone conducted tech inserted into her ear. "Phil, we need privacy. Can you cut Waterston out of our hair?"

"Like a piece of chewing gum," Phil replied, the feed active in Dan's ear, too.

"The Action Dudes will go on ahead," Toby said. "Laying the trail for Xander and myself. Then Bridget and Charlie, you bring up the rear. But please do not take this as my sidelining you. You will both be needed. I can only hope we do not have to fight."

CHAPTER FIFTY-FOUR

JULES HAD BEEN LYING BACK in the cabin for over an hour, and despite the engine hum and occasional seat vibration, he felt completely alone. Even in this state, he knew he was the only thing between Valerio, Emory, and a terrible outcome.

Valerio had briefed him and Horse on the resources available, and Jules agreed they should team up with the single Striovian unit Valerio had positioned in-country while still hedging his bets about the final destination. The nationless soldiers were to meet them on the ground, infiltrate the Donana site perimeter via dried mudflats, and hopefully complete their mission without detection. Valerio's efficient mapping out of the operation gave Jules a chill, as if he had expected Emory's betrayal in Ecuador rather than setting a backup plan in motion.

He stirred from his meditation and looked out the window as the green and black ground gave way to the once-marshy land, which was drying out at an alarming rate because of rising global temperatures, from which habitats like this were bearing the brunt. A plan of his own had taken shape, morphing, mutating into something else, now the reality of their incursion was upon him.

He took a deep breath and turned away from the window to concentrate. They'd made one pass over the target, which must have alerted Emory and his North Korean mercenaries, but it wasn't restricted airspace, so Jules knew they wouldn't shoot down a small plane on a hunch.

Since Charlie had rigged up the "puck" from her latest ground penetrating radar, Jules insisted on the flyby. Data arrived, making Valerio giddy and Jules tolerated the giddiness. The terrain didn't exactly match Richat or an island, nor the supposedly leaked documents from Prihya's conspiracy videos, and the GPR result was unclear.

"Are we concerned?" Valerio asked.

A glimmer of hope sparked in Jules's chest—if they could not find what they were looking for, then maybe Emory wouldn't either.

But no.

The land was far from perfect. This area of the Atlantic-Mediterranean plate lay on a subduction zone, so the plates would have moved thousands of times since the tsunami slammed into this coast. When Jules took a step back and zoomed out in his mind's eye, he could clearly see the landscape, how the hills undulated in a curve, dipping down to a central spot, then rising in an approximation of concentric circles.

Not proof of anything, but if Father Emory wanted to dig, it would be here.

"No drilling rigs," Jules said. "You see anyone?"

"No." Valerio consulted the e-tablet with the data processing, the forms of lines and what looked like walls manifesting out of the three thousand photos per square kilometer that had filtered through. "But then, you didn't see the Korean gents when you were stood right next to them in the rainforest, so there's that."

"True." Jules had no ego about things like that. It was just something that had happened, intel to factor into the present. "That's familiar."

He pinched the screen Valerio was holding and it enhanced the spot where he expected the center to be. A fuzzy rectangle took shape, shimmered, blurred, then focused.

"The Temple of Apollo," Valerio said.

"Or a hut some scientists left to nature fifty years ago."

"No... no, that's a buildup of minerals. A man-made building, secure from the ravages of nature, repelling what would normally rot it to dust, and—"

"Okay, okay, fine. Prihya's dumbass video turned out to be right somehow. I'm gonna guess Emory needs a way to activate it."

"And they need someone like you to do it?"

"Nah, the engineers in the Richat did it by killing the power from the orb. I think that's the point. The orb isn't supposed to power the city. It *holds back* the city, keeps it in stasis."

Realization sparked in Valerio. "Stored power. Like a capacitor. And the orbs are the resistors in the circuit, regulating the flow."

"Yeah, makes sense. Touch it, I can kill the power, but it gives a massive pulse. Or I can divert the power and turn it into something else, if I got the right conducting tool."

"Like the trident." If it were possible, Valerio grew even more excited. "Or the chambers you used in New Zealand."

"How do you know about—"

"My North Korean friends used them too, but they didn't have someone special like you and me."

"I ain't special and neither are you. Just have a quirk in our DNA, that's all. Ain't some mystical 'chosen one' crap, so don't start on that again."

"Fine. Be a moody boy about it. Shall we get on with things? Then you can enact whatever convoluted plan you have to betray me."

"You think I'll turn on you? After our agreement?"

"I do." Valerio squinted in a way Jules wasn't sure was sarcastic or melodramatic. "Are you seriously suggesting that if you have the chance to use me and then arrest me, you won't?"

"Of course I will. If I can."

Valerio laughed briefly and loudly. "Then we are nearing the end of our merry dance. You know how I hate spoilers, but I'll let you in on a secret: you're not getting out of there. You won't kill, and you can't escape without something very powerful coming to bear."

"There's always another way," Jules said.

"We'll see. Time to make everything go bang. I assumed you have a means of landing this thing?"

"Funny you should say that. But nope." Jules got up and opened an overhead locker, removed three brown packs, and dropped them on the floor. "You know how to check a parachute, right?"

Toby and Xander reached the rendezvous thirty minutes after the Action Dudes. It was a precarious approach, the dark certainly their friend, but engine noise would pierce the silence and carry over the wind for miles. Dan had suggested this as the last vehicle stage before walking, so they hiked in three staggered groups with a single expert in each.

Toby had already spotted the thick, rugged lines that looked like walls encroaching on the land. He might have missed them if not on high alert to the shapes in the night.

Not that these were their destination. This was merely the outer edge, the hors d'oeuvres before the amuse-bouche.

Would Jules see these? Which direction was he coming from? Would he mark them or ignore them?

Toby pushed harder as they crossed the barren ground, but Xander and their guide, Brad—short for something non-local and hard to pronounce—were very gracious about his slower pace. The chilly night kept him from sweating, and fresh air cooled his cheeks. They were likely red from cold and exertion.

Charlie and Bridget stayed a hundred meters behind because the staggered train gave each unit time to warn the others, should Emory launch an attack. After cutting Colin off, should he choose to interfere in his self-interested way again, Phil Locke was monitoring those airwaves.

And so, they climbed. Soft ground made the going tougher, and he had higher priorities than holding back the ageing process. Like traversing the remote plateau, undetected by any incursion of Emory's private army.

Toby saw a raised fist against the moonlit sky as Dan and Harpal stopped ahead.

"Down," came Dan's command.

Brad knelt. Xander did likewise. Toby bent his legs, feeling his knees creak, and supported himself on one hand before kneeling alongside.

Toby asked, "Why are we on the floor?"

"Movement," Dan replied. "Taking a wider route."

They resumed. When Toby and Xander reached the point where Dan had halted, peering into the depression of land ahead, it was clear that someone had arrived ahead of them. Lots of someones. Toby couldn't see the stick-man figures clearly, but he got the impression they were armed—the way they walked, carried themselves, the pattern of their movement.

They were guarding something.

"Militia," Brad said by way of explanation.

"Local?" Toby asked.

"I do not know. I do not expect it. We should have heard of them moving in."

"It is crazy," Xander said. "To think this is the site your Witnesses called home. *Another* Atlantean stronghold."

"Impossible, but true," Toby said. "That should be our motto."

Dan said, "The guards don't look military. Or big time mercs. Might be locals instead of the Koreans. Moonlighting cops, maybe. Hired to protect something they probably don't understand."

"You're sure they aren't military?" Toby asked. "Even militia?"

The term militia, in this sense, might also be construed as *terrorist group*, depending which government arm was speaking of them.

"I watched them for long enough," Dan said.

"Me too," Harpal added. "But that doesn't make them friendly."

They weren't sniping or bantering, which meant they were taking the situation seriously. Harpal was not a trained soldier, but he was more than capable of handling himself. He and Dan were both good people, though, so probably didn't need to hear what Toby said next.

"We should employ a non-lethal approach until they prove to be hazardous to life. If they end up being Valerio's or Emory's mercenaries, then they knew what they were signing up for. Do we agree?"

"Roger that," Dan said.

"Confirmed," Harpal said.

Bridget and Charlie both said, "Yes," at the same time.

Xander nodded, not that Toby believed he could fight his way out of a wet paper bag. Brad frowned—or the part visible above his scarf did—but said nothing.

"Okay," Toby said. "Then let's go forward. With care."

It was at that moment when the sky opened with a thunderous clap that shook the air, releasing a searing explosion of light that illuminated the basin. A cacophony of explosions and gunfire thundered around, crashing and cracking like a thousand drums pealing into the night.

"Oh, my," Toby said. "What on Earth is happening?"

"I don't know," Dan answered. "But it isn't us. My guess?"

"Jules," Bridget said. "It's gotta be Jules."

CHAPTER FIFTY-FIVE

Jules had never gotten emotionally attached to inanimate objects, but he admitted he would miss LORI's twenty-year-old Lear-jet. While he, Valerio, and Horse floated to the ground under para-chute canopies, he watched with a mild pang as the plane cut through the night on autopilot, flying over the military formation of men at the far side of Emory's destination. The first rocket shot upward in an orange streak and hit its target with a huge *thoom*. After the second hit, the jet spun, flinging debris in all directions, and fell into the hillside, where its fuel ignited and lit the entire plateau.

They could have set the autopilot to fly it in a more discreet direction, so it ran out of fuel over the ocean and sank without witnesses. But the risk paid off.

The flash and burn revealed their enemies' positions and numbers —a neat perimeter of fourteen men around a freshly blasted hole in the center—and Jules saw the best approach from the shallow angle before landing in a natural clearing. Valerio and Horse were already down, Horse cutting free and racing to view their target.

"Did you see it?" Valerio asked as he stuffed his and Horse's 'chutes back in the packs to avoid flagging their location. They just had to hope the explosion hadn't revealed their descent.

"The crater?" Jules said.

"Of course, the crater. They've been here longer than we expected. It means they're inside. They might already have found it."

"Don't matter. They can't do much with it."

"Are you sure? Remember what happened with me? In that pool?"

"You needed a catalyst to change your DNA. Me. And the bangles. Can't turn Emory into something else without—"

"How do you know he isn't already like you?" Valerio asked.

Jules snagged on the more intense tone. "You wanna tell me something?"

"I don't know for sure. I just feel like he has more at stake than getting his hands on a flashy weapon. Or a power source."

Jules had had the same thought, but he doubted it was as simple as Emory sharing the ability to activate the Witnesses' tech. "Whatever he's doing, that's the target, right? That's why we're here. Can't stop him if we ain't in front of him."

"Fine."

They set out on a trek to the heart of a wilderness guarded by what Valerio had thought of as his men for many months, North Korean ex-soldiers who'd fled after their leader's failed attempts to harness a dangerous defensive shield. Even though they were paid, those men wanted nothing more than to return victorious to their homeland. The terrain was rough, but a rare stroke of luck kept the moon too low to betray their position, instead casting a cold shadow from the lowland hills. Jules wore a thermal bodysuit underneath his padded coat and overalls, and their supplies were non-existent, aside from enough energy snacks and water to last half a day. Lighter to move. Faster.

Jules was more concerned about how hard he would have to fight his current allies once their common enemy was defeated. But he kept his concerns to himself.

Valerio appeared calm as they jogged, Horse obtained a thick stick he snapped from a tree, and Jules couldn't help but be wary of him being armed. He clearly had a use for it once they reached their destination.

Frequently, Jules noticed footprints in the soil and scuff marks on tree bark. Hooting and skittering echoed through from behind, in front, and to the sides. None of them said anything. The sounds could have been their imagination or nocturnal creatures investigating their intrusion, but Jules was certain they didn't go unnoticed.

Finally, they arrived at the outskirts of the plateau's center, where the crater they'd seen from above had been piled high. The men stationed at strategic points around it were heavily armed, and there was no way to eliminate them all without being seen or heard. Even in the dark, the North Korean contingent was clearly visible.

Too quietly to hear, Jules asked, "Are they a deterrent or are they supposed to suck us in to a gunfight?"

"Like they did at Richat?" Valerio said. "Hard to say." He gazed at Horse, who'd hunkered down beside them, his eyes alert, the stick held tightly like a short bo staff. "If he had all his faculties, I'd be looking to him for advice. But all I can do is tell him to go fight or help us sneak around."

"Can he do a bit of both?"

Deep in the blasted earth, Father Emory and his people discovered only mud, stone, and stale air. Prihya trailed behind and spoke only when called upon. She could only hope that, despite her helping the people who left Jules, Charlie, and Bridget to die underground, they would plow through with their usual bloody-mindedness. Jules, in particular, was unlikely to hand over responsibility. He'd see the benefit in going after her.

Unsure how much longer Emory would keep her alive, Prihya clung desperately to the hope that the plane crash into the hillside was merely a distraction, and that salvation was close at hand.

After Muzaffer's subcontractors' back-hoe diggers and blasts took four hours to excavate twenty feet, they hit a huge air pocket which expanded the hold to almost fifty feet, and Emory thought they'd struck gold. Again. Metaphorically speaking.

Prihya had warned them that it wasn't deep enough to hide a city from LiDar, geologists, and others like her, but they disregarded her advice. They left four radar pucks on the lowest level, pulsing and reading data in the hopes of receiving a signal revealing their objective.

Prihya followed the priest as he led his three acolytes through the tunnels, which were likely dried underground streams. She had speculated that the larger air pocket was once filled with run-off from those streams, but they were too desperate for a result to believe her on faith.

Returning to the edge of one dead stream bed, overlooking the larger air pocket, Emory stood deflated and said, "There's nothing."

Moses had been waiting in a different burrow with his abseiling gear attached, while Muzaffer and Hilla occupied another. The scene reminded Prihya of a network of ventilation ducts branching from an elevator shaft.

"It's here," Prihya said, determined to make positive use of her knowledge. "But a lot deeper. We need equipment like they had at Richat."

"No," Emory said. "We have something else."

"We're running out of time," Muzaffer pointed out.

Moses tested his line, and checked the remote that operated the winch to pull them out. "Muzaffer is correct. That plane crash was intentional. They are coming. And it isn't the police."

"You are scared?" Emory asked.

"It isn't cowardice to give a rattlesnake a wide berth, even if you know how to capture or kill it. Still be wary. If that plane crash was Valerio's doing, he may have other operatives nearby. If not, then we are looking at a group of civilians. But they are civilians who got away from us more than once. They are sneaky and effective."

"And do not forget Korea," Hilla said. "With help from the New Zealanders, they broke into a military complex. And destroyed it."

"The idiots running the complex destroyed it," Muzaffer said. "Toying with power they did not understand. Father Emory will guide us. The Forefathers want this for us."

Moses and Hilla bowed their heads in agreement and supplication. Prihya had witnessed similar behavior in the past, but never in the scholar-assassins. They'd exuded a more military air around Valerio, treating him as if he were a commanding officer; with Emory, they deferred to him as if he were some sort of guru, a spiritual guide. And their respect had little to do with the Roman collar he wore even when dressed more casually.

"They are probably here, one way or another," Emory said. "In fact, it is imperative they come. Once they understand the true power we will unlock, and the peace it can bring to the planet, they will want to help. You must stop them from killing me before I can show them the truth."

"What if it isn't Jules who comes?" Prihya asked as she snatched up her harness to step into.

"Your measurements are probably wrong, child," Emory said, helping her buckle up. "But your intimate knowledge of this place came in handy. I'm glad you changed your mind about Richat. That could have been awkward."

"The books from Tayos hinted at Richat. But that wasn't the destination, not the way I saw it. This is the real deal. *Here*." With her harness in place, Prihya swallowed back the enthusiasm resurfacing in her.

"I am sure you are correct. And, like Richat, the prize is in what Plato called the Temple of Apollo. But God Himself only knows what the Witnesses called it. Doesn't matter, really."

Ready to ascend, Moses's satellite phone pinged. He laid the controls aside and checked the readout. "Our off-site analysis confirms—movement. Unfriendlies closing in. And the LiDar units at the bottom have picked up something."

They all gazed over the edge at the ingenious setup below—four units scanning at once, collating data into a single computer, and transmitted via satellite to Emory's cult of fanatics. Or "scientific conclave" as he referred to it.

"Looks like she came through after all." Moses aimed a wide smile at Prihya as he put the phone away. "We've found it."

Was this really the spot? It seemed so anticlimactic to Bridget. No fanfare, no fireworks or volcanic eruption. Just, "Right, we're here."

Xander had seemed confident in his coordinates, but that didn't stop Dan checking them. Nor did it prevent Toby checking Dan had checked them correctly.

There didn't seem to be much around, and those guarding the area had been drawn away by the explosions and, possibly, something else.

"I reckon we can be sure the coordinates are correct," Charlie said. "But does this seem wrong to anyone else? Why is Jules bringing us *here*?"

Toby handed the shielded e-tablet back to Xander. "We don't have much time. The sun will be coming up soon."

"I don't like it," Dan said. "Got here a bit too easily."

"Easy?" Harpal said. "I'm knackered."

"I mean there were no hoops to jump through. No locked tombs, no puzzles, not even a bout of fighting. We should have met more resistance."

"Unless they want us here," Bridget said. "What if it's an ambush? Revenge against us? Or my dad?"

After a brief consultation with Dan, the three guides fanned out, cautious about the worry being voiced.

Bridget said, "I know he can be an ass, but we should trust Jules knows what he is doing. He insisted Xander bring us here, to this spot, where he's brought Valerio. Where Emory has Prihya hostage. We need to keep on track."

"But..." Toby huffed and shifted to a slightly higher vantage on this flat, unusual vista. "We've moved beyond what might have once been walls. Outside the city, perhaps."

"Maybe he's setting us up for a neat view," Harpal said. "Jules doesn't do small."

"Then why must we be here?" Xander asked.

Bridget caught the twitch of a half-smile at the corner of Xander's mouth. "Why do I get the impression you're being a wiseass? We only agreed to come with you if you were straight with us."

"And this isn't straight." Charlie squared off toward him.

Dan and Harpal also tensed, seeing the same now.

Xander pointed to the barren plain, away from where they'd seen and felt the explosions. "It is beyond the new walls. Not the old ones. Not the original walls, which we are interested in. There... This is why we come all this way. Why we wait for sunrise."

Sunrise was an exaggeration, although the sky to the east had lightened somewhat. Enough to cast faint but very long shadows competing with those stretching from the low moon to the south. They could make out a hill, black against a deep blue-black sky.

No, two of them.

Only, across the natural reserve, this protected land, the hills looked more like...

"Oh my god," Bridget said. "Twin mountains... projecting long, narrow lines... the shadows... look!"

All gathered to follow her pointing finger.

"Those shadows, they look so narrow from that angle. Coming this way, toward us. Like..."

"Pillars," Toby said.

"Pillars?" Dan said. "Like..."

"Like the Pillars of Heracles," Charlie said.

A surge of warmth filled Bridget, almost warding off the cold surrounding them. "Jules got this from Prihya. He understood the truth. And what has to be done."

CHAPTER FIFTY-SIX

HORSE AGREED to Jules's play, hesitating only to get Valerio's approval. The big man, who appeared to lumber around like an ape most of the time, crept forward as nimbly as a ballerina, keeping tight to the tall grass until the first guard spotted him.

Too late.

Horse thrust his new favorite stick into the man's throat, making him gag, then slammed an open-handed upper-cut into his chin, before grasping his head and twisting.

Jules heard the wet snap of the soldier's neck from where he darted silently beside Valerio into a shallow gully.

He whispered, "I didn't say kill anyone."

"You didn't say *don't* kill anyone," Valerio replied.

"I literally made it a condition before we jumped outta the plane."

"Huh. Really? That doesn't sound like something I would agree to. Must've slipped my mind."

Jules chewed the inside of his cheek. Too late for the dead man, and too late to recall Horse. He was doing his job.

Pinned to the ground, Jules peered over the gully's lip to see Horse engaging a second guard twenty feet away. Only, this time the man got a warning off before dying the same way as the first. Horse retreated loudly enough to divert attention away from Jules and Valerio as the alert spread around the perimeter. They quickly lost sight of him.

They belly-crawled forward and soon arrived at the explosion site.

Jules reminded himself of what Valerio had suspected: Emory hadn't come for a weapon or a power source, but for something else entirely.

The crater was a little more than ten feet wide and still warm. The pit itself was much wider and rougher than the drilled boreholes at Richat, but the deep excavation proved Emory owed their success to explosives experts. It was too deep to see into while lying flat, but a flicker below indicated human occupation.

Jules instructed Valerio to remain silent, then stared blinking into the shaft for a full minute, waiting for his night vision to adjust to the new shade of black. He soon noticed the holes where the explosives had revealed cavities—the ends resembling capillaries in bone. A steel cable had been lowered from the back of a modified pickup truck, and rope ladders had been daisy-chained together and secured to equipment on the other side.

Jules rolled away, keeping his eyes low to avoid any brighter objects stealing his eyes' night vision. "I'm going in."

Without pausing for Valerio's approval, Jules bolted around the barren dirt from his nine-o-clock position. Loose dirt crunched beneath his feet, particles of dust peppering his face. Stealing glances to his right to ensure Horse's diversion remained effective, he was determined to reach the three-o-clock point where the ladders and steel cable awaited him.

So far, so good.

Coming upon the vehicles, Jules slowed, crouched lower as he pressed on, and almost stumbled over another guard in full camo gear.

He threw a palm-strike, stunning the man with a non-lethal blow to the throat. The gun barrel lashed out in panic. Jules dodged, inserted one finger into the trigger guard to avoid a discharge, then spun his opponent around and used the submachine gun to choke him out.

Unconscious, not dead, he slumped to the ground.

Jules kept the gun, strapped it to his back, and quickly searched the unconscious soldier for other weapons, removing a knife. Finding no sidearm, he moved on.

It was now less than an hour before dawn, and Jules would be lucky to spend even half of that time in the pit. The steel cable hung freely over the side, but he couldn't see where it ended. There were no sentries on the other side of the pit, and the cable's angle likely prevented anyone from seeing it from above.

Only one way to find out.

Jules drew one of his batons and secured the grappling hook end to the cable, then hefted his body over the side and descended using the ladder. He had a quick escape option if anyone noticed him, the hook's claw tight to the cable. A moving target was difficult to hit, and a fast-moving target was nearly impossible for even the most experienced sniper.

During a stuttering descent, he counted the lights that occasionally revealed themselves. He counted three flashlight beams, implying at least three people.

However, there could be many more.

Jules checked on the capillaries he'd seen from above, concerned that the flashlights were coming from there, but the tunnels were empty. If he had to guess, they were natural fissures formed by flowing water, interrupted by the new hole.

He was almost at the bottom when he realized what he'd seen from the rim was not flashlights crisscrossing, but lasers communicating with one another. His eyes had adjusted to the darkness well enough that he could see the satellite dish hidden behind a computer crane, tilted so that the signal was directed toward a satellite. If it worked like Charlie's, there were multiple sensors and lasers firing data between themselves to form a single, coherent image.

Something whizzed over his head. He ducked, even though he couldn't see it, and swung on his grappling hook. Immediately, the tough clay-like wall sputtered with a cluster of bullets.

They'd have taken his head clean off.

Commercial suppressors simply dulled the gunshot, so the sound didn't travel over long distances; whatever was concealing these rounds must have been seriously heavy-duty.

He let out the bungee cord and as the claw slipped downward slower than Jules, the elastic rope fed through and allowed a faster descent.

Hitting the floor, he lay facedown, rolled to the side, and made himself as small as possible behind the satellite dish. Another spatter of bullets threw dirt up from where he'd been lying.

"Hello." Father Emory's voice echoed all around.

With nowhere to go except to reduce his target zone under the dish and hope beyond hope that they valued the equipment more than his death, he called back with the only reply he could think of. "Hey!"

"Are you shot?"

"Not yet."

"Good. Good. Then you will understand when I ask you to surrender your weapon."

Jules had little use for a submachine gun here, anyway. It was more important to pinpoint Emory and whoever was protecting him—the scholar-assassins, he assumed. And perhaps Prihya was close by, too.

First, he did something he was not remotely sure of. It was not a huge risk in terms of his life hanging by a thread, but as he untied one boot, he questioned whether he'd have taken such a risk—with so little data and next to zero certainty—in the time before LORI. Okay, he was positive he wouldn't have. But how far was he from such a gamble? Had he become an entirely different person? Had he never worked on a hunch before?

Or was the knowledge there, within him, at a subconscious level?

That would be unusual—his consciousness had always been front and center, so why would he—

"We do not have all night," Emory called. "Curious locals will descend soon, regardless of our official signposts."

Jules finished up, held the gun by the barrel, and extended his arm. He rose slowly so he could see past the dish, bracing himself for gunfire. Nothing happened. He tossed the weapon, linked his fingers behind his head, and looked upward.

"I'm unarmed."

The voice again was difficult to locate, but Jules found the most likely spot: two figures backlit next to the ladder.

Jules called, "What now?"

A whirring noise alerted him to a new line he hadn't seen before, black cord sequestered away from the obvious cable, with Muzaffer zipping down on a rapid carabiner. He cinched it to slow himself and came to a complete stop at the bottom. Moses and Hilla exposed themselves from where he began his descent, Hilla with a rifle stock in her shoulder, an eye to the scope, and a suppressor as thick as Julie's calf muscle; Moses held no weapon that Jules could see.

Muzaffer approached, a pistol at his hip, other hand extended to flap open Jules's coat, the gun too far for Jules to snatch. "Lose the belt."

Jules made wide, deliberate movements with his hands open. He slowly unclipped the belt containing his flashbangs and tossed it the same way as the SMG.

Emory issued another order: "Check his wrists."

Jules shrugged his coat off and raised his hands, showing his empty wrists.

"Where are they?" Emory asked.

"Where are what?"

"The key. *Your* key."

When Jules didn't respond, Moses gave a tut, followed by a grumble that sounded like, "Get me down there," and dropped from his capillary-tunnel to Emory's. Although sunrise was still some time away, there was a faint brightening of the sky that distilled the darkness, so Jules didn't have to squint as much, and his night vision was less important. Moses guided Emory and the other person, who turned out to be Prihya, to the edge of the near-sheer drop. Hilla remained perched, rifle poised.

Emory made a valiant attempt to free himself from the harness while maintaining his dignity, then marched forward, using Muzaffer as a makeshift human shield. While Moses widened his approach, Emory came to a halt with only half his body visible to Jules.

"Where are they?" Emory asked again.

"Where are what?" Jules replied.

Again.

Emory sighed, but it was an affectation. Jules sensed one of those annoying conversations coming where one side (Emory) wanted the other to admit they knew what was being said, but the other side (Jules) was being a belligerent teenager and enjoying the powerful feeling of frustrating the dude in charge. It was a bad habit, and one of his few highly illogical traits.

He enjoyed it too much to work on diminishing it, though.

"Jules, you carry the key with you everywhere."

"Not true," Jules said. "I don't have—"

"Shoot him," Emory said to Moses.

Moses steadied his aim toward Jules.

"Wait, no," Emory said. "Shoot her."

Moses turned his gun on Prihya. She squeaked a word that sounded like, "What?" and Emory held a hand that clearly meant *pause*.

"Well?" Emory said.

"You don't need her no more?" Jules said.

"I never really did. I just liked the idea of confirming our calculations. And of course, a hostage is always useful."

Prihya scowled at him. "But you said—"

"I know what I said. Now, you are far more useful as a bargaining chip." Emory shifted aside and closer to Jules, remaining out of any crossfire should Muzaffer and Moses need to pull their trigger. "You seem to be somewhat underdressed."

"There's a dress code?" Jules said.

Emory nodded toward Jules's foot. It was bare. "Prihya, why does your friend here have one naked foot?"

Prihya edged forward and saw what Emory was referring to.

"It's in the dirt," Jules said.

"Or soil," Prihya said, completing the line she'd fed him in Ecuador. "It's always in the soil. And always will be."

Jules's bare foot was standing on the connected bangles, and the tingle passing through his skin from the moment he pressed them into the soft dirt confirmed some sort of reaction was occurring. The gamble might be paying off. Or sealing them all under the earth, leaving Valerio to wander freely.

And where is Valerio?

"Okay," Emory said, exhaling with a calming tone, as if Jules were threatening them with a grenade after pulling the pin. "That's interesting. What, exactly...?"

"When I saw what the Forefathers were planning," Prihya said, using Emory's term for the Witnesses, Jules noted, "I realised there was more than one site. Just like you had. But that didn't mean any of them were safe. The rising saltwater might need to be held somewhere. If not in a massive cave like Richat, then..."

She petered out to allow someone else to finish.

Jules said, "In the soil. In the earth. In everything surrounding what's buried here."

Emory's mouth widened. Eyes bright in the gloom, he applauded slowly. "And he worked out just what you needed him to."

"Exactly," Prihya said.

The intensity of the tingle increased. No longer strictly speaking a tingle; more of a shock. Electrical tendrils zapped up through his sole, into his ankle, through the skin now, jagging through his muscles. His leg tried to spasm, but he held it in check.

Emory said, "Something's happening."

Moses and Muzaffer exchanged looks, Moses at odds with an instinct to take cover, enforcing the order to hold fast with a slow nod. Muzaffer obeyed and both men firmed up their positions, eyes drawn to the ground.

Jules flicked his gaze to his foot.

The ground glowed bright, red and green light interweaving like a complex circuit board, the channels branching out, then down, lower, until they vanished. Sparks spat and crackled under his foot, snaking around his ankle and climbing his leg like vines, alive and reaching, probing the new world, the air long denied them.

Usually, this effect was little more than a static prickle, but that was when he wore them on his arm, the internal smooth surface insulating him from the effects. Now, it crashed through him, around him, growing in size and intensity. It wasn't pain, exactly, but it wasn't pleasant either.

"That's it," Emory said. "Open the door. Then we will all discover the temple's secrets to peace on earth."

"Ain't going through no door," Jules said, teeth gritted against his spasming muscles.

"Jules, it's okay," Prihya said. "We'll work it out. We have no choice. We can't let Valerio—"

"That ain't what I mean."

Jules had felt the tremors before the others, but now the ground jumped. The soil undulated like water in a kicked bucket. All fell on their butts except Jules who was now stuck, melded to the bangles that had gripped onto the particles in the soil. It was all coalescing into one mass, connected through a form of magnetism, where particulate bonded to energy, which circulated through the non-reactive matter, and gelled it together in some semi-solid state.

"The door ain't opening," Jules said. "Time for the *temple* to come *up*."

The earthquake rumbled harder, throwing them around as they tried to regain their feet. Jules couldn't keep the glee from his voice.

"Get ready, folks. This is gonna be special."

Dan had learned a long time ago not to trust an earthquake when it came to LORI. Not that earthquakes were inherently trustworthy, but they were especially suspicious when exploring underground, inside some ancient building, and especially when that damn Jules was off doing his thing around forces that even he admitted he didn't fully understand. The team was making progress in getting Jules to stop wandering off alone, or so Dan thought, but it was still stupid and dangerous to go off on your own.

It was Bridget he turned to when he asked, "What's happening?"

"I don't know," Bridget answered, arms out to balance. "Is it like Richat again?"

Charlie struggled to keep her feet, the dry land shaking as she scrabbled for purchase on a cluster of boulders. No way she was going to climb high enough to share Dan's view from an adjacent rock.

He and Harpal were watching the world fall away. Half a click in front of them, a circle of earth disappeared. Then another circle rose around the hole. A small explosion—

No, that wasn't right. It wasn't an explosion, more a puff of air blowing out, like a giant whale expelling water as it surfaced. Sand, rocks, vegetation, probably more than a few animals, blasted into the air, then dropped and formed another circular depression, thrusting a new, wider section into the world.

"It's coming up," Dan said. "Must've got here way before us." He swallowed back a bitter taste as his jaw tightened and head bowed. "We're too late."

The group at the base of the rise had all taken one knee, the best position as the shaking subsided, to be replaced by distant heaves of ground rising and crashing. The guides, who had spread out to form a loose perimeter, stood firm.

Only Xander appeared animated.

Only Xander had a smile.

Only Xander did not appear dejected by failure.

"Old secrets. New world!" He leapt from his kneeling position and hopped around, arms to the sky. He was positively manic. "It's all true. The beauty, the engineering, it's all here!"

Between heaves, he launched up the rise, followed closely by Charlie and then Bridget. Only Toby remained behind, scouting around for a less steep alternative. He jogged the twenty yards to a kinder slope.

Charlie overtook Xander to settle by Harpal, then Xander and Bridget fast-crawled to perch near Dan.

Bridget gasped, putting her hand to her mouth. "It's..."

"Like Richat?" Charlie said.

"No, that was an accident, a wreck we disturbed. This looks... I dunno..."

"Intentional," Xander said. "Destiny. It is *controlled*. Someone with the will to see this through, someone who understands what makes the technology work."

"Nonsense." Toby crawled up beside them. He froze in place as another pocket of air blew a perimeter of earth out, then let it settle. "No one can control something on this scale."

"Of course they can. If they can build Atlantis, the pyramids, Babylon, the Incan empire, the mighty cities in the desert we have yet to uncover... if we can navigate the globe in sailboats, land on the moon, see into the heart of the universe... if you can decode ancient symbols and call it a language, if you can see into the earth using radar, find quantum communications, and defeat enemies superior to you because you hold the key to the Witnesses' greatest secrets...

surely raising this…" He spread his arms toward the walls forming out of nowhere. "Surely raising this is child's play."

All stared at him.

"Okay," Harpal said. "I'm glad I was here to listen to that live. For now, we have one simple question: *what* do we *do*?"

"This was something to do with that explosion," Charlie said. "The fighting we heard."

"Quite right." Xander lowered himself to his haunches. "But probably not what you think."

Dan said, "He knows more than he's letting on."

"I do."

Dan brought his gun around, not aiming at Xander, but the hint was stark. "Then how about you tell us?"

"Yes." Xander closed his eyes, paused, reopened them. "Jules and I wanted you to be part of this plan. You were essential, in fact. It is time you know your role in all this."

CHAPTER FIFTY-SEVEN

The temple was the first to appear. A series of platforms swished and swayed after that. Curved, most likely circular, but too large for Jules to see from ground level.

How on earth could this have worked?

Where Jules had feared the pit would collapse inward and bury them all, the bangles' expansion of energy blasted the existing walls outward, expelling matter in a massive volcano-like bloom, leaving the new crater's epicenter untouched; a sanctuary where they clung to life with thrumming hearts and disbelieving eyes.

Then they rose.

It was almost smooth, the only indication of resistance the grinding of stones and earth between man-made plates.

"How is this possible?" Moses asked.

Although it was probably hypothetical, Jules offered the only answer he could find, deep in the accumulated knowledge of his time with LORI. "They used magnetism a lot. Opposing poles to create a never-ending source of support. Released... I guess this is it."

"Stored for twelve thousand years!" Emory shouted. "All waiting for this moment."

"But they all still died," Muzaffer said, a hint of confusion.

Despite their predicament, Jules needed to emphasize the truth: "They were wiped out, or pretty much. Left behind the tech their warfaring factions developed... and the engineering... what we're only just discovering."

"Because they were inert," Emory elaborated, "no one ever found them... until now. Until *we* came along and proved ourselves worthy."

As the central mass rose slowly, the walls around it crunched up through the bedrock. As Moses tried to protect Emory, the priest cackled with delight, manic as his endgame loomed closer to fruition. Prihya, on her hands and knees, laughed the way someone might after narrowly avoiding a potentially fatal car crash by inches; she had been vindicated, and this was her victory lap. Hilla and Muzaffer stayed focused on their main task of covering Jules and Prihya, but they struggled as the massive, industrial-scale terraforming ruptured and tore through every visible surface.

As they neared ground level, as the world was reborn around them, a deeper creaking and moaning pierced the air. The platform on which they were standing groaned and squealed before tilting at a shallow angle. It wasn't enough to send them tumbling into the gaping moat-like canyon beyond the edge of their hundred yards of solid ground, but it was enough to make them stumble. Muzaffer's fall toward Jules triggered something inside of him.

A clear, unambiguous calculation, detached from the chaos around them: *he's vulnerable*.

Jules pressed his bare toes into the ground for purchase, discarded the four ways in which he could kill the scholar-assassin, and opted for the violent but non-lethal blow of leaping toward him and thrusting a knee into the man's jaw. Muzaffer's fast stagger forward and Jules's meeting him coming the other way doubled the impact and snapped Muzaffer's head back. He was unconscious before he hit the ground—whiplash and a broken jawbone for when he awoke.

In a fluid motion, Jules landed, ducked under Hilla's rifle, and swept her standing leg, placed his sweeping foot on the ground, and threw his heel back in a classic *ushiro* kick, landing his heel in her face, dropping her like her comrade.

In the three-and-a-half seconds those maneuvers took, Moses had ceased holding onto Emory and stepped in front of him, repositioned his pistol to fire, but it took significantly longer for him to draw a bead.

Significantly in Jules's world.

He'd be able to squeeze off a shot in perhaps a second more time, but it'd be inaccurate, and Jules predicted he'd want a kill shot, so it'd take at least two seconds. Jules gambled again, leaping to the side, rolling, snatching what he could from his discarded belt, and whipping a throwing knife—a three-inch blade designed for this exact purpose—into Moses's chest. It thunked home below his clavicle, discharging his gun with the impact.

Jules threw a flashbang his way, a small but piercing pop next to Moses's face, causing him to jerk and, hopefully, blinding him. Jules then charged, a second throwing knife by his side, ready to disarm the man and stab him in the thighs to deter pursuit.

However, pushing off in the usual manner resulted in a bolt of pain from his calf muscle. Instead of flying toward his target, Jules came to a halt, losing his balance as another heave shook the makeshift platform. He toppled over. He glared at the rebellious limb, noticing a bloody gash six inches below his knee.

Moses's wild shot had nicked Jules's leg, avoiding bone but gouging deep enough into the muscle to impede movement. Still, Jules could compensate.

Or he would have, if Moses hadn't recovered from the flashbang and the small blade still embedded in his chest—above his lungs and away from anything essential to life. His gun barrel was squared at Jules's forehead.

Jules said, "Damn," and awaited the end.

Prihya was terrified yet exhilarated as she dove at Moses, lifting off the ground as she yelled, "No!" and kicked out at the gun. It diverted enough for her to boot it upward, setting off another round which shot harmlessly wide.

"Ha!"

While she was not a skilled fighter, a year of lessons with a boyfriend trained in combat for a living had gifted her a solid grounding. She landed, adopted a tense fighting stance, and aimed another kick, this time at Moses' knee. But even a year was not enough to take on someone with his experience.

Moses twisted his leg so she missed, then backhanded her away, blowing the wind right out of her. She dropped, bog-eyed, and slapped onto her side. He brought the gun around.

Then cried out in pain.

Three wet chops sounded, and the gun fell from his hands.

Jules was back on his feet, using one of his throwing knifes like a stabbing weapon against Moses' upper arm, batting the gun from his grip. Then, in quick succession, the knife sliced into his forearm, thigh, then hamstring at the back of the knee.

Jules hopped aside, letting Moses crumple to the the floor.

No pithy afterthought, no glib remark. He was clearly somewhere else, mentally.

"Jules?"

He pivoted, taking in the section of city they were stood upon. Checking Muzaffer and Hilla remained unconscious, and that Moses was nowhere near a weapon as he groaned and attempted to stem the shallow knife wounds, Jules focused on Emory, who was on his feet, arms spread.

He said, "Jules, my fine young man. I knew you were capable of magnificent things, but—"

Jules snapped his wrist back, ready to fling the blade, but Emory shook his head and pleaded with him.

"No, no, no, there is much to do."

"We've stopped," Jules said, the throwing knife still prepped.

Emory twisted his head to view where they were—stiffly, hesitant, as if breaking eye contact with Jules would trigger the blade. Prihya knew differently; if Jules felt launching the knife at Emory would yield an advantage, he'd have done it by now. But that wasn't the point.

The point was exactly what Jules had said: They'd stopped.

Only, the buried city walls hadn't received that message. Whatever had disturbed the mass of negative power, the gears, or magnetic locks—Prihya still wasn't clear—continued to battle against the geological upheaval that had occurred since the comet strike ravaged the planet.

"The mountains, the hills," Jules said. "They formed centuries after the city fell. They're holding it in place."

"No," came a returning voice. "Atlantis will triumph."

Valerio and Horse were here. On an island of rock, surrounded by grinding, juddering platforms emitting unimaginable energy in its efforts to dig itself from its grave.

"You live?" Emory said.

Moses pushed back with his good leg, instinct to protect the priest seemingly hardwired. It confirmed what Prihya had observed: the scholar-assassins were not merely hired guns to the Church of the Forefathers; they truly believed in the cause, and Emory was their messiah.

Valerio wielded a handgun, Horse the type of submachine gun the Korean mercenaries had used.

"How are you alive?" Jules asked.

"I'm not actually sure," Valerio said. "Horse had made his way back to me, and he'd just stabbed this troublesome gnat of a soldier —another of my former employees, so, y'know, screw him—when we sort of fell into a big ol' pit that opened beneath us. Then there were all sorts of explosions and earthquakes and when we climbed out... wow! The last of the mercs seemed to have gone the same way..." He lowered his voice and winked at Emory... "Not many left, thanks to my man here, and they didn't seem that interested in engaging, what with all *this* going on." Back to normal... "So, yeah, seems a lot's happened since we split up, Jules. How about you fill me in, partner?"

Jules limped toward Prihya, which she found both curious and reassuring, although since she hadn't made up her own mind about who to throw in with, she couldn't see how Jules would side with her.

Was she the least bad option again?

Emory gave Moses a rueful nod, standing the soldier down in the face of dismal odds. They were a few feet below the tallest wall, the intermittent judders coming at almost regular intervals now, as the once-mighty city's outer circles pounded and struggled against the weight of the denser hills surrounding the plateau. Prihya, knowing only a little about this sort of thing, expected they would eventually break through, even if it took another twelve thousand years.

"If you can put our differences aside," Emory said, "then we can discover it together. All of us."

He stepped forward with caution, the worn and pitted form of the temple below them—brown from age but clearly delineated. It was the destination they'd all dreamed of.

Emory said, "I am truly gratified to all of you for bringing me this far. But we must unite. This, here, in the center of Atlantis, is where humanity enters its new epoch."

"Ain't there yet," Jules said. "Valerio, have you felt this?"

"Felt what?" Valerio said.

"The ground. The earth. People like us... it speaks through us."

Valerio gave a single, sarcastic laugh. "I don't feel anything."

"Flesh-to-earth." Jules pointed at his bare foot. "You need to feel it."

Valerio's eyes darted side-to-side before his mouth split a genuine smile. "Atlantis..."

"It's here. You can see it. But people like you and me... we can *feel* it."

Jules stepped back, as if awaiting an outburst or attack, but all that happened was Valerio's smile remained frozen in place as he narrowed his eyes in suspicion.

"What are you doing?" Prihya hissed.

"Trust me," Jules said.

Both waited.

Emory hadn't moved an inch.

Valerio held his hand flat and bent his knees. He didn't take his eyes off Jules for a second, lowering his palm toward the ground. It hovered just above it.

"I feel something..." Valerio checked on Horse, who kept the rest of the players in range. "It's like static."

"Go for it," Jules said.

Valerio touched his hand to the surface. Pressed down so it would leave an imprint.

Then, as if his touch set a fuse alight, another massive surge lifted them, bulging upward, and all lost their balance, tumbling across the surface, powerless to stop their fall over the edge.

CHAPTER FIFTY-EIGHT

Toby watched with no sense of control as the cracks in the earth deepened and the ground, rock, and sand fell away. The sight had silenced Xander from his excuses, and Toby had little interest in apologies or logic right now. A power source had activated. It turned a drill-like mechanism, cogs and gears, driven by what he assumed was a form of magnetism, forced apart by opposing poles, and grinding over millennia of sand and age. It spiraled before them, ascending from the middle, a series of platforms, awash with dawn light. Clearly ancient, the grey stones surged upward, and even with binoculars raised, it was impossible to see clearly through the storm of debris.

Clunks and booms echoed through the morning, the central platform coming to a halt above the sandstorm of dry earth and pebbles and what were probably millennia-old salt deposits. Emory's militia whom they had spotted before were in retreat, fleeing along a route they must have established already, their access roads and planning far in advance of LORI's. Still, their presence, their beating LORI to the location, had no bearing on the reality before them.

Toby said, "It can't be..."

Without much wind to speak of, gravity quickly took over, pulling the billowing earth and sand back to the ground. At their distance, they escaped the worst of the cloud, a dry, cool pyroclastic flow from the eruption of an inconceivable feat of engineering.

"I am sorry," Xander said in a tone that conveyed joy and despair equally. "Very, very sorry."

The construct before them took shape, a tower-block-sized series of platforms, concertinaing on top of one another. At first, Toby thought it an elaborate pyramid built with circular layers, but the size of each floor was different—steeper at the back than the front, allowing for easier access one way than the other.

A defensive setup perhaps? Minimal defense at the back to concentrate forces at the front?

Only, this was no fort, no military installation.

Toby could hardly breathe. "It's real. I cannot believe this."

Glancing at the others briefly, he found them all except Xander glued to binoculars.

"Are those... houses?" Charlie asked.

"I see... I think..." Harpal strained to see but found his spot. "They're like... baths. Like you get in Roman spas."

"And the terraces..." Toby couldn't help fall into professor mode. "What do you suppose they are?"

Because that was the key here. The reason they had been brought so late. The timeline stretched.

"If Jules is in there..." Bridget lowered her glasses.

"The force it took to lift those blocks," Charlie said. "It's... I can't work it out. Doubt I could with a calculator and an hour."

"We don't have an hour. He might still be alive!"

Before anyone could stop her, Bridget was gone. Over the edge of the rise and skidding down their promontory's sides like a snowboarder without equipment.

Toby said, "Damnit, get after her."

Dan was the first to move, but the others took little persuading to follow. Charlie slalomed at the same speed as Dan, with Xander stumbling in their wake. It was steep and soft, but not unassailable.

Unless you were an exceptionally out-of-shape, approaching-sixty armchair enthusiast like Toby. Harpal stuck with him, passing the three guides in turn, who had remained on point. When they reached Brad, Toby said, "Please, take your men. Report that we need transport away from here."

"But the militia," Brad said.

"They are gone," Toby answered. "This place... it isn't what we thought it was going to be. Please. Don't dally. Bring reinforcements."

Brad obeyed, retreating with the two men who'd brought them here, cutting short their wonderment in favor of duty.

Toby and Harpal made slower going of the longer, kinder slope, but Harpal made no protest to the way Toby handled it—sideways, foot after careful foot, speeding up only when no soil or sand threatened to slip. They made it to the bottom soon after the others who were ascending the rise to the construction's base layer.

Bridget had climbed onto the first terrace when Toby and Harpal arrived, closely followed by Xander and a panting Charlie. Dan kept watch, moving more slowly, more deliberately, in case what Brad had called "militia" returned.

Toby stared at the city in the wild. The stone was greyish brown, like sandstone, but smoother, and the light of the rising sun glinted off it, making everything appear sharper, clearer.

Whatever it was, it was one of seven layers that they could see, each with a steep stairway cut into it.

Seven *visible from this angle*, he reminded himself. They'd seen more than that.

Each terrace led to another a little higher, so that it resembled a stepped pyramid reaching for the sky. Only, it was uneven, as they'd observed from afar.

Bridget had ascended the first steps in a series of goatlike bounds, followed by Xander, Charlie, and Harpal. Dan insisted Toby went first. Once Harpal attained a good observation post, he followed.

Toby caught up, and then passed Bridget, because if he didn't get to the next section first, Bridget would be on the second and third before he could stop her. And they had no idea where they were headed. He wasn't even sure where to go. But if previous lessons were to be heeded, there was usually some form of security, a nasty surprise or test, waiting for them.

"This is crazy." Harpal ran next to him.

Toby was out of breath, and it was all he could do to gain the second, softer slope. The stone beneath his feet was smooth, and it seemed to help him to pick up speed.

"It's a series of terraces," he said.

"What do you think is inside?" Harpal asked.

"I don't know. A city. The Witnesses' Atlantis."

"Too small to be a city," Xander said.

It was not lost on Toby that Xander still hadn't explained himself, nor how he appeared so certain, so knowledgeable about where they'd chased Jules and Valerio.

"If you can make it further," Charlie said, jogging up beside him, "you can get to it."

Toby lost his footing, only pulling himself up by leaning on the stone. There were no banisters here. Over the crest of this staircase, he skidded down an unexpected slope, Charlie catching him.

This third level held what looked like houses carved out of the same building materials. If not houses, then certainly buildings. Accommodation. Rectangular pits that resembled public baths. Troughs ran the course of the next wall that towered over them to level four.

Bridget overtook, giggling as if this were a game, a race over an obstacle course. "See ya!"

"She's lost her mind," Harpal said, watching her scale a broken block to get her to the next terrace faster.

"Stairs," Toby said. "Let's stick to the stairs."

Charlie nodded, understanding. "We'll do it together." She went to the side, grabbing Toby by the hand to lend him extra support, gallantly making it look like simple camaraderie, then pressed on.

Toby and Charlie caught up with Bridget on the fourth terrace, this one with fewer buildings and more pillars and plinths, a series of troughs and furrows carved into the stone and what looked like half-cylinders—again, made from smooth, treated stone. Holes had been either bored or rotted into the channels, which had drawn Bridget's attention.

She had stopped, hands on knees, to recover her breath. "You're still here. Good. This is *incredible*."

"Where is the next one?" Toby asked through his panting. "The next stairs?"

Bridget didn't answer, instead running to the inset of the terrace, which was sloped now, not at a right angle as the previous ones were, scaling it to the next.

Toby sighed, then followed with Charlie. Unable to locate the stairs right away, they crawled after Bridget. The stone was less smooth here, more worn by time. It was cut, but not by modern tools, leaving grooves in the surface. Xander, Harpal, and Dan were close behind them.

Bridget reached the top, and then ran the length of the fifth platform to the first stairs they'd seen since level three. The stairs led Toby to another platform, the sixth, but there was no other floor above. Instead, this was a wide, flat rink. It offered a huge, expansive view of the surrounding land, including the mountains that Bridget had identified as Plato's Pillars of Heracles.

The others explored the same ridge, their forms small against the flat surface. Toby stopped before the drop, with the sandstone city peeling away at the bottom.

It *was* a real city, albeit much smaller than they'd observed on the feeds from Richat, a scale that Toby had never seen outside of a few of the bigger dig sites. The steps, or terraces, or whatever they were, were all different heights, which had made climbing difficult, but their differing cuts and angles had made it possible to ascend.

Bridget waved from atop the next level—the highest they had seen from below. "Toby! More!"

Toby didn't stop, summoning what he expected was the last of his willpower. Harpal and Charlie flanked him, keeping him going as the breeze got stronger this high up.

Arriving after Xander, Toby saw this flat level was even wider than the previous one. The next sections were far too steep to climb, forming the spiraling center like a huge temple, rising far over the city's platformed construction. They were standing at the uppermost level of what was, indisputably, a city. The highest level. The one that made it look like a huge pyramid with a single expansive floor and a whole series of smaller terraces climbing ever higher.

Before he could comment, new vibrations commenced. Not a violent shudder like an earthquake, but still clear and unambiguous. Their feet, their knees, their hips swayed. Disturbed earth filled the air, a cloying, dankness all around, like opening the door of an old house.

All spread out, assessing their situation. All except Bridget, who pressed on toward the central monument.

Toby called, "Bridget, you can't go running off like this."

She didn't listen, spinning away, ready to rush toward that pinnacle, the peak of this city. "Jules is here somewhere, and—"

Xander yelled, "WAIT!"

She didn't listen, staggering as the regular buzz of the vibrations continued.

"I see it," she shouted. "He has to be here."

Xander yelled at the top of his voice—more of a scream, truth be told—and Toby was shocked at the passion, his sheer desperation. "*Jules is not here!*"

"*This isn't Atlantis*," Toby called.

The others, who had seen what he'd seen, crowded around him.

Bridget halted, fifty feet away, and looked back at them.

Toby pointed upward at the peak of the city, where a rocket ship-shaped cone continued the height but was no longer a place for living. Below, a squared-off unit with pillars holding the roof aloft served as a block under the capstone. A building, an entrance.

But to where?

"I thought this was it," she said.

Then the stones at the very top turned. A colossal rasping noise grated out of the structure deep below them, guttural and resonant as it scratched and scuffed in movement that no one had witnessed in thousands of years.

"Get over here, Bridget!" Dan called.

For once, she obeyed. The brain-cloud that had clearly overtaken her common sense and critical thinking in favor of reuniting with Jules had been slapped away by the taxing scale of what they were witnessing.

The turns were slow at first, almost glacial, but as the first layers of earth jarred loose, spilling a curtain of flowing soil onto the flat level on which Toby had gathered with his friends, the mechanism sped up. It was never what Toby would have called fast, but as the majority of the debris from below overflowed down the back of the lopsided pyramid, it was clear to him what the purpose of its shape now was. He'd theorized when he could view it only through binoculars, but now he had no doubt.

"Jules was never coming here, was he?" Toby asked Xander.

"Sadly, no," Xander replied.

"He's gone to Atlantis without us?" Bridget said.

"Yes. But for good reason."

As the massive structure turned and growled, juddered and scraped, Bridget sounded more concerned about being left on the substitute's bench yet again. "It isn't fair. He can't decide what we get to find. He can't choose for us. Why the hell is he so goddamned arrogant that he thinks—"

"Bridget," Dan said, pointing.

Toby followed the finger to what he'd thought was a long-lost sight. One he never expected to see himself, despite being right about the location.

She turned, and they all stood in silence as a stream of water ran along one of the narrower terraces up above them. As the construct turned, its five-foot-wide scooped edges curling around the central structure like a serpent around a branch, the water flowed higher, reaching the top before spilling over.

The group dashed to the edge of the platform, excited, curious, and frightened to see where it led. The stream became an upward-flowing river, the wide channels lifting it from below, sloshing and crisp, filling the dry desert air with moisture and freshness, like a lake on a spring morning. If it failed and deviated, broke aside, they could be swept away, their bodies breaking as they bounced down this remarkable place.

Only, it didn't break. It worked exactly as it had been depicted in the stories Toby had read, the legends, the theories.

"It's an Archimedes Screw," Charlie said.

"Of course it is," Toby said.

The water, drawn from some unknown well deep beneath the desert floor, had no choice but to follow the motion of the screw's thread, reaching the top, before dropping. It cascaded down the furrows and steep platforms at the rear, much of it diverting through the grooves and gutters and half-pipes they had seen on the way up.

Racing from one edge to another, gazing over to the spread of levels below, the water distributed itself around the stone levels. It cascaded all around them, irrigation glistening in the low sun, feeding long-dead plants and crops, filling the cooling baths, and returning its excess to the ground to filter back into the well from whence it came.

"The city walls at the outskirts," Toby said. "We've known about the walls of Babylon for a long, long time. Even the gates are clearly marked. But the gardens... the *Hanging Gardens of Babylon*... were the only legend of the Seven Wonders of the Ancient World to have zero evidence for its existence. Too many descriptions... like Plato's writing of Atlantis, it was all third hand. But this..."

"Not Atlantis," Charlie said.

"No," Xander said. "Jules and I realised... Atlantis is nothing. A dead city from a past the Witnesses are not proud of... a time of war long gone. This is their true destination. This, my friends, is where you need to be. In the true Babylon."

"Then..." Bridget was stammering, almost unable to speak, dwarfed by the scale of the Archimedes Screw as it turned and drew water from the depths of the desert to feed plants and a people that no longer existed. She gathered herself and asked the question Toby had no answer to: "So where is Jules?"

CHAPTER FIFTY-NINE

JULES' heart pounded as he regained his bearings. This iteration of the Temple of Apollo—a name he knew was stupid to continue using but kept it straight in his head—was smaller than Richat. It was also more damaged because it had been stored underground in soil rather than in still seawater-infused salt and sand. It was stained a grey-brown and held its shape, and—unlike its larger cousin—the stairs were not half-buried in silt. There was still mud and dry earth fields scattered around, which Jules predicted would disperse once the city reached its full elevation. Only the swaths of mountains and hills throughout the national park kept it at bay, allowing the majority of the city to remain hidden.

When the mechanism pushing the city upward had surged again, they'd all rolled and dropped, then hit the soft terrain in front of the temple. Weapons had flown away, limbs had been tucked in, and heads had been held in hands. When they came to a halt, the more seriously injured held their ground, while the unconscious appeared to have awoken prior to the impact.

A similar effect to falling while dreaming, Jules assumed.

All were alive, and Valerio and Emory—rivals but unwilling to risk their wellbeing—stood, neither representing a significant physical threat. It was a tentative, nervous standoff, seeing whose muscle heads regained operational capacity first. In that, Valerio was victorious.

Horse was the only operative who was conscious and fully upright when the upswell tossed them over the edge, so seeing him glowering from Valerio's side wasn't surprising. Moses was out of the game, but conscious and taking in the scene, while Hilla and Muzaffer were recovering from Jules's assault, and Jules himself—who was unaffiliated with either party—was only slightly hurt and managed to get back on his feet. Prihya, whose allegiance was unclear, managed to join him.

"What now?" Jules asked. "Everyone fights each other?"

"I know the layout," Emory said, seeing Muzaffer and Hilla were both unarmed and still dazed, and Moses no use at all as he dealt with his painful but non-life-threatening injuries. "I know where to find the power source."

"And what stops me from taking it?" Valerio said with a pantomime-villain gleam.

"Ain't a power source." Jules limped forward. "And it needs a catalyst." He waggled his hands. "Unless you got a better idea."

"What are your terms?" Emory asked.

"No more killing anyone." Jules jabbed a finger toward Horse. "Am I being in any way unclear?"

Valerio hesitated. Were he or Horse armed, it may have been a different story, but he made a hand gesture that appeared to calm his big lunk of a bodyguard and nodded at Jules. "Fine. But if anyone holds me back, we're done."

Unlike Richat, this temple was either open to the elements or the doors had fallen off through the original damage or subsequent geological upheaval, so the five of them walked right on in. Just five people, wandering through an entrance, like a visit to a Walmart. If Walmart sold ancient weapons of interest to an apocalyptic cult leader and a mad billionaire intent on attaining more power than money could buy.

Jules hid his limp as best he could, the bullet having scorched his skin and nicked the flesh beneath. He detected no serious damage, but he would not want to face a full-strength Horse. And then he sensed something he could not name, could not fathom, but nor could he turn away.

Making his way through the temple, the pressure pounding

through him was almost too much to bear. He had been to many places in his life, and none had ever had such a profound effect. It reminded him of a planetarium, a theater without seats, a church without pews, the ceiling lower than expected—lower than Richat—and on the central dais was not a sarcophagus or altar, but simply a new level: flat, unspectacular, with a 360-degree view of the interior.

The walls were covered in faded murals, but the dryness must have preserved the substance, depicting an odd mix of epic battles and scenes of daily life in this forgotten corner of the world. He could feel the weight of the past pressing from all angles, the responsibility of getting the next phase right, making it hard to breathe.

Valerio and Emory were following close behind him, and he could sense their excitement and trepidation. He had promised to not interfere with their business, to show them something special, but this wasn't it. He had lied to them about his intentions, and now he was leading them to an unknown destination.

"The trident." Valerio pointed at the cracked, distorted picture of a towering warrior bursting from the ocean holding the glowing trident aloft. Then he indicated a different warrior, this one welding a sword as he faced an incoming army of naked men; amongst them, giants three times the size of the other humans marched. "Is that the sword? Is that what we were expecting?"

"Maybe," Emory said. "But it does not appear to be here."

They had reached the middle of the temple, where only old metallic strips of metal lay discarded. They had the shape of what modern people would recognise as swords, but there were two hilts crossing one another, and the blades appeared dull. Valerio bent and picked one up, grasping it in different places in the apparent hope it would glow.

It did not glow.

"Here." Valerio passed it to Jules.

It still did not glow under Jules's touch.

"No!" The billionaire literally stamped his foot as if commencing a tantrum. "This isn't fair!"

Horse tensed.

Jules eased onto his good leg, far enough from him to initiate a counterattack if needed.

"Here, in this temple," Emory said, "there lie ancient artifacts, frescos, more of the stuff of legend. The weapons that need a special touch to activate them are missing. Representations on the wall." He turned fully toward Jules. Pivoted to Prihya. "Did you know?"

"That the warriors of the past were real?" Prihya said. "Just jumbled up into legends? Hercules, King Arthur, that sort of thing? I'd guessed." She gazed around happily at the artwork. "All this... it's all you deserve."

"Can we go now?" Jules asked.

"No, we cannot." Valerio stomped around the dais, taking in the walls, the scattered weaponry. "Tell me what this is."

"This is an armory." Jules made sure he sounded bored. "A weapons rack, probably. Maybe a display unit showing the might of a defensive barracks."

"Wooden," Emory said, the penny dropping for him at last. "The wooden case rotted. But the metal did not."

"Yep. So... what's next? Wanna head to Egypt or something? Or should we go explore down one of those tunnels?"

They followed his finger to the passages leading away from the temple's main room.

"I saw plans for this place in the golden books, but the scale was off," Jules explained. "The Atlantis in Mauritania was similar, but that was a city state. A place full of the kind of assholes Plato warned his Greek followers about. This is defensive. More basic. At the entrance to the Med. They wanted to defend the people who lived there from the warfaring factions of their own civilization."

"Why?" Valerio demanded, voice cracking as he processed his error.

"Mankind sprang up in the far corner of the Mediterranean," Prihya said. "The Assyrian empire expanded fast during that time. So much knowledge. So much to explore."

"And there's all that stuff making the city rise," Jules added, again emphasizing the looming passages. "They must go to the heart of the city."

"Why are you being so cooperative?" Emory asked. "From what Prihya told me, this isn't like you at all."

"Hmm," Valerio said. "I hate to agree with a man I plan to kill sooner rather than later, but he's right. What's the ruse, Jules?"

Prihya had been the one to set him on this path, when she had spoken to him back at the Tayos library.

"The garden is the prize," he said to her. "Isn't it? *In the dirt.* It had more than one meaning."

"A place of beauty," Prihya replied. "In the cradle of civilization itself."

Emory finally realized what was going on. "You lied to us."

"No," Jules said. "Prihya brought you to Atlantis. We're here. It's what you wanted."

"And you brought me," Valerio said. "I wondered why you would do that, since you could have taken the airplane yourself or even brought Toby Smith along for the ride. But now I understand. You needed my touch to amplify the effect. To add to your power so the city could rise." He twitched as if waking from a half-sleep. "You figured it out in the Richat Structure... the trident needed more than one of us to keep the city in place."

"That was why you needed Valerio?" Emory asked.

"No," Jules replied, firing a lopsided smile at Valerio. "It's worse than that. For you."

Valerio stared back, his eyes slack and jaw tense. Again, Horse intuited a change in atmosphere, and switched up his alertness.

Jules told them all, "I needed Valerio to sell the ruse."

"Ruse?" Emory said.

"I brought him to Atlantis, yeah, and Prihya brought you. But Atlantis was a lie. It's a wreck. Destroyed. Empty. No benefit to Valerio. Or the Church of the Forefathers, or, frankly, anyone except someone like Toby."

"Who, ironically," Prihya said, sounding brighter now, "is at Babylon, if you followed the evidence."

Jules didn't need to answer. They all saw it.

He said, "I honestly don't care about any of that. I just wanna live. The real prize ain't some sword or trident. It's knowledge. And that's at Babylon. Where my friends are right now. While I'm here with you. Looking at the remains of war brought about by an overinflated sense of entitlement."

"And decadence," Prihya said. "Don't forget that."

"Oh, yeah, can't forget about the decadence. It was the main reason Plato wrote about this place—so the Greece of his age didn't repeat the past."

They fell silent. Digesting the confession.

"You are not normal," Emory said. "You could have led us to this place while you discovered what the Forefathers had brought with them."

"Normal is real subjective," Jules said quietly. "And while you can't choose who you are, you can choose what you do."

"Which means..." Valerio continued. "You're of *no* use. In fact, you're a liability."

There was a howl and then Horse charged at Jules.

CHAPTER SIXTY

THE LONG JOURNEY had been made more difficult by the intense secrecy and mystery surrounding their destination. Bridget understood why Xander had kept it from them and why Jules had duped them, but it sat in her stomach like a heavy meal that wouldn't digest. The conflict of intentions, the opposing methodology; she had no choice but to accept it and hope Jules had called it right.

"How did this happen?" Charlie said. "How did it... pop up like this? The power?"

"A guess?" Toby offered. "Something Jules did wherever he is right now sent a wave through the planet, like the neutrons transmitting the plague data a couple of years ago."

"No," Xander said. "I do not believe that is correct."

"Then what *is* correct?" Bridget asked.

"Better to ask what this place is. And why we are here."

The Hanging Gardens had been deserted for centuries. Those who were aware of the Gardens' presence had kept silent, either afraid or unwilling to speak of the secrets contained within, allowing it to fade into myth. All any theorist had to go on were stories from ancient scholars and explorers, as well as mysterious manuscripts and maps supposedly detailing the Gardens.

Bridget was both excited and apprehensive as she approached the entrance to the central structure. It was the first time any of them had even conceived that the myth might be real, and the sheer magnitude of the walls and the gardens took her breath away more-so than the physical exercise. Yes, the climb was arduous, her legs like Jell-O, but Xander's confession about the place—and that Jules would not be joining them—had given her time to recover.

"Oh, look," Charlie said with a gasp. "It goes farther than this building."

They all halted and took in the vista. Gushing water had dampened the sand and, now the dust had settled, the outline of the Garden's walls spread out beyond the lopsided pyramid. They must have once been huge, reaching into the sky like a vast fortress, with the gardens themselves stretching as a sea of green and gold to the twin mountains. The irrigation was a colossal maze, water flowing from the screw atop the capstone, but Bridget didn't believe it was simply a monument of floral beauty. There was a reason they were here.

Toby and Xander looked around in awe, Dan and Harpal torn between security and wonder, while Charlie couldn't take her eyes off the enormous screwlike tip spilling water throughout the structure.

Bridget said, "There seems to be an entrance."

The others slowly joined her in the shadow of the squat building under the waters' high point. Greek-style columns guarded the facade, although it predated Athens' Parthenon by centuries if not millennia; clearly, the Witnesses' architecture and engineering informed later civilizations.

They ventured forward.

All Bridget could hear was the slosh of water flowing through the mostly intact gutters, the occasional deep breath from her friends, and her own pulse in her head. Step-by-cautious-step, they advanced. A line of explorers, each with enough experience to hold in any celebration before they had gotten over the finishing line.

In the shadow of the plinth overhead, they paused.

No one spoke. They just stared into the open frontage, glimpsing what appeared to be a civilized interior—an anteroom initially, dulled by shadow. It was so incredibly well preserved, Bridget half-expected a scholar in a toga to wander out and invite them in for a cup of wine.

Without any of them seeming to move first, they all set off again, stepping over the threshold.

Before them unfurled a grand library, its walls made of white marble and its shelves filled with hundreds of ancient manuscripts, each one a unique history of its own. Some appeared bound in cloth, treated resin as Bridget had seen many times before. Others were metallic; some gold, some of a silver appearance, others an odd rainbow sheen like they'd been painted with gasoline.

It was as if they'd stepped into a museum. There were even reading stands molded into the floor, occupied by faded tablets and small artifacts—tiny vases that Bridget guessed might have been their equivalent of inkwells. The room smelled of parchment and ancient stone, and the domed ceiling loomed high above them.

Bridget and Charlie branched one way, while Toby and Xander slowly advanced the opposite, making their way around the library, exploring each corner and crevice. Soon, both pairs found themselves in the center of the room with the stunned-looking Dan and Harpal. Here, a great stone table dominated, as high as Bridget's chest and with a map of the Gardens on its surface, etched in gold. The tabletop was smooth to touch, and cool, too, sending shivers up and down her arms.

The map depicted the entire area, including the library, and was filled with hieroglyphs and symbols that Bridget could not decipher fully. Some were familiar, others obscure. Soon, her mind soared with wild imaginings of the secrets that the place could contain.

At the center of the map was an oval-shaped symbol with a zigzag running through it. Like many of the glyphs, Bridget had never seen it before. She knew it was important, though, as it seemed to be surrounded by less prominent whorls and symbols.

Was it the key to unlocking the mysteries of the Hanging Gardens?

She examined the symbol closely, trying to make sense of it, and soon realized its true meaning. She gestured over the tableau but couldn't quite reach to the middle. "This represents a sacred place in the Gardens. A repository of knowledge that only the Witnesses were meant to see..."

She scanned the other symbols, pooling her learning from other texts, and deciphering the code. This had always been her key role, not running around jungles or leaping out of planes. It flowed through her, like the water spilling all around, and this monument to learning felt more like home than anywhere she'd lived before.

"They hid it to guard from the violence that marred the Atlantean projects in Mauritania and Spain and, probably, elsewhere, too. Those had been constructed for dominance, for war. This place, their real mission when they left Tayos, was to distribute knowledge. Without forcing it on those who chose to go their own way."

Toby appeared to realise the truth, a deeper understanding. "Then this is why the Hanging Gardens were the only one of the seven wonders of the ancient world with no trace... because it was hidden intentionally. The Lighthouse of Alexandria and the Colossus of Rhodes are lost but have official records; the Great Pyramid of Giza still stands; the Statue of Zeus at Olympia is a UNESCO site; the Temple of Artemis still has fragments and columns... but not the Gardens. They were always speculation, the writings of people who claimed to have seen it or heard from people who had, but not one account matched the other. Visitors to Babylon, the city, never saw it. Most scholars assumed it was a brag, a status symbol. The same for dignitaries who had supposedly visited."

Bridget said, "The kings who presided over Babylon were guardians. Dressing it up in plain sight as a vanity project, then obscuring it from reality. When Babylon fell, they activated the fail-safe, dropping the gardens and library into the earth until someone like us dug it up."

She looked at Xander.

"Which brings us back to *how*. If it isn't Jules doing his thing somewhere else and triggering this place... what *did* make it grow out of the ground? It sure as heck wasn't anything we tried."

Xander pulled his lips into his mouth and stayed mute for a second. "Our mutual friend. Or, not friend, I think, but... associate. He said he had a resource to act on Jules's plan."

"Colin?" Toby said. "Colin Waterston was in on this?"

"We did not need Jules with us. And he felt he could serve our cause better the same way Prihya is doing—keeping the likes of Valerio Conchin and Father Emory Ballard focused on the bigger legend, where they seek power."

Dan said, "Asshat could've clued us in."

"Jules said he has got to know you all well," Xander said. "He believed you would not have come here without first ensuring his safety."

"Nonsense," Toby said. "We would have all discussed it—"

"And that would be a problem," Harpal said. "Xander's right, isn't he? Jules was right, too. No way we would've come here if we'd known for sure Prihya was... where is Prihya?"

"Spain," Xander said.

"Right." Harpal tossed his gaze around each of them in turn. "We wouldn't be here if we'd known the truth, would we?"

"Still," Charlie said. "It should've been our choice to make."

Bridget felt utterly conflicted. While she was furious at Jules for deceiving them, Harpal was correct that they would never have chased after this had they known Jules and Prihya were elsewhere. But Charlie was right, too; they should have been given the choice.

"LOOK AT THIS PLACE!"

Xander's outburst echoed back at them, the hard surfaces ringing his words all around and yanking them out of their fug, their annoyance at being manipulated.

Have we really become immune to these wonders? We're the first people in thousands of years to see this!

The group broke away from the table, a giddy atmosphere descending and gripping them, and pushing them out like a flower to investigate the room, to explore the incredible find. No one touched anything that wasn't metal or stone, just bending over or up on tiptoes, viewing the room that could have been built yesterday—it must have been sealed off somehow before the building emerged into the morning light, as it was almost entirely dust-free.

Bridget kept coming back to the table, finally boosting herself up for a better view. She traced her fingers over the lines, the carved picture and glyphs, the map, the...

She paused.

Translating this language was not even close to an exact science. She might have gotten the entire scope of their progress wrong. It wasn't like there was a key or an equivalent of the Rosetta Stone lying around.

Only, they hadn't gone completely wrong yet. So, why not assume she was reading this new information correctly?

"The Witnesses *were* here," she said. "But it isn't their final place, not the ultimate repository of their knowledge."

Her dour tone killed the party ambience, one at a time the explorers easing to a stop. Toby was first to return to the central table, the others following right away.

"What is it?" Toby asked as they waited for her.

"Instructions," Bridget said. "For us."

"Us?" Dan said. "Like, does that say, 'Dear Bridget' or something?"

"For the worthy," Bridget clarified. "For whoever finds this place."

"Don't be shy," Charlie said. "What are the instructions?"

"To accept this place but go no further. This is their gift to the world. Do not follow them. Their task is complete."

"Task?" Harpal said. "What task?"

"Might not be 'task' exactly." Bridget was seeing so many meanings, but the core of what they meant was unmistakable. "Could be 'duty' instead of task. Or even 'destiny,' but I kinda think they would've used 'destiny' before now, and I've never seen this level of clarity before. It's a super-simplified version of other writings."

"As if they think we're dumb?" Dan said.

"Or to be absolutely clear," Bridget said. "And it's very clear this is the end of the road as far as them sharing goes. After this, it's a warning. Danger. And death. If we go against their will."

CHAPTER SIXTY-ONE

JULES HAD ONCE BEATEN HORSE, back when he was the special forces operative Valerio relied upon, then recently underestimated him as a lumbering thug in the rainforest. This was the finale in a best-out-of-three scenario.

He stood at the center of the makeshift arena, dodged Horse's clumsy lunge, and pushed back with his good leg. Horse stumbled, but not far. His approach was wild and unruly, and his body was tense, as if he expected Jules's evasion but could do nothing about it. He glanced around the arena, his dull eyes surveying the audience of five.

Despite his troubles, he was still a tall, muscular man with a wide, square jaw and a cold, ruthless sneer as he turned fully to face Jules. He stood there, barely moving, staring with a deadly intensity. The man had attacked on instinct, rage having been balled up for hours before Valerio blew the dam and released every ounce of violence hiding behind his obedient mask. After an initial burst of mindless violence, the tactical instinct of a savvy spec-ops fighter clearly called the shots here.

Away from the pair, Emory's two henchmen—Hilla and Muzaffer—were as fierce and dangerous as Horse in their own ways. They had recovered from Jules's previous assault and were ready to jump in if needed.

"So, you all friends now or something?" Jules said.

"They'll pick up the pieces of whoever's left." Moses propped himself on a stair, his belt now cinched around the thigh where Jules had slashed shallowly into a couple of hamstrings. The pain must have been incredible, and he would never run properly again, but Jules had preserved the man's life while incapacitating him—perhaps permanently. "They do not need to endanger themselves."

Atop the stairs, where the altar had been in the Richat temple, Emory and Valerio watched silently. Prihya stood at the edge of the dais, watching with nervous anticipation. Jules hadn't been sure where her loyalties lay before, but he was certain now.

The moment between Jules and Horse stretched on for what seemed like an eternity, until eventually Valerio nodded, signaling the recommencement of the fight.

"Horse will take your people out, too," Valerio said to Emory. "He'll finish this one first, though."

Jules and Horse circled each other warily, like wrestlers looking for an opening. Jules kept in a catlike stance, the weight on his good leg, the ball of his toes its focus, ready to move.

Horse was the first to strike, a straight punch which Jules easily dodged, pushing sideways, then resuming his stance at a 45-degree angle, aiming a snap-kick at Horse's knee.

It missed.

Even injured, Jules was the more agile of the two, while Horse was more powerful. The two of them exchanged a flurry of blows, each move countered by the other. Jules had to shift position with each block, not strong enough to deflect Horse's punches with muscles alone, his own strikes thrown at obtuse angles to knock his enemy off balance. Neither could land a decisive blow, so Jules tried something different.

He waited for a decent lunge from Horse, used his functioning leg to spring up, rolled over Horse's back, and slapped him in the direction he'd been heading. At the same time the slap connected, Jules had ahold of Horse's wrist, which he dragged down, then up sharply. Horse spun in midair, appearing to defy gravity for a split-second—a variation on *kote gaeshi*, one of Jules's favorite aikido counterattacks—then Jules thrust his foot out, heel connecting with Horse's ribcage. Which wasn't anything to do with aikido.

Off the ground, Horse became vulnerable to the force with which Jules kicked him, as well as the effects of gravity. He flew out over the stairwell, dropped five feet while turning in the air with no idea which way was up, and slammed down hard, bouncing for at least ten feet along the rock-hewn steps. Something snapped, and the grunts of pain didn't bode well for a guy whose nerve endings had been dulled by previous injuries.

The audience was silent. And motionless.

Valerio glared at Horse, the big man bleeding from several places and striving to get to his feet to return to the fray. But something was clearly not working as it should—a broken bone or dislocated joint, or both.

Hilla and Muzaffer hustled to their leader's side, both facing Jules who lingered at the edge of the stairs' peak.

Jules had expected them to attack him right away, but all they were doing was holding position between him and the priest.

He said, "It's been cool and all, but I gotta go."

"No one is going anywhere." Emory spread his arms, pointing out the troops now filtering inside. They had survived the walls blasting partially from the ground and must have been drawn by the voices. "Surrender. And show us where we must go."

"That'll be a no."

Jules prepared himself for the pain in his calf and sprinted forward, grabbed Prihya's hand, and dragged her in the opposite direction, down the stairs.

Moses pulled a radio from somewhere and barked in Korean, which concentrated the newcomers on Jules.

As he and Prihya took the stairs two at a time, his wound protesting every jolt, he spotted Hilla and Muzaffer setting out after him, too. Checking parallel to himself, he found Horse up on one leg, but the other—the one Jules broke during their fight in India—hung at a hideous angle, as if it had suffered more than one break.

Hilla and Muzaffer were in hot pursuit, but Prihya managed to point Jules toward one of the passages branching away from the chamber.

"You're sure that's the right way?" he said as he arrowed toward the square, black hole.

"If it's where I think you need to be, yes." Prihya sounded earnest, and that was as good as Jules could expect. "You want to finish it, right?"

"Yeah."

"To live?"

"Yeah."

At the bottom of the stairs, running as fast as he could at a limp, he felt like he was in a small stadium, that most of the corridors he could see—and he'd counted six so far—would funnel spectators and civilians in here. For entertainment? For voting? Who knew?

Who cares?

"Then trust me," Prihya said.

As they ran, Jules realized where they were headed, and couldn't quite believe it—the bowels of Atlantis. They just needed to stay ahead of their pursuers long enough to do what he knew needed to be done here.

And to hope he could do so without losing his soul.

Poor old Horse, Valerio thought.

He was hurt badly, and Jules had again surprised Valerio. Horse had barely any nerve endings left, which meant he felt little or no pain, making hitting him redundant. Unless an opponent physically disabled him, Horse would keep on coming.

Jules must have figured that out.

Now, Horse was crawling up the stairs, bleeding, one leg dragged behind him and an arm cradled across his abdomen, like a dog struck by a car that didn't know it was likely to die soon.

Moses, Emory's main man, was in similar shape, but with fewer breaks, more cuts. He lounged there, as if waiting for an ambulance.

They must have brought medics with them, but there was no way to know if they'd survived. Ironically, it may have been one of the men Horse killed before the city crunched and gouged its way out of its grave.

With the handful of remaining Koreans now following Jules and Prihya, it left Valerio alone with Emory.

"Have you fully considered the powers at work here?" Emory said. "And what they might mean to us? Prihya and Jules have deflected us from the Forefathers' true home, but the energy source still remains. It can still be exploited."

Valerio shrugged. "I've guessed as much as I need. When Jules gets caught or tries to get away, I'll swoop in. I have a way with the lad. I think he likes me really."

Emory nodded slowly, eyes twinkling with amusement beneath his mass of white hair, before saying, "Well then, let's discuss strategy."

"Words, eh? You double crossed me in Ecuador. You've made it clear you and your sanctimonious cult view me as scum. Someone who should never be allowed a say in how this power is used. That... really hurt my feelings."

"The Church of the Forefathers is a *movement*, not a cult. And you showed you are more than capable of coming after me if I try to swindle you. Come. Let us be friends."

Moses said, "Don't trust him, Father. Our brothers will not be as inviting. And our Cardinal will certainly not."

"Cardinal?" Valerio said. "Meaning your *boss*?" He grinned at Emory.

"I can speak with our eminent leader and give him assurances. Valerio... surely you must see... if you toss me aside, others will replace me. Moses and his ilk are not loyal to *me*. They are loyal to our shared cause."

Valerio was tempted. As much as the betrayal had stung, it had stung far more that he hadn't anticipated it. He'd half-expected the North Korean mercenaries to stab him in the back, which was the main reason for his second unit of Striovians lying in wait as backup, but he'd worked with the scholar-assassins for a long time and thought he'd have picked up any extremist ideology. And Valerio hated extremist ideology.

Unless it was his own, of course.

Moses said, "Your resources are finite. Poor, even, since you fell out of the world to recover from your injuries. You didn't even know the Church of the Forefathers existed until I introduced them. And that was only because the time was right."

"I have other resources," Valerio said. "Not only muscle and firepower, either. Far more than my old broken friend down there, and some second-rate military refugees from Eastern Europe and Asia. I can find you and destroy you."

"Then why don't you?" Moses taunted.

Then Valerio remembered the swords nearby. The very old ones, fallen from some rotted weapons rack, as if someone had scattered them there on purpose. He slowly circled around them.

"You know what? Maybe I will." Valerio selected a sword from the ground. It was all metal, any leather or whatever they padded the handles with back then having long since decayed. "Yes, indeedy-do, that's my new obsession, my aim in life. To destroy the Church of the Forefathers and take a leak on the smoking remains." He struck a pose, sword outstretched. "En garde!" He giggled. "I've always wanted to say that."

"Your weapon is not particularly sharp," Emory said. "The blade must be quite brittle after all this time."

"It'll still hurt." Valerio hated to admit the weapon was really heavy, so adopted a more relaxed stance and tapped the blade on the floor twice, making a ping then a clang. "Feels solid to me. And the edge isn't completely dull. I reckon it'll go through flesh."

"Father," Moses said. "It is better this way. Defend yourself."

Emory stepped aside and snatched up a sword of his own, nearly dropping it as the weight swayed and pitched it back toward the floor. He looked disappointed, as if he'd expected to transform into Errol Flynn as soon as it landed in his hand. Once he got the measure of its balance, he held it upright.

Emory said, "We are not men of action, my one-time friend. This could be a very undignified fight."

Valerio pointed his sword at the priest and tried his phrase again: "En garde!"

"Okay, then," Emory said. "Let's see what happens now."

Prihya had trusted Jules to come, and he came. Although she hadn't been sure until he acted, he was very clearly on her side. He also seemed to know where he was going, so she trusted him again—this time with her life.

Using the bangles' red and green glow to illuminate the corridors through a five-foot halo, it kept them from stumbling over fallen plinths and unidentifiable pots and other items left behind all those centuries ago. The floor was covered with a finer dust than the coarse earth outside, yet the walls were still smooth throughout. The air was cool, too, clean yet stale. Not musty, but like a room that had not been used in years.

After a couple of left and right turns they now seemed to have been travelling on one passageway for a few minutes, a curve if she wasn't mistaken, but did not dare voice the question. Armed men had entered the building and couldn't be far behind, despite seeing no flashlight beams. The light from the bangles would not travel far, only noticeable if someone caught up with them.

No heavy footfalls yet, no shouts, not even the metallic clack of a weapon being handled. Maybe this curving corridor would bring them back out at the altar room.

Only...

It felt like the floor sloped downwards.

Is this a spiral?

Did Jules really know what he was doing?

It had been a turbulent and confusing week. Or was it more than a week now?

Didn't matter.

She had been kidnapped while on a Toby Smith mission, facilitated by Alfonse Luca. She wanted to believe the forces' main mission in the rainforest was rescuing her, but they all—including Jules—proceeded to prioritize the library. She understood their logic: find the Tayos gold, secure the position, and lure Emory and Valerio to them so Prihya could be rescued by a knight in shining armor.

Then, cornered, they abandoned her.

She wondered if Emory's seduction of Jules and Bridget had derailed their rescue mission. When that didn't work, Prihya had to survive on her own.

As she always had.

Years earlier, Valerio had taken her in, made her feel like her research mattered, like she counted for more than rabid followers praising her latest online theory and sceptics pouring scorn all over her like an acid bath. She had gotten her hands dirty, digging up real secrets that proved the establishment had lied for years.

Lied, in some cases, she reminded herself. Ignorant in others.

She'd been promised the scoops, but now she understood why they were kept secret. That was where her conflict churned.

Governments were corrupt and powerful, so they could not be trusted with ill-defined energy. It appeared only small, isolated departments, like the curator Colin Waterston, knew the full truth. However, a hardline, populist president or prime minister might well find the orbs and artifacts and use them to cement even more power.

If groups like LORI could find them, translate the texts, and move on to more extreme examples of a technology that even the Witnesses couldn't handle, so would the likes of Valerio, Father Emory, and whoever was pulling Emory's strings.

Perhaps burying it all was for the best, as the Witnesses did.

"Listen," Jules said.

"What?"

"Listen with your ears, not your mouth."

Was that a joke? Or was he really being rude?

Again, didn't matter.

She did as he said and fell silent. Tried tuning her ears to the eerie dark, and eventually heard it—a strange rumbling. Her sense of direction was awry, but she imagined it was coming from behind.

Jules spoke in a whisper. "It's coming from down there."

"We should go back."

"There's nothing to see there."

"No, but if those men are behind us, they'll find the source. We need to get back there before they—"

"That's not it, Prihya."

"What are you talking about? What's down there?"

"I don't know, but whatever is trying to push this city back to the surface must have some mechanism."

Prihya twigged what he was saying. "And a power source."

"Right," he said.

"And..." But Prihya was puzzled. "That's my point. We don't want them to have it, do we? We should draw them away or—"

Jules's face was sallow, his eyes sad, and mouth turned down. Even in the weak glow it was clear he was struggling with something.

Prihya touched his face, brushed his cheek with a fingertip. "What is it?"

He touched her wrist and gently removed her skin from his. "I have to stop them."

Jules turned and followed the passageway, his hand on the wall, moving more slowly. He was following the noise, and Prihya was still none the wiser about why they weren't running. It wasn't like they could barricade the orb or weapon—or the next dangerous object—away forever. And experience had taught her they couldn't simply be destroyed.

Jules halted.

Without a word, he held the bangles higher and shone them around a sharp turn. Then he broke them apart and placed them on his wrists so the metal flecks in the rocks turned off.

Yet, Jules was still lit up.

The sharp turn was the way in to another room. A room with its own light source.

He walked forward.

Prihya followed. "How did you know it was here?"

"Memorized the layout from Richat. When the city came up all mangled, it still had a basic structure. The orb was there. And it's here, too."

Light the color of the sun was channeled in through a sort of chimney and spread throughout the hexagonal room with mirror-plated walls. The basketball-sized sphere in the center was black, hovering over a carving of two hands cupped as if taking a drink from a stream, with a bracket over the top. A weapon or implement hung on each of the six walls, alternating green and red fluorescence that glimmered as if pulsing with electricity. The air was thick with ozone, like static in a storm, and there was a low-level buzzing or vibrating that she couldn't place. She knew from other people's accounts that the ball was silver when dormant, black and oily when active and floating against negative magnetic forces.

"Is this the same?" Prihya asked. "The same as the other rooms like this one?"

"Yeah," Jules said. It's kinda the same. But this time... oh, man, it is *so* different."

He was about to explain when the beam of a flashlight cut into Prihya's peripheral vision, and a hissed voice cursed in Korean.

The enemy had found them.

CHAPTER SIXTY-TWO

It was all too much to process at once. Toby would need months, if not years, of research to fully catalog this location. But there was no way he'd be permitted. Not with Colin Waterstone in the picture.

He announced he was taking a break and left the team to deal with the discovery of the century—this century or any other. There were only so many photos he could take, so many new ways to store books and tablets before his brain fried. He walked out into the open air, leaned against a pillar, and fished in his breast pocket for a packet of cigarettes he hadn't kept there in nigh on two decades. He sighed.

Weird how a habit like that can hibernate in the muscles for so long, then jump out at you from nowhere.

Just one cigarette. How much harm could that do?

Cigaretteless, he sat on a low wall, letting the breeze ruffle his ever-thinning, ever-greying hair, and breathed in the most mindful way he could summon.

Last Christmas, Charlie had bought him a subscription to an app that taught him how to inhale and exhale for different lengths of time and depths, to concentrate on sounds and feelings. It was supposed to relieve stress and bring one back into the present moment. It sounded like the hallucinogenic love-ins Toby had experienced while stationed in India in the 1970s, but he'd given it a shot. And it was effective. Up to a point.

He tried the basic technique again: six seconds in, ten seconds out. But he kept his eyes open. He'd be selling himself short if he didn't soak in the breathtaking view—the pyramidal base for the Gardens, the vista, the expanse of the walls far below. His ears and mind absorbed the flow of water, spilling in waterfalls now that the volume had peaked, gushing through cracks, or backed up through blockages, filling the air with a wet tang reminiscent of summer at Lake Como.

What now, Dr. Smith?

The walls of Babylon had been restored for tourists, although the original foundations were fiercely protected, despite decades of unrest in the region. Now, here they were, almost midway between the Euphrates and Tigris rivers, and equally out of bounds for an independent contractor like him. Like the Lost Origins Recovery Institute as a whole.

Might they at least earn a little credit? Was it enough to settle the score with Colin Waterston after they allowed Valerio Conchin to slip away?

UNESCO might take it over. Or Colin might form a cooperative of like-minded governments, a progressive alliance that could share the discovery, pool their resources, and even consider employing consultants with background knowledge on the subject.

After ten repetitions of mindful breathing, Toby conjured the image of Colin Waterston himself. The small, birdlike man had walked up the same series of staircases where Toby had chased an overexcited Bridget and was wearing a tan suit and fedora that made him look like the kind of stuffy imperialist fool who lived as if the British Empire were still a thing. This image of Colin had even adopted an Aston instead of a tie, which lent him an even greater pomposity.

"Hello, Toby," the vision said.

"Colin. How nice to see you. Do you like what we've done?"

"What you've done? No, no, my old friend. I believe we had something of a hand in it, too."

Four men in desert military gear marched up the stairs behind Colin. They were armed with British SA80A assault rifles, camo, and each were equipped with heavy packs.

Toby frowned. Stood. A shot of adrenaline blew away the mindful cobwebs, crashing reality into him like a truck full of lightbulbs.

You're real, he almost said, but held back.

"What's he doing here?" Dan asked, hustling out of the library.

The Royal Marine Commandos—for that was the crest on their uniforms—immediately pointed their guns at Dan. One of them barked, "*Put down the gun and get on the ground.*"

Toby whirled around to find Dan was carrying the gun issued by the smugglers, although—thankfully—he hadn't raised it. No matter Dan's abilities, he would not evade four commandos firing on a threat.

"Do it, Dan," Toby said. "And quickly."

Dan transferred the gun to his other hand, barrel first to show he was nowhere near the trigger, then bent his knees to lower his weapon to the ground.

"There are other weapons inside," Toby said. "But no one is a threat. Give me two minutes and I will ensure all firearms are made safe and surrendered."

Colin barely reacted, but the was definitely the hint of a snigger behind his face. The tiny nod was enough for one of the commandos to stow his weapon and approach Dan while the other three soldiers spread out to avoid hitting their teammate if Dan tried anything. Which he would not. Dan knew when he was facing good guys simply doing their jobs, so endured the pat-down without objection.

"What's the deal, Toby?" Dan asked.

"We're about to find out." Toby glanced at Colin for unspoken permission and another small nod granted it.

Toby returned inside, called for attention, and stood Harpal down, who had already heard newcomers outside.

"Give up any weapons, and I am sure Colin will corroborate our story."

"What story?" Bridget said. "That the greatest archaeological discovery ever is right here, and *we* found it?"

"I do not believe we would have found it without his intervention. Come. Let's play nice."

He led them out onto what he was starting to think of as a piazza —he could imagine people gathering here to discuss philosophy or military strategy or where to go next with a world intent on tearing itself apart. The Royal Marine Commandos remained cautious until LORI's weapons were secure, and all had been searched, then they stood back and let Colin do his thing.

Clearly, this had been the expected scenario, and Colin was loving every minute of bossing these intimidating men around. "Lovely day."

Xander sat amongst the group, the only one still smiling. The others had dealt with Colin before.

Toby asked, "Would you care to enlighten us as to how you did this? And our part in it?"

"With help from your newbie," Colin said.

"An ironclad contract," Xander said.

"Yes. Brief, but legally binding. He's really quite resourceful. Him and Mr. Sibeko."

"Let me get this straight," Charlie said. "Jules screws us over by freeing Valerio, then he contacts you—"

"I was already on the property."

"Whatever," Harpal said, picking up the train of thought. "He and Xander worked out that this was the Witnesses' main home after Ecuador."

"Yes."

Bridget said, "But he still went to the other location, the second Atlantis."

Colin rocked on his heels, speaking more kindly to Bridget than he had Toby. "Established to defend European tribes from the factions based on the African continent, I believe."

"He wanted to rescue Prihya," Dan said.

"Not *only* that," Xander said. "He believed taking Valerio would mean Emory and he would fight over the site in Spain. The Brotherhood—whatever his church cult is—would focus their attention there. This place... the resting place of the Witnesses' empire... would not fall into their hands."

Harpal said, "And you couldn't be certain Jules would succeed. If he was tortured and gave up this place—"

"Or stabbed me in the back and changed his mind," Colin said. "He's like that, young Sibeko. You never know when he'll go his own way. What if he'd chosen to switch sides?"

"He's a dick sometimes," Dan said. "But not that much of a dick."

"Paranoia," Harpal went on, "meant you wanted to secure the place, but red tape would keep you from doing it quickly. That's why you arranged to fly us to the gulf and put us on a fast boat up the Euphrates river. Smugglers, so you wouldn't be implicated."

Charlie shook her head with a tut. "We were a distraction. A backup. In case Valerio Conchin or Father Emory came along. They'd be busy with us, giving you time to get a defensive force in place."

"But your legal agreement," Bridget said. "You stipulated you'd give up the location in exchange for us being the ones to find it, while no one interfered with Jules heading the opposite way?"

Xander had been roving over the faces of all present. Now, he focused on Bridget. "He could think of no better guardians of the place his mother died protecting. *This* is her legacy."

"He left the library for us to find." Bridget shivered, sniffed, and did not cry.

Nor did Toby. "But the power required to do something like this. It can only be attained by the orbs that are so dangerous. And only Jules whom we know of can activate them."

Colin gave a curious frown. "Really? You think the gene pool is so specific that only a single 'chosen one' can create a circuit between the orbs and the earth? A single being who can will its energies into being?"

Charlie said, "That sounds suspiciously specific."

"Oh, it is." Colin raised a finger as if just remembering something, beckoning as he crossed the piazza between the four troops sent to guard this new site. "Here."

He held out a hand to the nearest Royal Marine, who stared at him. Colin snapped his fingers and pointed at the binoculars in a case strapped to the commando. The soldier sighed and rolled his eyes. Only when he received a visual *go ahead* from his commanding officer did he open the hard case and hand Colin the binoculars from within. Colin narrowed his eyes at the man, who simply held his gaze until Colin broke away.

He passed the glasses to Toby and pointed at a gathering of vehicles at the far end of the extended walls.

"The entrance was difficult to find, but based on your chap's recollection of the plans in Tayos, we managed to blast our way in."

Toby lifted the binoculars to his eyes. "The explosions we heard."

"Indeed. We brought the cars around so you would understand how much work we have put into this." Colin clapped Toby on the back and plucked the binoculars from him, shifting his line of sight to an armored military transport. "There. Give her a wave."

At the bottom of the pyramid-like garden, the vehicle surrounded by more commandos, Toby spied a familiar figure. The only woman among them. The only person not in full military gear, the sole concession being a ballistic vest over her bright orange overalls.

The last time Toby had seen her was in Scotland. Montrose, to be exact. She'd gone against her president's orders, violated international laws, British laws, and tried to steal an energy source that Colin had kept secret from everyone, including his own government.

"General Zimina Yanovna," Toby said, passing the binoculars to Dan. "Of course, you would use a paranoid ultra-nationalist to do your bidding."

"She holds the same abilities as young Sibeko," Colin said.

"And she's cooperated?" Harpal said.

"For several months, yes. We know a lot more about this tech than we ever could have hoped."

"Still looks like a prisoner to me," Dan said, lowing the binoculars. "That's a fetching Guantanamo orange she's wearing."

Colin gave a reproachful shrug. "She has almost escaped a number of times. But always resumes her work when she has been sufficiently chastised."

"Chastised?" Charlie said.

"Once we had Richat as a marker, and Mr. Sibeko's remarkable memory giving us more detail, we explained the situation and, once here, we got Yanovna involved. Blasting out a hole in a country she wasn't even sure of. Ancient passageways, a new chamber, a shiny, fresh sphere. She was happy to help."

"Happy?" Toby said.

"Okay, hopeful. Bearing in mind Striovia's proximity to Russia, and the big bear's willingness to flex its muscles with its former Soviet colonies of late, she welcomed our assurances that we would do all we could to prevent Russian ambitions from spilling into her little country. There have been hints we might even sponsor Striovia's bid for NATO membership if she cooperated."

"So, what happens now?" Toby asked.

"We secure this place. The United Nations, UNESCO, and the Iraqi authorities will meet to decide how much information is given out, and when. It cannot be a secret for long. If nothing else, it's visible from planes and satellites, so..."

Colin swallowed back an obvious nugget of discomfort.

"There may be some opportunities for outside consultants with specialist skills and knowledge. But they will have to work within strict boundaries."

Toby's smile stretched wide but didn't stop at his mouth. He felt it spread deep within himself, through his chest to stimulate his heart, and out through his stomach to warm him even more than the rising Middle Eastern sun.

"Which leaves one question," Colin said. "What, exactly, is young Sibeko with the magic touch doing with Valerio Conchin?"

CHAPTER SIXTY-THREE

THERE WAS no time to think, even at the speed Jules's brain worked. They only had one shot. Well, two, but he still wasn't sure he could take the second option.

Pressed against the mirrored wall on the side of the doorway, keeping him and Prihya out of the line of fire, he checked out the weapons attached to the walls. They could've been real, deadly, linked to the energy that crackled around the room, or they may have been ceremonial.

Prihya said, "The trident again?"

"Maybe. We gotta use the weapons for some kind of advantage." He studied them for a moment, taking in the trident and spear, the two swords of differing lengths, the orb in the center, and the two hooked weapons that resembled nunchucks. "I could use the trident or spear, I guess. But if they ain't conventional builds, I don't have time to learn how they work."

"Not conventional? Like, you could zap them?"

Jules drove away the juvenile image of blasting energy out of the tip of a spear like a ray gun but could not deny he had half-hoped for that.

He bladed himself to the wall and darted one eye around the corner, then whipped it back in case someone tried a potshot.

The ten-foot passageway from the corridor to the orb room was empty except for two men either side of the entrance. When Jules popped his head back out—again for less than a second—he spotted other beams, other shadows, including Muzaffer. Which meant Hilla was there too, and at least four additional Korean troops.

Jules turned to Prihya. He saw the fear in her eyes, the concern and worry that this may be the end. He felt the same, but he had thought his way out of tougher spots than this.

He couldn't rid himself of thoughts of Valerio and Emory, the two men vying for the secrets this place held, and the weapons they thought would imprint their vision for humanity on the world. Not to mention the orb. The power source, channeling quantum energy and controlling the magnetic forces and highly reactive rocks—such as those in his mother's bangle—might be worthless if applied to modern tech, so it was doubtful either man would transform immediately into a despot standing astride the world as the populace bowed before them.

That didn't make it safe, though.

He recalled the shield that had caused so many problems, how he'd had to play GI Joe to infiltrate a military complex with Dan, Harpal, and Prihya's ex, Tane. If he hadn't penetrated that facility and allowed Dan and the others to kill many breakaway troops, how many others would have died?

"How many people you think'll die if some power mad egomaniac gets ahold of this and brings Atlantis all the way back online?"

Prihya looked from the orb to Jules. "Is that a hypothetical question, or do you expect an answer?"

"Valerio's still got his resources worldwide. Emory with his extremist cult."

Jules let his head drop. If he and Prihya fell here, either Emory or Valerio would likely acquire what they were looking for.

"You are trapped," came a woman's voice—Hilla, presumably, although Jules could not recall hearing her speak more than a couple of words before. She was a pilot, although clearly more than capable at other actions. "You cannot escape."

Muzaffer called, "Work with us, and we will be merciful."

"Yeah," Jules shouted back. "Like that's gonna happen. I mean, it's not the most reassuring of phrases. *Work with us, and we will be merciful.* You gotta work on your sales pitch."

"Jokes?" Prihya said. "Now?"

"Dan's fault. He's a bad influence on me."

Jules's chest spiked as his brain formed an idea. It was a risk, but his lightning quick mind had kicked back into gear.

"One grenade," Muzaffer said. "You die."

"And you take out this room," Jules replied. "You know what it means to your boss."

No reply.

To Prihya, Jules said, "I only got a few seconds before they come pouring in."

Prihya pushed away from the wall. "How do you know?"

"They got no choice. It's the only play left. And they know I don't wanna kill anyone."

"I don't either. But if you tell me how, I'll give it a damn good go."

He remembered the time at Montrose when they had encountered the same type of orb. He recalled how they had managed to use it to their advantage but paid a price.

Could he replicate the effect here? Without hurting himself?

"I got an idea, but it's a risk. Might hurt. Are you with me?"

Prihya held his hand. "If I get to see where the Witnesses really travelled to after Atlantis was wiped out, I'd literally cut off my own arm."

"Then hold tight. This is gonna be rough."

Emory and Valerio stood before one another, swords extended. Valerio had never needed to train as a fighter. For much of his life he'd been too sick to exert himself, and—frankly—he'd always had staff to perform such tasks as lifting and carrying, repairs and decorating, shooting and stabbing enemies. The occasional garroting. So, it was little wonder that when the two men clashed blades, it was like a tame high school play.

At first.

The edges bit into each other, chipping a shard out of both blades, then scraping down one another like fingernails on a blackboard.

Valerio shivered as he backed away.

Emory said, "I read a thing a while ago about swords. Sword fighting, in particular."

"Oh?"

"That it was more swinging and punching and kicking. Slamming the blades together is for the movies. It just damages the metal."

"Old metal at that." Valerio held his up, examining the deep V-shaped gouge in the edge.

"Yes."

Valerio lunged, thrusting the sword at Emory, who staggered aside, feet scrabbling to get away and swinging his own sword in Valerio's general direction.

Valerio came at him again and the ancient weaponry clashed in the air, this time sending sparks flying.

Valerio said, "Ooh, pretty," and swung it again.

Emory tried to duck but fell instead. It had the same effect, though, the attack cutting only air. Unfortunately for Emory, he also fell.

Valerio swung the sword over his head to bring down on Emory, but the priest parried the blow with his sword, again the two weapons slicing into each other.

Then Valerio's blade snapped.

"Crap."

Valerio tossed the nub of metal attached to the hilt aside and darted away from Emory.

The priest was on his feet and chasing after him, when Valerio dived to the floor and grabbed the first weapon from the stash left on the ground.

A metal lance or spear. It was ten feet long with a wide, flat business end, which appeared dulled by time. Emory wielded his broadsword like an axe, and the would-be warriors traded jabs, thrusts, and slashes.

Valerio reflected that they must have looked rather comical to the two trained fighters reduced to spectating—and Horse had returned, battered and broken, to the top of the staircase. Just watching instead of dragging himself to Valerio's aid.

"Hold on a second," Emory said, one hand out, sword pointed at the ground.

"What?" Valerio asked, although he was thankful for the break.

Both were sweating and red-faced. The few times Valerio had played any kind of sport, it had been the same way—strong start, then the exertion turned him into a vomit-tasting heavy breather with more sweat than skin.

"How... long... have we been going?" Valerio said.

"About a minute," Moses said. "Father, finish him."

Horse's head snapped around at Moses. The pair were twenty feet apart, and it didn't look like either man could stand, let alone fight.

"Just give me a minute," Emory said. Then, pointedly at Valerio, "I told you this would be undignified."

"Yeah." Valerio tightened his grip on the spear. "Let's have a rest."

Emory exhaled a long breath.

Then Valerio charged, thrusting his lance-like weapon. It sunk into Emory's side a couple of inches—not deep enough to do much damage, but plenty to deliver pain and suffering.

Valerio pulled out the spike and Emory stumbled back, dropping his sword.

Valerio stepped forward, stabbing his lance against Emory's chest, but it just cut him and damaged his clothes. Emory tried to fight back, but his movements were sluggish and uncoordinated. Despite how blunt it was, Valerio quickly gained the upper hand, and Emory turned and dashed back toward the stash of weapons. He stumbled to the floor and crawled on hands and knees, grimacing against the wounds.

But Valerio tossed aside the long, not-so-pointy weapon and hurried forward. With Emory injured, Valerio overtook him and decided to try something different.

He bent over and, still heaving against his lungs, scooped up an item he hadn't thought to use before: a metal handle as long as a sword with a rounded stone end, like a mace without the spikes.

"Nice."

Valerio stepped back and raised the club.

Emory shut his eyes.

Valerio sensed the air ripple with anticipation as the club

descended. The impact was so vicious that the ground beneath his feet shook, and he felt something within his opponent break.

Emory slumped to the ground, his body ragdoll-slack, breath rasping.

In the distance, Horse yukked and clapped his hands, despite his own injuries. The fight was over.

Emory had been defeated.

Valerio walked over to his former friend, listened to the man's tight, weak breaths, and looked him in the eyes.

"I'm sorry," Valerio said.

Emory nodded, and Valerio brought the club down on him again. And again. And once more to be safe.

It was gross, but Valerio couldn't remember a time he felt more exhilarated. Killing a man. By hand.

"Oh, mama, that was good. I guess I'm not sorry."

Horse applauded faster. It looked like it hurt, and Valerio was glad. The big lunk had hauled himself back up the stairs with his leg and arm broken, possibly his collar bone, too.

Valerio said, "You know, you at least could gave crawled over there and thrown me a better weapon than a blunt spear and fragile sword."

Horse frowned, a look of shame in his eyes. He shrugged and pointed between the two men.

Valerio realised what he meant. "You thought I wanted to fight him myself?"

Horse nodded.

"No. I did not want to finish it myself. Look at me. I'm all sweaty. I hate being sweaty."

Horse lowered his head.

"Never mind. We have something else to attend to. Come on."

With Horse dragging himself behind, Valerio paced over the floor, approaching Moses. Still prone on the floor. Unarmed. Vulnerable. Valerio decided he would beat this man to death as he had the priest.

"I can help," Moses said.

"But will you?" Valerio asked. "No, I think Horse and I should kill you and be on our way to where Jules is surely securing the orb with brilliant precision as we speak."

"You may find I do not die as easily as a soft priest with no experience."

"Let's see."

Valerio heaved the club over his head to bring it down on Moses with all his strength. Moses jerked forward, extended a hand, and grabbed the handle. Even though he couldn't stand, he yanked the weapon out of Valerio's grasp and retracted it to hit back.

Valerio was about to retreat when the ground made a high-pitched whining noise. Everyone froze, the noise getting louder. Sound waves reverberated through the ground and air until an unbearable sonic boom deafened them.

Then, with a pulse that thumped right through Valerio's chest, the entire world turned white.

Jules's hands were shaking as he gripped the hilt of the short sword, his chest tight with a mix of dread and resolution. He peered out from the shadows of the entry point, his heart thudding in his ears. Nothing had changed. Two Korean soldiers guarding the exit, vague movement behind.

"I can't give it up," he called into the dark.

"Neither can we," Muzaffer replied, unseen.

"The world is broken," Hilla said, also unseen but likely to be the tall outline leaning out from behind one of the statue-still troops who would follow their orders to the last. "We can fix it."

Jules wondered if it would be easier because he couldn't see them. Most of them. If they were lined up before him, their souls open in their ignorant expressions of fealty to a man who ran their movement. Their sect.

Their cult.

Jules said, "I've met too many people like Father Emory and Valerio Conchin. Valerio is the guy who keeps bouncing back and popping up, but... Emory, he's a breed like we got in the US. Speakin' good words but doin' bad things. It's too obvious."

"What is obvious," Muzaffer said, "is you are trapped. You are unarmed, or you would have shot at us by now."

Jules weighed the sword in his hands, flicked his gaze to the orb, and his stomach tightened again.

"Last chance," Jules called to them. "Back off. Go away. Give this place over to the Spanish government and we all walk outta here."

"Enough!" When Jules craned his neck to look out, he found Muzaffer and Hilla had advanced to the middle of the stunted corridor to the orb room. The light from the room cast their shadows long and thin behind them, and the company of mercs flanked the pair.

Jules wiped a tear from his cheek. His hands trembled, gripped around the sword-shaped tool, which was glowing brighter the more enraged and despairing he felt. He didn't think he could let go of it if he tried.

"Jules?" Prihya said. "I can hear them. Are they..."

"They're coming."

"You can't fight them with that."

"No." Jules pushed away from the wall. "But that doesn't mean we die. Stay close."

Jules hooked an arm around Prihya, and they walked toward the orb, huddled like lovers on a beach. She said nothing, plainly trusting him.

He wondered if this was how it felt for Dan. If it was how Harpal dealt with confronting the enemy at the barrel of a gun or setting an explosive he knew would tear someone apart. Ruining lives through his knife assaults or broken bones in hand-to-hand combat was not the same as taking a life intentionally, but it would still be heinous in some people's eyes. Jules had only taken one life before, and that was an accident, one he felt responsible for. He'd been crushed by guilt because even those far-right Nazi types could be redeemed.

Could the same be said of Muzaffer and Hilla? The North Koreans who no doubt saw Jules as a mortal enemy after what he and the team did to their stronghold?

Valerio Conchin himself?

Could any of them serve a positive purpose in society if they survived today?

"You cannot get out," came Hilla's voice. "We must kill you both if you do not cooperate. Please give it up. Now."

Jules and Prihya reached the glowing black orb, floating above the two cupped hands. He pivoted to see the cadre of the strange church's point guards enter and spread out to aim at him.

He said, "Hey. I warned you."

Then he thrust the sword into the orb's black surface. It felt like stabbing a blunt knife through flesh.

CHAPTER SIXTY-FOUR

In the days to come, it would be one of the most extensive investigations the scientific community had ever seen. Anything from satellites orbiting the Earth to sensors installed to detect animal migration, as well as cellphone footage, CCTV in cities, and eyewitness statements, would be analyzed by intelligence agencies around the world.

Nobody would know the whole truth.

The shockwave roiled at the speed of thought, slamming into the soft bodies in its immediate vicinity and effectively liquifying every sack of soft organ and shattering every hard obstruction, including bone and fillings.

It continued up and out, a dome of pure energy—uncategorized by scientists of the modern era—a combination of kinetic force, electromagnetic static, and the unknowable gravitational forces that surround the event horizon of an ultra-dense singularity.

Once past its epicenter, the blast quickly lost much of its potency, absorbed by the bedrock surrounding its trigger point, yet still pulverising every single body within the substructure trying to rise up through the Donana National Park.

In the aftermath of the initial sonic boom, one man, Moses, had patched himself up, pushed toward a discarded submachine gun, and was halfway to the exit ladder to pursue Valerio and Horse, who had retreated to grab supplies from the surface. But the bones in his one good leg, like every other bone in his body, fragmented into shrapnel as the wave lifted him up, slammed him against the wall, and dropped him to the ground, already dead.

On the surface, an impossibly small fraction of time later, both Horse and Valerio were on the move. Horse's limited pain perception allowed him to use a crutch to support the leg that didn't work, and his one good arm kept him going. His instinct to follow the man he saw as his master, friend, and father was the most powerful motivator within him, even more powerful than his own survival. So, it came as quite a surprise when something hit him from behind and below, like a bus careening through him. The only sensation above the pain was the impact, but he was aware that none of his limbs would obey his commands to move. First, the world turned bright white, his master-friend-father appeared confused but unharmed. Then, as a result of that final vision, as Horse's world turned black, he was relieved. And happy.

On the periphery of the Atlantean site, lighter vehicles shook, and some turned over, heavier ones shuddering as their windows blew out, and supplies blustered across the plain.

The roiling circle of energy expanded farther, and trees swayed as if in a hurricane. Trunks cracked on the older ones and they crashed to the ground.

Out even farther, beyond the national park, civilization beckoned, but the wave saw no reason to stop now. Light bulbs popped, electrics overloaded, and the villages' lights all winked out.

When the dome reached the first power station, it plunged an entire region into darkness. Cell towers failed. The internet died.

Then the rest of the country went the same way.

Then it reached Portugal.

Then France.

Power failed in hospitals, nuclear power stations, military complexes, airports, but all emergency processes kicked in as expected. Once the wave was past, it did not stick around to do more damage.

It cut into the Atlantic Ocean, rippling the water without assailing it with the violence it inflicted upon anything electrical. Boats bobbed harder, though, as if caught in a storm, and every radio instantly cut out, along with the burning of every light on board.

Since the kinetic energy was weaker by the time it reached the first airplane, it inflicted only severe turbulence and a power outage. But because the wave was similar to a solar flare, and weaker at the high altitude, all modern aircraft were protected, and after every passenger's stomach performed a massive scoop like the world's most terrifying rollercoaster, backup power kicked in, and pilots all over Europe received a round of applause.

Three seconds after Jules blew the sphere's protective skin, CERN in Switzerland detected the energy signature and those instruments that did not instantly shut down sent the operators into a frenzy of panic and delight. Many thought they'd experienced a nearby gravitational wave—perhaps an undetected star within the Milky Way going supernova—but they would soon learn it was nothing of the sort.

As the curvature of the Earth lengthened with distance, the wave's potency quickly ebbed. Affected less by gravity and more by data-heavy neutrons—which do not have mass—it continued upward and out, so the lowest point, closest to the ground, was the first to dissipate. Southern Britain suffered outages, as did Belgium and parts of Netherlands, although by the time it reached Poland, the populace experienced a flickering of lights and a temporary loss of internet. Rebooting the routers soon restored normal service.

The weak pulse passed over the International Space Station and anomalies were picked up in Hawaii and Chile, China and Australia, but no sooner did it wreak its damage than it ended.

The Witnesses had travelled the modern world, left a footprint, then fallen back to sleep.

In the orb room, Jules woke up dazed, exhausted, but conscious. He had a killer headache, and a vague memory of enacting a theory from a long-trapped memory. It had lingered in his subconscious, the physics of this place, the energy signatures, the way it protected the handler.

"You're awake."

Jules blinked at the voice, at the soft touch of skin on his cheek. Lips crushed against his, warm and welcoming, and even though he was barely conscious, he was happy. He allowed the kiss. He returned it.

Glad Bridget had forgiven him.

This phase of his life was over. He could enjoy his time now. Indulge in a relationship if she'd have him once the adrenaline wore off. Because, although he could affect his behaviour, he knew he could not change his core self—the logic, the swift thought processes that informed his impulse, his—

Wait...

How long had he been unconscious?

His eyes snapped open, blinked away the crust that had formed, and he guessed he'd been out a long time. Hours, maybe longer.

And it was not Bridget kissing him, but Prihya. She pulled away, wide-eyed and shocked.

Shocked at his surprise, probably. At the suddenness of him pushing her away.

"Oh," she said in a small voice. "I'm... sorry. I wasn't thinking... I—"

"No, no, carry on." Colin Waterston was here, along with two men in Royal Marine uniforms and full tactical gear. "You youngsters deserve a break."

Jules ached all over and lacked the strength to reassure Prihya he held no ill will toward her, that intense situations resulted in intense feelings. She'd never hinted at affection toward him, nor him to her—nothing serious, anyway—so he wrote it off as confusion and deep-seated emotion.

A female medic pushed through the men standing over him, and Jules realised there were lights on. The higher he climbed from his slumber, the more he saw: portable lights, CSI-type techs in suits, the security.

"How long...?" Jules croaked.

Although he couldn't finish the question, Colin answered it.

"The energy wave kicked out a lot of power grids, but satellites pinpointed it to this park. The damage to the landscape made it rather simple to locate the epicenter, and we came in—with permission from our Spanish friends."

"They just let you?" Prihya said.

Colin ignored her. "Tell me, how are you still alive?"

Jules was sat upright now, the olive-skinned woman examining him strapping a blood pressure cuff to his upper arm.

He said, "Still alive? How many dead?"

Colin pondered a moment, totting up in his head. "Eight in this room. One up in the temple. And Valerio Conchin's bodyguard has passed away, too. We came across him a couple of hours ago."

Muzaffer and Hilla. The Koreans. Moses. And Horse.

"Valerio?" Jules asked.

"No sign as of yet. But there's a lot of ground to cover. If he was caught in the worst of it, we'll find him."

Jules doubted they would. He'd been changed years ago, made like Jules. Valerio might have been hurt but his genetic makeup would likely have protected him.

"No one else?"

"There's a big infrastructure bill to be met," Colin said. "But no deaths beyond the walls of Atlantis." He ran through the extent of the EMP-like wave.

"As the Witnesses must have intended," Prihya said. "A failsafe to take out anyone invading their Atlantis for evil means. But the comet crashing into the ocean destroyed it before anyone could wage war."

Colin waved her off. "Plenty of time for stories later. How come you two didn't end up like... like the poor corpses we've removed from here?"

Prihya was brighter than Jules, clearly having been awake for longer. His theory had worked better than hoped.

He said, "Being connected to the orb when it ruptured... it protects the person actin' as the trigger. A headache, a blast to the consciousness... maybe it had affected me more than Prihya because I got the... what do you call it?"

"Magic touch?" Colin offered.

"Ain't magic, but sure."

The medic finished her examination and told Colin in Spanish that Jules could be moved.

The soldiers helped him up and he leaned on one as they accompanied him out, promising he'd soon be reunited with the Lost Origins team. And at that, Prihya looked embarrassed.

Jules offered her a wry smile and a firm nod that he hoped conveyed all was still good between them.

But the longer he thought about what he did today, the more devastated he felt. Through the brightly lit passages, up to the temple, the memories of that day were strong. Vivid. If he'd done things differently, then the scholar-assassins, the mercenaries, Horse, and maybe—if he was dead—Valerio Conchin would not have had to suffer the ultimate fate.

And they'd perished at *his* hands.

It wasn't even self-defence. He'd been in worse scrapes where only his life was at stake, and not resorted to such extreme measures. But the wider issue, the question of how many innocents would have perished had either Emory or Valerio accessed this level of power, had weighed too heavily on him.

In the end it was a simple calculation.

A sum.

If he failed, more than the ten people he'd killed would die. And those individuals were probably more worthy of life than those people lost today.

Was that the logic Dan used? Harpal, too? Charlie?

It was something he'd have to work through, accept, and eventually forgive himself over.

As he emerged into sunlight, to the multi-agency camp of Spanish law enforcement, UN, Interpol, and medical facilities, he questioned every action he'd taken since departing China.

He'd always thought he was the only one who could unravel the mysteries of where the Witnesses came from and where they went. It was his right, given what he'd lost as a child. His mother had cherished the bangle, and the fierceness with which she protected it pointed to her knowing its significance. It had been his right, his destiny, to solve that question.

And yet, coming here, in sending Xander to take LORI to the

true destination, he'd let go of the notion of finding the ultimate prize. He'd given it up, passed the privilege to people he believed would do the right thing, the way he would, that they would protect it if Jules had failed to make it back.

He'd done the right thing, too. He *had* to believe that.

But did he lose himself in the process?

CHAPTER SIXTY-FIVE

Colin Waterston's speed and thoroughness in arranging immunity from prosecution for members of the Lost Origins Recovery Institute was impressive. The team would face no charges for illegally entering Iraq or possessing unlicensed firearms. Xander was reunited with his daughter in France, and the Chinese removed his name from their list of people of interest (although he was still not welcome in the country). Prihya was to be treated as a victim during her time in Father Emory's care. And Jules faced no criminal prosecution about the mysteriously widespread event, which was now declared a natural phenomenon caused by a volcanic event in a region long thought to be dormant. Jules was relieved that such a threat had been removed, but this did not make him any less concerned about his actions.

Bridget's parents provided a lawyer, who in fact added the news that all deeds related to the artifacts and monuments discovered the previous week were considered null and void in terms of protection. Anything related to the events leading up to the rise of the Gardens of Babylon was considered off-limits throughout Europe, Africa, Asia, and the Middle East. Only the US government refused to ratify the legal documents, but Colin claimed they were throwing their toys out of the pram because they would not be in charge of the upcoming operations. They had a seat at the table, but Colin, who had been lavished with praise, was the man in charge, with several hand-picked colleagues and law-enforcement agencies as partners.

With no legal threats hanging over them, Toby gathered the group in the Chateau, and the Demon Hub had never felt more like a war room about to host a debriefing.

Jules had spent a lot of time alone. He hadn't cried or lain awake wringing his hands. He was as satisfied with his decisions as he could be, and even a week later he believed he'd done the right thing. But he didn't want to be near people. He told them he needed space, and they'd allowed him that without visible judgement.

Now, as the last person to enter and find a seat, he looked around and adopted the friendly smile he'd practiced before leaving his room, and left the final one for Bridget, for whom he added a, "Hey."

She held his eye a moment before turning away to land on Toby.

Jules had never been good at disseminating emotions, other than in an academic way, so complex feelings were a mystery. He didn't know whether Bridget was mad at him for flying off to Spain and tricking them into going where they'd always wanted, or if his isolationist choices since returning had insulted her.

He'd talk to her later.

Toby took the lead, his university professor's manner perky and authoritative. "I have had much time to reflect. And while we wait on the red tape to grant us permission to join the excavations and cataloguing, we have an abundance of new data to run through. But first, let us get up to speed, and make sure we are all on the same page."

They all spoke. They gave their accounts, the parts where others weren't present, anything to fill in gaps. Jules and Prihya spoke for the longest.

Jules gave a more detailed narrative regarding the machinations between Valerio and Emory, and his decision-making process that led to wrecking the power source that had tried to lift Atlantis into the light and effectively murdering eight people. Dan insisted it was not murder, as the deaths were fully justified, as demonstrated by the Spanish courts and the international legal system. Jules knew he should be satisfied with the rationalization but was yet to feel it inside.

Prihya explained her role, how she'd meshed her older theories about Atlantis with what she saw at Tayos and hinted at it to Jules. She'd held back anything about a site beyond Atlantis from Father

Emory, having faith that either Jules would work it out alongside LORI and claim it for the side of the angels, or that he'd keep Valerio as far from it as possible.

As Prihya spoke of her faith in Jules and his ability to decipher the maps and codes, Bridget fell still and watched her carefully. Charlie, too, appeared wary, as if the pair still didn't fully trust her, despite what had transpired.

Prihya admitted, too, that although she believed LORI would not screw her over entirely, it had been tempting to throw in with the Church of the Forefathers, especially when Jules and the others escaped without her. All had been explained on that front since coming out of the national park, but she hadn't known it at the time.

"And this cult," Charlie said. "What do we know about it?"

"An offshoot of hardline Catholics," Harpal said. "I tapped up sources in the intelligence community, but there isn't much. They keep their heads down. They're flagged because of a few extremist beliefs but no worse than a lot of churches and religious types—they're not keen on homosexuals, feel abortion is murder, races shouldn't interbreed, that kind of thing. But no violent intentions."

"Other than the crazy priest kidnapping people," Prihya said.

"They've disowned him, and they condemn the actions of one rogue clergyman." Harpal shrugged to emphasize how he didn't believe that. "But, MI6, the CIA, and Interpol all have them on watchlists. If they do anything suspicious, it'll flag."

"It wasn't Father Emory running them," Prihya said. "I never learned the name of the leader, but I think it's someone close to the Vatican. He might be hard to pin down, especially if he still works there."

"It would make sense," Toby said. "They emerged from the Church, so having someone inside to keep an eye on the Vatican would be an advantage."

Jules said, "Anything on Valerio?"

Harpal shook his head. "No. He hasn't surfaced. After his bodyguard died, I guess he either wandered off and got lost in Donana, or he made it out and went to ground. He has resources in pretty much every country. Wouldn't be hard."

It was Horse whom Jules felt particularly sorry for. The scholar-assassins were fully aware of their actions; Horse had been reduced to the role of a dumb, thoughtless henchman, a childlike mind in a near-unstoppable body. Only the man's deeds from before he suffered his head and spinal injuries kept Jules from eating himself to death with guilt; had Horse been fully compos-mentis, it was unlikely he'd have done anything differently. He'd always been loyal to Valerio.

"Which brings us to our future role," Toby said.

All sat a little straighter.

"We will be allowed to help decipher the texts, the maps, and whatever else comes of what the powers that be are referring to as 'the Babylonian Library.' What we cannot do is act on that information. For example, we cannot go searching for any other sites revealed by our translations without permission."

Bridget said, "Even though we know there's at least one more?"

"Yeah, I'm not clear on that," Dan said. "How do we know about it?"

"Bridget read the map's warning," Charlie said. "And now Toby and Bridget have pieced something else together."

"The final resting place of the Witnesses," Bridget said. "It isn't the Hanging Gardens of Babylon, or Atlantis."

"Yeah, I think we all got that," Jules said.

"Let us *finish*, please." Bridget sounded curt, adding the *please* with the willpower of a stressed schoolteacher. "Toby?"

"Yes. Quite. The Witnesses were indeed peaceful. But this other race who were bent on conquest were the instigators of the orb technology, and what scientists today class as quantum physics. Back then, who knows? Maybe they thought they were conjuring magic. Certainly, the people they enslaved or conquered would have seen it that way."

"And the cataclysm just wiped them out?" Charlie said.

"Some of the writing we have disseminated suggests they were seeking a way to reproduce. They lived longer than humans but were a small tribe. We do not know why."

Jules's gears turned and he threw out a scenario. "If they wanted to advance humans enough to consider having babies with them, I guess they went infertile for some reason. Inbreeding, climate... being that close to those balls of energy?"

"Whatever the reasons," Toby said, "the Witnesses were like Switzerland. They chose never to force another race to change. But the others, the same people who split from the Witnesses... let's call them... let's go with Father Emory's phrase, the Forefathers? Any objections?"

No one had any. To Jules it made sense to denote the two sides—Witnesses and Forefathers.

"They were powerful, too," Toby went on. "The Witnesses didn't want war with the Forefathers but would fight if the Forefathers gave them no choice. And the actions of the Forefathers on the African continent—advancing certain tribes, selective breeding to produce a giant, obedient slave class—"

"The giants' bones we found," Harpal said.

"Correct. Their inhumane practices meant the Witnesses had no choice but to intervene, to side with the next swathe of the world on the Forefathers' list—the Europeans. They built their own advanced city, less opulent than the Forefathers, to then serve as a defensive measure."

"But in the middle of it all," Bridget said, "the comet wiped them out. All of them. The war never came. The Atlantean cities were sunk. It ended the possibility of the Witnesses surviving."

"Or did it?" Toby said.

Again, the room focused with a hush.

"It is possible the Witnesses lived on. The warning Bridget deciphered—about how this is as far as anyone should go, that no one should look for them. Because death awaits. What if that didn't mean they were retiring to die out?"

Charlie considered it. "You mean, what if they survived? Maybe bred...?"

"People with the touch, like Jules and Zimina, must have come from somewhere. Some lineage where the genes remain dormant except for a select few."

Jules saw the logic. To a point. "After so many generations, the gene pool is so diluted, ain't no way to see the Witnesses as anything other than gone."

"You're certain?" Bridget asked coolly.

"Don't mean they didn't settle down somewhere."

"And," Dan said, "there's still the other stuff Valerio thought was out there."

"Which brings me to two possible ways forward," Toby said. "Have you heard of the Garden of Eden?"

"Sure," Jules said. "Adam and Eve, the snake, apple. Who hasn't?"

"The Garden of Eden is the place life first evolved, a mythical place for which every religion and, indeed, folk tale has an equivalent. We see it today as Mesopotamia, and give it a nickname like the cradle of civilization. It's where the earliest signs of human habitation are found."

Prihya said, "I don't think Valerio was interested in protohuman fossils."

"Which brings us to the other legend. How many swords can the world imbue with mythical power? Damocles, Excalibur, and the rest. I believe, and Bridget agrees, that the Witnesses moved on from Babylon, and hid their most dangerous secrets with them."

It went on for a while. Longer than Jules usually tolerated, but he held his tongue and let Dan and Harpal banter about how they were in need of a nap and how Toby just liked his own voice too much. Jules usually edged the talks toward a briefer delivery but today he let it flow over him. He was still tired, and there were too many possibilities to make firm plans sitting in a room full of hypotheses and theories that no one could verify without getting out there.

And since that was currently forbidden, it was all talk.

When Margarete broke in with coffee and pastries—homemade, of course—the team accepted the chance for a quick break, and Jules sat alone. He watched as Prihya poured over the mock-up of the map Bridget had tried to reproduce, which had carried the warning about going no further than the Babylonian Library, but she'd admitted it wasn't close to accurate. She didn't have Jules's eidetic memory, so it was broad strokes at best.

Jules waited until Bridget wandered away from Toby and Charlie, then approached her, carrying a strong espresso. He knocked it back like a shot of tequila and placed the cup on a desk.

"Hey," he said.

She faced him. "Hey."

"I'm sorry."

"What for?"

"I've been distant," he admitted. "I guess... I thought I should feel more guilty about killing Horse and the others."

"You don't?"

He remained still, almost stiff. "That's kinda the problem. I do. But not like I expected to. When I ran that Nazi guy off the road, he died, and I couldn't accept it. Now, I took out a buncha guys and it's like... sad. But they deserved it."

"You saved more lives than you took. Maybe it's the scales that are telling you you're good."

Jules had considered that. Even if it wasn't a conscious thing, more subconscious, it'd make a lot of sense. Or it was hiding, sleeping in his psyche, ready to pop its head up and cripple him when he was least expecting it.

"So, look," Jules said. "Back in the rainforest, we said we wanted to, y'know, explore things. Between us."

"We did," Bridget said.

"And we got a few options. Garden of Eden, a sword in a stone." He smiled. When Bridget didn't return it, he said, "You wanna explore things more? With me? Maybe at a bar?"

No response.

He said, "Just the two of us?"

She inclined her head toward Prihya who was talking with Toby across the room. "Are you sure you wouldn't rather be exploring with someone else?"

Jules frowned. "Why? No. Why would you think that?"

"Because..." Bridget patted Jules's chest. "The commandos who raided the city in Spain had a live feed on their bodycams. We were watching. We saw you two kissing."

Jules's voice wavered, his throat tight. "No. No, Bridge, I thought it was you."

Bridget widened her eyes in disbelief as she stepped back. A heavy tension filled the air, and her lips parted slightly, trying to find the right words. "You... you know that's kinda making it worse, don't you?"

"Oh..." Jules dragged his fingers over his close-cropped hair.

He'd messed up. If he'd spoken with her sooner, opened up instead of shutting the door in everyone's faces, he might have explained things. Now she'd had a week to stew, it would be harder to—

"Relax," Bridget said, grinning. She turned and took a couple of steps away, and Jules could not help watching her figure leaving him. She glanced back, pausing to catch his eyes far lower than her own, and smiled coyly. "I'd kinda guessed, but Prihya told me all about it. You can beg forgiveness properly tonight."

"Tonight?"

"Seven p.m., Le Bouchon du Village. Wear something nice."

Le Bouchon du Village.

The Village Cork.

A bar?

"You mean...?"

"We've all got some healing to do," Bridget said. "Why not start over a nice glass of wine?"

EPILOGUE

The night-reckoning was coming, swift and sure as the winter wind. Its very darkness seemed to have a purpose, a design that whispered of some strange destiny, one as still and silent as a tomb.

In the gloom of the night, a lone figure made its way through the desolate nightscape, into the shadow of the Pakistani prison. A guard on the outer wall had noticed her and called out, because no one should be trespassing on the exclusion zone. This was, after all, a high-security facility, where level-one criminals—including skilled Taliban fighters—were housed. But a second guard placed a kind hand on the man's shoulder, whispered in his ear, and both turned their backs.

The figure continued swiftly, the darkness cloaking her from view.

The trespasser approached a small door in the prison's outer wall. A moment later the bomb-proof, steel door glided open and another figure in a long black robe and hood emerged from the black. The trespasser beckoned to the figure.

The newcomer followed her, their steps soundless as if walking on air. The two wraithlike women moved through the forecourt, their shadows merging in the darkness, until they reached a barren road, and the prison was a toy fortress in the distance.

A flatbed truck idled on an embankment, which required no communication. The trespasser and liberated prisoner climbed on board, lay on the carpeted flatbed, and waited. Thirty seconds later, the vehicle fired up with a quieter sound than one might expect from something that looked so old, then it drove away.

Neither woman spoke, nor even tried to see the other's face. The former prisoner would know that faces might not be desirable at this stage.

They travelled for two hours, both conditioned for such journeys, until they reached a dilapidated town that appeared abandoned. Goat huts dotted the hills, but no animals were apparent. Houses without roofs or doors zipped by, and the road was more potholes than tarmac.

They reached an alleyway between a half-collapsed wall that once surrounded a market or some sort of large shop and a three-story building that appeared more intact than most.

As the pair disembarked the truck, dust filled the still air, and as their anonymous taxi drove away, the dry, powdery grime soon settled. The two women stood in silence, hoods low over their eyes.

The figure who had led the other from the prison led the way again, into the building to the left, its door oddly resembling a western saloon bar, and the figure in the black robe opened it and stood aside. The freed prisoner entered a small, bare room, where a third figure in yet another robe pushed back his hood revealing on oddly youthful face of what was clearly a middle-aged man. He was tall and not conventionally handsome, yet he carried an air of authority about him.

"General Yanovna," he said in a low voice. "Very nice to finally meet you."

Yanovna dropped her own hood back and nodded, her gaze never leaving the man before her. "And you are?"

"I am Valerio Conchin. I aided your incursion to the UK some time ago. Unfortunately, I could not prevent your apprehension. I have invested considerable funds into uncovering your location and facilitating your handover."

"Not that I am ungrateful, Mr. Conchin, but I expect some reciprocation is expected?"

The man continued. "I am here to take you to a place where you will be safe and protected. I have organized a team of highly efficient forces to ensure your security. In exchange, you will lead those forces in the search for certain artifacts that will assure the future of humanity is not in the hands of people like... the Russian or American governments."

He paused and looked at her, his gaze never wavering.

"Do you understand what I am saying?"

Yanovna nodded. "I help you find more of the things like I helped bring to the light in Iraq, and you guarantee the freedom of Striovia?"

The man smiled. "Good. Then let us go."

He motioned for her to stand, then led her out of the room. The woman who'd broken Yanovna out followed. They walked through the alleyway to a waiting car. Valerio opened the door and motioned for her to get inside. The other woman, whose face remained hidden, got behind the wheel.

As the car pulled away, Yanovna shivered, her heart pounding in her chest. She was being taken away, forced into something new, something unknown. Something infinitely better than a Pakistani prison, visited monthly by that insufferable British idiot who kept trying to bribe her into cooperating with him. That last time, when she'd been bundled off to partake in what should have been a glorious event, she'd been dumped back in the prison as soon as it was over.

She would have helped. She would have advised them.

All they had to do was formalize Striovia's right to independence, but the cowards could not do that.

So, she had no choice. She had to take that chance.

"Why the robes?" she asked. "It feels... weird."

"Oh, it is weird," Valerio said. "But I needed partners. We both need you. And you—I'm hoping—will put up with a bit of silliness if it means the men who enjoy that sort of thing can get you the power you need."

"Security," Yanovna corrected him. "Not power."

"I stand corrected."

The car drove for another two hours, stilted conversation and unanswered questions punctuating the silence. When it finally stopped, Yanovna stepped out, finding herself before a small, forgotten-looking building that seemed to be built into the side of a steep hillside.

The man nodded. "This is it. Your new home."

Yanovna looked around. "Where are we?"

"The border."

"Which border?"

"Pakistan-Afghanistan. A deserted region of little strategic significance. And less expensive to turn eyes away from than having a high-value asset simply walk out of prison."

Yanovna was unimpressed with this man's constant references to money. If it were a problem, he should not have spent it. No, he would not have parted with it if it was not worth the investment.

"This is to be my new home?"

The building was old, with crumbling walls and a sagging roof. It seemed to be a relic from some forgotten era, its shattered windows staring out into the night like the empty eyes of a corpse. But Valerio seemed pleased, and he ushered her inside, the robed woman following.

The interior was sparsely furnished and smelled musty. The man showed her a small room at the back and opened the double doors to a passage that must have burrowed deep into the hillside.

Yanovna said nothing as she forged on, a minute of walking bringing her to a grand-looking door of heavy wood and cast iron fittings. Valerio took a black, baseball-sized sphere from under his robe and raised it.

"They insist I use this. It's part of the ceremony."

"Ceremony?" Yanovna said.

"To induct you into the Church. If you want to lead the logistics and military side of our crusade, it's a crucial formality."

"You seem less than enthusiastic."

"Like I said, it's a bit silly, but it serves my purpose."

"Which is?"

Valerio gave nothing away. He used the ball as a door knocker, banging on the wood four times before stepping back and lifting his hood again.

The door opened.

Yanovna stepped through and stood with her feet firmly planted in the dust of the ages. They were underground, in a cave. Spreading before her was a church, the natural, cavernous dome of a ceiling towering above. The damp air clung to her skin, and she shivered, despite the fires burning on the walls. Pillars loomed, melding into the arching contours high above her, ancient and mysterious, built by hands predating the Christ which the men and women in attendance appeared to worship—and far older than the two very Muslim countries either side of the border.

In the center of the church-cave a fire burned, its bright orange flame crackling atop a pile of logs. Around it in a half circle, dozens of men and women wore robes resembling those of Vatican Cardinals, only these garments boasted dark purples and blues, gold and silver threads woven through.

The worshippers turned towards her, their faces hidden behind masks like long-beaked birds, the eyes of some glinting from behind the slits.

With Valerio and the woman waiting by the entrance, Yanovna followed the man who'd opened the door toward the assembly, reasoning that if they were going to sacrifice her to some god they'd better get it over with quickly or she'd take at least a couple with her.

The fire blazed beneath a vast hole in the roof, smoke drawn up through the chimney in a manner she thought foolish.

Wouldn't that draw attention?

Or were they truly so isolated that it simply didn't matter?

The crowd made way, at least twenty adherents, parting for her to approach a man at the center of it all, backlit by the flames, and the only one not wearing a mask. He folded his hood back a centimeter or two, just far enough to see his face.

"You are the leader?" Yanovna asked.

"And you will be our general," the man said with what Yanovna took to be an Italian accent.

"If I am convinced you are on the correct side of history."

"Oh, my dear General, history is exactly the point here. I am not only the leader of the Church of the True Forefathers, but I am also the world's savior. Some call me a visionary. Whatever I am, I have long-renounced a past of violence and selfishness. I am simply a man who first came to the Church as they were splitting from the Vatican, and through keeping my promises to recover relics and Out of Place Artifacts—'OOPARTs'—to aid them in their task, I have risen in esteem and importance."

Zimina Yanovna had never stood for blowhards, but she sensed the man's boasting was honest. While he was clearly full of his own *self*-esteem and *self*-importance, he knew of the artifacts she sought, and with Valerio Conchin facilitating things like her escape from prison, perhaps this church could be a means to an end.

"Let us get your ceremony done," she said. "Then we can get to know each other better."

Valerio watched, containing his amusement at the ridiculous ritual whilst in a very satisfactory position. With Emory dead along with their prime agents, Valerio's knowledge and experience, as well as his vast resources throughout the world, made him a valued partner, his spat with Father Emory forgiven in the wake of the priest's failure. To prove himself, all he had to do was deliver them someone with a special touch.

"We could have brought them Sibeko," Renata said from under her hood.

"You know why I didn't," Valerio said. "This was more expensive, and more difficult, but Sibeko is mine."

"When *I've* finished with him."

"In time, yes." Valerio didn't risk going after Jules, since part of the deal in handing him over would be that Valerio would be allowed to handle him afterward, as he saw fit. But, if the hunt went on too long, or Jules refused to cooperate, Valerio's patience would run thin and snap in close succession. "Yanovna is the better choice. Easier to control. It's a partnership."

"And when they betray her?"

Valerio looked at Renata and waited for her to turn her face to him, the raised scarring across one cheek still an angry red.

He said, "By that time, we will have found the weapon and eviscerated Sibeko and his friends."

"You are sure we will find it?"

"I'm not messing around now. No more Mr. Nice Sociopathic Billionaire. We will kill Jules Sibeko and his team the next chance we get."

"I used to believe in all this." She flicked a hand toward the gathering where Yanovna currently knelt on a cushion while the leader fed her a sip of wine—a close cousin of the Catholic Communion ceremony. "Now, all I want is vengeance for my husband. For my friends."

"And that, Renata, is why you are the only person I trust, now Horse is gone. And please, trust *me*, I don't care about finishing Jules myself. He's yours. I promise. All you have to do is be my right hand. Loyal to me. Not them."

She returned her gaze to the formalities, but Valerio suspected she was not seeing anything but the blood she planned to spill.

She asked, "In that case, where to after here, boss?"

"Where else would we travel in search of the legend of Excalibur? To England, of course."

As the short ceremony wound down, the wine having been drunk and chunks of bread eaten, the men and women filed out with practiced smoothness. Even Valerio and his female agent had departed, leaving the Church's leader and General Yanovna alone.

"So, I am in the club now?" Yanovna said. "Do I get your name, at least?"

"Indeed, General." The Church's leader pulled his hood down all the way, and he held both her hands in his, an oddly familiar gesture. "My name is Alfonse Luca. And we are going to be very good friends."

COMING SOON...

Book 6 - *Sword of the Last King* - is the final instalment of the "Witnesses" arc.

While the Lost Origins stories are planned to continue beyond book 6, it feels like the right time to bring this story to a final conclusion.

To stay up to date with news on book #6's release date, with cover reveals, and my own updates, please consider signing up to the newsletter below:

addavies.com/lori-news

Alternatively, follow the author page on Amazon.

NOVELS BY A. D. DAVIES

Lost Origins Novels:

Tomb of the First Priest

Secret of the Reaper Seal

Curse of the Eagle Plague

Guardians of the Four Shields

Gold of the Lost Empire

Adam Park Thrillers:

The Dead and the Missing

A Desperate Paradise

The Shadows of Empty men

Night at the George Washington Diner

Master the Flame

Under the Long White Cloud

Alicia Friend Investigations:

His First His Second

In Black In White

With Courage With Fear

A Friend in Spirit

To Hide To Seek

A Flood of Bones

To Begin The End

Moses and Rock Novels:

Fractured Shadows

No New Purpose

Persecution of Lunacy

Co-Authored:

Project Return Fire – with Joe Dinicola

Standalone:

Three Years Dead

Rite to Justice

The Sublime Freedom

The Dead and the Missing

From the UK to Paris to Asia, and back again – a girl's life hangs in the balance.

Through his successful corporate business, Adam Park once used his expertise, money, and technology to penetrate the murky British underworld where he rescued missing and vulnerable people. Now, secluded amid a quiet life of surfing and travel, his former mentor sends a new client his way, one Adam cannot turn his back on.

To survive ruthless traffickers, confront corrupt law enforcement, and return the girl safely, Adam must burn down his concepts of right and wrong, and draw upon violent facets of his psyche that he has long denied exist.

His First His Second

Meet Detective Sergeant Alicia Friend. She's nice. Too nice to be a police officer, if she's honest.

She is also one of the most respected criminal analysts in the country, now assigned to a cold northern town, investigating the kidnap-murders of two young women. Now a third has been taken.

But Richard—the father of the latest victim—launches a parallel investigation, utilising skills honed in a dark past that is about to catch up with him. As Richard's secret actions hinder the police, Alicia is forced into choices that will impact the rest of her life.

The 1st book in the Alicia Friend series is out now!

Project Return Fire - By A. D. Davies & Joe Dinicola

An inadvertent trip through time... A battle to decide the fate of mankind... One chance to set things right...

Deep in the Juras Mountains, Johnathan Santarelli's team of Army Rangers investigates a radioactive anomaly. Suddenly Santarelli and his men are transported to 1945 in German-occupied territory!

Far from their loved ones, the Rangers want nothing more than to preserve the timeline and get home, but when an elite Nazi unit captures future technology, and the Rangers are confronted with younger versions of important people from their present, they question if this trip was a coincidence after all. Before long, the U.S. team realizes it has a higher duty: stopping the Third Reich from turning the war in Germany's favor.

Before they return home, the team must battle the Nazis for the future of time itself...

Printed in Great Britain
by Amazon

39632282R00260